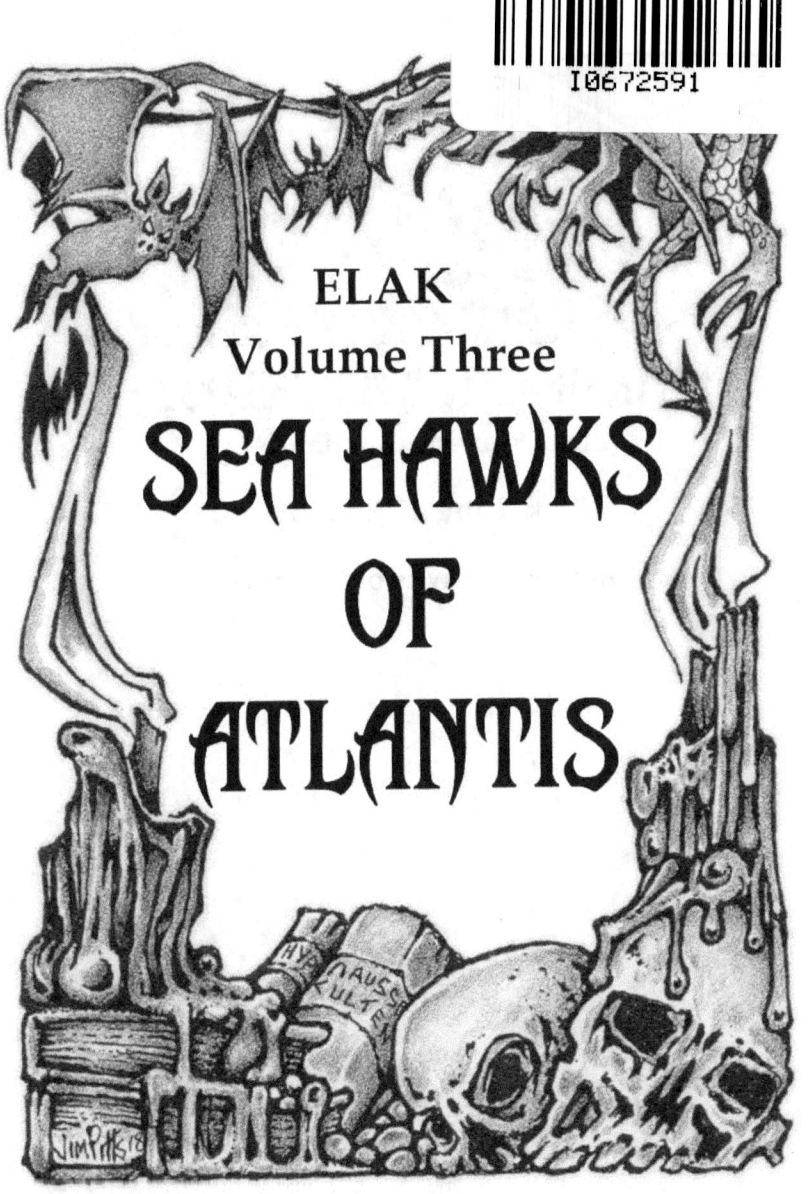

ELAK

Volume Three

SEA HAWKS

OF

ATLANTIS

ELAK OF ATLANTIS TRILOGY

Elak, Warrior of Atlantis

Elak, King of Atlantis

Elak, Sea Hawks of Atlantis

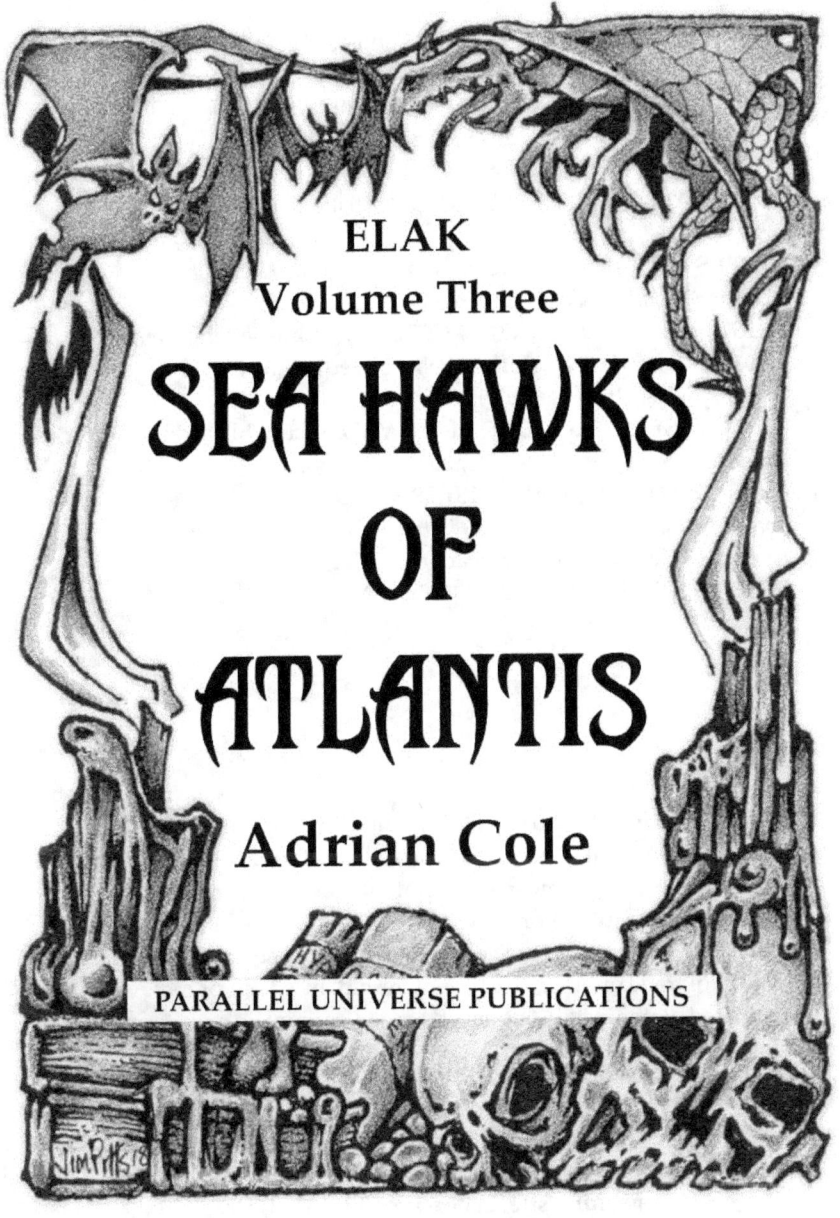

ELAK
Volume Three

SEA HAWKS
OF
ATLANTIS

Adrian Cole

PARALLEL UNIVERSE PUBLICATIONS

THE SWALLOWER OF ISLANDS Published here for the first time

JEWELS OF THE SEA HAG First published in *Tales from the Magician's Skull*, Special #2 (USA) 2022

PRISONERS OF DEVIL DOG CITY First published in *Swords & Sorceries: Tales of Heroic Fantasy Volume 5*, edited by David A. Riley, Parallel Universe Publications (UK) 2022

THE CURSE OF BLOODBONE ISLAND First published in *Heroic Fantasy Quarterly*, (USA) 2023

GOD OF THE DREAMING ISLES First published in *Swords & Sorceries: Tales of Heroic Fantasy Volume 6*, edited by David A. Riley, Parallel Universe Publications (UK) 2023

WHEN THE SEA GODS RISE Published here for the first time

ISBN: 978-1-7393674-7-3

**Parallel Universe Publications, 130 Union Road,
Oswaldtwistle, Lancashire, BB5 3DR, UK**

To David C Smith,
who once, like me,
wrote swashbuckling adventures for Zebra Books
way back in the misty past

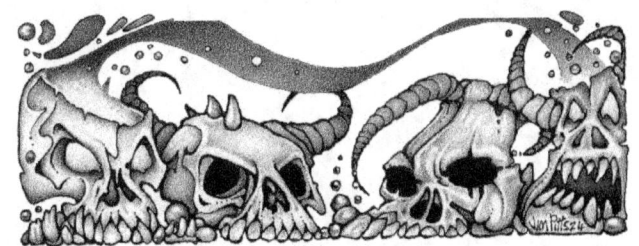

CONTENTS

INTRODUCTION: A WORD FROM THE AUTHOR

Recently I contributed a piece to the excellent book *Robert E. Howard: How He Changed My Life*, (Rogue Blades Entertainment, US). In this, as with other contributors, I talk about how I came across the work of REH and how it went on to influence and, in some cases, define, aspects of my own fiction. It wasn't a one-off event, and even today, the repercussions of REH's work continue to have that impact. *The Elak of Atlantis* is one very obvious example. I'd discovered REH's work in the 1970's along with an entire raft of Sword & Sorcery yarns, and these included Henry Kuttner's Elak tales, which originally appeared in *Weird Tales*. I could see how the young Kuttner was inspired by, in particular, Conan, and how he'd come to create Elak as a homage to REH.

Time moved on until, in 2006 I was approached by writer and editor Robert M. Price, to see if I'd be interested in writing a brand-new story featuring Kuttner's Elak for a magazine Price was launching, *Strange Tales* (originally a companion to *Weird Tales*). I duly wrote the yarn, *Blood of the*

Moon God, and it appeared in the subsequent first issue of the revived magazine in 2007. It was inspired by Kuttner's Elak yarns, which as I said were themselves inspired by REH's Conan. So indirectly here was another impact of REH on me.

Since then I have gone on to write a good many new Elak stories, and in writing them I have always striven to remain faithful to the spirit of the old pulp sagas. My Elak is no "new edge" sword and sorcery. He's not "new pulp". Although I have eschewed the less acceptable "politically incorrect" aspects of the old pulpsters (which belong to another age, another mind set) I have used Kuttner's world (and Howard's) and thrown in H. P. Lovecraft's and a few others for good measure. I've been conscious of Kuttner's anachronisms in his stories (not least of which is a recurrence of Vikings!) but I've wanted to use Kuttner's Atlantean world and not change it, so there are Vikings in my yarns. I've added to Kuttner's world and expanded it along lines which I hope will be seen as acceptable extensions to it. And I've brought back some of Howard's Valusian elements, as my take on all this is that Elak's world and Kull's are the same, separated only by thousands of years. I hold the view that the Picts introduced by Kuttner were descended from Howard's.

In my Elak saga, of which this is the third (and very probably final) volume, you'll find the kind of old school stories you would have read in the pulps, and you'll recognize the characters, settings, sorcerers, monsters, *et al.* And the emphasis on the yarns can be summed up, I sincerely hope, in one word: Fun!

In bringing this extravaganza to you, I am indebted to a number of stalwart supporters and enthusiasts, whose encouragement and support have been vital to the rebirth of Elak, the legend. The series is, consequently, dedicated to them, and in particular I'd like to thank:

Morgan Holmes at *Castalia House*
Bob McLain at *Pulp Hero Press*
Howard Andrew Jones and **Joseph Goodman** at *Tales from the Magician's Skull*
Adrian Simmons at *Heroic Fantasy Quarterly*
Jason Ray Carney
David C. Smith
David A. Riley and Linden at *Parallel Universe Publications*
Trevor Kennedy and the gang at *Phantasmagoria Magazine*
and
Jim Pitts, who has been illustrating my work for almost 50 years!

I'd also like to thank the Estate and Agents of Henry Kuttner, who gave their blessing to my writing new Elak stories.

Adrian Cole, 2025

THE SWALLOWER OF ISLANDS

Once King Elak had completed his unification of the Atlantean continent, he and his many people enjoyed a period of rebuilding and peace. Elak the wanderer had reached his thirtieth year and at last settled for a time in his magnificent new palace in Epharra, capital of Cyrena. With his bride, the former pirate queen Shiveeri, at his side, Elak maintained control of the sea lanes, while the pirate islands became for the most part outreaches of the new Empire, developing legitimate trading and exploring the more distant shores of their world. Even the fierce Pictish tribes of the northwest were no longer hostile, though they generally kept to themselves and their remote domains. Their celebrated king Borna died, and his son Kaa Mag Borga remained a staunch ally of Elak, received more than once at court, where he was feted by the Council for his part in the subjugation of Atlantis' enemies.

It was a time of new prosperity, though the men of Atlantis were watchful, knowing their world would never be entirely free of danger and creatures of darkness, whoever craved their own empires.

- Helvas Ravanniol, **Annals of the Third Atlantean Empire**

Chapter One: From the Island of Shadows

Dalan, the High Druid of Atlantis, most prominent and powerful of his Order, spent a part of his day in the royal palace in the capital, Epharra, visiting the secluded temple of Ishtar, mightiest of Atlantean gods. After he had made his obeisances and offered prayers for the well-being of the Empire, its ruler, Elak, his family and all those who lived and thrived under the dragon banner, Dalan retired to a private tower, where the holiest of the relics and sacred instruments of power were housed. Studying these, sealed in their golden caskets or glass-fronted cabinets, he considered their individual histories, and in many cases the part he had played in them. Most prominent of them were three cases, bolted firmly to the inner wall, their steel housing decorated simply with runes forged long before the present Empire rose to eminence. The cases contained the three most powerful weapons in Atlantis' armoury, these days rarely taken from their hallowed beds.

The first contained the great staff Dalan had often used before it had been richly empowered by the crimson jewel of the ancient Valusians, given to Dalan by the last of their sorcerer kings, Amun Thuul. Dalan well remembered the last time he had used the weapons, at the cataclysmic battle of Skaafelda, where Atlantean and Pict had crushed the assault of the alien sea people, the Orugllyr and their sorcerers. In recognition of their fabulous powers, both staff and jewel were kept here now, awaiting the day when their immense energies were needed once more to protect Atlantis. On either side of the case, the many blades of lost Valusia and her Slayers were carefully stacked, also in readiness to combat the powers of darkness.

Beside the first case resided a second, equally as large, housing another of the three great staffs of power. This had been named by the treacherous Holy Prime, Kallarok of the Protectors in the far eastern continent as The Rod that Brings the Thunder, the Scourge of the Night. Dalan had used it to devastating effect in the overthrow of the black gods served by the man-apes of the White Mountain. Now, it too had been locked away in readiness for a time of great need.

Dalan faced the third case, knowing it was empty. It had been prepared for the final staff, last of the terrible set that, combined, would bestow upon their wielders the ultimate defensive power, the gift of Ishtar, only ever to be used against the coming of the doom of the world, the gods from the stars and their swarming horrors. This staff remained a legend, and had not resided in the care of Man for years without number. Dalan's Druidic brothers had secretly scoured the world for it, but no word of it had come back to Atlantis. Its absence was a constant source of anxiety to Dalan. He knew that when the powers of darkness mounted their ultimate onslaught, the staff's power must be entwined with its fellows in the defence of Humanity.

*

As he left the temple of Ishtar, Dalan made his way to the royal courts and was quickly met by a courier, who bowed low and began a garbled, anxious message. "Slowly, Gerontes," said Dalan with a smile. The young man's eagerness to please, combined with his awe of the High Druid, often confused his messages, but Dalan had a soft spot for the boy and his dedication.

"A ship has come," said the youth, trying to control his excitement. "From the southeast."

Dalan masked his immediate unease. Of all the seas controlled by Atlantis, the southeastern waters and their innumerable islands were those where troubles most frequently reared their head.

"The captain is Morgaal, from the pirate islands."

Dalan nodded. He had met the towering seaman, a former Viking from the far northeastern lands, and a loyal servant of Queen Shiveeri, who had once been his captain in her pirating days.

"There's an island. Grimfallas. It is populated by no more than a few people. They're terrified. They say it's going to be eaten."

The Druid would have smiled, but he knew that somewhere behind this strange statement would be an underlying truth, and almost certainly one that presaged ill. "I'll come at once, Gerontes. Go ahead and let the King know I'm on my way." He watched the youth rush off, thinking of Grimfallas. Also known as the Island of Shadows. A place of ill omens and past terrors, where a major pirate community had once been swept to its doom one single night in a local storm that legend implied was conjured by demonic forces from beneath the waves. These days few sailors visited the place.

Elak and Lycon, together with Shiveeri and some of the Councillors were gathered in one of Elak's private audience chambers, where Dalan joined them. He read the mood at once, one of concern and uncertainty. Seated around the central table in the hall, where they had met many times to discuss policy and strategy, the company had received Morgaal, who inclined his head as Dalan entered and took up his own seat.

"I gather you've come from Grimfallas," said Dalan.

"I have, lord," said the bearded seaman. He turned to Elak, who indicated that he should re-tell his news. "It's no place I'd have visited through choice, but when I was passing it, my ship picked up a man cast on to the rough waters – they're mighty troubled in those parts – and with great difficulty we revived him. Another hour in the water and he'd have perished. He was one of the last surviving people on Grimfallas, where they'd rebuilt the small citadel and its temple. A terrible evil has come to the island. I believe it's the beginning of something far more dangerous. A proper threat to the Empire."

Chapter Two: The Lost Staff of Power

Although Morgaal had already given his report to the company, they listened closely as he repeated it in his gruff tones for the High Druid's benefit. "That near-drowned inhabitant of Grimfallas, Pannartas, told us that he and his people had lived on the island for a year. They'd been working in the ruins, carving stuff out of the huge cliffs. Making a new home for themselves. The fishing around the island is what brought them there, being as he said, a marvellous bounty, worthy of the risks they took for it. They wanted to establish a small port. Thrive on trade with other islands. Probably would've done it, too, but for one thing. They got too curious. Right in the heart of the ruins, they found a great many tunnels. Led deeper into the guts of the island. Grimfallas is shunned for good reason. It had its secrets."

"They uncovered them?" said Dalan.

"So Pannartas said," Morgaal went on, warming to his report. "They followed the longest tunnel. Reckoned it had been constructed and strengthened by human hands, long in the past. A bunch of explorers reached a place that was hewn from a cavern far beneath the ocean's floor. Amazingly old, a place of marvels, rich in treasures, statues, furnishings and any amount of jewels and precious rocks. A place fit for gods, or at least a tribute to them. Waiting to be taken to the surface."

Dalan glanced at Elak, whose serene face wore a knowing look. The King and the Druid had found themselves in such places of wonder on more than one occasion, and it inevitably led to complications. Elak's eyes met Dalan's, and in the King's expression, those very words passed across the chamber to the Druid.

"For such things," said Dalan, "there is always a price."

Morgaal snorted. "The gods enjoy taunting us. Those worshiped on Grimfallas were no exception. The men who'd come into the lost temple reckoned they could feel them in the air. Didn't stop them from being greedy. They took things. Gold, jewels, and the like." Morgaal turned to Dalan. "And weapons," he added.

Dalan sensed there was more to this. "Weapons? Such as?"

"Swords fit for kings. Knives with jewelled handles. Spears. They only took some. Most was left. Pannartas said there was one weapon, a long staff. From the way he described it, it was like the thing your Druids told us all to watch for."

Dalan's eyes widened. "Staff?"

"Pannartas said it sounds like the staff you bear, lord. With all the carvings on it."

Dalan and Elak faced one another, stunned by the words. "Where was this?" said the High Druid.

"Left in the cavern. Soon after the men fled, the storm came, like it had been sent to punish them for thieving. It was that violent the whole island shook, and the rebuilt parts of the city fell into the sea when the cliffs just slid away. The islanders were all drowned, all excepting Pannartas."

*

Elak and Shiveeri were alone with Dalan and watched him pace up and down in the private room, his face a cloud, his fists clenching and unclenching in frustration. It was unusual to see him so agitated.

"You think it is the third staff?" Elak asked.

"There's every possibility. Its description fits. How it came to be on Grimfallas is a mystery, but the details of the staff's past is shrouded in rumour and myth."

Shiveeri grinned. "There's only one way to find out. Man a few ships and sail out there. Send a small fleet if you need to."

Elak nodded slowly. "If there's a chance that it is the missing staff, Dalan, we have to investigate. It'll be dangerous. Grimfallas is notorious. But no island is impregnable."

Dalan temporarily ceased his pacing. "Yes. A small fleet. But you cannot lead it, Elak. If what Morgaal said about the storm and whatever dark gods these are that protect the island, it would be far too much of a risk to your life."

"Or yours?"

"I have to go. I must take one of the other staffs with me. If the gods and their servants have the use of the staff on the island, only one of the others can cancel out its power. I will take the Valusian staff of Amun Thuul. The Scourge of the Night must remain here."

"If you took both, would that not doubly empower you?"

"I fear the risks involved. If all three staffs fell into the hands of the enemy, I'd fear for Atlantis."

"I should go," said Elak. "This is far too important to delegate, even to my best warriors. Lycon should come, too. In the past, the three of us have been a match for anything the enemies of the Empire have thrown at us."

"The Council will never allow it," said Dalan.

"The Council do not order me –"

Shiveeri was gently laughing, seeing an old argument rising and about to flare. "There's something else you should consider."

The two men turned to her. "Oh?" said Elak.

"It could be a trap. Whoever is behind this could be using the staff as bait. With you three worthies as the prey."

"She's right, of course," said Dalan.

"How would you get to the island?" said Shiveeri.

"The Royal Wing," said Dalan, referring to the great flying lizards from the island of Illyrin, which had been used successfully on previous missions.

"They'll expect that," said Shiveeri. "And if these dark powers can bring storms down upon an island, the skies will not be a safe place."

Elak was suddenly grinning. "I think it's time that Kellomar returned from the shadows."

Dalan frowned at him, the reference clearly eluding him.

"My assumed name. Lycon and I will simply be ordinary sailors on one of the ships sent to Grimfallas. No one need know who we are. It's worked in the past."

Dalan's frown became a deep scowl. "It'll be one time too many. That's my worry, Elak."

Shiveeri shook her head. "My husband is a pirate at heart, Dalan. You should know that by now."

Chapter Three: Intruder by Night

Moonlight silvered the choppy waters as the small Atlantean fleet left Epharra and set sail for eastern seas. On the rail of the *Red Gull*, Morgaal studied the rise and fall of the tide, with its shrinking backdrop of the land and craggy rocks. A dozen ships had set sail, and on this craft, Elak and Lycon were secreted among the crew, which had been picked from the very finest of the King's warrior sailors. Dalan was on board the expedition's leading ship, the *Fox*, protected by the powers in the staff he carried as well as a double crew of Epharra's finest. The Druid had protested Elak's involvement in this quest to the last, but eventually had to give way to the determination of the King. Morgaal grinned ruefully at the waves, admiring the King's spirit

Something out beyond the ship's side made the huge renegade Viking lean forward, eyes narrowing as he tried to focus. Yes, there was a small craft there, arrowing through the waters as if propelled by secret ocean powers. Morgaal could see several figures at its sharp prow. The vessel, although a large rowing boat, had raised its single sail, and was profiting from a strong wind. In moments the craft would come alongside the warship. Morgaal looked around, but none of his fellows were at the rail. The lookout, high on the main mast, would doubtless be focusing his own gaze on the seas ahead of the *Red Gull*, watching the other members of the fleet. Morgaal tossed the prepared rope over the side and watched it dangle inches from the creamy waters.

The smaller boat knifed towards the *Red Gull's* keel, and with formidable dexterity, the first of its crew reached out for the rope, gripped it and swung out over the spray. Swiftly, lithe as a cat, the figure climbed upward. Once it was clear the figure was safe, the craft swung away, dipping below a trough of waves before being swallowed by the darkness as it made its way back to the shore.

Morgaal waited for the figure to reach the rail and thrust out a huge paw to grip its hand and help swing the climber aboard. It was clad in black from head to foot, wearing a tight-fitting mask through which only the eyes were visible. The big sailor began pulling up the rope, curling it as he did so, preparing to drop it and secure it in the scuppers. The climber clapped him on the shoulder wordlessly, the gesture marking its gratitude. As the two of them turned, they found themselves facing a rapier, whose length gleamed silver in the moonlight.

"What treachery is this?" snapped a voice from the shadows as a sailor stepped forward, his sword's tip weaving a slow circle, poised to strike like a serpent.

Morgaal shifted in front of the intruder, though he was careful not to go for his own blade. The huge Viking's face dropped when he realized it was no ordinary sailor he faced, but the King himself, secreted on board under the false name of Kellomar. Morgaal knew well enough just how fast Elak was, and that the King would open his throat in a moment.

Behind him the lithe figure danced to one side, its own blade suddenly drawn, ready for conflict. Elak smiled grimly and nodded his head, indicating the group of armed men with him. If this was to be a fight, it would be an unequal contest.

"If you want to test my blade," growled the intruder, "do so alone, warrior. Or do you not have the heart?"

Elak paused for a moment, then threw back his head and laughed. "You know you already have my heart, Shiveeri," he said and Morgaal blew out his breath in a great gust of relief.

Shiveeri cursed softly. "You knew it was me."

"That outfit does nothing to hide your form, and who knows it better than me? Besides, that voice! You'd need to deepen it to deceive anyone."

She put up her sword and pulled off her mask, but she

was smiling now. "Don't punish Morgaal. I threatened him with dire reprisals if he didn't assist me in this affair."

"I suppose there is no point in my asking you what in all the Nine Hells you are doing here?"

"Save your breath. You didn't think I was going to sit uselessly in Epharra while you and the others enjoyed yourself? I'm as good with a sword as any of you. And you can put that to the test if you dare."

Elak shook his head, but smiled. "No, that won't be necessary. Very well. Since you are here and there's no way we can dump you overboard, you'd better come below."

"I'm glad we understand each other."

*

Later, in the company of Lycon, Elak and Shiveeri discussed the planned landing on distant Grimfallas. Lycon, delighted at Shiveeri's arrival and Elak's completely unnecessary anxieties about her safety, found it impossible to keep the grin from his ape-like features, and Elak glowered at him to no avail.

"Can we land in safety?" said Shiveeri.

Elak shrugged. "From what Pannartas the islander says, the quayside to the port may have been washed away by the storm. It was one of the few places where anyone can get on to the island. It'll be treacherous and will certainly try the best of us. When we arrive at the place, we'll know more."

Days later, when the fleet circled Grimfallas, the chances of getting ashore looked bleak. Overhead the skies were in perpetual turmoil, lowering in massed cloud banks that fizzed with lightning, shimmering with powers that suggested sorcery, the work, it seemed of the gods who protected this sinister place. Its shores from all approaches were intimidating, great walls of chiselled, slippery stone, spume-washed and sharp, and there seemed to be no place in the milling seas at their base where any ship that dared attempt to move in close would be risking destruction. The expedition looked fated to fail before it had even begun.

Chapter Four: The Things from the Sea

Elak and Shiveeri woke with the dawn and on deck were greeted with an unexpected sight. The sea, so turbulent the night before, was like glass, unnaturally so. A weird pinkish light shimmered on its surface, while above Grimfallas, the clouds had vanished with the night, leaving blue skies overhead. Lycon joined Elak and Shiveeri at the rail.

"You can almost smell the sorcery," he said.

Elak was watching his fleet, each ship motionless, as if frozen in time. "What does it mean?" he breathed.

"It gives us a better chance of landing," said Shiveeri. "But again it also suggests a trap."

"You think something wants us on Grimfallas?" said Lycon. "Do you think they know you are here, Elak?"

Elak was about to reply, when there came a shout from the mast. The lookout was pointing seaward. Mist drifted across the still seas a few miles away in a great band that obscured the western horizon. It writhed, as rich a pink colour as the sea itself, as though something lit it from below rather than the dawn, which was rapidly turning to gold behind the island. As Elak studied the oncoming mist, he caught sight of shapes within it. They were rising out of the water, scores of them becoming hundreds, things that took to the air like flying fish, though these were no fish.

"Ishtar!" gasped Lycon. "What are these?"

"Jellyfish?" said Shiveeri. "Although they are not like any I have seen before."

Elak called out to his sailors, who quickly prepared to defend the ship. The massed creatures from the deeps formed a cloud as they approached. Their dark green bodies, bulbous as sacs, cross-veined and transparent, trailed long fronds and tendrils, and they drifted on air currents as easily as gulls. Each one was the size of a large hound, and Elak feared their delicate, root-like tendrils would carry a deadly sting. He looked to either side of him, to where his other ships were readying for this bizarre blizzard. Dalan would be at the rail of one of them, his staff raised in expectation of what promised to be an onslaught.

Quickly the clouds of aerial horrors, swarming like bees, reached the ships and began circling them, lifting higher into the still morning air, threatening to drop down among the warriors. Several bowmen released their arrows, some of which struck home, bursting the sacs of numerous jellyfish, which plummeted to the sea, but they were simply replaced by more of them. Waves of these began to drop down, tendrils flicking at the defenders, and where these caught one, their stings did their terrible work, bringing an agonizing death to Elak's warriors. The conflict became a crazed exchange of weapon and tendril, countless scores of the jellyfish being brought down, either by steel, arrow, or fire, as bowmen ignited fire arrows to deadly effect. Elak could see, though, that the outcome of this grim struggle would be decided by numbers, for the sea creatures were still rising up from the water in vast quantities. They formed a solid cloud.

He saw Dalan, whose staff of power glowed crimson, its light spearing outward in lethal bolts, burning into the assailants, and the main body of them swirled around the fleet like a miniature storm, though it continued to grow in power. The ships were forced away, back from the main front of the aquatic army, and Elak realized the *Red Gull* was heading inexorably towards the shores of Grimfallas. Were they being driven?

The sea remained like glass, and the waves that had burst so spectacularly on the rocks the night before, remained small, mere ripples lapping softly at the shoreline.

"I think you were right, Lycon. They want us to land. See – the damaged quay." Elak pointed to where the former port had collapsed, leaving the shells of houses and other buildings, and a short quay that was broken and deeply cracked, as though what remained of it was about to crumble into the waters.

"Then it *is* a trap," said Shiveeri.

"Yes," Elak said with a nod. "But we must get on to that island." Turning, he gave sharp commands to Morgaal and his oarsmen: at once they had the ship heading for the quay. Word was passed down the line of ships and immediately Dalan's craft also headed for the island. The rest of the ships held their formation. Around them the thick cloud of jellyfish pulled back, as if waiting for a new command from some invisible source.

Shiveeri pointed to them. "See! They have achieved what they wanted, Elak."

He was nodding. "It seems my identity is no secret. We are all known to whatever commands these things."

"Then we should avoid Grimfallas," said Lycon. "The lost staff of power would be a prize beyond value, but what use would it be to Atlantis if we are lured in and killed?" There was no fear in his voice, and Elak knew Lycon would be the first into battle on any front, but there was no time for deliberation.

"We need that staff, Lycon. Without it, Dalan fears the balance of power would be with our enemies. We have no choice. We must land and deal with whatever they fling at us."

At his shoulder, Shiveeri grinned. "Well, we didn't come here for the fishing."

Chapter Five: Death Weed

Elak and Dalan's ships eased shoreward, the Druid holding aloft his staff, from which a brilliant halo of crimson light suffused his craft and its warriors. There were places along the battered quayside where it was possible to tie up the ships, and this was speedily done, enabling both crews to disembark. Dalan joined Elak at the forefront of the landing party, having listened to Shiveeri's comments about this likely being a trap. "We must enter the island swiftly. For now, the staff will protect us from the worst of any attacks. But I doubt an attack will come among these ruins. I do know the third staff is here on Grimfallas. Its power reaches out and this staff I carry senses it."

"Where is it, exactly?"

"At the very heart of the island. There will be a way to it. It is waiting for us."

"That's not necessarily a good thing," grunted Lycon.

A shout from beyond where the first scouting party had entered the ruins signalled that a path had been found, winding up to a narrow chasm, where two great walls of rock had split apart. The company moved forward, bathed in the softened crimson glow of Dalan's staff. It did nothing to dispel the feeling of deep unease that also cloaked it, for there was an atmosphere here akin to a battlefield, where countless warriors had died. Most of the islanders had perished in the supernatural storm that had devastated the place, and elements of its fury still hovered among the smashed buildings like wisps of smoke, and a sense of malevolence hovered over the company like a cloud of gulls. Of living gulls there were none, nor any sign of life. The only movement was the sluggish drift of the sea, thick as oil.

*

On the deck of the *Grayshark*, out in the narrow bay beyond Grimfallas, where the fleet had been instructed to wait, Corfundal, its captain, studied the largest of the islands. From a distance he saw the two ships tie up at the quay and figures climbing on to it before disappearing into the rocks. The glow that suffused them winked out, so the captain assumed they had found a way into the island.

"I fear for them," said the gruff voice of his helmsman, Dattric, beside him. "The King should have taken everyone bar a skeleton crew for each ship. Ishtar alone knows what sorcery is harboured in that place."

Corfundal studied the skies. They were clear, the aerial threat of the jellyfish dispersed as if it had never been.

"What is that?" said Dattric, pointing to another island, the closest islet to Grimfallas. It was small, little more than a great chunk of rock, pointing upwards like a thick finger, the home for squadrons of sea birds, judging by the accumulation of white droppings that coated it. There was not a single bird to be seen, but there was life there, emerging from the sea around it.

Corfundal, intrigued, went to the mast and clambered upward effortlessly. Like all young sailors, he had learned the ropes of sea-craft and spent endless hours as a lookout, so hauling himself up to the highest point of the mast was second nature to him. From up there he could view the bird islet better.

He gasped. All around its base, a weird kind of weed was encroaching, sliding upwards from the sea, glistening in the bright sunlight. Yet no weed could have moved so swiftly! Corfundal watched as tendrils emerged from it like long whips, and rose up to the highest part of the islet.

They clamped around the crest like grappling irons and below them more of the extraordinary weed rose up, a solid bank surrounding the islet, like a single organism, a monstrous denizen of the ocean. Corfundal realized now that it was not composed of weed, but something more substantial, more fleshy, compounding the impression of its being a uniform entity. It must be huge, a leviathan. He watched in stunned amazement as the thing seemed to *shake*. Gradually it began to subside, but as it slid back into the waters that were now heaving and churning as though in the throes of a vast whirlpool, *it took the islet down with it*. A single tall column of water was flung upwards as the last of the sea creature and the islet slipped under the waves, and as it sank, all signs that the islet had existed had gone, as if it had been swallowed.

*

Dalan's staff lit the way into the chasm, and from high above came the sounds of flying things, flapping and croaking as their shadow territory was disturbed. Beside the Druid, Lycon had attached himself to him on strict instructions from Elak, as the Druid's personal guardian. Lycon carried a long spear, renowned as he was for being a master of its use, in spite of his protestations to the contrary. Elak had, however, dismissed these, as he'd good reason to recognize Lycon's unique skills with the weapon, having previously seen them put to stunning use.

The King and Shiveeri followed close behind, occasionally nodding to each other, but saying little. Their bond was another unique thing in this company, their minds attuned, their strength trebled by their unity, in conflict as much as in love.

Slowly the company, comprised of some fifty of the finest Atlantean warriors, moved upward into the heart of the island. It was cold in this chasm, like everything else about Grimfallas, an unnatural thing, more than hinting at dark elements, as though the island were either alive or housed forces that coiled like vast serpents, gradually roused from sleep.

Light from ahead at last alerted Dalan to the exit, and soon the company stood on the lip of an opening on to a spectacular panoramic view. This was the heart of Grimfallas, a vast expanse of stepped rocks, cliffs and what might once have been enormous buildings, temples perhaps, to unknown gods. These rose up in a ragged circle, a vague, crater-like hollow, whose floor fell away into immense green depths, choked with alien verdure, what looked to be an impenetrable carpet that covered the entire area. The encircling cliffs had the ominous look of a gigantic ring of teeth

Dalan turned to Elak and Shiveeri. "What we have come for," he said, his face grim, "is below."

Chapter Six: The Heart of the Island

Elak had his men spread out along the ridge, searching for a way down into the immense green cauldron, vividly highlighted by the sun which now blazed in an azure, cloudless sky. It soon became apparent there were no steps or stairs, or any artificial pathway cut into the rocks to enable a descent. The drop was sheer, as though the only creatures capable of traversing it would be avian, though no birds flew in this enclosed, silent atmosphere. There were several huge vine-like growths swinging from the cliffs across the void, attached to a distant jutting central tower of stone. Its bizarre shape made it impossible to discern whether it was a natural phenomenon, or something constructed by whatever beings had once lived here. These would have pre-dated by centuries the colony of people on the outer rim of Grimfallas as attested by the crumbling condition of the rocks. Various stone projections from the central tower clung to it like petrified mushrooms, although they could have been buildings, now overrun by choking banks of ivy-like plants.

"We'll find what we seek inside that place," said Dalan.

Elak nodded. "We'll need to use the thickest of the vines to cross." He had the word spread to the company, and however appalled anyone might have been by the prospect of going over the vines, no one demurred. Soon afterwards Dalan chose one of the thickest, several feet in girth and hung with thick fronds and mosses. The Druid stepped on to it. Solid and unmoving, it promised a reasonable bridge, although it was thickly woven with vegetation, misshapen ferns that had seeded themselves along its entire length, shrubs and vividly coloured flowers. The unique stillness of the surroundings was like the paused breath of a god, a spirit of the verdure.

"The way has opened for us," Elak whispered to Shiveeri. "It is indeed a trap. Otherwise the whole place would come alive. It is strange, being this far north of the jungle continents."

"Yes. Almost as if it had broken away from them and lodged here."

"Something protects it."

Nothing changed as they crossed the great void, feeling the thick vine shift at their weight. On the far side, they stepped from it onto a wide ledge, rock that was clear of vegetation. Behind this a tall opening in the stone had been cut and chiselled, its frame a frieze of strange, embossed pictograms and carvings, inter-linked with unfamiliar creatures, things that had no limbs and whose heads were bulbous, studded with globular eyes. They appeared to writhe about the sculptured frame, sinister and malefic. Their meaning was clear, a warning to anyone thinking of setting foot beyond the portal.

Dalan lifted his staff, the crimson glow strengthening as he did so, and the frieze shivered at the light's touch, as if the alien forms it harboured shrank back from it. "I sense a response within the cavern," said the Druid. "The third staff is there, waiting. Ready yourselves," he told the company. "Whatever else is inside will be hostile."

"Madness," muttered Lycon, but he never moved more than a few feet from Dalan.

The Druid stood to one side, raising his staff, for as long as he did so there was no threat from the stone guardians of the gateway. Elak posted a number of guards outside the entrance and led the way within, which was lit by an invisible source, possibly phosphorescent fungi or jewels set in the high roof, otherwise locked in shadows. A passage led upward, broad enough to allow four people to climb abreast of one another. Elak and Shiveeri, with one warrior on their outside flank, led the way, swords gripped, prepared for any hint of an attack, though none materialized. They were in a winding tunnel, cut into the heart of the tower and, looking back, they saw Dalan and Lycon bringing up the rear of the column.

Light above increased, a sharp glare, and they came up to a level area spreading before them like the great floor of a palace, polished and ornately decorated, the creatures depicted in vivid splendour therein as unfamiliar and bizarre as the ones in the portal below. Elak suppressed a shudder. He had seen things like this before in his wanderings, things that had drifted down from the stars and embedded themselves in the depths of the ocean. It was evident now that this place had never been the lair of Man, even in his earliest form.

The walls around the gleaming floor were lined with statues and sculptured shapes, perfectly preserved, intricate and brilliant in their workmanship, like frozen living entities, tributes to another world. Some were beautiful to look upon, while others prompted only revulsion, their gaping, tendril filled mouths monstrous and hostile. Where there were eyes, these shone eerily down upon the company, fixing it with stares that spoke of a great hunger, evil desires that filled the company with dread.

Elak calmed his nerves with difficulty. Coming here had been a huge risk, but Dalan had told him there was no choice.

The far wall was devoid of statues or decoration, a thick, black void that could have been an opening into a stellar gulf, hinting at distances beyond imagining. Vague light began to shimmer there, and presently a long slab of stone was limned in its glow. Stretched upon it was a figure. At first Elak and the company took it to be another statue, but it moved, gently swinging off the slab to stand, a man-shape of medium height, wearing a plain dark robe. It carried a staff, the twin of that held by Dalan, though it seemed to be little more than a cut bough of wood.

"Welcome, Atlanteans." The voice was powerful, enhanced by the acoustics of the great chamber, echoing around the walls. "Welcome to the ending of the days of Man."

"Who are you?" said Elak, his own voice a ringing challenge.

"I am the voice of Xeraph-Hizer, who you have named the Leviathan Lord. Soon you and all your kind will feed him and his fellow Sea Gods. What began so long ago among the stars will reach its ordained conclusion here in your world. The oceans, the blood of the Old Ones, will claim it for all eternity."

Chapter Seven: The Coming of the God

The robed being opened its arms, and behind it a wall of water rose up, a line of mingling fountains fifty feet high that shimmered and gleamed, the waters falling somewhere beyond the floor, drained away by an invisible channel. Sounds made by the cascading wall were muted and as the Atlanteans watched in amazement, a section of the immense curtain flattened out to form a window as smooth as glass, wherein vague shapes and shadows moved about like a scene from beneath the ocean. A landscape rippled and took shape, a strange, alien place, lit by a spectrum unknown to human eyes, and a sky in which clusters of brilliant stars winked and blazed, and where vast moons slid by in a dizzy procession, their surfaces riddled with lines like twisted hieroglyphs. Wedged into the jagged rocks and escarpments of the landscape beneath the racing moons, towers rose up, carved from the naked stone, though these were like no towers ever viewed on Elak's world. Between them floated monstrous creatures, trailing countless filaments, while bird-like shapes swooped and dived.

"See distant Xalkara, mother of worlds, cradle of the sea spawn, where the Star Gods sit in regal majesty," said the robed figure. "Their children soar among the stars, and together they have crossed the abyss of timeless space, to swim in the deeps of your world."

The vision changed to show the oceans of Elak's world, both its continents and all its islands, teeming like the seeds of a vast plant.

"The sea will claim them all!" cried the robed figure. The face within the hood was blurred, its eyes hidden in darkened sockets, its mouth a gaping hole, toothless, its lips shrivelled. "See, their fate begins!"

Thrust up from the panoramic view of the sea, several islands rose like leaning slabs, bare and windswept, outposts of the northern archipelagos, where only the colonies of birds had made homes. As Elak and the others watched, the seas around one of the islands churned and from those white waters erupted scores of long frond-like growths, wrapping themselves around the island.

"See! The children of Xeraph-Hizer feed!"

The island jerked under the colossal pressure of the things that clasped it, like a great fist squeezing the water from a sponge. Up rose the island, rising like an immense whale, and as it did so the fronds continued to wrap around it, inexorably dragging it back down into the water. One by one all the islands succumbed to the same fate, and when it was over, the sea fell calm. There was no sign of the islands ever having been there.

"Soon, this island of Grimfallas will suffer the same fate! One of Xeraph-Hizer's deep dwellers will rise and take it!"

*

While Elak, Shiveeri and the company stood mesmerized by the shocking revelations within the cavern, the guards left outside became aware of sudden movement beneath their feet. They turned to see the huge vine, the natural bridge across from the far side of the island's interior, shaking wildly, as were the others that criss-crossed the void. Like an immense spider web, the complex of vines shook as if an earth tremor had them in its grip, and several split and tumbled far down into the green depths. Slices of rock shook loose and slid downwards, and even the thickest of the vines, including the bridge, exploded as they snapped under the colossal pressures brought to bear on them.

Chaos filled the whole of the jungle around the base of the jutting central rock, the vegetation thrashing as if gripped and shaken by monstrous, invisible hands. The guards leapt back as the edge of the platform crumbled and fell away. They realized they were stranded here, with no way down. Swiftly they ran inside to alert Elak and the company to the disaster, the thunderous sounds crashing on their ears like a sudden storm.

*

Corfundal was again perched high up on the mast of the *Grayshark*, watching the shores of Grimfallas. To his absolute horror he saw the same massive fronds emerge from the sea that had wrapped around the bird islet and dragged it beneath the waves. Surely the same fate could not possibly befall Grimfallas! It was far too large. Yet those tendrils, massive banks of weed, were multiplying at a fantastic speed, burgeoning up from below. Corfundal gasped as they slapped at the two ships moored to the distant quayside, and within mere moments they had battered both vessels to destruction, and all that remained were a few spars and chunks of wood, floating on the surface. None of the men on board could possibly have reached the shore.

Dattric had clambered up beside him. "By all the Hells!" he gasped, seeing the horror unfold. "Can we save any of them?"

Corfundal squinted in the sunlight. "I see no one. All dragged under the sea."

"That weed is surrounding the island! Is that possible?"

Corfundal nodded. "This can only be the result of sorcery. No living thing can do that. Grimfallas is a large island. Surely it cannot be dragged down like that smaller islet." Yet as the two men watched, numbed, they wondered if they were wrong.

*

Inside the chamber, Elak and the company studied the spectacle on the wall of water, where the same scene looked upon by Corfundal and Dattric was now displayed.

"Our ships!" gasped Elak. "The men!" His voice was filled with horror.

"How can we fight this abomination?" shouted Lycon. He stepped forward, roaring his frustrated defiance, shaking the long spear he had brought. His fury boiled over and, unable to contain himself and taking a short run up, he dashed forward, drew back his arm, preparatory to hurling the weapon at the cloaked figure.

Dalan was visibly aghast. "No!" he yelled. "We dare not lose the spear! It is what the enemy wants"

But it was far too late. Lycon flung the spear and it tore through the air in a blur.

Chapter Eight: The Unleashing of Power

As Lycon's hurled spear tore into it, the robed figure

exploded in a confusion of dazzling light, its staff sent spinning across the floor to land in front of the wall of water. Elak and his companions shielded their eyes against the glare, while chunks of darkness rained down around the place where the figure had been. Amazingly there were scores of them, and as Elak watched he saw several of them break up into even smaller pieces. As his eyes adjusted, he realized the shadow-things were enlarging, becoming the size of dogs, with numerous legs. The first of them wriggled forward, centipede-like, and he met it with a swipe of his blade that cut it in half. Beside him, Shiveeri was also desperately fending off others.

"The sorcerer's staff!" cried Dalan. "Recover it!"

Lycon, dazed but shaking himself, ran forward, his own sword now wreaking havoc among the mass of creatures, barely enough to keep them from swarming over him. His size belied his speed and amazingly he reached the fallen staff and managed to grab it before others covered it. His spear had been almost melted by its impact with the robed figure, while the exposed end of the staff glowed, a similar crimson to that of Dalan's. Lycon flourished it and it burned off several of the creatures trying to drag it back from him, and they melted away like hot gobbets of fat.

"Elak!" Dalan shouted above the sudden roaring of the water wall, which shook now as if it would collapse, threatening to wash the entire company out of the cavern. "Use your staff!" The Druid held up his own, and its vivid glow pulsed, bathing the waters in its light, apparently holding it back. It bulged like a huge sac threatening to burst.

Elak did as bidden, cutting aside more of the shadow-things, and forcing his way close to where Lycon stood, legs braced, holding aloft the sorcerer's staff. Shiveeri protected him as Elak swung the staff and shook loose several more of the creatures, which burst into flame. Dalan used his staff to incinerate enough corpses to create a path to them both. He turned to look at Elak, a grim smile of satisfaction on his gaunt features.

"That is no ordinary staff," the Druid told him. "I deceived you, Elak. It is the second staff of power, the Scourge of the Night. and now we hold all three."

Both Elak and Lycon gasped. Neither had known that the staff given to Elak was the second staff. They had thought it had been left in Epharra, where it would be safe. Risking two staffs, Dalan had said, would be too much of a gamble. It had been a worthy trick to bring it, though, doubtless conceived to deceive the powers in this place. The shadow-creatures, amassed now in their scores, drew back from the three figures and the light that shone vividly from all three staffs they held. The Atlantean warriors closed in on them, a further protective wall, and as they did so, they, too, cut at the creatures, many of which went scuttling back into the hidden recesses at the back of the cavern.

Dalan faced the roaring waters. "Let us test our combined powers against this vile agent of Xeraph-Hizer." So saying, he directed his staff at the centre of the water wall, Elak and Lycon doing the same. Light streamed from the three staffs, combining to create a circle of white energy in the centre of the wall which gradually expanded until it had covered the whole shimmering mass. The roaring ceased abruptly and a sudden silence fell over the company. Then, like shattered glass, the water fell, drained away like a mirage.

Elak and his companions drew back, the last of the shadow-creatures, slithering away in molten form, lying in lifeless, gelatinous pools on the stone floor. Dalan motioned the company back towards the entrance, where they waited. Elak could feel the surging energy within the staff, but its unnatural power filled him with deep unease. He could see by Lycon's face that he felt the same discomfort. It was a relief when Dalan's staff ceased to glow, and what remained to the three men were seemingly no more than three simple staffs.

Before Elak could comment, Shiveeri pointed to the cavern entrance, where a distant rumbling came to his ears and the ground shook as if an earthquake might have been triggered by the release of their powers. Behind what had been the wall of water was a large area of utter darkness, an inner cavern perhaps. More thunderous sounds were coming from within it, from far below, at what must be the heart of the island.

"Is it volcanic?" Elak gasped, turning to Dalan. "We'll be fried alive if that's lava rushing up from the core."

Dalan shook his head. "No. The power of the three staffs has stricken those that fester in this island. Xeraph-Hizer's servant is wounded. We must finish the work. Come." He strode purposefully towards the black emptiness. Elak, Shiveeri and Lycon followed, though it took a great effort to master their fear. Behind them the warriors waited, confused and uncertain, also sensing what seemed like the imminent collapse of the entire chamber. Not one of them, however, would abandon their king.

*

Corfundal remained at the masthead, watching the island of Grimfallas with ever mounting horror. The colossal, massed banks of weed, or whatever that growth was, had spread almost to the peak of the cliffs, preparatory to beginning what must be a swallowing of the island similar to that he had witnessed with the others. From somewhere above Grimfallas, light rose upwards in a column, as if a strange beacon had been lit within the island, its rays released to the heavens. This was accompanied by a muted roaring within, as though some vast beast was giving vent to its anger.

Was the island *shaking*? Or was that the result of whatever actions this monstrous aquatic force had taken, an impossibly immense hound shaking a rat?

The sea round Grimfallas swirled in gigantic eddies, its out-flowing waves threatening to overcome the fleet, but the ships held steady. On the island the matted weed banks abruptly began to slide back down towards the churning waves, repulsed by something, and Corfundal was relieved to see that Grimfallas was not being dragged down with them. They were releasing their grip. Slowly whatever it was that had gripped Grimfallas withdrew, and once the waters had reclaimed it, the sea ceased its boiling and settled, becoming gradually calm once more. Corfundal knew, though, that none of the crews of the two ships berthed at the quay had survived.

What of Elak and his companions? Surely they, too, could never have survived inside that stricken island.

Chapter Nine: Descent into Chaos

Dalan, Elak, Shiveeri and Lycon stood on the brink of an immense dark well that fell away into invisible depths, though the sound of a tumultuous sea rose up from it. Around them the pall of darkness was held back by the glow from the three staffs the men held aloft. Each throbbed with powerful energies, linked to one another, and they were no longer bare shafts of wood, but a complex mass of embossed sigils and pictograms that shifted, imbuing the staffs with seething life. Light from the three staffs combined to throw off brilliant nimbus around the figures, and presently Dalan directed his staff downwards into the abyss. As he did so, the other staffs dipped, as if pulled by magnetism, working in harmony with Dalan's staff.

Light speared from the nimbus, a white bolt that lit up the great drop, revealing its curved sides, smooth as glass, searing a path deeper down until it struck the remote floor of the tunnel into the heart of Grimfallas. In spite of the depth and distance, the detonation roared, even more light exploding, and the tunnel shook, cracks writhing in its wall like live things. For long moments Dalan continued to direct the staffs, pouring more energy downwards until a final explosion rocked the ground and almost brought the group to their knees. Slowly everything fell still.

The three staffs ceased their outpouring of energy until only their tips glowed. Elak gazed into the churning well of light. By its shimmering luminescence he saw that the walls of the pit had crumbled in places, revealing a rough procession of shelves that formed a crude ancient stairway, though one never shaped for Man's use. He turned to Dalan, who was nodding.

"We must descend," said the Druid. "There is no other way back off the island."

Elak summoned his warriors, and the entire company began the dubious descent. Progress was dangerous and treacherous: as parts of the crude stairs crumbled, several warriors came close to falling to their doom, only saved by the quick-mindedness of their fellows. Overhead, in the pitch-black vault of the upper tunnel, where no light from the outside world intruded, a sound like low thunder rolled, a threat of the imminent and complete collapse of the riven walls. Below, the dazzling light weakened until it became a sullen glow, and the sound of the sea, less stormy, came upwards.

By the time the company had reached the bottom of the stair, the seas that had breached the underground caverns of Grimfallas had stilled, forming a salt-sea lake which lifted and fell gently, its surface reflecting the light from the staffs.

Around this huge central grotto, a wide shelf curled, its far edge leading to an exit out into natural daylight. Dalan indicated it, but as he did, the waters burst upwards as a dark shape breached them, a huge, saurian creature with a tapered head and a mouth that opened wide to reveal banks of long, curved teeth.

"Xeraph-Hizer's servants aren't done with us yet!" snarled Lycon, waving his blade in defiance.

Dalan reacted the swiftest, plunging his staff into the waters, where it discharged more light, though far less than previously. "Quickly!" he shouted to Elak and Lycon. "Swords are no use against this spawn of the deeps."

Elak and Lycon drove their staffs into the water, and as the light from all three fused, the sea glowed a rich crimson, as if the blood of the creature was oozing from it. The long head snapped back, the massive body turning and thrashing the waters, which slapped up against the rock ledge in a sequence of buffeting waves. Elak could see the eyes, twin saucers, wide with feral horror, filling with pain as light coursed through the body and shook the long tendrils that were clawing at the warriors.

Each of the three staffs suddenly felt cold, their light extinguished. Their powers had been exhausted. Elak waited for the renewed attack of the saurian, the head lowered into the water, about to smash into the ledge and sink its rows of teeth into the Atlanteans. Yet as Elak watched, the eyes glazed, opaque as glass, and the body of the sea beast shuddered, rolling over to reveal a corpse-white belly.

Lycon sagged, breathing heavily. "The gods took us to the brink, but they appear to have spared us," he said.

Dalan watched the saurian slide away beneath the water, which had ceased rising and falling. "We need the clean sunlight to renew the power of the staffs. In this darkness, they will pall and become corrupt, which is exactly what Xeraph-Hizer desires."

They wasted no more time in getting to the exit, clambering out on to rocks and into the afternoon sunlight. The sea was calm, its waves lapping at the shore. Far above, at the pinnacle of the cliffs, a slight mist had formed, and whatever storms had threatened had dispersed.

"What was that thing?" said Shiveeri.

"Xeraph-Hizer drove it up from the seabed. The Leviathan Lord controls everything in the depths in these seas. If he himself had risen, we would never have beaten him back without greater powers of our own."

"Why did he not come?" said Lycon. "The being I killed with the spear said he would rise."

"The Leviathan Lord has the power to become many things. He can use even a small part of himself to create servants, such as the thing within the cave. The enemies of Atlantis have made several attacks on us. Perhaps to test our defences. My fear is that, when their stars guide them, they will merge and launch the ultimate assault. If they do that, we will need all our own powers to withstand them. We won a great victory at Skaafelda, but there will be more such conflicts, and they will be worse."

"He assumed it would be easy to snare the second staff," said Shiveeri.

Dalan nodded. "Had he known that all three were here, he would have used far more power to take them. Even a god, it seems, can underestimate his enemies."

"Meanwhile," said Elak, putting an arm around Shiveeri with a broad smile, "there is something to warm our hearts!" He pointed to where several of his fleet were rounding a shoulder of rock. "Corfundal and the others have found us."

The company waved enthusiastically, and to their relief the ships veered shoreward, soon to lift Elak and his companions to safety.

Epilogue: Worms and Maggots

Elak and Shiveeri sat in one of the luxurious palace gardens with Lycon and Darruvia, enjoying a rare moment of peace in the sunlight. There were glasses of wine and wide bowls of fruit on the low table. Lycon, far less disposed to over-indulge in the wine than was customary for him, picked up a bright apple and polished it on his robe. Elak grinned at him and Lycon, amazingly, blushed.

Dalan joined the company and sat with them, enjoying the view of the Bay of Gold, where the many ships of Epharra rode gently at anchor. For once things seemed tranquil, the shadows of Atlantis' many enemies withdrawn.

Lycon let out a sudden growl of disgust. He held up the apple. "Just my luck," he said. "I picked the wrong one." Laughing, he was about to toss it into the nearby undergrowth in one of the flower beds, when Dalan held out a hand. Lycon tossed the apple to him.

Dalan examined it. After a while he held it up. "You see here what has all the appearance of a beautiful fruit. And yet, as Lycon has discovered, there is a worm within it."

Elak and Shiveeri exchanged covert glances. They knew the High Druid was about to reveal an astute observation.

"That voyage," said Dalan, "to Grimfallas, was the last in a long line of adventures, Elak. I think we were very fortunate to come away with our lives, and with the three staffs. As Shiveeri said, Xeraph-Hizer assumed he had us in a trap and would simply relieve us of the second staff. Our luck, though, cannot go on, and must not be tested again. We must be on our guard, more than ever. Every move we make must be weighed and calculated."

Elak grinned. "It pains me to agree, Dalan, but I see that you, and the Council for that matter, are right. No more wandering."

"Your movements now will be under the eyes of strange gods. The snares lay for you will be far more effective than what has gone before. However, there are ways to study our enemies." He held up the apple. "In this little world, there are worms and maggots who thrive. It is to their equivalent in our world that we must turn now."

Lycon screwed up his face. "Maggots?"

"People who will not be noticed, burrowing away out of sight. Men and women who are too insignificant to earn the attention of the gods, however deviously they scheme."

"Spies," said Elak.

"We need eyes and ears in every port, on every remote island."

"Men and women," added Shiveeri, "who can sail and are not afraid of peering into the darker places."

Lycon laughed. "Men and women like us!"

JEWELS OF THE SEA HAG

With the third of the great staffs of power housed safely in Epharra, Elak was again able to focus his attention on affairs of state and to administer his vast Empire. Dalan's suggestion to him that he should build a network of spies and informers which could travel secretly throughout the Empire, seeking news of plots and potential threats from Atlantis' many enemies, was put into effect, and the High Druid wasted no time in recruiting for the network. While this was served by those loyal to Elak in high positions, it was at its most effective when it drew upon the seemingly innocuous resources of men and women from the humblest of backgrounds.

- Helvas Ravanniol, **Annals of the Third Atlantean Empire**

Chapter One: The Secret of the Cliffs

The small fishing port of Tarrenus nestled among weathered bays on Cyrena's northern coast, fifty miles east of Epharra. Its buildings fitted jaggedly under the brow of tall cliffs, its jetty running out in a curve, following a sweep of shoreline to Seafire Island. Warehouses, boat yards and a solitary inn cluttered the jetty's end. Once this had been a notorious meeting place for various pirates and brigands from far and wide, but in these peaceful days, its custom centred on less dubious activities. The new king had promised to reward adventurers flying the Atlantean flag, and paid handsomely for their trade, even advancing them resources to set themselves up in their ventures. Most sailors had set aside old quarrels, and in many cases ships leaving here were crewed by those who once would have been at one another's throats. There were still rivalries and disputes, but less mysterious deaths and mayhem, and generally a goodly supply of ale steadied things.

For young men, eager to learn the skills of seamanship and launch out across the great, wild ocean in search of treasure and fabulous realms, Tarrenus offered an exciting starting point. Experienced captains, both those dedicated to Elak's regime and those who remained on its rim, were always on the lookout for fresh crewmen they could mould to their own persuasion. The less scrupulous captains took to their company many a rogue and rapscallion, secretly mourning the passing of the old days, when freebooters served private flags. They knew, however, the King had set up an efficient spy ring. Very little got past its eyes and ears. When a captain overstepped the new boundaries set by Elak, punishment was swift and effective.

Artugol and Volnus, two youngsters in the final months of their teens, had spent the day on the northern, seaward side of Seafire Island. It had been a grey, drizzly day, the crags and overhangs of the coast slick and shiny, a danger to all but the numerous sea birds nesting here. The two youths had climbed countless demanding ascents, testing themselves fully, rejoicing in the sheer exuberance of their endeavours. More than once they had felt the cold breath of death on their necks, but they worked as one, their extraordinary sharing of skills the blend that made them almost unique among islanders who thrived on such challenges. Artugol was tall and wiry, able to find the narrowest of channels, clinging to the rock faces like a gangling spider, while Volnus was stocky and muscular, his strength invaluable, swinging his companion across dizzy drops, or preventing Artugol from a fatal fall whenever he overreached himself, which was too often for Volnus's comfort.

Artugol sat on a narrow shelf, high above the boiling foam of the ocean smashing against the rocks far below. He produced a thickly woven bag. "Let's find something to eat." Around him, wings beating the air in a frenzy of anger, sea birds massed in clouds, shrieking raucously, beaks snapping, as they protected their nests from these hated intruders. The youths edged along the precarious ledge and found several nests, from which they took a few eggs, always making sure they left more than they took. The bag was half full, the eggs carefully wrapped and packed in thick strips of material against breakage, when they left the shelf and entered a narrow cleft which led like a chimney to the clifftop. Inside its shadows they were safe from the jabbing, frenzied beaks.

Volnus called to his companion, already several feet above him. "Hold, Artugol. Don't be in such a hurry to leave. You missed something."

Artugol swung round, laughter masking his impatience. "Enough is enough. We've eggs here to keep us fed for a week."

Volnus was probing a small crack, using a snapped-off root. "Forget your belly for a moment. I saw light strike something." He dug earth and a handful of rocky shards from the widening crack, leaning back with a gasp. Carefully he reached in and pulled out a sparkling object. It was the size of a small egg, glistening and shimmering strangely.

Artugol dropped beside him. "Gods of the deep, is it a diamond?"

Volnus held it up. "Look at the light reflecting! I think it must be."

Artugol pointed to the crack. "There are more! Get them out!"

"Gently! I don't want to lose them." Again Volnus used the root, painstakingly excavating a dozen more objects. They were perfectly circular, seemingly artificially shaped and polished.

"Must be worth a kingdom!" said Artugol. "Here – slip them in the bag. Cover them with the eggs. We'll have to think how we're going to pass them on. My friend, we'll live like princes!"

Having satisfactorily bagged their plunder, the youths scrambled to the daylight, laughing as they returned to Tarrenus. Had they taken a final look at the wave-blasted rocks under the crags, they would have seen figures rising from the spume, wraiths shaped from it: twisted, bloated things, their forms writhing like troubled fog, features blurred, the black orifices of mouths wide in silent screams, either of pain or fury.

Chapter Two: Terror from the Sea Fog

As the two youths traversed the narrow jetty to Tarrenus, they felt a sudden coldness in the sea air. Evening was closing in quickly, a damp fist. Fog swirled around the shifting waters. A powerful wind whipped up abruptly and the youths exchanged glances of deep unease. They understood well the ways of the ocean currents, tides and dramatic changes in the weather along this exposed shore, but tonight there was something indefinable in the air, a brooding otherness, a hint of the unnatural. They quickened their pace, crossing the half-way point of the stones as a gust slapped a wave against the jetty's base. Water erupted and a cloud of salty mist enveloped them.

They looked back, gasping. The fog, a churning grey mass, contorted itself violently, and from its coils a number of shapes emerged, bloated figures with swollen heads, black pits for eyes and wide, gaping mouths filled with utter darkness. The youths broke into a sprint, Volnus clinging tightly to the bag and priceless contents. Both knew instinctively it was the latter which had attracted these ocean horrors.

Overhead the roiling banks of cloud sank, about to obliterate all vision, but the youths accelerated, fuelled by seething terror: they felt the potential icy grasp of spectral claws, moulded from the fog. Something screamed at their shoulders, a nest of disturbed aerial fiends. Volnus might have tossed aside the bag, hoping to deter the malign pursuit, but some atavistic urge forced him not to do so. Instead he gripped it tighter and roared defiance.

To their relief and amazement, the youths crashed through the doorway of a small harbour store, kicking it shut and barring it behind them. A huge force battered itself against the outer wall of the building, shaking its foundations. The low roof beams quivered, releasing thick clouds of dust. Fortunately there were no windows, yet the horrors outside intensified their efforts to demolish the walls. The store was temporarily disused, and the youths knew if it had not been, that door would have been securely locked. When the place was used, amphorae of rare, southern wines lined the walls and chests of likewise valuable goods were stacked here. The place had been designed to keep thieves out and its considerable resistance to any such cemented the youths' safety now. They could hear, through thick stone and heavily slated roof, the wild efforts of the fog creatures to batter their way in. There was barely enough light to see by.

"What are they?" said Volnus.

Artugol shook his head. "Some kind of guardians, maybe. Of these jewels. Dare we keep them? Should we just toss them out?"

Volnus shook his head, and Artugol recognized the obstinacy.

"Will this store hold through the night?" Artugol went on breathlessly. "No one will venture to our aid in this storm. There's no other exit. The store is partly built into the cliff behind." They'd escaped death but only to trap themselves. "Put the bag by the door. If they break in, they can take it and hopefully ignore us."

Volnus gripped the bag even more tightly, a determined expression on his face. "No! Our future depends on these stones. We'll never get another opportunity like this. It's the gods' way of telling us. Nothing is won without a price."

Artugol groaned at the familiar obduracy. "If they get to us, Volnus, we'll be –"

"Listen!"

They froze, ears straining. The din outside had died down. Strangely there was not even a hint of the storm, no breath of wind.

Artugol frowned. "They're like huge hounds, sniffing around us in silence, waiting, trying to trick us. If we open the door, they'll be on us. If we're to frustrate them, we must remain here until daylight disperses them."

Somewhere above in the heaving night sky, a tremendous crash of thunder reverberated, and again the walls of the store shook. It was followed by another, the sounds intensified by the renewed shrieks and screams from the gathered demonic forces. A tumultuous battle was raging between natural and supernatural elements. The youths shrank down, fully expecting the building to be smashed, stone by stone, as the ferocity of the conflict rose to a crescendo.

"How could we possibly have unleashed this!" gasped Volnus, although his fingers yet gripped the bag. It would take a sharp blade to pry them loose.

When the chaos ended and silence fell again, the youths remained on their haunches among a few rejected pots, their ears ringing. Finally Artugol rose, suspicious of the silence.

"The door!" said Volnus, his voice a harsh whisper.

Artugol focused his gaze in the dimness. To his horror the door had swung inwards, its thick wooden bar snapped in two. Torchlight streamed inwards, flickering in sudden gusts of wind.

Two figures stepped into the room, not ethereal creatures shaped from fog, but warriors, fully armed and protected, wearing rounded helms. One raised a lantern.

"Ho! Who cowers there? Come out in the name of the King!"

Artugol whispered. "Elak's men. See, their insignia."

Volnus thrust the bag surreptitiously behind the largest of the amphorae. He and Artugol went before the warriors, hands held out, demonstrating they were unarmed.

Several warriors had entered; they stood in an intimidating line. Another figure, garbed in thick robes and bearing a tall staff, pushed gently past, sizing up the youths.

"The game is over," he said in a cold voice. "Deliver to me what you have found."

Chapter Three: The Sea Hag's Curse

"Found?" said Volnus. "We're sheltering from the storm. There's nothing here but broken pottery."

Artugol looked at his friend in puzzlement. Volnus was never usually this assertive in the face of authority. His fists were clenched, his whole manner one of rebellion.

"He's a Druid," Artugol whispered.

"I am Dalan, the King's Druid!" said the robed figure, his staff faintly glowing, as if alive. "Do not waste time. Bring me what you've found!"

Volnus drew back at the power in that voice. Reluctantly he went to the hidden bag and brought it, handing it to Dalan.

"Come with me," Dalan went on. "Quickly, before the next wave of attack."

The youths had no choice, seeing the grim faces of the armed men, whose blades looked all too ready for use. Silently they trooped out behind the Druid into the early dawn light. The tempest had abated, but a heavy, white mist clung to the town, jetty and sea, corralling the group. Dalan held his staff aloft. The air fizzed, reeking as though a fire had recently been extinguished. Out in the mist, vague shapes pulsed, imprisoned within it, striving angrily to shred their way free.

The Druid watched the aerial horrors keenly. A halo of light surrounded his staff and by its glow the party made for the jetty's edge. A large sailing ship loomed from a bank of mist, oars and belling sail proclaiming it to be the King's vessel.

Dalan led the way down a narrow set of steps on to the craft. As they followed him, the youths heard distant shrieks and screams of protest as the mist creatures attempted to renew their assault. The staff, however, held them at bay as the company boarded. Artugol and Volnus were taken below to the Druid's private quarters and presently the youths felt the ship shudder as the crew cast off.

"Where are you taking us?" said Artugol.

Dalan bid them sit and dropped into a tall seat, setting his staff aside. His hood fell back to reveal flowing, grey hair and a lined, alert face that spoke of great age and wisdom, so typical of his kind. He did not smile, but his expression softened.

"You are safe on this vessel," he said. "If you'd remained in Tarrenus, those demons would have sucked the life from you. Where did you find the jewels?"

Artugol explained and as he did so, Dalan nodded. "The King sent me on this mission. I have seen such jewels before." He pointed to the unopened bag, which he had dropped lightly on a small table. "There are believed to be many such clusters along these shores, and on some of the remote northeastern islands."

"What are they?" said Volnus.

"They were spawned by a creature from the myths of Atlantis's far past, a corrupt queen, who ruled her island kingdom like a goddess, worshiped by a primitive tribe. She may have been an outcast from the continent, or a renegade from the mysterious islands that throng the northeastern ocean. The ancient Druids knew her as Barzangis, the Sea Hag. After a violent conflict and terrible clash of powers, she was drowned, her corpse sent to the deeps. It was said she drew on cosmic forces from beyond the earthly plain and at the end, used the last of them to shield herself from death, although she took upon herself another form, something that has survived the eons and which lives yet, deep in her subterranean lair."

"The Sea Hag," said Artugol, suppressing a shudder. "All sea folk know the legends. Our mothers told as such tales to scare us and keep us from roaming far from the shore. She is real?"

"The jewels are like eggs. The Sea Hag secreted them along the boundaries of her kingdom, promising one day she would hatch them and unleash her vengeance on Atlantis and whoever ruled it. Some were found nearer Epharra, in another cliff. The aerial demons fed on them and were transformed. It took particularly deep magic to destroy them." Dalan looked away for a moment, as if seeing something dire in his mind's eye. "Many good men were lost, but the demons were snuffed out."

The youths studied the bag with fresh unease. "Those jewels – eggs –" said Artugol. "Are they *alive*?"

Dalan nodded. "If the demons had taken them, a fresh transformation would have occurred. For certain the Sea Hag intends to use every jewel she secreted, simultaneously. There may be thousands. If she does, it will require all of the King's power to withstand the invasion."

"How many clutches are there?" said Volnus.

Dalan's face clouded. "We cannot say. Nor where they are. In time, we would find them all. But there is no time. Soon the Sea Hag will attack. We may not contain her. Unless –" He let the word hang between them like a spell.

Artugol and Volnus stared at one another, mouths dry.

"Unless we find the Sea Hag and deal with her in her ocean lair," said Dalan. "Which is where you can help."

Artugol gulped. "Us? Take on the Sea Hag? Your pardon, master, but we'd be little better than sand flies! We have no powers."

"You're adventurous, cunning, athletic, and you know the seas and how to sail them. The King needs spies. Men who can join a reiver's crew and keep a sharp lookout without being conspicuous. I need eyes across the ocean. And reports. No more than that. Find where the Sea Hag is buried. For King Elak."

Chapter Four: She-Wolf of the Seas

The *Arrow* was a sleek and swift craft, carried across the waves at speeds few could match. Crewed by fifty, who either bent their backs in harmony, pulling at the oars, or rested and let the many winds of the ocean bell the single sail and plunge the craft through the swells like a knife. The steersman, Zendullo, swore loudly as he piloted the ship, cajoling the winds as if he could shape them to his will: in response, the *Arrow* rose and dipped, a match for all but the heaviest seas.

Among the crew were Artugol and Volnus. Dalan had negotiated their places with the craft's mistress, Eskarra. She was a daughter of a pirate clan that had sailed these tempestuous northern waters for decades, inheriting her role as mistress of the *Arrow* from her mother, whose reputation for ferocity and determination to better the efforts of any male rogue was well known across all seas, until a sudden illness had ended her illustrious life. Eskarra, barely out of her teens, was already developing into a she-wolf no less formidable than her mother. Artugol and Volnus found that out very early on and over the following weeks at sea.

"She drives her men hard," Artugol said softly to his companion as they bent their backs at the oars. "If we don't strike land soon, I swear I'll pass out."

Volnus grinned, though the efforts he made at the oar were evidently taxing even his strength. "She reserves her toughest demands for you and I. It's a test. She never wanted us on her ship."

"She fears Dalan. He has the power to impound the *Arrow* and curtail her wandering."

Both were conscious of the figure standing on the deck at the *Arrow's* prow, its back to them. Eskarra was not tall, a slender young woman, whose arms and legs were bared to all weathers, deeply bronzed, muscled, though not excessively. She wore her raven hair tightly bound; her ears exposed to reveal two golden earrings. Although the ship rose and fell as it sliced the waves, spume flying over it, Eskarra remained unmoved, the men beside her waiting for orders, which they carried out without hesitation. The word was Eskarra could match anyone with a rapier, her favoured blade, something she had in common with the legendary Elak. It was said that she only smiled when she was fighting.

"I doubt if she fears anything," said Artugol. "I wouldn't want to be the subject of her displeasure."

"Then you might want to be wary of your gaze." Volnus's grin widened.

Artugol almost lost the rhythm of the oar. "Meaning?"

"The way you look at her."

"Silence!" roared the oars master, Ormullah, a swarthy giant with a face like thunder and enough scars for a regiment. "You're not on a fishing trip now! Less mouth and more effort. Pull, you scum!" It was a tribute to the man's vocal chords that he was heard over the blasts of the wind. Artugol had been warned that this great bear of a man had been a powerful pirate captain, the most irascible and untamed of the free rovers, his fleet the scourge of the southeastern waters before he had finally agreed to ally himself to the King's cause. No one was sure how the transformation had been achieved, although it was whispered Shiveeri, the Queen had played a part in it.

Artugol bowed his head as if he had been caught in an embarrassing act, and was horrified to see that Eskarra had swung round, hearing Ormullah's roar. Her eyes fixed on the two youths, an eagle eyeing its prey. Lithe as a cat she swung down from the deck and moved among the rowers, stopping beside Artugol and Volnus.

"Come with me. Ormullah! Have these two replaced for an hour." She strode down the deck to her quarters at the rear of the vessel, a low, narrow cabin, and disappeared inside. The youths followed, watched by the amused eyes of the rowers, some of whom blew them mocking kisses. Artugol was furious, but Volnus laughed.

Inside the cabin, Eskarra faced them brazenly. Volnus closed the door, shutting out the blasting wind.

"There's an island ahead, not three leagues away. We'll shelter there for the night," said Eskarra. "It may not be safe. We believe it's uninhabited. There are ruins, once a pirate stronghold, long before Elak's time. Now there are only ghosts." She said it without fear and equally without scepticism.

"Legends?" said Artugol. "Or actual ghosts?"

Eskarra grimaced. She was a harsh mistress of the seas, and though young, to Artugol her responsibilities and seriousness augmented her wild beauty. Fierceness and possibly anger gleamed in those golden eyes. "We'll find out," she said. "If this is a place where yet more jewels are buried, we'll dig them up."

"Won't that invite the demons of the sea fog?" said Artugol.

"Probably," she snorted. "Now – show me what Dalan gave you. This jewel he said would lead us to the Sea Hag's trail. The one she will want to recover."

Volnus was momentarily taken aback by the girl's bluntness, but he nodded and carefully slid a leather sheath from his belt. As he flipped open its top end, a dirk's haft was revealed, grey metal with a dull brass pommel. Volnus laid the long weapon on the table, tapping the pommel. "Disguised," he said. "That's gold, enclosing the jewel. Dalan destroyed all the others we found. The gold has been impregnated with spells cast by the Druid. Otherwise the fog demons would have found us."

"When we go ashore," said Eskarra, "we'll need to make use of it. Will you bear it against the demons, or shall I?"

Volnus picked the dirk up possessively and wrapped it in the leather. "It has fallen to me to do this."

Artugol barely concealed a grin. His friend took his responsibilities very seriously and no one, not even the belligerent she-wolf of the seas was going to change that.

"Very well. But don't disappoint us. You make good spies, tucked away like mice in a barn, but what will you be like when the blades are out and the blood flows?"

Artugol wanted to retort, but he knew Eskarra was right to question their skills. In fairness, neither he nor Volnus had ever been tested in battle. A few skirmishes with other youths, and any amount of exercise with weapons would count as nothing in the murderous cut and thrust of a sea fight.

Chapter Five: The Island of Terrors

The storm had abated as the *Arrow* slipped into the small bay. Clouds churned away eastward, leaving the night sky revealed like a vast, star-pitted dome. A thick slice of moon cast a rich glow over the island's jungle terrain. Nestling deep down under the foliage the twisted shapes of an old fortress poked up like grasping fingers. Silence clung to everything, the more potent since the passing of the storm. There was a single, crumbing jetty, sand heaped up along half its length, but there was enough depth in the waters that lapped it to provide a safe berth for the *Arrow*, whose crew tied her up.

Eskarra led a party ashore, the two youths beside her. All weapons were drawn, save the dirk that Volnus carried. However, once he had stepped on to the crumbling paving slabs of the jetty, he felt a growing warmth in the concealed blade. There were broken buildings, crammed together in their ruination, the narrow streets choked with fallen bricks and lintels, as the tiny port straggled the steep slopes behind the shore, in places obliterated by the mass of encroaching verdure.

"There's a central temple overlooking the place," said Eskarra. "We'll make for there." Undaunted by the hostile feel of the terrain, she led the way over the rubble and the crew followed her, two of them bearing lanterns which threw the humped masonry into even weirder, tormented relief.

Artugol shuddered. This place felt as though it had poked through from another realm, a world far removed from his own. Shadows shifted within its bleak confines and an alien coldness plucked at his neck and scalp. He almost welcomed a human attack, flesh and blood enemies he could lock swords with. The climb was awkward, and several times men stumbled. Eskarra was undeterred, face drawn in a grim visage of effort. They reached the broken-down temple, where thick trunks bored into it, pushing it to one side, dislodging one of its walls and dragging down much of its elaborate roof.

"What unspeakable gods were worshiped here?" Volnus whispered.

Artugol was about to reply, but saw Eskarra's withering glare, admonishing them to silence. They went under the overhanging arch where once twin massive wooden doors had sealed the place. They now hung to one side, mouldering and worm-infested, their hideous carvings made even more ghastly by their decay. Inside, lit up by the guttering lanterns, the floor stretched away, oddly smooth and free of detritus, as if freshly swept. Broken columns and collapsed beams cluttered the walls, and starlight gleamed from great gaps in the ceiling, picking out the smashed ruins of two statues, gods long abandoned, headless and forgotten. Long creepers trailed from above like great roots or weed at the bottom of a lagoon.

Eskarra had her men search the interior, setting two to guard the entrance. It did not take long to establish there was no sign of recent habitation. "We camp here for the night," said Eskarra. "We can defend this place readily enough." Word was sent back to the ship and soon afterwards the remainder of the company came to the temple, leaving a skeleton crew aboard the *Arrow*.

"This is the island of Noomakis," Eskarra told Artugol and Volnus. "Once part of a pirate alliance, it was brought to ruin in a battle with creatures from the deeps. These were destroyed, but they left their curse here, as you can see. Neither man nor monster has returned since."

"You think there are Sea Hag jewels here?" said Artugol.

She nodded. "Dalan said so." She watched as her men pitched their rudimentary camp, checking to see that everything was done to her satisfaction. "In the battle fought here, many of the men who died fell victim to the fog demons. They come from some other realm and, through the power of the jewels, possess those they destroy, sucking the life from them and replacing it, thus taking on physical form. But it is their weakness, for as such, they can be destroyed, cut by steel, or burned."

"Will they attack us?" said Volnus.

She showed her teeth in a mirthless wolf's grin. "I hope so. The Sea Hag will send them, and when we dispatch them, their spectral remnants will lead us back to her lair. That jewel you carry will be a beacon to them. She'll want to recover it. So – reveal it. Let the night feel its power."

Volnus almost demurred, fearing what might come upon them from out of the pulsing darkness beyond, yet he knew if he did not obey, Eskarra would likely take the dirk by force and use it herself. Gently he pulled out the leather scabbard and revealed the dirk. Its pommel shone like bright new gold, dazzling. He gripped its haft and raised it like another lantern. Beams of light danced from it, flinging up grotesque shadows around the hall's rim. As one, the men leapt to their feet, weapons drawn, waiting.

Eskarra's grin was almost demonic in that light, transfixing Artugol. "The jungle never sleeps," she said. "And it is wide awake now. Can you hear?"

He gasped. The listless night breeze had become a swirl of sound, a rush of wings, a horribly familiar wind. Presently the two guards at the temple's entrance gave a shout, pointing into the jungle. Something moved down in the pitch darkness. Creatures were climbing up the jagged streets and over the ruins. Man shapes, physical beings, not the demons of the air that Artugol and Volnus were expecting.

"Hah!" laughed Eskarra, brandishing her rapier in eager anticipation. "Just as was promised. They've come for a fight – for the blade and the lost jewel within it. Well, you sea rats, let's see what you're made of!"

Chapter Six: Fiends from the Sea

The mingled moonlight, glow from lamps and Volnus's beaming weapon washed the jungle in garish light, revealing the things that stumbled from the trees, vaguely human, glistening like fat slugs, dripping with salt water. Evidently risen from the ocean, their weed-like hair was plastered to faces and necks, where gills pulsed: their webbed fingers were spatulate and grasping. Their misshapen heads, leached white and rounded with fish-like eyes, bobbed to and fro, like those of aquatic reptiles. Eskarra and her crew stared in horror as they realized the men who had been left behind to secure the *Arrow* were among these oncoming horrors. Their transformations were not yet complete, but already they were morphing into something alien.

First among them was the huge bulk of the oars master, Ormullah, whose mouth opened in a shout as he raved, either against being possessed, or in the drive to force an assault upon Eskarra and the others. She and her men were appalled at having to defend themselves against their changing fellows, desperately avoiding killing them or cutting them down, but what little humanity remained in the former sailors was riven by their transformation, fuelled horribly by a dreadful blood-lust as the battle was joined. There was no alternative – former friend or foe, these creatures had to die.

Artugol and Volnus were in the thick of it. Claws groped for the shining dirk that Volnus swept this way and that in cutting swathes, and where it tore into the flesh of the attackers, they blazed and dripped hot, fatty blood. The battle was fierce, but the sea denizens and converted seamen were a poor match for the barbaric energy of the crew, who, spurred on by panic in the face of such monstrous opponents, doubled their usual efforts. Eskarra had chosen them well, for they were as deadly with their blades as any cut-throat wanderers of the sea lanes. The mangled corpses of the sea fiends mounted, many cut to ribbons, others charred to smouldering hulks by the dazzling light from the dirk that Volnus wove so effectively among them. Eskarra's warriors fought back tears of sorrow and utter frustration as they cut down former friends, in some cases men who had once saved their lives.

Artugol shared no such misery and found himself strangely revelling in the fight, his rapier darting before him, swift as a serpent's tongue, ripping into the eyes of the enemy. How many swarmed up from the deeps and the path to the temple was impossible to say, and the *Arrow's* crew were forced inside. They withdrew in a carefully coordinated movement, but ultimately their experience was too much for the wild, stumbling of their opponents. As suddenly as it had begun, the insane battle ended. The remainder of the ragged assault died away and the beaten sea creatures slithered or hopped down through the darkness to the waters that had spawned them.

The crew, exhausted, were sullen in victory. Eskarra allowed them a moment of subdued celebration. She studied some of the fallen around her, piled outside the smashed doors of the temple. The look of cold fury on her face made Artugol start. She saw his reaction, lowering her slick blade.

"Some of these were our brothers," she said. "Not just those we left on the *Arrow*. The jewels of the Sea Hag must be here, working their foul sorcery. You see now what our lands face, and why Dalan was so appalled."

Artugol nodded and would have answered, when a cry from among the crewmen alerted him and Eskarra.

"What is it?" said Eskarra

Two of the crew were standing over a victim. It was the unmistakable figure of Ormullah, who had fallen in the skirmish, a deep gash at his side, which he yet struggled to staunch. He gazed up at Eskarra, his eyes wild, tears of blood on his cheeks and in his thick beard. He was fighting whatever monstrous energy sought to bend him to its will. The retreat of the sea creatures had weakened its grip and something of the man remained, its fires yet blazing.

"They overpowered us," he said through bloodied teeth. "They crawl into your flesh and bones -"

Eskarra bent to him, thrusting a small jar of water at him. He drank thirstily. "We'll have you stitched up yet," she told him.

"It burns!" gasped Ormullah, yet fighting an inner battle. "Yet I'll speak of what I know."

"Rest first," said Eskarra, gripping his shoulder. "I'll not abandon you, old friend."

Ormullah shook his head, spraying more drops of blood. "They use us, but in so doing, we see their minds. I understand things. I can see."

Artugol and Volnus were also kneeling, ready to support the fallen man, whose eyes widened as though something vivid had opened up in the skies, a vision of something beyond them all. Ormullah raised an arm that was already a deathly grey. "Up there!" he gasped. "The path leads to the island's peak."

Eskarra turned and looked upwards, but there were only the suffocating black banks of jungle and high in the lurid moonlight, a blunted cone. "The volcano," she said. "It has slept for centuries."

"Hollow!" said Ormullah. "It leads far down into the earth."

Artugol and Volnus stared at each other. Was the wounded man suggesting they go up there and – *descend*? Eskarra may have thought the same. Artugol caught the flash of horror on her face. Warriors of the sea were not fond of delving below the earth.

"Why should that concern us?" Volnus asked Ormullah.

"The Sea Hag's lair!" he growled. "I have seen it! Far below the island and out to sea, under deep caves and grottoes. It could never be reached by ocean divers. But up there! There is a way. It will take us to her palace, and the heart of her treasures. The mountain sleeps, its fires gone, its ancient lava solid."

"Rest," Eskarra told him again. "By the first rays of dawn, we'll ascend. What of the *Arrow*? Did those horrors destroy it?"

"No. She rides the waters, neglected but secure. The Sea Hag's vermin assumed they would absorb us all." He laughed in defiance. "I am not done with them."

Chapter Seven: From the Earth's Mouth

As dawn broke, Eskarra sent a small party back to the *Arrow*. Ormullah's last words before unconsciousness claimed him was that the sea horrors had subsided once more into the ocean deeps. Eskarra's ship was unmanned and would for now be ignored, its skeleton crew safe from the grim transformation that had been their companions' fate. The Sea Hag, Ormullah warned, would focus all her attention on the raiders on land. These followed Eskarra through the upper streets of the ruined city and into the jungle. There was a narrow path, almost overgrown, and it was only with Ormullah's insistent guidance that the sea warriors were able to chop through the clinging fronds and ferns that hid it. The sun was high in the east as they broke from the greenery and stepped onto the black loam of the volcano's lower flanks. Steep banks of boulders and scree stretched upward towards the peak, etched against cloudless, azure skies.

Artugol and Volnus flanked Eskarra, while Ormullah, only partly conscious now, was carried by two of the sturdier seamen. Occasionally he opened his fevered eyes and muttered further instructions, saying there was a way to the lip of the volcano, where the means of descent would await them. His body shook, soaked in sweat, and the pallor of his skin had turned a sickly grey. Even so, his strength had not completely deserted him and he fought desperately against whatever possessed him.

"If the wind rises," he murmured, "be wary. The air demons will be drawn to the jewel. They will try to bend its powers to convert you, but the Druid's power will block them. However, there are other jewels in the volcano, and you will not be so safe from them."

"What does the Sea Hag want?" said Artugol.

Ormullah shuddered. "The jewel you carry. And you – all of you! New warriors to be converted to her massing army. Perhaps she sees in you a fierce potential as fighters. You've shown formidable mettle here."

Eskarra, her sword gripped tightly, studied the rough terrain. From this height she could see beyond the jungles to the sea. A deep tranquillity had settled over the waves and the air remained still, no breeze stirring. "Too perfect," she said.

"What's the plan?" said Artugol. He felt like a rabbit

exposed to the claws of sky eagles, but masked his fears. He had surprised himself in the night's conflict, setting fear aside as he fought, but this deathly silence scratched his nerves. Beside him, Volnus seemed more relaxed, although he carried the dirk with the jewel, and evidently would not release it unless he had his arm cut off.

"If what Ormullah says is right, we go down," said Eskarra. "Does anyone want to go back to the ship? I suspect a small party, sneaking into the Sea Hag's lair, may do better than a noisy company. Speak up! Who is not with me?"

No one said a word.

"What about you two? You've done Dalan's work well. There's no need for you to risk your necks further."

Artugol almost succumbed to the temptation of an easier future, but could not bring himself to step away from the girl and the intensity of her determination. He knew she'd woven a spell over him equally as potent as that of the embedded jewel in the dirk.

Volnus clutched its sheath more tightly. "Dalan meant me to be the carrier of the jewel. I am – linked to its power.""

"Very well, let's get moving," said Eskarra, and recommenced the climb.

Artugol looked briefly at his big companion, puzzled by his words, but Volnus looked as stoic and dependable as always. If the jewel was exerting anything more than fascination over him, it did not show.

By mid-afternoon, they had reached the summit. The lip of the volcano's crater was a jagged line of rocks, crumbling and treacherous. Beyond them the inner walls plunged dangerously, dropping hundreds of feet to another rim of stone, giving way to a vast hole, sunk into complete darkness. There were numerous volcanic islands in these seas, most of them smoking, whether gently or with boiling clouds, presaging minor eruptions, when lava spewed forth in great gouts of light and fire. Yet here there was not even a suggestion of smoke.

Ormullah was set down with his back to a blackened rock. He opened tired eyes and gazed down into what seemed an infinity, a night without stars. "That is the way," he said.

"Is there a path?" said Eskarra. "We can't descend these slopes. One slip and we'd plummet into that chasm."

"They'll come," said the oars-master.

Artugol scowled. "He's delirious. And you're right, Eskarra. We can't climb down." He and the others concentrated on searching the crater rim, searching for a clue that might reveal any path, but the scree was unbroken in a perfect circle, slippery as polished glass, with no suggestion of anything to prevent a slide to oblivion.

From behind them, on a higher ridge, a lookout called down. "Clouds approaching!" The panic in the man's voice was clear, and at once everyone had gathered into a defensive formation, swords ready for any attack. Overhead the first wisps of cloud drifted in at speed, followed by an initial thick bank. Artugol knew immediately what it meant. The air demons had found them.

They swooped down like hawks, diving but twisting aside as Volnus held aloft the dirk, thin beams of light scattering from its jewel, drawn by the aerial horrors. These swerved to avoid it, held at bay by whatever sorcery Dalan had locked into the jewel. The bright sunlight dimmed as the massed air creatures created an overhead whirlpool of cloud and shadow, their gaping faces leering through it like ghosts from another realm.

"We cannot stay here!" cried Artugol. "We'll have to fight our way to safer ground."

Eskarra cursed, though she nodded, about to shout instructions when something made her turn. She gasped at what was emerging from the great pit. Artugol and Volnus also gaped, wondering if this was real or a vision triggered by yet more sorcery. It was as if they looked down not into the emptiness of a crater, but to ocean deeps, a submarine region where things shifted on invisible tides. Rising from them was a monstrous creature, a rounded dome, trailing thousands of glistening fronds, a protoplasmic mass with the proportions of a whale. Whatever aquatic intelligence powered it appeared to be focused on the group of warriors.

Chapter Eight: The Gulf Beneath the Island

Simultaneously with the huge creature's appearance, there was an abrupt shift in the terrain, as though far down within it something had exploded and torn loose. It caused an immediate slide of rocks, sand and ash, and the entire group tumbled downwards, unable to get a grip or prevent being sucked into the vortex. Artugol's mind reeled, plunged into darkness as though he had been smothered by a dense cloud. He cried out, but silence also surrounded him. He fell outwards and for long moments drifted like a broken doll in a coldness as if he'd been tossed over the side of a ship, spinning and held by a drifting oceanic current. Something sticky wrapped itself around him, partially crushing him and he felt himself being drawn along, snagged in weed or undersea growths. The darkness intensified.

Gradually his inner eye focused on wafting shapes and gliding forms that moved around like dreams, splitting apart to reveal visions that made him dizzy. He discerned an amazing city, spreading across vast distances, its angular buildings soaring up from the ocean deeps, with colossal denizens weaving along impossibly wide streets. Around him in the paradoxical submarine skies, other shapes flapped, some singly, others in massed shoals. He could barely discern Volnus, Eskarra and others of the *Arrow's* crew, spinning gently, floating on this dense current of air, helpless in its whirling course. Slowly they were all sinking down into the fathomless maw of the crater. Bizarrely this was no ocean swell. It was air, somehow thickened, cloying and almost solid, soft as clouds and yet substantial as earth, powered by forces beyond normal understanding, alien sorcery, perhaps.

The darkness eased as, with all sense of time dislocated, Artugol opened his eyes. He was sprawled across a clammy surface. He forced himself to his knees, pulling gelatinous, mucus-like secretions from him in slick strands. Around him, on a gently curved surface, the remainder of his companions also stirred. As they got to their feet, uniformly dazed by their experiences, Artugol saw the curved walls of the crater around them and realized whatever they stood upon was still sinking. Far overhead, the sky receded. A host of smaller shapes floated across, more fish than bird.

Volnus stood groggily beside Artugol, still gripping the dirk. Its light had faded, but he held it poised. Artugol saw the crew had retained their weapons, though as yet they were not under attack.

"That creature," said Volnus. "It gathered us all to it. We descend."

Eskarra was beside them, tensed for any assault. "The work of the Sea Hag. Those aerial demons drove us onto this thing. The air in this crater is almost as thick as the sea. Did you experience visions?"

Volnus shook his head. "Just a blur, vague shapes."

Artugol knew his companion to be less imaginative

than him. "The city?" he said.

"Whoever built it came from another world, spawn of stars beyond any night sky we have seen," Eskarra replied. "I have heard of such legends. Here, time may be ruptured."

Artugol remained dizzy. This was knowledge beyond things he had learned as a stripling among the wilds of his shores. The company could only gaze at the spinning walls as the descent continued for an age. Strange light seeped up from far below, alien to the sunlight of the upper world, an aquamarine glow in which yet more shapes wriggled and squirmed around the falling creature. At last the featureless walls changed, their composition of twisted rocks apparently hewn from the native substrata, unimaginably huge columns, supporting the mass of rock above. The first buildings came into view, and their scale made the travellers reel.

No earthly creatures could dwell here. No human powers could have carved these monstrous blocks, or set them together. Not all the glorious cities of Atlantis or of all the ages before her could have fitted into this mind-jolting vastness of construction. And yet, there was no sign of habitation within the towers. Such creatures as drifted through windows the size of palaces and along terraces beyond visual assimilation were simple things, like the minor denizens of the oceans known to the Atlanteans.

Ever down into the weird light the great creature sank, dropping between two mountainous banks of carved stone, within whose halls the secrets of eternity were embedded. The creature sank at last to the floor of the crater, gently deflating, spreading wide across the sandy bottom like a thick carpet. Its invisible heart trembled, pulsing softly.

"Come," said Eskarra, impatient to be free of it. She crossed the clinging surface and the company wove between low banks of settled fronds, mindful of their potential to sting, which must surely have brought painful death. Beyond was an opening in the great wall of a building, apparently the only way out. However, the company was wary of being manipulated.

"We've been brought here for a purpose," said Artugol. "We could easily have been destroyed."

Eskarra nodded. She pointed to the opening. "Can you hear anything?"

Two of the seamen went forward and presently called back. "The sea!" one said. "We hear its waves."

"A sea beneath the sea!" said Artugol.

Eskarra wasted no time, leading the company into the opening, a wide chasm within the building that ran in a perfectly straight line through the wall's dimly throbbing light towards the unmistakable sound of waves breaking on a shore. Some distance down the chasm, the walls gave way, opening out on to a pale beach, its pebbles bleached, massed banks of weed tossed up against the edge of the constructions. The inner sea beyond the waves shimmered to a far horizon, lost in pitch darkness. On its turgid waters, close to shore, a single shape waited.

A small, sailing craft, with no sign of a crew.

Chapter Nine: The Power of the Deeps

Eskarra gathered the men around her, whispering instructions. "If we allow this craft to bear us across, it will be to the Sea Hag's lair. We'll be caught like rats in a trap. Let's take the ship and find our own way across. Everything depends on surprise."

Moments later they had all waded out and clambered aboard the empty vessel, whose hull was shallow: no enemies were skulking here. The oar banks rested quietly, so the crew sat at the benches and at Eskarra's signal pulled the craft from the shore. It moved swiftly, as if gliding across ice. Once they had left the shore, the rowers turned the craft to a new course parallel with the curving shore, taking advantage of the deep shadows. Overhead the ceiling of this unimaginably vast cavern was lost in darkness, and a low line of surf broke like whispers on the rocks of the sweeping beach. Eskarra stood in the sharp prow, scanning the empty sea, Artugol and Volnus beside her.

They had not travelled far when the first tugging began. Something was beneath the boat's hull, a strong current turning it, trying to force it, they realized at once, back to its original predetermined course. The rowers put their backs into the work, striving to assert their strength and keep to the plan of a stealthy passage. At first their efforts succeeded, but whatever submarine force gripped them increased, forcing the prow out toward the open sea. Its horizon was distant, obscured, but the waves began to undulate as though a silent wind piled them up. Progress became impossible unless the rowers propelled the craft away from the land.

Volnus again held the dirk high so that light from its single jewel pierced the waters around them. At once he drew back in horror.

"What is it?" said Artugol.

"A sea beast! I saw its eyes, as large as cartwheels! And its many arms grip us."

Eskarra called for a spear and drove it unhesitatingly down in the now churning waters. Three more followed it, the only such weapons they carried, and although something shuddered, causing the boat to veer sideways, it was only momentarily deflected. The waters around it foamed and from them burst a score of quasi-human shapes, mere-beings with extended arms and curved talons, using them like grappling hooks to pull themselves onto the deck.

The sailors dropped oars and took swords to the affray: in moments the clash of steel and claw rang out loud as the first wave of invaders was repulsed. It was, however, impossible to beat back renewed attacks and steer the craft. For a while it wallowed in turgid seas as the ferocity of the battle increased, fuelled by the sheer numbers of the creatures from the deeps. As the fighting intensified, blood slick on the deck, the ship moved ever more quickly out into the subterranean sea, accelerating as the aquatic monster that impelled it exerted unrelenting power.

Several men were lost before the chaos ended, as suddenly as it had begun. The mere-creatures slid over the side, leaving a score of their dead behind them. Eskarra's crew kicked the corpses overboard, resigned now to the ship's new course. The wounded were tended and fortunately no one was so badly hurt that he could not continue. Fifteen of the company remained, their grim faces set with determination to see this voyage through to its bitter end. Eskarra's mouth was a hard line, her eyes cold as marble, a lava of anger churning inside her.

There was no day or night in this place, just a faint glow from far rocks, possibly the result of sorcery. Time condensed and the ship moved on quickly, covering league after league, until, when almost all of the crew were on sleep's borders, an obscure shoreline pasted itself along the horizon, rising up in a thick, black band, suggesting high cliffs. Cut into them was a small city, a collection of great stone buildings, much like those the company had negotiated originally.

Eventually reaching the narrow harbour fronting this place, the company again saw no life, just partially ruined, decomposing structures, apparently abandoned. There was a quay, with wide ramps leading up to it, but no steps. Whatever dwelt here did not move on human legs. The ship slid on to one ramp, its hull creaking as it ground to a halt.

Eskarra led them ashore, pausing at the quayside, where surprisingly nothing had emerged to meet them. She pointed to a narrow alley leading away into the buildings at one end of the quay. Swiftly they ran, taking shelter within its cold shadows. Artugol watched their rear, but there was still no pursuit.

"This must be the Sea Hag's lair," said Volnus. "She's somewhere in this citadel."

"Find a way through these streets," said Eskarra. "We must disappear, then study the place without being discovered."

They wound inward like maggots in a vast carcass, climbing upwards along slick passageways that had the feel of drains, not streets. Darkness closed in, but there was enough hint of light to see ahead. They could hear the shifting of large shapes within the engulfing walls, and heard strange susurrations as though water swirled below. They began to feel as though they had, after all, been pursued, but stealthily, and what followed them was itself clinging to secrecy.

Gradually they were rising, moving into a central core. Rounding a curve, they debouched on to a narrow terrace, creeping into brighter light to peer over its low wall to the circular chamber beyond. This soared upward to a vaulted ceiling, with jet black cylindrical walls dropping to a vast well. Bright phosphorescent light gave this a bizarre, alien look, like the surface of a remote, interstellar world.

From the waters, a wide shape humped upwards, cascades falling from scales and fins alike, and a huge head shook itself, massed tresses of weed-like hair spraying crystal droplets. Two enormous eyes opened, baleful lamps, their gaze hostile and not remotely human.

"The Sea Hag," said Artugol, his breath almost frozen with fear.

Chapter Ten: Across the Void of Space

As the small company looked down on the emerging colossus, water pouring from its broad shoulders, they each felt their minds invaded by a deep, commanding voice, opening them to visions as clear as the external world. Gripped by amazing vistas, they could not move, the huge eyes of the Sea Hag pinning them like flies to a board. They gazed upon an alien sky, where countless crimson stars burst like the embers of an interstellar explosion, and beneath which a city of soaring towers groped at the stars, among which shifted the incomprehensible shapes of its denizens. In the coiling shadows, diabolical gods from beyond all human knowledge pulsed with the energies of remote suns.

Artugol watched as numerous creatures poured from the city, flapping skywards on wide, leathery wings, faces burning with a hunger for conquest among the stars. And each face resembled the next, for these were sister beasts, spawn of a single birthing in that blackest of cities. Offspring of some hideous deity, they had been charged with subjugating new worlds, numerous and far-flung. One of them had traversed the gulfs of space and at some point in the dawn of Artugol's world sunk herself deep under its ocean, preparing for her own spawning. In those fathomless grottoes she had found the outlawed Barzangis, the Sea Hag, and occupied the near-dead renegade, a perfect receptacle for her power.

Soon she had sown the first seeds, the clutches of bright jewels. Where these had hatched, on remote isles, far from Atlantis and other centres of civilization, they had exuded vapours that had poured into their unsuspecting victims, transforming them into aerial demons that Artugol and the others had later seen, as they spread across the ocean realms.

Creatures of this world, the voice of the Sea Hag told the travellers, *you have been tossed and blown by a casual fate, subject to no other plan than simple procreation, the whim of the elements. No longer! Soon my spawn will spread across your world and all its inhabitants will evolve to a new pattern, arising from the primordial mire in which you wallow, bringing you to the edge of unrealized powers. You will be the fuel which projects me to the fulfilment of my promised godhood and immortality.*

Artugol found his innermost, hidden thoughts probed and exposed, focused by the mental intruder on his family, specifically those he had lost: as a child, two older brothers, killed in wars with the eastern sea raiders, and soon afterwards, his mother in a new childbirth. His life had been a hard one, the people among whom he dwelt often subjected to premature losses or death. This star-born creature seemed to be offering him a haven from that, a new form of life in which he would be absorbed and protected. The voice had become seductive, the possibilities it offered alluring, almost beyond resistance.

A shout beside him snapped him out of the semi-drugged stupor. It was Eskarra, whose own thoughts had been similarly snared. Artugol realized she must have found something within herself to resist, raising her rapier in anger and determination. Volnus, too was coming groggily out of a daze, his stoicism a bastion against this insidious assault on his emotions.

You will be the first of a new wave of conquest! came the mental voice of the Sea Hag to them all. *I have seen how strong*

*you are, a tribute to your nation! I need such warriors to carry my
own. You are a fitting choice for the glory awaiting you in the
name of the Old Gods. See, my fresh spawning is complete!*

The company as one looked down into the waters
boiling around the base of the huge creature, where
countless jewels rose up in glittering masses, light as huge
bubbles, luminescent and sparkling. Artugol realized there
would be as many jewels here as there were grains of sand
on the beaches of the continent, more than enough to enslave
every man and woman alive. He tore his gaze away from the
twin moon eyes of the Sea Hag, who had now risen up on a
level with him and his companions.

Volnus had drawn the dagger given him by Dalan. Its
embedded jewel, now a rusty colour, its light dimmed,
seemed a trivial thing, no match for the superhuman powers
surging from the waters. Volnus gazed at the faded jewel as
if it spoke to him, recalling whispered words of instruction
from the Druid. With a sudden shout of realization and glee,
Volnus flung the dagger out into the chamber. Both Artugol
and Eskarra cried out in alarm, fearing the Sea Hag had
commanded this. They watched in horror as the blade spun
end over end and struck amidst the jewels.

For long moments nothing happened: the only sound
was a sonorous booming of laughter as the Sea Hag lifted
her long arms threaded with spines, dripping venom. Her
laughter was cut short, however, and those great orbs
turned to study her jewel hoard. Where the dagger's jewel
had touched those closest to it, they had lost their shine,
dimming at once, likewise becoming rust-coloured. They
burst, the diminishing of bright hues spreading, a virulent
plague released, implacable.

The Sea Hag screamed in agony as the waters around
her boiled with released poison.

Eskarra leapt up on to the balcony's narrow wall. "Artugol!" she yelled. "The eyes! Take her eyes!"

Volnus would have dragged his impetuous friend back, fearing catastrophe, but Artugol leapt up beside Eskarra, sword poised like the sting of a huge insect. At a nod from her, they both leapt out across the space separating them from the vast face of the Sea Hag. For a fleeting moment that face contorted into something remotely human, a dim memory, perhaps, of the thing that had once been Barzangis. Shutting out a wave of pity, Artugol and Eskarra simultaneously plunged their blades into her eyes, Eskarra to the left and Artugol to the right. The creature screamed like a swarm of banshees, flinging her head this way and that in sheer agony as the fluids of her eyes poured from the ruptures made by the swords. Eskarra and Artugol were tossed aside, each crashing back over the low wall into their dazed companions.

They staggered to their feet, looking over the wall. Already the Sea Hag was sinking back into the water, which fumed and steamed as the jewels turned a dark, lightless shade, the spreading power of Dalan's sorcery within the corrupted jewel having done its murderous work. As the black waters closed in, the two ruined orbs ran with blood, draining of power and life, the last thing to be sucked under.

The watchers were almost deafened by the dreadful sounds below, the very air roiling like a storm and as they gazed down into a scene of utter madness they saw, rising from the boiling waters that churned with the countless erupting jewels, the great face of the Sea Hag twisting and morphing horribly, as if invisible hands were pulling at it, attempting to rip it apart. As it changed, bloodied and warped, another set of features flickered there, super-imposed upon it. Other eyes stared up at the three figures, eyes filled with pain and something else, memories, perhaps of happier days. For it was the visage of the queen, Barzangis.

For a while she stared as if pleading for forgiveness, mercy, and something more compassionate. But then her gaze melded into anger that grew into a colossal fury, and the waters burst up over her. The last vision the three figures had was of the broken Sea Hag, dragged down to final destruction, the price of her ambition and cruelty.

Epilogue

"How did you break that trance?" Artugol asked Eskarra as they re-boarded the ship. There had been no pursuit, and whatever things crawled or slithered through this desolate citadel had returned to their hidden sanctuaries. "I felt myself sinking inevitably into its promises."

Eskarra looked away to the horizon. "Like you, I have lost family. Nothing the Sea Hag offered me could assuage that pain."

Artugol would have said more, but he saw Volnus gently shake his head, as if to say, there will be another time to speak of this.

The big man knelt beside the still form of Ormullah. "We've stemmed the flow of his blood. It's clean. Gods willing, he'll rise again to take up his role as oars master."

Eskarra nodded grimly. "Our work has only now begun." Her eyes fell on the two youths, a little of her former ruthlessness gleaming there. "If nothing else, the Sea Hag made men of you."

Artugol gripped the hilt of his blade. The Sea Hag may not have seduced his will, but Eskarra...well, she he could follow. "So – where next?"

PRISONERS OF DEVIL DOG CITY

While Elak kept to his promise to the Council to eschew his wanderings and directed his attention to matters of court in Epharra, his newly formed and secretive groups of spies travelled far and wide across the oceans, among them Eskarra and her ship, the Arrow. *There were, however, other eyes upon them: dark, scheming powers with their own lust for expansion and ascension across the world of the Atlanteans.*

- Helvas Ravanniol, Annals of the Third Atlantean Empire

Prologue

By midday the storm brewing on the northern horizon had chosen not to veer off west, but to turn south and bear down menacingly on any ships in these waters. The *Arrow* found itself battling against waves of increasing turbulence. A sleek, swift craft, she cut through the rising swell, spray flying, oars lashed, sails doing the work, although if this wind continued to strengthen, a port would be needed, or an island with a sheltered southern inlet. Such islands as dotted the rough seas hereabouts tended to be ringed with treacherous reefs, with coral banks like rows of serrated teeth to snag and rip open a ship's hull.

Zendullo, the steersman, knew these waters well and eschewed the opportunity to take the ship into any of the sparse makeshift harbours, where the dangers would come from rebel pirates, invariably spoiling for a fight. Nevertheless if the *Arrow* came to grief here, she was far enough off the sea lanes to have become stranded with scant hope of rescue. Zendullo scowled at the boiling northern clouds, turning to the slender figure of Eskarra beside him. For once the feisty captain had wrapped a waterproof cloak about herself against the blasts of wind and driving spray.

"We should turn south," he bawled above the roar. "I can hold her steady if we let the wind drive us. Get back to the mainland."

"Aye, do it," she yelled back. "I like a challenge, but that storm hints at sorcery. Let's not tempt fate."

Zendullo expertly adjusted the helm, using every ounce of his prodigious strength. The waves fought back like live things and Eskarra's comment about sorcery froze his blood more readily than the mad buffeting of the wind. Each time Zendullo tried to pull the ship around from an easterly bearing to a southern one, wind and wave combined to defy him. The storm front was erratic, but its one constant was its bizarre determination to force the *Arrow* on a course it had apparently decided for it.

"Well, Zendullo, are we turning south or not?" shouted Eskarra.

"The sea's in no mood to be bested, mistress. If I'm not careful, she'll tear the rudder off. We can't use oars in this weather. They'll be ripped from the oarlocks. This storm isn't natural. I fear it's going to take us where it wills."

"Will it drown us?"

"Not if I let it carry us."

Eskarra grimaced at the misting eastern horizon, brightened by bolts of lightning from skies that had lowered almost to the waves. "Very well." She wondered, though, to what dread destination they were being driven.

Chapter One: At the Sea's Mercy

Artugol sat with Volnus and the fifty other crewmen, hunched down under the stiff blow, heads cowled. This was their second voyage as agents for the Druid, Dalan, closest adviser to the Atlantean King, Elak, and a man who was steeped in lore and power, second to none in the rapidly burgeoning new empire. Dalan's messengers had contacted the two youths and given them instructions that had set them on this hazardous voyage, employing Eskarra and the *Arrow* as they had done a few short months previously when they had defeated the Sea Hag. The pirate girl, as respected a captain as any others of the loose federation of buccaneers, had smiled a rare smile at the prospect of another tilt at fortune in uncharted waters, and her gritty crew had been all too eager to get to work.

However, as the storm swirled around the ship and towering waves flung them like a missile through swollen waters that would have buried many a proud war galley, Artugol cursed repeatedly, wondering if the adventurer's life really was the one for him. Volnus, far less tall but near twice as stocky and, according to him, possessing better sea legs, laughed at Artugol's miserable expression.

"Missing the comforts of shore already?" said the big man, grinning like a shark.

Artugol spat and wiped salt from a two-day stubble. "I should think even the sea gods have taken shelter from this muck! Much more and we'll end up on the bottom. And why aren't we heading back to the mainland? A porpoise would drown in this!" And our chances of finding Cloudrace Isle and Kesrak, the former cutthroat who now espouses peace with Elak, grow slimmer with every nautical mile, he thought.

"We'll be no good to the pirate's envoys if we fetch up on its rocks as corpses!"

"Cheer up. Even this storm won't make a corpse out of Eskarra. Look at her, Artugol. Standing at the helm, defiant as a goddess. Make a fine wife for someone."

Artugol scowled at his burly companion, who could jest, even in this madness. Artugol would have retorted, but Ormullah, the swarthy giant oars-master was coming down the line, bawling instructions as he came. Since fully recovering from his brush with death with the Sea Hag's sorcery, he had become even more demanding of the crew. He knelt beside Artugol and Volnus. "We can't steer south and we can't get a bearing on Blood Island and the pirate hold there, which is supposed to be our first port of call."

"So where in the Nine Hells are we heading?" said Volnus, above another vicious buffet of the wind.

"Slightly north of east."

"That's open ocean! In this? We'll never survive!"

"No choice. Something is taking us there. So keep your heads down and be ready for a rough landing."

"Dammit, Volnus," said Artugol. "The King won't thank us for this diversion! We'll be out on our backsides for failing his orders."

"Relax," said Volnus. "Who's to say we won't come back the richer, for the King as much as ourselves! Go with the flow."

"Go with the – Are you insane? The Gods alone know what is dragging us to that place."

A few seemingly endless hours later, the two men and the rest of the bruised and battered crew peered through a lull in the storm's madness at an island, a knuckled green fist rising from seething waves. Artugol watched appreciatively as Zendullo wrestled back control, seeking a night harbour. The sea thrust the ship forward into a wide bay, where alarmingly the waves were suddenly sucked back rapidly, casting the Arrow onto exposed, glistening sands, half a mile from shore.

"We've been beached!" cried Artugol, looking over the side of the ship in horror. Beyond the ship's stern, flat sands disappeared into the distance, where fogs curled and writhed, huge banks of cloud serpents at the new tide line. The storm had abruptly moved out to the invisible ocean, its crackling lightnings diminishing.

"Sorcery," grumbled Volnus. "The air reeks of it. Coming from that island, or I'm the son of a Pict."

Artugol laughed. "Aren't the Picts our allies now?"

Volnus nodded. "Even so, you better hope we don't meet any."

"How are we going to get free of this sand bank?" Artugol called to Zendullo.

"A freak tide grounded us here. We'll need another to float us."

Eskarra glared at her crew, raising a hand for silence. She was about to issue instructions, when a cry from the masthead drew everyone's attention. The lookout, who had shinned up the mast as soon as the Arrow beached, pointed back at the churning mists.

"Something's coming."

Artugol and Volnus looked beyond the stern. Eskarra was craning her neck. "Everyone get under cover. Whatever forces brought us here might be hostile. Ready with blades!

And keep silent." In moments the entire crew crouched under the ship's rails, peering through its timbers, weapons in hand. Artugol and Volnus could see the stretch of sand directly behind the ship: shortly they observed a lone figure crossing the open expanse, two creatures on either side of it. Both men gaped, but said nothing, mouths dry.

It was a woman, by her armour a warrior, dressed in a combination of glittering silver plate and jet black. The haft of a broadsword rose from a filigreed scabbard at her belt, and silver chains hung from her neck, catching the first evening rays. Her legs were encased in lightweight, flexible steel and she wore a protective helm, exposing only her eyes, and allowed a long tail of black hair to hang down her back. Her hands were gloved: in each was a length of thin chain, leashes for the creatures accompanying her. These were also jet black, huge cats the size of lions, their eyes a scintillating green, gem-like. These beasts opened their mouths to reveal rows of brilliant teeth, pointed daggers. All three beings were slick, dripping wet, as if they had emerged from the sea itself.

As the warrior neared, Artugol realized she was not coming to the ship: her path would take her some distance from it and on towards the island. Soundlessly Artugol and Volnus watched as the warrior and two big cats paused, heads turning towards the *Arrow*. The animals sniffed the air, emitting long, low growls that froze the blood. Everything about those muscular bodies suggested raw power: those claws could shred a man effortlessly. However, the woman turned again to the island, as though something there had attracted her. Ignoring the *Arrow*, she led her creatures across the upper beach, eventually disappearing into the undergrowth beyond.

Chapter Two: The Living Jungle

Shortly after dawn, Eskarra picked a handful of warriors to accompany her exploration of the shore, including Artugol and Volnus, who tried not to look too apprehensive. Those left on the ship complained grumpily, particularly Ormullah and Zendullo, until their mistress shouted them down. She led the small company out on to the sand. "Remember," she said, "something brought us here, and it wasn't chance. Hopefully we'll replenish our food supplies and find fresh water, but be careful what you touch."

The mysterious warrior woman had not returned, nor were there signs of anyone else emerging from the sea mists. Cautiously the party reached the edge of the vegetation and moved along it, looking for an alternative path to any taken by the warrior woman. The island had awoken, the sound of birdsong and drone of insects a steady backdrop to what seemed just another sleepy remote wilderness.

"Perhaps she was also lured here by sorcery," Volnus said softly to Artugol.

The latter nodded. "Did she really emerge from the sea? I couldn't see another ship back there."

Volnus grunted, not wanting to consider the implications. He moved ahead in silence. They found a rough path and cut aside the low vegetation on either side, beginning the penetration of the interior. The trees were closely packed, not a kind familiar to the crew. Their trunks were semi-transparent, their hues mottled, more like skin than plant, their branches tangled as seaweed, as dark in colour, and exuded a saline smell, like tall banks of exposed kelp. The path rose steadily initially, then zigzagged upwards, negotiating a much steeper climb. Looking back, Artugol and Volnus saw the bay below, a vast expanse of sand, with the *Arrow* way out in the open.

Overhead, through thinning trees, they saw the rugged outline of an escarpment, the rim of the volcano. Eskarra announced her determination to reach the crags, and Artugol moved up close behind her, with Volnus at his shoulder.

"If you get any closer," the big man whispered, "you'll risk treading on her heels."

"She's the captain, you ape. We're supposed to guard her back."

Volnus grinned. "Of course. But you think she needs it? She's worth ten of us."

Artugol knew from earlier experiences that Eskarra fought like a tigress, but he just grunted. If he was to be master of his own destiny, he'd rather be in the front line than twiddling his thumbs back on the *Arrow*.

Reaching the crest of the climb, in late afternoon, they came out through a weathered gash in the uppermost rocks to stand on a narrow plateau which gave them a view not only of the sea but also of the interior. The island was indeed a volcano, apparently extinct and inactive for many years. Its rim curved away in an unbroken circle, its crags and outcrops resembling a ring of gigantic teeth, irregular and cracked. Inside the vast crater, the strange vegetation had taken complete control, humping skywards, an encircled jungle, deep green and intensely matted, a huge blanket, tightly woven, covering every inch of the depths.

"We're not going down into that, are we?" said Volnus, forgetting himself and raising his voice.

Eskarra frowned at him. "If there's a path, we'll see. Where's your spirit of adventure?"

It was Artugol's turn to grin inanely at his companion. "Yes, Volnus, what are you afraid of?"

"Are you serious?"

Eskarra ignored them and set a number of men as lookouts. They were already scanning the sea's horizon, where the banks of fog had been blasted away by the recent storm. There was nothing to see out on the waterscape, no other islands, and no hint of other shipping. The tiny *Arrow* was the only sign of human life. A few sea birds drifted on the air, resentful at having their nesting sites disturbed.

"We'll camp under the rim and look for a safe way down in the morning," said Eskarra. She picked a few men to accompany her in a search, Artugol and Volnus included.

Volnus again breathed in his companion's ear. "She likes you, too."

"Mind you don't trip on these rocks and crack your thick skull open."

"Keep silent!" Eskarra hissed back at them, and in spite of himself, Artugol had to suppress a grin.

They investigated the upper slopes of the dead volcano's rim for the remaining hours of daylight. Rainfall had gouged a number of natural tracks downwards into the choked jungle mass, and although most of them were treacherous with disintegrating, sliding scree, a few offered reasonably safe descent. It was the forbidding arboreal expanse that made progress difficult, even by daylight. The bizarre silence of those birdless trees reinforced their impenetrability. Yet everyone felt the irresistible lure of the place, seduced by it.

Sunset in these latitudes was sudden, the great golden orb abruptly dropping below the horizon, taking with it the sky's glow. The cloudless heavens were studded with stars, and the air quickly chilled. At the ridge camp, tucked comfortably into a rock overhang, the crew had lit campfires and broken out meat rations.

Volnus grumbled. "That jungle below looks as dead as

the volcano, like a graveyard. We'll be eating gulls' eggs again when our meat's gone."

After they'd finished their meal, Artugol and Volnus sat among the rocks, watching the crater's impenetrable darkness. It was mottled suddenly by an unusually vivid moonlight, its curves and swells like a frozen sea. In that eerie glow, abrupt movement suggested itself, a swell, as though waves coursed through it.

"By the gods!" Volnus gasped. "I swear it's – alive!"

Artugol was about to ridicule him, but he, too, saw an entire area of the jungle shift. "Must be an illusion." They stood, craning their necks.

Eskarra appeared beside them. "What's happening down there?"

"The trees are parting," said Artugol. "There! See."

In the moon glow, they saw more clearly. Whole banks of the jungle had pulled back, branches waving, living tendrils, more animal than plant.

"It's the moonlight!" said Artugol. "The trees are reacting to it."

"As if scorched," murmured Volnus.

Eskarra nodded, stunned by the grotesque spectacle, as the jungle that had completely covered the crater's floor was drawn back further, its branches and leaves pulled towards the surrounding rim, where caves and openings offered sanctuary to it. Soon nothing remained of the foliage.

What was now revealed had the watchers gaping in amazement.

Chapter Three: Jaws of Death

It was a city unlike any other seen before by Artugol and his companions. Its buildings appeared to have been partially undermined, uniformly leaning at precarious angles, towers and blocks dropping into the crater's unfathomable darkness, where the streets were clogged with shadows. The upper reaches of some towers had crumbled, ripped apart by tendrils of the jungle as it closed over them in its diurnal movements. Even so, the style of less damaged towers, vast rectangular blocks, were unrecognizable and had an outrageous, alien aspect. Their contorted windows were set at oblique angles, offering no view of what lay within; strands of weed hung from their sills like fronds in shallow seas. Artugol wondered if this place had been built for human habitation.

Below the watchers, curling down through the rocks, a roughly hewn stairway fell away. Eskarra called to her men. "Bring torches!"

"You mean to enter that place?" said Volnus uncomfortably.

"Better now than when the jungle covers it. Who knows what treasures we might find."

"Yes, Volnus," said Artugol. "Unless you'd rather stay up here on guard?"

"No, no. I'm ready for anything." His expression, however, suggested otherwise. He wondered about Eskarra's determination to explore, as though the island had enchanted her.

Eskarra gave Artugol an unexpected grin, and he felt himself flushing. Soon after she led several of them down the winding stair. Moonlight exposed the way until eventually they came to the first street, where the torches repulsed the shadows. Chunks of masonry and mounds of dusty rubble choked whole sections of the street, which wound like a canyon into the city, as they clambered over the spoil. Total silence smothered everything, as though sound was unknown here.

"Mark our passage," said Eskarra softly, her words amplified, ringing back from walls which soared to the remote moonlight. Artugol and Volnus used their swords to scuff patterns in the dust as they passed into the huge maze, a trail they could follow back out later. Here every building looked identical. Some distance in, the company heard something, every ear pricking.

"Is that baying?" whispered Artugol to Eskarra, close beside her. He was pleased that she'd not objected to his proximity. She nodded.

They all paused. The silence closed in again, but as soon as they were on the move, the distant sound returned, with more than a hint of a hound's howl.

"Look!" called Volnus, pointing down a narrower passage lined with huge, cracked columns. These were uniformly topped with vaguely human statues, possessing heads resembling hounds or jackals, their anthropomorphic shapes cast in obsidian, impervious to erosion.

"Are they gods?" said Volnus.

"I've heard of such things," said Eskarra. "Some of the older pirates tell of a lost race who worshiped such gods, though they're not of our time." The party continued down the chasm, only its torches penetrating the pitch darkness, in time reaching a wider area, circular and more open, although the twisted architecture yet loomed overhead like thunderclouds. Here, no debris had accumulated, as if it had been deliberately swept clean. The torches picked out more statues, these little bigger than living men. They, too, were dog-headed, eyes highlighted by the flames, gleaming like living things.

Somewhere nearby there was another elongated howl, in its aftermath everyone tensed, swords drawn in readiness. Artugol heard low snarls down one of the streets.

Something was approaching. And from another street. And another! He knew they were surrounded.

Scores of eyes in pairs, reflected the torch glow. Low growls came from each of the streets leading like spokes from the circular area. The party arranged itself into a defensive grouping, waiting silently. Artugol and Volnus automatically stood shoulder to shoulder, close to Eskarra.

Gradually the shapes materialized, large hounds the size of ponies, with muscular, canine bodies, padding forward, tails lashing. These were fearsome enough, but the heads of the dogs caused Artugol to give vent to a uniform gasp: they were quasi-human, with hybrid faces that resembled people. They slavered, teeth uneven, long tongues dripping with saliva, eager to feed. In their eyes was a look of desperation, sorrow almost, as if they had once been something very different, something now trapped in these monstrous shapes. One by one they sank onto their bellies, watching their prey, waiting.

"Why don't they attack?" whispered Artugol.

"They're dogs," said Volnus. "A pack, like wolves. They'll have a master."

The largest of the statues moved. Stone cracked, as if becoming malleable, softening its features. The head, with its pointed snout, was that of a jackal-like creature, its bejewelled eyes morphed into living orbs. The face turned, staring at the *Arrow's* crew. It was a curiously human, yet feral stare, withering and aggressive. The living creature snarled, and as one the circle of hounds rose, preparing to spring.

Eskarra shrieked a challenge of her own and Artugol, Volnus and the men roared their defiance, holding up their glittering blades. Then it began, as the hounds leapt in, the first of them spitted on the blades, while others tore into the humans, bringing some of them down, fangs closing over windpipes and ripping them out in a welter of blood. Artugol was a blaze of energy, Volnus equally as galvanized beside him, as swords cut and slashed with abandoned ferocity, the warriors imbued with the strength of terror, wreaking sheer havoc among their assailants. It was crimson madness and the hounds, for all their power and ferocity, were slowly being butchered. Behind them their demi-god master watched in silence, unmoved by the slaughter.

When it was over, a score of the hounds had been cut to pieces, disemboweled or decapitated, and not one had survived. They lay in deep pools of blood, some twitching their last. Artugol gasped for breath, almost exhausted, Three of Eskarra's men were lost. The others closed ranks, dripping with sweat and blood, waiting.

"We're being tested," said Volnus. "The real contest hasn't started yet."

As if to confirm his grim words, the jackal-headed creature lifted its snout to the heavens, emitting a long ululation. Its meaning was clear. It was calling others from the darkness. Soon there were more sounds from the streets. There were scores of the beasts, advancing like a swarm, preparing to sweep the intruders before them — it threatened to be a total massacre.

Chapter Four: Servant of the Goddess

The first huge brute leapt at the warriors, whose swords drank deep of canine blood, cutting and thrusting with terrible effect. For a while Artugol and Volnus spearheaded the stemming of the tide, but sheer weight of numbers was inevitably going to destroy the entire company. The distorted faces of the beasts, that had a deeply unnerving human quality to them, leered maniacally as powerful jaws and rows of dagger-like teeth caused havoc, tearing men and women aside, working through the line; there seemed no likelihood of respite as the creatures came on in a flood. Yet they paused, drawing back and padding around the warriors, licking their wounds, tongues lolling, mouths frothing with blood. Beyond them their master watched in silence. He raised a fist in readiness to urge the massed pack forward again, but there was a shriek behind him, followed by a snarling even more blood-curdling than that of the hounds.

Artugol looked over the mass of oncoming dogs to see what had caused the commotion, to one of the lighted streets. A fantastic vision met his eyes, for two sleek black shapes, each as large as the biggest of the hounds, was ripping and tearing into them, using claws like knives and teeth that were spraying blood from the leaking wounds of their victims. Behind them, using a broadsword, was the armoured woman from out of the sea fog. So ferocious was the attack on the dog pack that all of them swung round, momentarily ignoring the pirates, racing to defend their fellows.

Artugol watched in amazement as the woman swung her blade from side to side in a blur, a scything movement that slashed into the furred bodies of the dogs as if she were cutting swathes of wheat. It was murderous and irresistible, no matter how many of the hounds flung themselves into the fray. Their dead and dying were heaped up on all sides, the two huge cats as deadly as their mistress, too fast to be bitten, too powerful to be dragged down.

The hound master, apparently deterred by the horrific spectacle, withdrew into the darkness of another street before anyone had noticed. His retreat was a signal for the hounds to abandon their attack, and as one they broke apart and streamed off in confusion, leaving behind a thick trail of blood and countless carcasses, some twitching in their final throes. From the welter of gore and mutilated bodies, the two huge cats emerged silently, eyes fixed on the crew of the *Arrow*. Artugol, Volnus and all the company prepared for a renewed bloody contest, hearts beating with terror.

The warrior woman sheathed her sword and spoke a harsh command. At once the two black cats dropped to the paved slabs, stretching out as if the fight had been forgotten, licking their fur casually. The woman calmly pointed to the butchered dog-creatures.

"They were like you once. Men and women who were lured to this accursed island by the magic of another time, another dimension. How many of you fell?"

"Five," replied Eskarra instantly. She knew every one of her followers.

"You must decapitate them. It is the only way to prevent the transformation."

"You mean – into these horrors?" said Artugol.

"Yes. The creature at the heart of this island is a prisoner here, but he retains much of the old magic of his era. Sorcery uncommon in your world. He is using it to attempt to escape his fetters. If he creates enough followers here, he will break free, and if he does, your world will be in dire peril."

"Who is he?" said Volnus.

"I will show you."

"And who are you?" said Artugol.

The warrior woman's eyes fixed on him and he felt his nape hairs stiffen. The two huge cats lifted their heads and growled menacingly. Artugol's blood froze.

"I am Nefertari, servant of the cat goddess, Bastetis, who rules in a place beyond the walls of your world. She is the prime adversary of Sutmekk, whose lore-master, Zolotec, was cast out of their world and chained here, long ago in the deeps of time. Zolotec has brought these monsters to life. His master is a god of storms and of hounds and jackals, the emissaries of his reign. Zolotec wields power delegated to him by Sutmekk. Zolotec will never rest until he has freed himself."

"What of he who controlled the hounds?" said Artugol.

"Returned to the stone and clay of the island from which he was fashioned by Zolotec to be the vessel of his powers, controlling the devil-dogs. Men and women of your world, shipwrecked here, or drawn by the lure of treasure, were turned into beasts, Zolotec's slaves. Only death can release them from that sorcery, unless my powers can aid the wretched creatures. Come, there are things you must see."

She turned on her heel. The two great cats rose and padded behind her, long tails lashing. The pirates moved away from the carnage, glancing at the fallen hounds as they went, regarding them with pity for what they had become. Ahead of them, Nefertari walked in silence through streets that sloped and curled ever downwards, towards the city's heart. There were occasional distant howls, but no further attacks.

At length the company entered a tall, arched door that led to a circular series of steps, the concentric levels of a former auditorium. This circumvented a vast chamber, its far side in darkness. Artugol and the others looked down: the floor there was a perfect circle, its stones inlaid with complex patterns and motifs, craftsmanship of another, long-lost age. But it was not this fabulous art that drew the attention.

At the chamber's centre, a solitary figure was chained up, feet spread and manacled so they had little room to shift position. The arms were also manacled, chains dangling to the stones where they were firmly embedded. It was a human figure, no larger than a normal man, though its head was misshapen, elongated like a hound's, with dog-like ears and a snout. Its eyes, though, were human, its expression undoubtedly fashioned by human misery. As it gazed up at Nefertari, it bared its teeth in a brutish snarl, a deep growl escaping foam-flecked lips. Anger boiled visibly and it seemed that the creature's chains would snap under its volcanic anger.

Chapter Five: The Deeps of Time

"You have come to taunt me, accursed sorceress!" Zolotec snarled, the words distorted.

"No! I have come to put an end to your cruel use of human slaves. Too many have fallen under your spells. I will make your surviving devil dogs human again."

"You and your god made me what I am! You chained me here without pity and left me to rot across the ages. Your evil transcends mine by far! You were jealous of my powers. You wanted them all for yourself, Nefertari."

Artugol, Volnus and Eskarra stood together and listened to the argument in silence, awed by the evident powers filling the air around the two figures like heat from a furnace, heat that could all too readily burst incandescently to life, scorching anything close to it. As the company watched, the two big cats went down the steps, bellies to the floor, eyes fixed on Zolotec, whose terror at their proximity showed in his twisted features. The animals growled ominously, sitting on their haunches a few feet from him, awaiting Nefertari's command.

"You are ever a deceiver. I will remind you how things were," she told Zolotec. "These warriors should hear the truth." As she spoke, a wall of white mist rose up in a thick curtain directly behind the prisoner. It shifted and coiled, images forming upon it, revealing a huge window to another place, in a time before Atlantis had risen from the sea.

Artugol felt his head swimming as his mind followed the dazzling array of images: he knew instinctively they were from some remote era. A vast city sprawled, soaring to unprecedented heights above a green world, housing hundreds of thousands of people. In its highest reaches colossal temples boasted an entire pantheon of lost gods. These awesome beings, striding through their immense corridors in magnificent splendor, had come from the stars, or through other portals of time and dimension, making the city a focal point for their gathering. Many of them wore the shape of beasts, some of them anthropomorphic, seemingly human, though with animal characteristics. All were worshiped by lesser beings, ranging from demi-gods to the lowly life of the world, the seething humanity that filled the streets, harbours and surrounding jungles of this immense focus of divine power.

Among the gods were the jackal-headed Sutmekk and Bastetis, the cat goddess who moved with feline grace, and among all the gods, these two strove for overall mastery, their powers vast, surpassing all their fellows. Long did their conflict endure, waged discreetly away from the palaces of the gods, where their highest servants carried out their commands in efforts to undermine and ultimately bring each other down. This turbulent contest alternatively raged and simmered over countless epochs, an age in human terms, and whole nations were brought into the wars spawned by the terrible explosion of wills.

Artugol recognized the figures of Nefertari and Zolotec, principal servants in the swirling madness, as they hurled their armies, human and otherwise into the cauldron of discord. Sutmekk, determined to gain ultimate power, exercised increasingly more terrible forces, pillaged from primordial depths and interstellar chasms: he became more deeply steeped in evil, warped and corrupt, so that other gods, appalled by his dangerous course, leaned in favor of Bastetis. Light and darkness in their most terrible aspects rocked the universe of these gods and all who served them.

Sutmekk's greed was his undoing, and although he could never be destroyed, only subdued, the majority of the gods and goddesses, sympathetic to Bastetis, brought the jackal-headed one to heel. Zolotec, his champion among demi-gods and mortals, was chained, Nefertari made his jailer. Sutmekk could not be banished from the palaces of the gods, but his powers were restricted by the unified will of the other gods. Zolotec, however, was banished, sent far from his own time and place to here, where Atlantis stretched her power across the seas.

"Lies!" screamed Zolotec, straining at his chains.

"No," said Nefertari. "Since your incarceration, you have again attempted to use forbidden powers, luring human servants here, transforming them, building an army, seeking one day to free yourself and challenge the human empires of this world. You would have had Atlantis bend the knee to you. It was ever your way."

Behind Zolotec the great bank of mists and its window shimmered, slowly dissolving. He sank down, exhausted, all remaining powers sucked out of him.

Artugol snapped awake from these dream-like visions and a quick look at his companions told him they had similarly been mesmerized. They sat or sprawled on the concentric steps around and above the arena, waking as if from drugged sleep, yawning and stretching cramped muscles.

Zolotec gave one last roar of defiance and rose, muscles bulging as he strained at the chains. "I defy you to the death!" he yelled. Something crackled in the air around him and his cry of fury was echoed by sounds beyond the chamber. Abruptly another pack of devil dogs burst in through the many portals, preparing to assail the intruders. Artugol gasped—the entire company was never more vulnerable than now.

Nefertari raised her hands, claws gleaming, and called out in a tongue that no one recognized, before flinging a bolt of blue light down at Zolotec. It struck him on the chest and burst into a cloud of bright sparks, smashing him to his knees. As he collapsed, the pack of devil dogs fell silent for a moment, but then began going through a demented twisting and turning, a mad, uncontrollable parody of dance, their howls filling the huge chamber. One by one their bodies morphed and they rose from being on all fours, shape-shifting through layers of pain, back to human form. At the end of their agonized transformation, they stood even more dazed, as unstable as the crew of the Arrow.

"It is done," Nefertari said, her two black beasts again beside her. "And for you, Zolotec, there is a new realm prepared, far from here, in another time."

"I'll be glad to get back to familiar sea lanes," Volnus told Artugol.

Eskarra leaned towards them both and whispered. "I recognize some of those men, twisted though they have become. They serve Kesrak. Perhaps he is in this city, too."

Beyond them, in the shadow-hung tunnels, more howling had begun, louder than before. The city swarmed with prisoners as a hive swarms with bees.

Nefertari called to Eskarra. "Take your men and these wretches back to the Arrow. I have further work here with Zolotec."

Eskarra wasted no time in obeying and with Artugol and Volnus led the entire company out of the chamber. The confused ranks of Zolotec's freed servants followed behind, as if trapped within a dream.

Nefertari went down into the arena to confront Zolotec for a final time.

Chapter Six: Hell Hounds

The company, now swelled by the released men and women who had been Zolotec's creatures, wound its way through the street canyons of the city to the stair to the rim of the huge crater-city. Bright moonlight beckoned over the heights, as it became a race to climb out of the crater before the strange jungle plants overspread it again. Artugol and Volnus looked back at the press of bodies. These people were still dazed, their minds unable to comprehend what had happened to them. Artugol wondered how long some of them had been prisoners in their transformed shapes. All were naked, although it seemed to mean nothing to them, their physical senses apparently numbed. They obeyed instructions like cattle gently goaded onward, but within them all there must yet be a spark of will to survive their bleak ordeal.

Eskarra spoke to two of the men she had recognized. "You are Kesrak's followers?"

Both nodded, recognizing the name, though they yet seemed confused.

"Is your master on Cloudrace?" asked Artugol.

Both men shook their heads. "No. His ship, with all of us aboard her, was driven on to the rocks of this place. We were all – taken. Changed," they said, shuddering at the horrific memory.

"Where is Kesrak now?" said Volnus.

"Somewhere among the creatures that throng the passageways of this accursed city. The last of our crew are there, changed like him."

Artugol grimaced. "We have to find them and pray that Nefertari's powers can restore them. The eastern confederation of pirates won't sue for peace with Elak if we don't have Kesrak at their head."

Eskarra nodded. "This ragged company," she said, indicating the rescued men, "will be no match for the dog packs. They need to get back to the ships."

"Perhaps a couple of us, disguised in some way, might seek out Kesrak," said Volnus. He looked pointedly at Artugol, who grimaced but nodded.

Eskarra considered his words for no more than a moment. "Very well. I'll send our men back with these others. We'll take up the hunt."

"You should go back with your crew," said Artugol.

"No," she snapped. "I'll not shirk the task." With that she went to some of her men and soon after they were leading the company back up the winding stairs. Eskarra came to Artugol and Volnus. "The three of us," she said. "let's move." There was clearly not to be any further discussion.

They returned to the dusty corridors of the city, where dim moonlight speared down from above, barely showing the way. They smeared themselves in dirt, hoping that by doing so they would not only create an entirely disheveled appearance, but also go some way to disguising their human smell. Somewhere below them, they again heard the baying of the dog packs.

Their path led through a narrow stone maze until they debouched on to a high ledge. Light pulsed below and they looked into a wide pit, which may once have served as a meeting place, possibly a temple. Its columns and walls were pitted and broken, long decayed, and overhead its thick rafters were sagging, in places fallen in, so that light suffused the crumbling ruins. And in that space, countless dog-beings had been herded. They squatted on their haunches, or lounged on the steps, quietly gathered, waiting for their master's commands. Occasionally one would lift its head and emit a howl, answered by others, although the ferocious-looking creatures kept their distance from each other. Amazingly, no conflicts broke out.

"They're waiting," said Volnus.

"As long as Nefertari controls Zolotec," said Artugol, "these creatures will wait to be commanded."

"There!" said Eskarra softly but urgently, and pointed to one of the larger beasts. "I see in its features something of the pirate ruler, Kesrak. I'm sure it's him."

They found a stair down from the ledge and descended silently, their eyes never leaving the dog pack below. Some of the creatures growled, but made no move to rise. As the three companions came to the last step, swords drawn and prepared for any attack, the beasts remained relaxed. Kesrak, or what he had become, was not far from the foot of the stair, sitting on its haunches. As the three figures closed in, it lifted its great head, its crimson eyes glaring, more than hinting at a threat. The jaws opened and saliva hung from yellowed fangs.

"Kesrak," said Eskarra. She repeated the name, and the third time she said it, the beast stiffened. It studied the three figures, as though determining whether to rise and attack. Around it, scores of other hounds began to register a sudden hungry interest in the intruders.

Eskarra and the two men found themselves surrounded, their uncouth clothes being sniffed by the quasi-human hounds, whose tongues lolled and whose eyes glared balefully. Swords gleamed in the vague glow and for a while the fate of the intruders hung by a slim thread.

"Kesrak," Eskarra said to the largest of the beasts. "You know me. I am Eskarra. You and your crews have fought alongside mine in the past. Remember!"

The huge head lifted, and for a moment a strange expression crossed the twisted features, imbuing them with a little more humanity. A deep growl rumbled down in the beast's chest and Eskarra's sword point rose, ready to thrust home if an attack came.

"You must leave this place," she said. "Come with us and let the others follow."

Slowly she moved back, Artugol and Volnus going with her. Kesrak and the pack closed in, but padded forward, apparently obedient to the instruction. There were snarls and further growls among the creatures, but their leader yet had some sway over them. Not all of these creatures had been part of Kesrak's original crew, but in their crude, primal way had accepted him as their leader in this place of darkness. Step by step, careful not to make any sudden moves, Eskarra and the two men edged back up the passage, their blades yet raised, their shirts soaked in the sweat of anticipation.

Chapter Seven: A Window on Time

In the early morning light, Zendullo and Ormullah leaned on the rail of the *Arrow* and studied the movements on the beach by the distant shoreline.

"They're coming back," said Zendullo. "Yet there seem more of them."

"Who are they?" said Ormullah. "They are not properly clothed – see, they have taken leaves and grasses to cover themselves. And where is Eskarra?"

Slowly the company came across the wide expanse of sand, until its leaders called up to the crew of the *Arrow* and explained something of what had happened.

Tarakeen, one of the returning seamen, indicated the massed ranks behind his companions. "They are from many ships, snared by the sorcery of the island. Some have been here a long time. Their own ships are somewhere among the sand banks."

"They look in need of clothes," said Ormullah. "We'll see what we have below decks. Where are Eskarra and our two young recruits?"

"Watch for them. They are bringing others."

Zendullo leaned close to the giant oars master. "I hope this army doesn't decide to make a play for the *Arrow*. We'd be heavily outnumbered."

However, the newly arrived men of the island looked anything but hostile and to a man sagged down into the sand, apparently exhausted. Tarakeen and the crew of the *Arrow* clambered back on board, helping to find spare clothing and distributing it. An hour later more figures appeared on the shoreline and Ormullah was first to recognize them, crying out with relief. Eskarra and her two companions waved, coming forward.

"Gods of the Deep!" gasped Zendullo. "What are those things with them? Are they human? They walk on all fours."

"Be ready to fight," said Ormullah, leaping down on to the sand, and a score or more of the pirates joined him, their blades singing.

When Eskarra reached them, she raised a hand. "They have followed us from the heart of the island," she said. "They have not attempted to harm us. These are Kesrak and his crew, with others. They were turned into the beast-forms you see by the sorcerer of the island." She explained briefly what had happened. As she did so, Artugol and Volnus watched over the strange pack, but one by one the beasts dropped down on to their bellies, apparently waiting for something. The Kesrak creature also dropped, its own feral eyes yet fixed on Eskarra.

"Nefertari will come," she told her gathered crew. "She will attempt to free Kesrak and these others from their curse. Then we can all be on our way."

The day had waned towards evening when Eskarra's prediction proved founded. From the island trees and across the beach now came the imperious figure of Nefertari, holding a slim, silver chain, which ran to a neck collar she had placed on her prisoner, Zolotec. Like the dogs he had created, he now padded along on all fours, cowed and beaten, head lowered, matted hair plastered to his head, his eyes dull. On either side of Nefertari, the two huge black cats stalked silently, eyes fixed on the massed dog pack, though they made no attempt to harass them. Kesrak and the others all rose, ears quivering with alarm, but they remained stock still, as though waiting for a storm to burst around them.

Nefertari raised her sword and the late rays of the sun caught the blade, reflecting numerous spears of brilliant light which dispersed among the dog pack, each beast stricken and for a moment howling in shock and pain. Artugol and Volnus leapt back, but to their immense relief saw that Nefertari was freeing the last of the cursed dog-creatures, just as she had done in the city. The weirdly disturbing transformations were occurring once more, and as the dazzling light faded, men emerged from the chaos, naked and dusty, struggling to stand, or falling, dazed, to the sand. Among them was Kesrak.

Clothes were quickly flung to the bemused company, and the restored humans dazedly dressed themselves.

Kesrak faced Eskarra. "We owe you much," he said. "You cannot conceive what horrors we have endured under the commands of that fiend!" He pointed to Zolotec, but the prisoner remained oblivious to his surroundings.

Nefertari lowered her blade and sheathed it, but she then raised both arms and appeared to be uttering an invocation to the skies. The effect was immediate, for sudden banks of cloud swirled overhead, creating a vortex that opened like a window. As one the numerous watchers below gasped, amazed at the vista that opened, a huge window on to what must surely be another world or time. A vast city sprawled there and trees spread on all sides in majestic avenues, paved and straight.

"What place is this?" said Artugol.

The racing winds dispersed and the air was still. "You are looking into your world's far future."

As one, the company gaped at a trio of incredibly huge structures, built using countless stones, each a construction the size of a small dwelling, rising up to a central point, perfect pyramids. These had been painted in vivid colours and the final, capping stone, itself pyramidal, blazed in the sunlight, a brilliant golden beacon.

"The sacred land of Kemet," said Nefertari. "This city is the heart of its greatest empire, where even gods walk its sublime highways and temples."

"Why have you brought us here?" said Eskarra.

"To seal the fate of Zolotec."

The city came into focus, causing more stupefaction among the observers, for it superseded anything they had ever seen in their own time. It was not just the extraordinary size of the place, but the awesome majesty of the buildings and colossal statues, mostly of human figures, men and women bedecked in marvelous costumes and headpieces, rows upon rows of them spread along wide avenues, where chariots raced to and fro about their business. Temples rose, supported by enormous columns, most of which were decorated in splendid artwork, brightly painted, and huge walls bore dramatic scenes of battle, depicting perhaps the history of these people.

The swirling clouds combined with the arrival of a sudden sea mist to wrap around the gathered company, which now found itself standing not on soft sand, but on the hard flagstones of a great plaza, at the edge of which gigantic statues rose intimidatingly, dog-headed sculptures reminiscent of the creatures of the lost city at the heart of the island. The company stood in the shadows of these terrifying shapes with renewed fear, but Nefertari prodded Zolotec forward across the burnished stones of the wide floor. The air was absolutely still: every slightest sound whispered clearly. The humans experienced a feeling of minuteness, as if they were ants. Huge steps rose into the mist, above them another statue, wreathed in clouds of incense from several immense cauldrons around it.

Nefertari bowed her head in obeisance to the shape within the clouds, and an enormous face was revealed, that of another dog-headed god, with sharply pointed ears and an elongated snout, an open mouth and rows of teeth. It had been painted with such skill it seemed alive. Nefertari's two great cats dropped to their bellies, motionless as stone.

"Great Sutmekk, who walks in the world of men, I honour you. I have brought your servant, Zolotec, to you. He who was cast out for sins against the gods."

Chapter Eight: To the Death!

The eyes of the huge face gleamed as the humans beneath the colossus felt the living gaze, until the clouds of incense shifted, obscuring it. After a long silence a figure, itself human in size, stepped from the clouds. Sutmekk had taken the form of a man; atop the stairs, he studied the company, his gaze imperious and arrogant.

"Nefertari," he said, voice deceptively soft, with no hint of anger. "You are either brave or naive to bring my servant to me in chains. What does this affront to my prestige mean?"

"Zolotec defied the authority that imprisoned him in the far past, in the time of these people. He used the dregs of his sorcery to transform them into devil-dogs, building an army with which he intended to free himself and serve great harm on that world. I ended that perfidy."

"On whose authority did you act? I presume your mistress, the goddess Bastetis, had a hand in this outrage?"

"Great Sutmekk. I know that in this age, far, far in time from Zolotec's prison, you and the gods walk in the world of men, here in Kemet. You no longer war with one another. There is peace between you, Bastetis, and all the gods."

"Bastetis is in the distant city of Bubastis. The gods have indeed set aside our disputes— in this age we no longer seek each other's destruction. Why are you here, with these assembled mortals?"

"To return Zolotec to you. I implore you to put an end to his crimes. If he acts in your name, then free him from whatever commands you once gave him to show such contempt for humanity. He turned them into dog-beasts, forced to his will. Shall I show you how they were, under his evil sorcery?"

Sutmekk grimaced. "Spare me that horror."

"Perhaps they can be allowed to witness your sagacity and humility."

"Humility! You bear all the conceit of your mistress.

However, I admire your nerve. Very well. Unchain Zolotec."

Nefertari did so. Zolotec remained with head bowed.

"Let us see your human face, Zolotec," said Sutmekk, waving a hand airily. Zolotec's face blurred, then revealed a new face, that of a middle-aged man, the features strong, though haggard, wrought by pain, the madness of incarceration.

"Remove your mask," Sutmekk told Nefertari.

She acceded, revealing her great beauty. Her long black hair, the precise colour of the pelts of her two huge cats, fell below her shoulders, framing a young face and eyes that blazed with determination and hauteur. Zolotec looked at her, stifling a gasp.

"You recall your past, Zolotec," said Sutmekk. "All that befell you and this woman. You were not always eager to destroy each other."

Zolotec spoke at last. "No, great Sutmekk. There was a time when we shared much."

"As I recall, you did so in defiance of those you serve," said Sutmekk.

"Yes, until she betrayed me and sought ultimate power for herself!"

Nefertari bridled, cat-like, as if poised to spring. "A lie, Zolotec. I shared everything with you. Were you as generous with me?"

Sutmekk had descended the wide steps, standing above them. "I have set my differences with Bastetis aside so that Kemet benefits from peace. If you are to dwell among us and enjoy its benefits, you must do likewise. That, or be destroyed. You will both dwell either here or in Bubastis, To decide, we will have a contest."

Nefertari straightened, a hand gripping the hilt of her sword. "Gladly," she said.

"No, no. You and Zolotec must cease aggression towards one another! Let the mortals play their part in this. A contest between two of them." Sutmekk pointed at Eskarra, with a wry smile. "You will be Nefertari's champion. And you," he added, indicating Artugol, "will stand for Zolotec."

Artugol drew back. Fight Eskarra? That's insane! But his mouth was too dry to form an objection.

"If the woman triumphs, you will all go to Bubastis and be subject to Bastetis' rule. If the man is victorious, then you remain here, under mine. We need to conclude this protracted business, so the fight will be to the death. Begin when you are ready." He sat nonchalantly on the steps and waited.

Artugol exchanged glances with Eskarra, shaking his head slowly. She was frowning, evidently equally horrified.

"Come, come, get on with it," the god barked. "These matters are always best settled with a sacrifice to the gods. Begin at once, otherwise I shall conduct sacrifices from among the other mortals, and I will continue until you begin."

Eskarra drew her blade and nodded for Artugol to do the same. The two of them stepped out into the open, circling each other cautiously.

"I warn you," said Sutmekk, "I will hear any whispered words. Demonstrate a genuine desire to kill your opponent. Fail me and I will sacrifice one of your colleagues. I want to see a real fight! Begin!"

Artugol and Eskarra exchanged sword strokes, skilled enough in the use of their weapons to appear to be attacking each other with serious intent. Artugol was fast, but did enough for Eskarra to anticipate his moves and deflect what to any casual observer would have seemed a murderous strike.

They did this for a while before Eskarra took the offensive, likewise giving Artugol time to avoid being run through. Both drew blood, mere nicks, visually messy but harmless.

Backwards and forwards they fought. Beyond them Volnus, Kesrak and their crews watched impotently, dreading the moment when one of the antagonists must succumb.

Sutmekk yawned. "You'll be here beyond dawn at this rate! You're pulling your killing blows. I give you a final chance before I start sacrificing the others. If necessary, I'll kill you all!"

Eskarra glanced at her crew. They were men and women who had fought for her, willing to die in battle, but not like this. This was no way for them to be rewarded. Others had died out on the seas or on the islands. She could not bring herself to let them perish here.

She lunged at Artugol, closing with him, and he realized what she wanted – to die on his blade and sacrifice herself. Again he turned his sword at the last moment, but she had anticipated his move and their weapons clashed. Hers went tumbling on to the paving stones. Sutmekk rose, clapping his hands in expectation of a death.

Eskarra's face was inches from Artugol's. She nodded to him, waiting for the steel to run her through. But he turned his blade, proffering its haft to her.

"Let it be me who dies," he said to Sutmekk. "My life for theirs."

Eskarra took the sword and set its tip under his heart.

"What are you waiting for?" said Sutmekk. "Strike, girl. Resolve this wretched dilemma!."

"Both of us," she whispered to Artugol. "Pick up my sword. If we cannot live as one, we'll die together."

Her meaning burst inside him like fire. He turned to

face the god. "You've taken mortal form, Sutmekk. Then I challenge you. You fight. Fight as a mortal fights, not with a god's power. Dare you risk such a thing? Are you brave and honorable enough for that?"

Sutmekk stared at him in bewilderment. Then he laughed, a long, drawn-out howl, the baying of a wolf or the cry of a jackal. "I'm a god! I don't fight like a mortal, you fool. Although your absurd gallantry amuses me. It's love, of course. Ironically it's something that you, Nefertari and Zolotec, once shared. Learn something from these young mortals."

"Take us both," said Eskarra. "Spare my people. Send them back to their time. You'll have your sacrifice."

Sutmekk smiled. A sudden and complete change of mood possessed him, as whimsical as the shift of the wind. "Well said. You shame the gods with your selflessness. Yes, yes, you and your people can all go. As for Nefertari and Zolotec, go to Bubastis. Serve her, both of you. Let the wounds heal in peaceful Kemet. Probably one of the gods will grow restless and begin some ridiculous new dispute in the future. For all its power and glory, Kemet will not last. In the end it will be you mortals who survive. You'll outlive us and replace us with new gods. Such things have been prophesied often." He turned and walked back up the steps. At the top he looked down again.

"Go – go! Have done with it. I will provide chariots for you, Nefertari and Zolotec. You may enter Bubastis in joint splendor. If you begin your dispute anew, Bastetis and I will sacrifice you."

Epilogue

The clouds rolled in and the extraordinary view of Kemet's city were again blotted out. As sea mist and clouds dissipated, only the vast expanse of sand remained, the sun a fiery ball close to the western horizon.

"I think it best," Eskarra told Artugol, "if we did not speak of what we endured in that place. Not for now."

Artugol smiled. It was enough for him to know that whatever existed between them was alive, discreetly hidden perhaps, but a powerful force, the thought of which filled him with a will to live beyond anything he'd felt before. His pleasant thoughts were interrupted by the voice of Kesrak.

"Who are these two men who braved the hellish city with you, Eskarra? My life belongs to you all, and those of all my followers."

"This is Artugol, and this, Volnus. They are on the King's business, which is to see you and discuss a treaty with you."

"Ah, then they were expected. A treaty, with Elak? Well, he shall have one, I promise you. It will be an honour to serve."

*

Later, amidships aboard the *Arrow*, Volnus was polishing his sword as Artugol watched the sands of the beach where already the crews were searching out their scattered, wrecked craft, beginning what repairs they could manage, though some ships were utterly ruined..

"You know," Volnus said, "one thing does disturb me about the future. Sutmekk spoke of gods being outlived by man—how even he and his fellow gods would be forgotten by our descendants, replaced by newer gods."

Artugol looked skyward, where lonely gulls wheeled. "It seems incredible."

"So what happened to our gods? The gods of Atlantis –

they did not exist in Kemet and that world. Sutmekk's pantheon had displaced them. Is that the fate of our world? To pass into oblivion, to become myth and legend?"

Artugol laughed gently. "Well if so, my friend, it's up to us to write the legends. Sutmekk spared us all, so let's take advantage of that. We've the King's work to do."

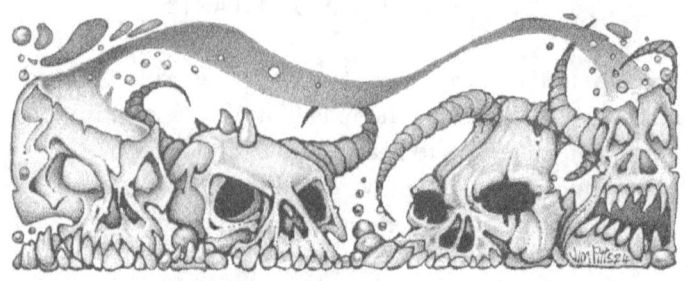

THE CURSE OF
BLOODBONE ISLAND

Sea rovers adventuring in distant waters face many perils, and not merely human enemies, but also the hybrid servants of dark gods, creatures from hidden lairs both above and below the ocean, and more besides. There are also potentially fatal diseases that can strike like a curse, bringing low the strongest of warriors. There is not always a cure for such frightful slayers, and if one can be found, it is a rare thing, a priceless jewel among treasures, won at considerable risk. As the Arrow *voyaged far from the better known sea lanes, the dangers of exposure to such nightmares ever increased.*

- Helvas Ravanniol, Annals of the Third Atlantean Empire

Prologue

Under the watchful eye of the Atlantean moon, the sleek privateer, the *Arrow*, was moored at the quayside of the small port of Ulumar, far from the main sea lanes of the young Empire. Below deck, in the captain's cabin, Artugol cursed softly, leaning over the narrow cot. Volnus was crumpled up in it, barely contained, one leg flung over its side, arms over his face. Artugol's companion had not improved during the day, clearly worsening. The mud swamp fever was killing him. The word in Ulumar was that few survived its rigors. Artugol and Volnus were young men, barely out of their teens, with a reasonable life expectancy, provided they didn't get carved up in a sword fight, or chewed to pieces by any one of many beasts that populated the islands of the north eastern ocean.

They'd been lucky thus far in such skirmishes, but this damned fever frightened Artugol. Volnus was in an unnatural sleep, his flesh slick with sweat. For a big man, his frame seemed to have shrunk, his muscular arms oddly pale, as if the great strength was being leached from them.

Behind Artugol the narrow door creaked open and Eskarra entered. She was young to be a captain, but her strength of will and skill with a blade had won her the position and there were few other captains among the sea rovers who could command a crew as she did, fewer still who did not respect her. She put her hand on Artugol's shoulder, face betraying obvious concern for the man in the cot.

"No better?" For once her voice was not hard, her tone sympathetic, and it was difficult to imagine her as the fiery character who strode up and down the deck of the *Arrow*, metaphorically booting the crew into action.

Artugol shook his head. "Have we tried every surgeon in this poxy port?" he said testily. "If we don't do something for him soon, I fear the worst. It's been almost a week."

"There's news. Come with me. I know you don't like to leave him, but the crew will look after him."

He knew the *Arrow* was never left unattended. Its motley band of pirates, men and lasses, were hardened seamen, and this ship was their home; they carried with them every essential they needed for a life spent almost entirely on the high seas.

On deck the bright moonlight glimmered, and a cool ocean breeze drifted over the tight harbor below ragged cliffs. Onshore, Eskarra turned to Artugol. She was of slight build, her hair tied back from a face burned by the sun, and her simple shirt and trousers would have deceived many into thinking she was an easy opponent, whereas in truth she was far more dangerous. Artugol, like all the ship's company, was also simply clad. He was several inches taller than the girl, a lean islander who'd spent most of his youth toughening himself up on the crags of his home islands. His eyes held an eagle's stare.

Eskarra's mood was, as usual, difficult to read under her own stern gaze. She was an independent young woman, proud of her pirate crew, and at first she had not welcomed the advances of the new Empire under its King, Elak, who desired to curtail as much privateer activity as possible. However, the promise of pardons for all and opportunities to fight for the new King, - particularly against those pirate fleets still to bow to Elak - with their potential rewards, had won her over. Artugol and Volnus, servants of Elak, had become accepted members of the crew, fighting hard and well alongside it.

"There's an old seaman who has unique knowledge of the islands," Eskarra said. "Most think him mad, a simpleton at least. But in his more lucid moments he's able to talk about places he's seen, some of which are little more than legends. Usually I'd not waste my time with him."

Artugol nodded, preoccupied, and followed Eskarra's lead. They negotiated a cramped maze of side streets, entering an inn hardly bigger than a domestic dwelling. Several men and women had squeezed therein, sharing their drinks, swapping tales of their seafaring. A few eyes followed Eskarra and Artugol, relative newcomers to

Ulumar, but these were enlightened times since the new King became enthroned at Epharra.

Slumped on a high stool at the end of the bar like a crumpled doll, a lone figure sipped his ale, muttering to himself. He seemed mesmerized by whatever vision he'd conjured from a memory stretching back innumerable decades, judging by his emaciated, wizened shape. Eskarra brought Artugol to him: the incredibly old man swung round, eyes ablaze as they pierced the youth, almost in fear.

"This is Varzarras," said Eskarra, indicating the oldster. "He's not been to sea for years."

"No! Never again!" Varzarras hissed, shaking his head, his long, white hair moving like weed in a current. "I dare not. Too many enemies. Too many creatures of the deeps ready to suck me down."

At another time, Artugol would have laughed. Instead he leaned close to Eskarra's ear. "You brought me here to meet a madman?"

"We must pick the jewels from the pebbles," she said. "Varzarras, this is Artugol, friend of the man who has fallen ill with mud swamp fever I told you about."

Varzarras frowned, face a mass of wrinkles; his eyes lit up. "Oh, yes! Bring me more ale. It fortifies my memory."

Eskarra went for the drinks, while Artugol sat. "What do you know of this fever?" he asked.

"Lost many seafaring friends to it. It strikes in the night like a fog, drifting in, working its foul magic."

"Yes, I know that much," said Artugol impatiently. "But how is it cured?"

"I was once a man of power, before the deep sea horrors discovered me and began their filthy crusade against me and my fellows."

Eskarra returned with mugs of ale. She nudged

Artugol's arm. "Let him ramble. He'll get there," she whispered.

"All of my companions died of that accursed fever! However, the sorcerers cultivated a plant. The crimson orchid. A rare thing, beautiful, with a scent that no perfume could match. It grows in only one place known to man."

Artugol brightened. "Where?"

"Hah! The gods mock us, do they not? On one island this plant grows, hidden in its jungle heart. Some tried to bring it back, to help the sick, but madness claimed them."

"Where is this island?"

Varzarras recoiled in unfeigned horror. "Once a paradise, it has become a place of legends and sorcery, shunned by man, a tormented place where only a lunatic would set foot. A grim death awaits any who visit it. Or will you dare go there?"

"Where is it?" Eskarra echoed Artugol.

"I will tell you for a price. Bring back one flower for your stricken friend, and one for me. I had powers once. The crimson orchid will restore them! I will enjoy the fruits of youth again!"

Chapter One: The Forbidden Island

"Bloodbone Island," said Eskarra. Around her, sitting or squatting on the narrow deck of the *Arrow*, her crewmen and women either gasped or exchanged uneasy glances, as if their leader had uttered an ancient curse, hinting at something better left to its private darkness. Eskarra raised a hand. "These north eastern islands abound with legends about it. There's said to be a terrible curse laid upon it by evil gods from the far past. A grisly fate awaits anyone setting foot upon it."

"I know of it," said Ormullah, the huge oars master. "It's everything it's said to be, truly accursed. No one has ventured there in living memory, or if so, they never came back to speak of it." He stood with folded arms, a grim statue, face clouded in a scowl that would have cracked stone.

"You know its legend?" said Eskarra.

"Said to have been raised from the deeps at the end of the cataclysm that drowned most of the original Atlantean continent, it was the home of a race of mutant sorcerers, who were equally at home undersea as on land. They used powers forbidden to them by the ocean's darkest gods to build their citadel, not from rock and stone, but from the bones of men. In the chaotic aftermath of the cataclysm, many thousands fled the inundation, and in the waters surrounding their black island, ship after ship struck its shores. Crew after crew succumbed to its poisoned magic." He spat into the scuppers to underline his disapproval.

Artugol was surprised at Ormullah's revelation. It was unusual for the big man to say much, other than to bark orders, but it was clear from his mood that the place he spoke of alarmed him with its mysteries.

"The sea gods unleashed their anger on the sorcerers, furious at their abuse of power. One night they sent power of their own to bring about their downfall. There was an unearthly storm, as violent as those that had accompanied the cataclysm. The seas churned, their very beds flung apart, and on the island, stone and earth turned to boiling mud. Like the red-hot lava of a volcano, the mud poured down from the mountainous heart of the island, engulfing everything in its path to the sea, on all sides.

"At the end, the entire island and everything on it had been turned to mud. The place became as arid and treeless as a desert. All things, living or shaped from earth and stone, were changed, fused into that mud mountain. Deep into the very bowels of the earth below the island, the mud hardened, down to the sea bottom. Solidified, it locked in the sorcerers, crushing and destroying them."

"Then it's just a barren rock?" said Artugol.

Ormullah shook his head. "For a century it was thus. Not a single windblown seed landed there and rooted. No man dared go close. In the seas around it there was life, and who knows what frightful guardians, but it swallowed ships and crews who dared those waters. When life did begin anew, it was said to have been raised by the gods who'd destroyed the original life. From the mud rose vegetation, trees and other sprawling growths, but like nothing found elsewhere. A nightmare realm. The Nine Hells offer nothing worse."

As Ormullah ended his bizarre description, the company murmured, no one grinning or chuckling at the oars master's severe expression.

"I've heard stories about Bloodbone Island," said Eskarra. "My mother, who was an enterprising adventurer, sailed close to it. She told me of the things that swam off its shores, and of the unnatural growths in the deeps around it. She never set foot on it, and I know of no one who has ever done so. But I also know this much – it has its treasures."

Inevitably the pirates perked up at the word. Come hell or high water, the hint of treasure always brought a gleam to their eyes.

"Treasures worth having are always guarded," said Eskarra. "Some by demons, and other such monsters, or sorcery, or by kings and their armies. And some," she added, with a deliberate and challenging glare at the company, "are guarded by legends. Legends so powerful they are enough to trouble our sleep at night.

"So it is, I believe, with Bloodbone Island. I've no doubt it's a dangerous, malevolent place, but who can match our steel, or ferocious resolve? You didn't join my crew to be coddled. You are warriors."

The implication behind her words was not lost on anyone. Now there was laughter, though nervous, and even Ormullah stared at his captain with more than a little apprehension in his gaze. Gods, did she mean to sail to the island?

"Below this deck," Eskarra went on, "Volnus lies in the helpless throes of mud swamp fever. You all know Volnus and have fought beside him. He and Artugol came to us as novices in our trade. But they quickly showed their mettle. They've risked their lives for us, as we have for them. We are nothing if not a united ship. Is that so?"

Everyone was quick to agree, some raising their fists in acknowledgment.

"When one of us is in peril, we all stand with them. So – on Bloodbone Island, there is something which can heal Volnus. A unique plant that grows nowhere else. Its perfume, inhaled and taken into the body, can overpower the mud swamp sickness. It can save Volnus. Without it, he will die. And if we can harvest the plant, it'll protect us all from that accursed illness. An even rarer treasure!" She let her words sink in and for long moments there was deep silence as the crew digested them.

"Who is with me? Who will sail to Bloodbone Island to find the crimson orchid?"

Surprisingly it was Ormullah who was first to raise a fist. "Volnus and others like him saved my life when Zolotec's sorcery almost finished me. I owe it to Volnus. Bloodbone Island fills me with dread, but I stand with the captain."

Zendullo, the steersman, almost as large as Ormullah, likewise pledged his support. "Turning our backs on this venture would shame us. I will go." There were murmurs of surprise around him. He was usually the first to grumble if the *Arrow* was to be sent into dangerous waters. She was like a member of the family to him.

"If anyone wants to quit the ship while we're anchored here in Ulumar, now is the time to do it," said Eskarra. "At first light, we sail."

Chapter Two: Reefs of Death

When the *Arrow* sailed, it was with a full compliment. Terrors aside, everyone was ready to take their part, though the usual cheery atmosphere among them was for once subdued. As they sailed further into northeastern waters, passing the last of the populated islands, their apprehension was drawn taut as a bowstring. After several days, with a light swell on the open ocean, Bloodbone Island came into view. To Artugol's surprise, its outline was not flat and bare, but jagged with trees and other growths. Time had finally eroded the island's rock defenses and allowed seeds to germinate: the place seemed overgrown, as though the vegetation had run amok, smothering everything, right down the cliffs to their bases, choking fronds dipping into the sea like ropes of weed.

Zendullo, at the helm, called out in concern. "Reefs, captain! We'll not get close this side of the island. The whole approach is riddled with reefs, and they're packed together. They'll rip the bottom out of the ship if we try to navigate through." His voice was filled with barely subdued outrage at the thought. The crew knew Zendullo's love of the ship far transcended any he might have had for his companions, and several grinned at the thought.

They had no choice but to circumnavigate the island, which was some fifteen miles in diameter, its centre rising high in huge green buttresses to what once must have been an active volcanic cone. However, they returned to their starting point without earning even a glimmer of hope of breaking through the reefs. These encircled the place perfectly, too perfectly, it seemed, as though strange powers had set them there. No ship of any size dared approach the shores. The coastline offered a second problem: cliffs, rarely dropping below fifty feet, also ringed the island, their growths suggesting an impossible climb.

"How do we get ashore?" Artugol asked Eskarra. His impatience was clear to her. "I'm used to scaling cliffs, but these look more dangerous than anything I've seen before. Are those tendrils alive? They seem to be moving, yet there's no breeze to speak of."

She would not allow herself to be fired by impetuosity. "Varzarras told me there is a channel, a deep cleft in the rocks on this southern side. We can't take the *Arrow* in, but a small craft can do it."

"A handful of us?"

She nodded. "The *Arrow* will have to anchor outside the reefs." She turned to some of the crew. "Prepare a rowing boat." She called out several names and those named stood forward, three men and two women.

Artugol recognized them as among the ship's toughest fighters. Each of them grinned, more than eager to be part of the landing party. "I'll go," Artugol said.

"And I'll lead," said Eskarra, though she grimaced as she studied the waters curling around the ship and the shadows of the nearby reefs.

"Let me go in your stead, captain" growled Ormullah, the oar master. "It's too much of a risk."

Eskarra ignored his concern. "There!" she said after a protracted silence. She was pointing at a large piece of driftwood, a long, broken log. It swirled and bobbed in the current; they watched it as it was slowly pulled on an erratic course to the shore, between reefs. "Varzarras said to follow the drifting logs and branches, which mark the shore-bound currents."

Once the rowing boat was lowered, its small crew embarked, Artugol settled in the prow, watching as other chunks of maritime debris swung to and fro across the bow. He called out to the rowers and slowly they guided the craft between the first of the threatening reefs. Whatever growths comprised them, they had not formed the common coral of these waters, which was vivid in its colours. These were a sickly yellow, as if diseased, their formations oddly uniform. In places they bulged out from their main body like the bloated fingers of an undersea denizen, motionless but deadly.

The rowing boat was tossed to and fro by the whim of the currents, steered somehow between the grasp of the reefs, and the rowers prepared to use their oars to push the craft away from the reef. They knew that one error of judgement could mean the crushing of the boat's keel, and if that happened, they would have no choice than to abandon it.

Eskarra was bent over the side, studying the waters beneath. "Strange," she said to Artugol. "I see no fish. No weed. No sign of life."

"Such reefs are normally teeming," he said. "What does it mean?"

"Bloodbone Island's curse runs far out."

Gradually the boat bobbed and wove towards the island, its passage growing more erratic, twice almost bringing it into collision with the reefs, until a sudden wave got under it and propelled it too far to one side. The rowers rammed their oars downwards at the reef, expecting them to strike brittle coral as they worked to push away, but instead they got no purchase, slipping alarmingly, the rowers almost tumbling over the side at the unexpected lack of resistance.

"Solid!" cried one of the rowers. "Smooth as glass."

The boat was caught by another wave and flushed towards more of the reef's groping shapes. It struck, but like the oars, skimmed over them.

"Sand banks," said Artugol.

"Too solid," said Eskarra. "It's mud. Varzarras spoke of it and Ormullah has already warned us of the mud flow that engulfs the island. It must have come out this far. Row!" she yelled at the crew, picking up a spare oar and handing another to Artugol. Again they rowed, more frantically, and now the sea worked against them like a live thing, trying to slide them against the yellow mud banks, which in the distorted light below the water writhed and grasped at their prey, a voracious sea horror coming to life. Oars were snapped and the boat bumped more than once on the mud, but it corrected itself and the crew worked the currents, pulling away, each time more effectively until at length they came inside the ring and into placid, clear waters that offered a view of the empty bottom. This close to the island, with the cliffs rearing up like the huge green towers of a fortress, they could see the cleft that led within. Its inner walls were dark, but devoid of vegetation, as if the monstrous axe of a god had descended, cleaving the rock in two.

Eskarra, beside Artugol, at last smiled. "The old madman was right," she said wryly.

The tide surged and the rowers fought to keep the boat stable, but they skillfully used the movement of the waters to line the boat up, directing it into the chasm. Once past its mouth, they were in deep shadow, the cleft some fifty feet across, leading into waters that slopped and gurgled ahead, where only the faintest beams of light cut down from the heights. Apart from the soft sounds of the oars, silence prevailed. Here there were no raucous sea birds as would fill the skies on other islands. It was like entering a vast mausoleum.

Chapter Three: A Reivers' Daughter

It had been a long, drawn-out afternoon on the *Arrow*. The sea was unusually calm, flat and gradually dulling to gray as the westering sun buried itself in cloud on the horizon. Zendullo, the steersman, paced up and down, checking and re-checking every rope and stay on the craft, all of which were considerably less frayed than his nerves. At the prow, the huge bulk of Ormullah stood like a sentinel, as unmoving as a statue, eyes glued to the island, no more than a mile north of them. For the dozenth time, Zendullo went to the oars master and testily asked him the same question.

"Any movement?"

Ormullah shook his head and scratched at his tangled beard. "Not even a bird. Apart from that vegetation, it's a dead rock. Cursed is right. Damn it, Zendullo, I should have forced her to let me go with them."

"Two days, she said. Then we send the other boat in. At least they negotiated the reefs."

"How's the youth?"

"The same. I worry, though, that Volnus doesn't eat much. Forcing a few spoonfuls of gruel into him isn't going to keep him alive for long. Cursed fever don't kill him, lack of food will."

"You know he's a King's man. The two of them are. Elak's High Druid, Dalan, negotiated with Eskarra to have them join our crew."

Zendullo nodded, leaning on the rail and watching the silent isle. "Crew knows it. Resented it at first. Eskarra never liked having to deal with the King's men. Mind, those youths have earned their place with us. They've risked their lives for their shipmates, King's men notwithstanding. No one begrudges Eskarra's determination to help Volnus. You think his being Elak's man is why she set's his life so high?"

"That's part of it."

"You know her better than the rest of us, my friend."

Ormullah managed a rare twisted smile. "I knew her parents. Kerroch was the hardest man I met, but even he succumbed to another pirate's blade. And Dershiva never recovered from his loss, ferocious reiver though she was. Sickness carried her off, but Kerroch's death broke her heart. I swore to her on her death-bed that I would protect Eskarra's life with my own, no matter what."

"You loved Dershiva?" Zendullo was the only crewman who would dare ask.

Ormullah's smile brightened, his eyes fixed on something that clearly lifted his spirits. His stern features uncharacteristically softened. "Of course! Which of us did not? There was never another woman like her, not that I've known. Apart from Eskarra. She is so like her mother. Probably even more stubborn. But she has a heart, Zendullo."

"Kicks us and berates us, but she'd stand beside all of us. Artugol and Volnus included."

"Yes. Artugol has a special place, I think. You must be aware of how they look at each other, how they sometimes touch, though she's discreet. Perhaps she fears it is weakness to show desire for a man."

"You think them lovers?"

"I think they will become so."

"This is all about that, then?"

"Probably. But she watched her mother sicken and die. A fighting woman like that should have a better death. Eskarra has carried that with her on every voyage. Volnus is an unfortunate reminder."

"Tomorrow," said Zendullo. "Day earlier than agreed. You go in. If she wants to feed us to the sharks for disobeying her, let her."

Ormullah clapped him on the arm. "It would be worth it to get her and the others out alive."

*

The eyes of the rowing boat's crew accustomed to the poor light. Up ahead they saw an end to the cleft, which opened out into an inner bay, an area some two hundred yards across, the water flat and seemingly tideless, lapping at a bizarre shoreline. Walls of sheer rock rose up beyond it, partially overgrown, but with open surface areas that were pocked with cave-like openings, possibly burrows, though nothing stirred within them. The shore itself was bare, its gleaming banks of mud dried hard as rock, sculpted into unnatural shapes that had all the crew gasping. It was as if a company of artisans had fashioned these, attempting to create a life-size village, with dwellings and a crude quay. Yet the work had failed to achieve its goal – this place was a mockery, a grim ruin, its buildings twisted and tormented into something grotesque and unnerving.

"The wrath of the gods fell here," said Eskarra. "The mud flow from the upper island engulfed everything, alive or otherwise."

Artugol studied the mud banks as the boat drew close. They looked soft and unstable, but as the oars were used to probe them, they proved to be as smooth and solid as polished marble. Even so, stepping ashore, Artugol shuddered.

Chapter Four: Night Monsters

The rounded mud flats curved in a miniature bay and rose in globular tiers to humped and twisted shapes that had the vague appearance of constructions, mangled buildings. Beyond them the jungle reared, massed greenery so profuse it had knotted and tangled itself into a seemingly impenetrable wall, almost solid. Strange flowers and fruit hung in abundant clusters and in a few places the trunks of immense trees showed through, their wood dark and gnarled, more like rock than plant. Up and up the greenery soared, ringing in the tiny bay, the uppermost branches overhanging and trailing great loops of vine and knotted vines, with ferns the size of trees burgeoning out from all sides. It would have been fabulous had it not been so sinister.

Artugol bent down and examined the floor of this amazing place. The hardened mud had set, tough as the granite cliffs he had known as an islander. "It seems hardly credible this mud must provide all the sustenance for the jungle," he told Eskarra. "I suppose if it's some kind of volcanic loam, that would explain it."

She nodded, studying the sky far overhead. "The sun is dropping outside. We'll camp. Varzarras said we'll have to climb up near to the rim to find the flower. We'll do that tomorrow." She called to her reivers to fetch brushwood, anything to feed a fire, and everyone set about searching.

Two of the men found a crude pathway, where a thick

finger of mud had probed the undergrowth before hardening. At its end there were low-hanging branches and the men chopped into them, cutting and trimming material. They laughed and joked as they worked, mainly to counter the eerie silence that had clamped down, but they were nervous, constantly studying their surroundings. One of them, Neyhal, mistimed a cut and his blade bounced back from a sturdy branch, nicking his forearm. A trickle of blood ran from the cut, and he licked at it, grunting with brief annoyance.

"Some hell-hole, this," he snorted. "And us here on the words of a madman. Likely he dreamed the whole thing up."

Beside him, Druach nodded. "Probably. Sooner we get back on the *Arrow* the better."

However, they put their backs into the work, gathering a sizable bundle. Neyhal thought no more of the cut, but it continued to dribble, until several drops fell, landing on the hardened mud. By the time the two men had finished their work and carried their spoils away, Neyhal had left a small trail of blood spots. They gleamed like jewels, spreading briefly before being absorbed by the mud. When its rounded bulge shuddered, like the hide of a large animal, there was no one to see the unnatural movement.

At the camp, where larger branches had been raised and bound together to form a crude lodge, a fire had been lit, and as thick smoke rose in a curling plume, there was enough heat to warm the company, which sat around it and chewed on the sliced meat they had brought. It was salty and almost raw, but they were hungry enough to enjoy it. There were pools of cool water behind the banks of mud, clean enough to drink.

Gradually the company fell asleep. Eskarra and

Artugol took the first watch, sitting a small distance apart from the lodge. Already the sky had darkened, and the smoke tendrils disappeared into it.

"You and Volnus have been friends for a long time," said Eskarra.

Artugol nodded. "Born a few months apart in our village. We learned to crawl together. Never been separated since."

She looked serious, but Artugol was used to that. Whatever life she had lived, it had made it difficult for her to smile often. In the short time he'd served under her, albeit as the King's representative, she'd generally been difficult to engage in conversation. Her intention to help Volnus now had been a pleasant surprise. "We'll save him, I promise you," she avowed.

He sat close to her, though he was always careful not to encroach. He wanted to hold her and tell her what was in his heart, something he'd hardly dared admit to himself. Perhaps intuition had already revealed that secret, but she mostly kept a certain distance between them. He sensed she was attracted to him, but told himself it was wishful thinking. Volnus was the one who knew how to charm the women, but Artugol always found it hard to overcome a natural shyness. He disguised it with gruffness, but not everyone was fooled. Volnus, of course, teased him brutally.

"You fear for your friend," said Eskarra, about to say more, but he turned, certain he had heard a sound beyond the rough lodge. The two of them rose swiftly, silent as cats.

In the darkness, on the trail that Neyhal and his companion had walked, the spilled blood had seeped deep down into the mud, softening it, feeding it like nutrient. In response to it, the mud had altered. A small section of it bubbled, melting, turning to something far more malleable. The power surged along the mud flat and more areas bubbled, pushing upward to create shapes that leaned and swayed upright, clumsy statues, formed by invisible, inexpert hands.

The humped structures behind the camp were bathed in the subtle glow of the campfire, adding to their alien look, and shadows seethed within hollows that could have been windows.

"This was a city," said Eskarra. "Buried under the mud flow, along with everyone who dwelt here. Who knows how many of them are under us, entombed?"

Artugol gasped as he saw something stumble out from one of the cave-like openings in the structures. Squat, naked and hairless, it shambled forward, its head a flattened blob on shoulders without a neck. There was no face, just a few features, hollows for eyes, a vertical smear of a nose and a gash of a mouth. From this uttered a groan. The crude man-shape sniffed the two humans before it, its dark mouth opening wider, and it raised its bulbous arms and clutching fingers like fat worms.

Eskarra called her reivers awake: instantly they were on their feet, used to coming out of a shallow slumber at sea in response to a challenge. Neyhal, who had barely managed to sleep at all, his wound of the day a nagging pain, was first to his feet, shouting at the others. Artugol rushed to meet the oncoming creature, slicing at it with his rapier, but the blade whanged off that thick skin. To his horror he saw several more of the monsters shuffling out of the buried buildings, all reaching out hungrily for their human prey.

Chapter Five: A Taste for Blood

The reivers fought frantically as a score or more of the shambling horrors closed in, snatching clumsily at them, fortunately slow-moving, their actions not well coordinated, as if human endeavors were unfamiliar to them. Artugol tried several times to pierce their slippery, partially formed hides, but fruitlessly. He and the others were pressed back. Neyhal seemed to be the focal point of their attention, and as his own sword arm rose and fell, equally as ineffectively as Artugol's, blood seeped anew from the wound he had given himself earlier. It had worsened, and three of the monsters crowded in on him, drawn to the scent of the blood.

"Protect Neyhal!" cried Artugol, realizing, and the reivers attempted to get between him and his attackers. However, several others also pushed forward, totally fixed on Neyhal, so that it was impossible to shield him from their groping fingers. Inevitably he was knocked to the ground and buried under a rush of bodies.

Druach, closest to him, shrieked his anger and chopped with his war axe, bringing it down in ferocious cuts on the backs of two of the attackers. It struck resoundingly, but might have smitten stone for all its lack of penetration. It did serve, however, to knock one of them aside. For a moment Neyhal struggled to rise and free himself, but one of the creatures had clamped its mouth to his bleeding arm. It came away dripping blood, and Artugol saw the wound had become a long gash, bleeding copiously. It sent the creatures into a frenzy, like sharks fighting over a bloodied victim at sea, tearing and rending.

The first of the creatures drew back; in the firelight, its entire body shone with a weird new energy. Inside it, shadows were coalescing and Artugol understood what they were. "Bones!" he gasped, pointing.

Eskarra nodded. "The blood," she said. "Once consumed, it changes them." She and the others drew back, watching the transformation of the creature, and then more of them that had fed on Neyhal's blood. Their shapes were altering, becoming more human, although they were yet parodies, their bodies contorted, malformed. Their faces developed eyes and other features. At best they were like the work of an experimenting sculptor, incomplete and lacking the final touches that would make them less nightmarish.

Druach, horrified by the rending of Neyhal, who seemed about to be cannibalized by these monsters, rushed at the creatures and struck at them anew, but they brushed his axe aside as though it were a frond. Eskarra and Artugol both yelled at him to keep back, but so deep was his fury that he kept at them with his war axe. It was impossible to restrain him and inevitable that he would also be wounded. As soon as that happened, he was attacked by four of the stumbling horrors and they pulled him to earth, their mouths clamping on his leaking wounds.

"Withdraw!" shouted Eskarra. The remaining four did so quickly, backs to the crackling fire.

"We'll have to take to the boat," said Artugol.

Eskarra cursed. "If we quit the island now, we'll never get ashore again. We stand and fight!"

"See, even more are coming," said Dendric, the other surviving man. He bore a huge scar across one shoulder, but it did not seem to have diminished his strength. He was right. A fresh swarm of the devils had awoken, pouring from the houses and forest, their pending attack irresistible.

Artugol bent down and picked up a short branch protruding from the fire. It blazed, its sap acting like oil, and instinctively he waved it at the first of the creatures. Immediately it fell back, stubby hands raised against the heat and light. Artugol pressed forward, jabbing the flaming torch at more of them and the effect was instantaneous: they were afraid of fire. The reivers realized at once, each taking a firebrand. Quickly they formed a short wall and forced the creatures back. By now there were at least a hundred of them, most in their basic, mud-figure form, with others developing into the quasi-human shapes. All drew back, crowding the shore area.

"If we can repulse them," said Eskarra, "we can take the path into the heights. We'll cut fresh branches as we go and keep torches lit."

Carefully the five of them worked their way beyond the clearing to the area between the strange buildings, the mud creatures held at bay, though only out of reach of the fire. They clearly had no intention of relinquishing the pursuit. Artugol briefly studied the twisted buildings and saw they, too, were changing, their outer layer of dried mud dissolving, running like great tongues of molten muck. The city, like its denizens, was slowly transmuting, as though all the spilled blood had released the ancient magic of the gods.

"Here's a path!" called Brenna, one of the warrior women. She was stocky and bore as many scars as Dendric. Her fierce expression made it clear she had no intention of going back. She pointed to a passage through the leaves and thick bracken, cutting at it with her sword, glad to have work for it. The others joined her, using their torches to hold back the following creatures, Artugol thrust hard at the chest of the first and instantly it burst into flames, burning with an extraordinary intensity, scorching the vegetation on either side. Whatever was trapped inside the mud form screamed horribly in agony.

While its companions pulled back as one, unable to pass the blazing inferno, the reivers made their way up the steepening path in desperate haste, hacking aside creepers and undergrowth. Out in the forest, nothing stirred, the darkness beyond the glow of the torches starless and deathly silent. Some distance below the group, the flames burned on, but none of the mud creatures were following, constrained by the blaze. Up ahead, the low mountain's bulk loomed, an even darker stain on the nightscape.

Chapter Six: Citadel of the Fallen

As they climbed, holding aloft their torches, the reivers studied what little they could see in the glow. Around them, the mountain was silent; sounds of pursuit quickly receded far below them. They remained on the hard mud path, twisting and turning ever upward like the winding of a huge serpent, the gradient steepening. When they had gone far enough, they paused to cut fresh branches, trimming them and strapping them to their backs, in readiness for when their torches sputtered out. If there was any life on the island other than the horribly revived mud beings, it did not show itself or otherwise indicate its existence.

Artugol followed close to Eskarra at the head of the party. He could see her face in the glow, its features pulled into a grimace of anger and sadness.

"Two men lost," she hissed. "We must not fail in this business."

Brenna moved forward. "They knew the risks. We always do, Eskarra. You can't shield us all from the things we challenge," she said.

"She's right," said Dendric. "We all know the risks."

"Still it comes hard when our companions die," Eskarra said bitterly, then fell silent. Artugol knew better than to comment, though he wanted desperately to offer her some kind of comfort. At times like this she seemed more unattainable than ever.

As they got closer to the rim of the crumbling caldera, the forest became no less matted, the vegetation spilling over the rim on both sides, a choked barrier of root and branch, vine and creeper. Dawn was seeping into the eastern clouds, its light tipping the edges of the jungle, adding a bizarre, bloody tinge to motionless leaves. The path cut down through a narrow rift, its sides flaking, the only place apparently devoid of plants. Underfoot, the hardened mud was thinning. It gave way to earth and loam, comprised of the falling leaves of the ages.

Beyond the cleft, the reivers came out into a flattened area, a small plateau, ringed by more trees and weed-choked rocks that had an unnatural geometric feel. As the company entered what appeared to be a time-worn amphitheater, the five warriors stared at their surroundings, seeing in the moss-hung rocks the recognizable shapes of statues, not of men but of disturbingly strange creatures, possibly sea dwellers, with long, snaking arms and extraordinary aquatic features. They had the look of guardians, opposing any further progress, created, possibly by denizens from below the waves, given the marine nature of their bodies, shaped like nothing previously seen by the reivers.

"Were these the gods of this place?" said Artugol softly. "The ones who vented their wrath on the sorcerers of the island?"

Eskarra nodded. "That or their servants. Varzarras said there is a central temple, the heart of the island kingdom. It is there we shall find the crimson orchid."

The other three reivers had been searching warily among the statues, cutting at the undergrowth. Brenna called. "Here! The path goes down again, though the steps are overgrown."

By the increasing light of dawn, they all saw the open bowl of the extinct volcano. It was filled with jungle chaos, a great green lake of verdure, fathomless, not a bare rock protruding. Life here was almost impossibly rampant, so choked and congested with vegetation that it seemed remarkable it could have survived its own furious conquest of the land. The path widened out into a series of deep steps, somehow resistant to the rabid jungle growth, yet slippery with lichen and mould. They led to the ruins of what could have been a temple.

The company clambered down to it, careful to hold on to their brands. Halfway down the dangerous stairway, Artugol turned and looked back upwards into the partial dawning light. He was appalled to see even more statues looming above, these much larger than the ones in the amphitheater. Their faces were far more horrifying, something from the worst sea nightmares imaginable. Those frightful gazes suggested the demonic, and their arms, elongated and ending in frozen, grasping suckers, reached out in a fixed threat, a promise of a bloody death.

To his horror, Artugol thought there was movement among the malevolent sculptures. Their numerous eyes were alive, picked out by the brightening dawn, the silence of the jungle broken by the cracking of rocks. Quickly the five reivers dropped down the steps and under the shadow of the first temple block. As one they looked back. Dawn had broken through and now the statues were lit up. Their heads did move! A score of them creaked as if on mighty hinges, and those hungry eyes turned skywards, watching the oncoming day.

"They are night creatures," said Eskarra. "Varzarras said so. Their sea gods swam in utter darkness, far down in the remotest deeps of the ocean. They will not harm us by day. Their movements will be very restricted. Dawn has not come too soon."

It quickly became apparent that she was right, for the statues had frozen once more, faces twisted in frustrated fury, as if held in thrall to the sunlight. The reivers ducked under the portal and entered a temple thick with dust and shadow, though the torches threw its interior into sharp relief. Whatever had been here was broken and spread about the rubble-strewn floor. Mounds of leaves had turned to soil, sprouting weeds and trailing ivy that had been captured by other growths hanging down in festoons from the shattered roof.

"Search every corner," said Eskarra. "The flower should be here somewhere."

They split up and began looking, wandering through a maze of rooms, some of which were too choked to enter, others roofless, yet more in danger of collapsing. As the morning wore on, Artugol began to feel a sense of despair. They had come here on the promise of a madman. Now, surrounded by this alien place and its ruins, its sense of death and destruction, he wondered if the flower really existed. Had Varzarras simply dreamed up his visions? Were they fact or simply legends?

Entering what had once been a larger hall, he gasped, and the truth hit him like a cold wave.

Chapter Seven: Lair of the Sorcerers

Eskarra had visited three low chambers, all lit partially by shafts of light from the disintegrating roof overhead. So far, nothing but rubble and ruin. There were mushrooms and other shadow growths, but no sign of the promised flower. This room looked as if it once had an elongated sunken bath in its centre, now choked with bricks and tiles, fused together with more fungal growths. There were a dozen or more holes in the walls, several inches across, possibly old pipes, gaping at her like surprised mouths. She was about to quit the room when she heard sounds within the pipes. Something rustled, possibly a strong draught. Perhaps the pipes fed air into the chamber when it was undamaged. Or water. A few thin vines hung from the lips of some pipes and these trembled now, gently at first, but then more violently. Something was coming.

Eskarra stepped back, sword poised. Rats? Other creatures, disturbed by the human intrusion after so many years? When a shape thrust its blunted head forward into the light, she gasped. Serpent! Yet unlike any she had seen before. At once she stepped back and gave a shout. In response, more serpents emerged from the holes, a dozen nests. These creatures were fat and twenty feet long, constrictors that could hold and crush a human body easily. Shocked, she stumbled backwards, almost falling into the sunken area. She let out a shriek which echoed along the passageways as the first of the serpents attacked her.

She used her sword effectively, timing her cut so that it bit deep into the thing's neck, its vital juices frothing and spilling. Yet even with its head half severed, it came at her. All the frustration and furious anger at the loss of two of her companions fuelled Eskarra now, and with a second swipe she sent the serpent's head flying into the dust. Behind her, rushing into the room, Brenna, Tormea and Dendric found themselves also confronted by the serpents, as a score of them came at them in a united attack. The reivers' horrified reaction almost undid them as they took in the terrifying spectacle. Instinct fueled them, however, and as they backed off, they all hacked and stabbed at the weaving heads, feeling their blades cut deep and not rebounding uselessly as they had when striking the mud creatures in the fight by the shore. Yet the odds against the reivers were stacked against them.

They retreated out of the chamber with Eskarra.

Tormea, the taller of the two women, slid one of the branches she had trimmed from her back and used it to drive between two of the loose stones that formed the crumbling archway around the door. Tormea's muscular arms bulged as she gave a jerk and the stones slid outwards, followed by the immediate collapse of part of the arch. In the confusion, with dust billowing outwards, the serpents momentarily drew back. Tormea rammed her makeshift staff into more loose stones, levering them out and completing the destruction of the arch, which crashed down, bringing a huge section of roof with it. One of the serpents got through, writhing in agony as tons of stone rained down on its back half. Eskarra drove the point of her blade up into the soft flesh beneath its mouth and tore it open, spattering herself in blood.

The doorway was completely sealed. Eskarra wiped muck from her face and gave Tormea a grim smile. As the four reivers turned, they heard a shout from beyond and quickly ran in response. They came into a much wider chamber, where they saw Artugol. Beyond him, leaning over, thick with cobwebs and dust, was a large statue. It was of a human, an important figure, judging by its carefully sculpted robes and medallions, and the stone-wrought finery circling its arms. Even partly obscured, the face was recognisable.

"Varzarras!" cried Eskarra.

Artugol nodded. "One of the sorcerers, perhaps a king. He did know the secrets of this place."

"Then we're not on a fool's errand," said Brenna.

"No wonder he wants an orchid for himself," said Eskarra. "Not so mad."

"There's a door behind the statue. I've cleared some of the rubble from it," said Artugol. Quickly the others joined him and soon they had shifted enough detritus to reveal the wooden door and heave it partially open. Light spilled in, enough to see there was an outside courtyard beyond, although it was richly overgrown, choked with plants hanging from high above.

"It must be here," said Artugol as they forced the door wider.

Eskarra set Tormea to guard the exit as the rest of them got busy at once, cutting away the wall of greenery and other plants, flowers of brilliant hues and extraordinary blooms. The air was rich with the sweet smell of released perfume, clouds of motes dancing in the brilliant sunlight. Exhausted, the reivers paused. As they did so, Artugol cut aside the fronds of a rubbery bush, to reveal a small, more open glade. Around it, seemingly untouched by the rampant weeds and tendrils blanketing everything else, a dozen crimson flowers were open to the sun, drinking it in.

Eskarra stood close beside Artugol, gripping his arm. "These are what we came for. These will save Volnus."

He put an arm around her, then realized he may have overstepped the mark. But to his amazement she turned and kissed him lightly on the lips. There was no time to react. They went to the flowers, kneeling down.

"Gods, that perfume!" he gasped. It was heady, its sweet scent powerful.

"Be careful," she said, but she, too, caught the powerful scent. Both of them felt themselves on the point of swooning, turning to raise their hands to the others. However, they were also caught unawares by the extraordinary strength of the emissions of the flowers, dropping to their knees. In moments, all four of them were lying prone in the thick grass, victims of an unnatural sleep.

*

Ormullah growled like a bear, glaring at Bloodbone Island in frustration. "The afternoon wears on. They've already spent one night there. I should go."

Zendullo nodded. "Aye, as well go now as ever. Take four with you, and watch that tidal race. You saw how Eskarra crossed over."

The huge oars master wasted no more time, and soon the second rowing boat had been lowered. There was no shortage of volunteers for the crossing. The westering sun was low, evening imminent. On the island, the jagged cleft was a tall, black stain, its inner darkness pulsing with invisible terrors.

Chapter Eight: The Hell-Spawned Gods

No sooner had Artugol, Eskarra and the others fallen into the drugged sleep of the orchids, than they were adrift in the dreams powered by their exotic perfume, for each sleeper, a similar experience. Artugol felt himself tumbling slowly in the ether, the air around him bright, falling gradually through clouds, dropping deeper into the embrace of the sea. Strangely it grew lighter as he fell, not darker, as ocean abysses would have done. Far below, wrapped in huge fronds and trailing streamers of weed, the towers and structures of a city spread out on the seabed, and through the endless forest of weed, fantastic alien creatures drifted like coloured bubbles on a breeze. Silence closed in the extraordinary vista, and the atmosphere, whatever it consisted of in this dream state, was calm and relaxing. Turning, Artugol saw the floating body of Eskarra and the other two reivers. Each of them waved languidly as they all sank slowly downward.

Several floating creatures nudged past, huge unrecognizable entities with multi-hued domes that glowed, lit from within. Shoals of oddly shaped fish flashed as they turned in the sunlight from above that was as bright as if it cut through air rather than the sea. Artugol and his companions, who had lived on and by the ocean all their lives, were well used to seeing mysterious creatures flung up in storms, sometimes dredged from far below, but the things that swam in these waters were unique to them, like visitors from another dimension. The dreaming minds understood that what they were seeing, scenes from long ago, a hundred years or more, events that had shaped their present.

Beyond the city, rising up behind it like a vast cloud, a sea-bed mountain soared, dark and featureless, its rock gnarled and pitted, in places sheer, in others a mass of apparently fused globules of cooled rock, creating an enormous natural structure that reached for the distant sky beyond the waves. Artugol understood instinctively that this was Bloodbone Island's underwater foundation. As he and the others drifted closer to the mountain, hanging like discarded dolls over the underwater city, they sensed something else, a living presence within the mountain. Something incomprehensibly colossal. Somehow they knew what it was – one of the gods that the race of sorcerers had offended. Indeed, their sorcery had trapped it within the mountain, and they were leeching its otherworldly powers, making themselves quasi-divine, but in ways that would have appalled humanity. They had risen up on to the island and created their citadel there, and built it not from stone but from the bones of men.

Artugol felt the intense anger of the god-being trapped in the mountain, its impotent fury emanating outwards like heat from a furnace. For decades it had been imprisoned, weakened by the vampiric feasting of the sorcerers. Yet its desperation had not been ignored. From far off in the uttermost deeps of the ocean, other creatures stirred, beings unknown to Man, which had roamed the very floors of the ocean since its early formation, beings that had been spawned around a distant star, refugees from wars beyond human understanding. They had fled some world-shaking catastrophe to this world's ocean bedrock but now they were coming, in answer to the call of their trapped fellow. Artugol's mind veered away from contemplation of these Hell-spawned immensities, knowing it would lead to madness for him and his companions. He sensed unbelievable size, as though mountainous beings were about to emerge from the darkness. He felt Eskarra's hand clutching at his and together they drifted mercifully further away from the city, up into the emptiness of the ocean.

Below them they knew the fate of the city was sealed. From limitless oceanic distances, the monstrous god-beings came and vented their vengeance on the sorcerers, unleashing their dreadful, cynical powers. The mountain shook, blurring as the waters around it clouded, and numerous sea creatures fell to the ocean floor, blasted apart by the horrific clash of powers. In the utter confusion, Artugol and his companions drifted through a silent darkness, wafted away from the chaos. Eventually they emerged into the light, floating once more in the ether above Bloodbone Island, although what they now saw remained in the island's forgotten past.

Its high citadel, up on the peak and the paths that led from it down to the city at its shoreline, seethed and boiled with a molten flood, a golden mud-flow, gushing endlessly from the caldera, as if the sea bottom had risen ever upwards, transformed into this gelatinous landslide that carried all before it. Nothing below the crater rim survived the flow, down to the sea and beyond it. Underneath the waters, down the side of the mountain, dark brown runnels of mud blended with the rock, creating an illusion like dried wax spilling down the sides of a candle holder, but on an extreme scale.

In the citadel itself, high above the boiling sea, the last of the sorcerers vainly sought to hold back the powers of the beings they had abused. Locked inside their innermost chambers, they waited. For days the storms outside raged, like a new cataclysm, an upheaval almost as devastating as the previous ones. The creature they had trapped was freed at last and together with its hell-spawned rescuers, made its way back out into the vastness of the ocean and ultimately down into its fathomless abysses, where no man could venture. When the sorcerers dared to emerge from their lair, they found that guardians had been set around the rim of their citadel, monstrous demi-gods that waited for them, hungry as slavering hounds. The sorcerers could not pass that circle, and remained trapped. Their powers waned, until only one last source remained – the crimson orchids. These, brought from some other, unknown dimension, gorged on the molten mud burgeoning out from the crater, feasting on that wild sorcery. The flowers imbued the survivors with enough of this to enable a small handful to flee Bloodbone Island and out to the world beyond. It was a desperate, forlorn flight, for all of the once mighty sorcerers succumbed to madness and either died, starving on remote, barren islands, or were snared and executed by angered seamen who had lost friends and family to the abuses of the sorcerers in their pomp, and whose bones were now rotting under the mud of the island.

Only one survived—their last ruler, Varzarras, himself close to madness.

And on the island, the volcanic mud released by the angered gods sealed everything but the inner temple, and nothing could grow. Only the crimson orchids and surrounding plants lived on, but locked away, their powers impotent. Guardians were set about them, the monstrous statues, the serpents, and other, unseen horrors. Around the coast, other guardians dissuaded roving sailors or anyone foolish enough to try to land on Bloodbone Island.

All these things, this violent, terrifying history, the dreamers watched, understanding. Something shook them now, a physical presence. Artugol was the first to awaken, rough hands shaking him. He saw the anxious face of Tormea above him.

Chapter Nine: Flight from Madness

"Thank the gods!" said Tormea as the last of her companions woke from the drug-induced sleep. "I was afraid you were all lost."

Artugol struggled to his knees. "Quickly," he called to the others. "All of you – pull your scarves around your noses and mouths. Inhale as little of the flowers' perfume as possible."

As they all did so, including Tormea, Eskarra was rising and nodding. "The sorcerers," she said, her voice almost muffled. "They gave themselves terrible powers, superhuman strength, longevity, powers of the mind."

"The gods don't want the crimson orchids taken from here. Their powers are too dangerous to release into our world," said Artugol. "We must act with great caution."

He turned to the crimson flowers, preparing to use his blade to dig a single orchid free of its soil.

"Wait!" cried Brenna. "Surely It's too dangerous!" She looked to Eskarra, whose scowl had deepened. "After what we have seen, dare we take any of the flowers back?" Brenna went on. "What if they send us and the entire crew of the

Arrow into that drugged sleep? None of us might awaken."

Tormea and Dendric were nodding, feelings written clearly on their faces. "Aye," said Dendric. "Surely we cannot risk that? There's more horror here than we could have foreseen."

Artugol turned to Eskarra, an agonized look on his face. "But what of Volnus? Only the crimson orchid can save him."

Eskarra's expression was equally pained. She stared at Artugol as the others drew back in confusion, though their views now were obvious.

He leaned close to her, speaking softly. "You can't just abandon him. There must be something. If we could take one plant, sealed in a bag. Once it has been used on Volnus, we can burn it." His eyes stared into hers. He knew this was to be a test of any potential future relationship between them. If she refused him now, they could never be anything more than ship companions. He understood that she knew it, too.

"And Varzarras?" she said.

"Nothing for him. His life was spent in deceit. Let him pay for that."

She nodded and whispered so that only he could hear. "Take one plant and hide it inside your shirt. If the others realize, they may try to kill you. The crew, too. Go on. I'll shield you." She pushed past him and pointed with her blade to the exit. "Go back," she told Tormea and the others. "We need to get away as swiftly as we can. Night will soon be upon us and the guardians will wake."

As one they went back into the ruins. Artugol surreptitiously dug up a plant, muffled it in a small bag he had brought and slipped it inside his shirt where it would not be noticed. He followed Eskarra, wanting to thank her discreetly, but she ignored him, concentrating on their passage through the thickening shadows. Beyond the old temple the small company came back to the steps leading up to the crater rim. It was lit by the fading embers of late afternoon. They had been unconscious longer than they'd realized—it would soon be dark. As they climbed, several of the ancient statues loomed over them, their extended arms seeming to reach down, imbued with hungry life, eager for human blood. Somewhere inside each of them, stone ground on stone.

It was a demanding climb, the old stairway steep and broken by gnarled limbs of ivy, but the company climbed over the rim. No sooner had it done so than the reivers heard louder cracks behind them and the snapping of branches, the vibration of the ground. The statues, free of sunlight, were awake—moving. The gods of darkness, horrors deep under the ocean the dreamers had seen, had poured their energies into the stone itself. Tormea had kept one of the torches burning, now lighting others, until all five of the reivers carried a fresh firebrand. There came a unified ululation of fury behind them in the knotted trees and undergrowth, testament to the anger of the pursuing guardians.

"Light and fire!" called Eskarra, leading the company. "They abhor it. Keep the torches high." As she spoke, something tore through the air above them, a mighty appendage, ripping at treetops and tearing them aside. However, the company sped on like rats in a run, coming again to the hardened mud trail. It gleamed in the torchlight, like the sweating hide of a great beast. Downwards they sped, almost slipping and falling. In the haste and confusion, a single torch was inadvertently dropped, sputtering on the mud.

Artugol glanced back and saw to his horror that the mud was melting. The fallen torches had ignited something in it combining with the powers of the old gods, creating a fresh slide, small but increasing in volume, and it followed them down the mountainside. He exhorted his companions and they rushed at breakneck speed, also feeling the shifting of the mud slide, reactivated again after so many years. Overhead something vast and winged swept around them like a cloud, dipping down, but deterred by the blazing torches. On either side of the trail, other huge shapes blundered through the undergrowth.

All their powers will concentrate on preventing the flower from leaving the island, thought Artugol. He held the concealed bag close to his chest, almost stumbling, but doubly determined to get away.

Somehow they got to the lower part of the path without anyone tumbling into what would surely have been their death in the knotted verdure. The mud path had widened and they had outdistanced the oncoming mud flow, at least for a while. However, their exit on to the beach was blocked off. The mud creatures they had fought earlier had not left. Some had fallen to the fire, but the remainder, scores of them now, gathered like an immense herd, and it had one unified purpose. They gazed at the fugitives from distorted human faces. Then charged.

The torches swung in blazing swathes as the reivers fought in sheer desperation, setting alight shape after shape, until a conflagration lit up the beach, its backdrop the former buildings of the city that had been its port. Already, in the earlier fire, countless blocks and towers had been freed of the no longer solidified mud, and their own dire secrets had been revealed. They had not been constructed of brick and stone, but were hewn from bone. Human bone. Countless thousands of them had been fused together, melded into the bizarre architectural nightmare, and in some places there were towers built from nothing other than human skulls.

Artugol and his companions stood shoulder to shoulder, the city and its demented defenders ablaze, the mud bubbling and boiling. On the lower shore they saw their rowing boat. It, too, was ablaze, quickly being incinerated, and with it all hope of a return to the *Arrow*, far out in the bay.

Chapter Ten: Fire and Bone

They got close to the shoreline, torn between making a stand and risking taking to the water. In the end they were reluctant to toss aside the firebrands, knowing they would almost certainly be unable to reignite them. They waded out, waist deep, but the transmogrified creatures pressed forward, groping blindly for them, driven by a relentless desire to smother them and undoubtedly reduce them to their own physical forms. It was how they trapped all those unfortunate enough to be wrecked on Bloodbone Island.

However, the mud around them had softened, the fires in the bone buildings and along the path of the mud slide from higher up intensifying so much that in places the mud boiled away, revealing layer upon layer of human bones, a thick carpet ringing the cove. Artugol and his companions were horrified to see so much human devastation, evidence that thousands had died here over the years. Behind the heaped bones where towers had crumbled and left yellowing mounds of skulls, pyramids of those human relics leaned into the night sky, the trees snapped and crackled, some burned, huge fiery torches, others falling. Out of the inferno slithered several huge shapes, their forms distorted by the waves of heat. Guardians of the upper temple, slaves of the sea gods, they burst through the masses of bone and skull, scattering them like spoil, and lumbered on to the beach. They swung their massive tendril-like arms like clubs, carelessly smashing scores of the mud beings aside, even though they served the same purpose. The guardians, crashing through the conflagration had inevitably set themselves ablaze, yet it made little difference to their inexorable advance.

Madness reigned, fueled by time's corrupting process, so the function of the guardians and mud beings became perverted to the point where they blindly thrashed against each other as well as the fleeing humans, embroiled in a lunatic furore of destruction.

Eskarra said to Artugol, her head close to his ear, "The guardians are set to keep things in, as much as intruders from landing. In the dreams, that became clear. The last powers of the sorcerers must not be released."

Artugol nodded. He knew the plant must not be allowed out into the wider world, "Once I've used it to help Volnus, I'll burn it."

She looked at him in apparent doubt, and he wondered if she would actually fight him for the flower. Had she changed her mind? Would she abandon Volnus after all?

"We'll never swim to the ship, not through those waters," she said. They could both hear the sea churning out in the bay, beyond the great crack – as though events on the island had disturbed it, waking other powers beneath it. The mud slide, they knew, went far out, so if it was also transforming, it would be a deadly trap; there was no way to avoid its clutches.

More of the mud creatures came forward, stumbling into the water, but the reivers yet resisted, stabbing at them with their torches, repulsing them. The first of the guardians heaved up behind them, but it was already sunk deep into the seething mud, unable to free its lower body. Abruptly a score of the mud beings swarmed over it like insects, and the fire spread as if igniting oil. Clouds of foul black smoke billowed upwards, covering the beach as the monstrous guardian toppled. Behind them others paused, only their hellish eyes visible in the choking mayhem.

"We'll never hold them back," said Artugol. "We have to swim."

But as he spoke, the water beyond him burst upward, writhing shapes limned in the firelight. The undersea mud was disgorging more of the amorphous things, and like twisted sea creatures, they headed for the reivers. Artugol flung his firebrand and it struck the first of them, bursting into flame. For a short time the new assault was held back, but it would not be for long.

"Discard the flower!" said Eskarra. "It's our only chance."

Artugol was wracked with indecision. If he threw it away, Volnus's life went with it, otherwise they would all die. He reached into his shirt.

A distant shout rose above the roar of the flames, across the waters.

Artugol turned, squinting into the night. Beyond the first group of aquatic mud creatures, he could just make out a long shape on the tide. A rowing boat!

"It's Ormullah!" said Eskarra. "He's disobeyed my orders, but for once I can't fault him for that."

The reivers waved their torches and at once the rowing boat knifed through the water, evading the grasping hands of the things beneath its hull, making for the shore. Artugol and the others flung the last of their burning torches at the mud things, driving the assault back. The men in the rowing boat fought off all attempts to overturn it, racing forward. It swung round and at once Eskarra was pulled aboard, followed by the others.

"No time for explanations," said Eskarra. "Just get us away from this hellish island."

Ormullah laughed, but he studied the shore and the massed creatures, many of which had melted into the layers of bone that carpeted everything. Of the huge guardians there was no sign, but up in the skies, deep-throated sounds hinted at some aerial threat, smothered as yet in the clouds rising from the boiling waters. It was a tortuous row back through the cleft and out into the bay, but the underwater attacks subsided. At last the boat reached the *Arrow*, everyone dragged aboard, exhausted.

Artugol wasted no time in rushing down into the cabin where Volnus lay, close to the point of death, for the swamp fever had not relented. Eskarra stood behind him as he took out the small bag and revealed the crimson orchid. He let its perfume waft under Volnus's nose so that the fumes were drawn in by his slow breathing.

When it was done, Eskarra handed him several jewels and coloured stones that might have been valuable, "Enough to sink the bag," she said. "Perhaps the gods of the island will accept them as recompense. Better to let it lie on the sea bed, far from shore."

Epilogue

As the *Arrow* sped further from the smoking Bloodbone Island, Artugol discreetly dropped the jewel-weighted bag containing the flower over the ship's rail. He and Eskarra watched it disappear into the darkness of the depths. Overhead, where thick clouds churned, lowering like the balled fists of the gods, the sounds of aerial creatures broke through, calling like gulls. Something had followed the ship from the island. As the *Arrow* moved further away from where Artugol had disposed of the bagged flower, the pursuers descended from above, their shapes indistinct in the gathering sea mist, though one of them plunged into the waves and was lost to sight beneath them.

"It seems the orchid is destined to return to the island," said Eskarra.

"Yes, though its work for us is done. Volnus is recovering and stable."

"You're angry with me," she said. "You know, in the end, I would have abandoned him. I had to think of my crew. I could not risk sacrificing them. As captain, it was a decision I had to face."

"You have responsibilities. Sometimes they overrule personal matters."

If she had more to say, there was no time, for the lookout called from the mast. Before long another ship was seen on the horizon, likely drawn to these waters by the huge pall of smoke rising from the island. By the markings on its wide sail, it was a ship of the King of Atlantis.

*

Emmaneus, primary Druid of Dalan, High Druid of the King, watched Volnus as the youth ate, propped up in his cot, eyes alert, strength visibly coursing back into what had become a wasting body. "You seem in good health, Volnus. Are you well enough to board my ship?" Emmaneus had a brusque manner, openly impatient to get on with his business.

Volnus reached out for the meat slices on the adjacent table. Chewing one hungrily, he nodded. "Yes. I need to wash the stink of the last week off me."

"You're fortunate. Few survive mud swamp fever. You have the constitution of a bull."

"Dying from the fever would be an ignominious way to pass."

"I want to set sail for Epharra before the end of the day."

Behind the druid, in the door to the narrow cabin, Artugol and Eskarra watched the exchange, both relieved to see Volnus' evident recovery. They withdrew quietly and went up to the deck, into the early morning light. Alongside the *Arrow*, the sleek vessel of the King had been tied up. Uniformed sailors went about their daily chores on its deck.

"Emmaneus is Dalan's right hand," said Artugol. "Volnus and I are being recalled. We're to sail with Emmaneus to the capital. Apparently the King wants to meet us and thank us for the various missions we've undertaken for him."

"Then what?"

"More, no doubt. The new empire is young. The King has many enemies."

Eskarra nodded, gazing out at the sea. Bloodbone Island was far below the north eastern horizon, not even a smudge of cloud to mark it. "Our days together have been chaotic, but interesting," she said.

Interesting? Is that how you'd describe them? "Yes. In truth, I'd rather they did not end."

She shrugged. "You're obliged to go. I have my ship and crew. My priorities lie with them."

"Perhaps you'll be commissioned to carry Volnus and me again."

"The King sets his own priorities. They may clash with mine."

"And mine?"

"You've no choice. You're the King's man. He commands, you serve. You must arrange your life around that."

Emmaneus emerged from below deck, easing cramped limbs, his gray robe stretching over his portly shape. "I won't ask you for details of how you brought about his recovery." He studied Artugol and Eskarra for a moment, as though he knew what had occurred on the island. "There are places in these seas that are off limits. Better not to visit them."

Eskarra nodded. "My ship will always be at your service. We acknowledge the King as our ruler." She managed to make her smile convincing.

Emmaneus allowed himself a brief smile. "Good. He did marry a pirate lass, you know. And all of Atlantis regards it as a fine match." He turned and called out orders to his sailors, and they made ready to part company with the *Arrow*.

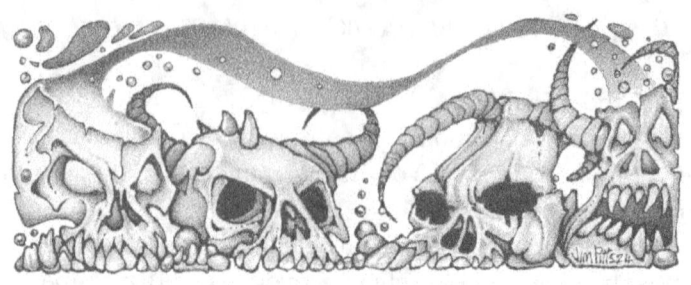

GOD OF THE DREAMING ISLES

During the reign of King Elak of Atlantis, the world was a turbulent place, populated with many kingdoms and empires, as well as smaller states and island confederations, not all of which desired to be a part of the Atlantean unification. There were numerous gods and demigods scattered throughout the world, not a few of which had transported themselves from other stars, even other dimensions. Their conflicts were often no less volatile than Man's, which, ironically led to confusion and a weakening of their desired control over lesser mortals.

- Helvas Ravanniol, **Annals of the Third Atlantean Empire**

Volnus emerged from the hatch of the Atlantean sailing vessel, a powerful war galley, and squinted up into the daylight. He and his companion, Artugol, had been brought aboard the vessel by its commander, the Druid Emmaneus, right hand of Dalan, High Druid of the King. It had taken Volnus over a week to get over his attack of mud swamp fever, a hazy period of days when he could barely recall anything apart from waking briefly, his mind a complete blur, or slipping back into feverish dreams that at times had him raving, at others crying like a child.

Artugol had been scanning the eastern horizon, where the *Arrow* and its tigerish captain, Eskarra, had disappeared days since. Already the youth missed her and what they might have become. She said they'd meet again, but when would that be? In these vast oceans, it could be half a lifetime away. The thought made his heart ache with misery.

He turned to see his burly companion staggering amidships and went to him, giving Volnus a hefty cuff which almost sent him reeling.

"Back on your feet at last!"

"Steady there, you oaf. You'll have me over the side. It'll be a while before I can stand up straight. I need some food inside me."

Volnus laughed and other sailors joined him, enjoying the latest banter between the two young men, who had hardly stopped baiting each other since Volnus had recovered consciousness, even though he'd been too weak to rise. The fact of the matter was, they were all immensely relieved to see Volnus alive and well. Surviving the deadly fever had been a close thing, and more than once they had feared him close to dying.

"It's a relief to see daylight again," he said.

"Well, enjoy it while you can," said Artugol. He pointed to the northern skies, where huge banks of clouds were unfurling at a rapid rate. "That's a storm heading our way. We'll never make it back to Epharra before it overtakes us. Looks like being a big blow, too."

They heard the pilot, roaring out instructions from the helm. "Batten everything down, boys! That storm will burst long before we can fetch up on any nearby islands. We're going to have to ride it out. Get the sails down and be quick about it!"

Quintas, the captain of the fighting ship, shouted his own orders and the uniformed crew ran to and fro, their preparations for securing the craft slick and efficient. He turned to Volnus and pointed to the hatch. "Get yourself down below, man. You're not in any fit shape to work the ropes. And *eat*! You've lost half your weight this last week or so. Eat!"

Volnus swore under his breath, but did as bidden. Already the wind had got up, unnaturally violent, and was piling up the first of numerous waves, which came rolling in towards the vessel, threatening to tip it end over end. Kranidas, however, was as good a helmsman as any in these seas and brought the craft into a more manageable position, though it rose and fell as the seas became increasingly tumultuous. Artugol watched Volnus get awkwardly below, then swung round to his next task. As he did so, a heavy gust caught him, like the punch of a god, and lifted him almost off the deck. He was tossed against the rail, grabbing at it, his fingers slipping on the wet surface.

Emmaneus saw what had happened and could do no more than watch impotently, horrified, as Artugol stood up, only to be caught by a curling mass of spume as yet another wave crashed sideways on to the ship. Artugol seemed to be snatched by white claws of surf and swung up and over the rail. Emmaneus howled like a wolf and ran forward, impeded by his soaked robe of office, almost tossed out into the maddened waters himself. All he could see out there was a cauldron of furious waves, churning chaotically, reforming to batter anew at the hull. There was no sign of Artugol.

"This is no ordinary storm," said Quintas, standing at his side. "I swear I saw the faces of demons in those cursed waters."

"They have taken Artugol," said Emmaneus, shaking his head in disgust. "Those seas are mountainous. We've lost him."

"Kranidas must ride this out. He'll not turn us about, otherwise the ship breaks her back."

"Are there no islands nearby?" asked the Druid.

"None that we can land on. The Dreaming Isles are said to be in these waters, but they are the graveyard of all who approach them. The mad god, Dagnann, who guards them, drowns everyone. That or the sea monster, Ceraphis, whose vast coils are said to wrap around the reefs and outer atolls of the Isles. Better if the storm blows us out to sea, far from this abominable region."

"We must save the ship."

"And Artugol? Are we to abandon him?" The captain's anger vied with his knowledge that many lives were threatened by this freak storm.

"If we dare to approach the Dreaming Isles, we will all of us be snatched and taken down into the afterlife."

"Do you think Artugol was singled out? Why not others? Many were exposed to the waves."

"It may be that Dagnann will have his bounty. Artugol may have been enough."

Quintas swore. "Then we'll defy him! We'll ride this storm out, and then search for Artugol. If he lives, we'll snatch him back from this mad god. If not, we'll free his corpse and bury him like a king."

Emmaneus nodded, though he knew a rescue was a forlorn hope. No man could survive once immersed in those wildly surging waters for more than a few minutes. If they were not beaten to a pulp by the violence of the waves, they would be frozen in the icy cold.

*

Artugol hit the water like stone and desperately fought

the buffeting waves as he was instantly dragged down in to their icy grip. He twisted and turned, battered and cuffed, and could feel his grip on consciousness slipping as he struggled to hold his breath. The more he tried to force his way back up to the surface to win another vital lungful of air, the more the merciless sea drove him downwards: darkness began to close in on him, a palpable force that crushed his body in a deathly embrace. Fragmentary images of his short life blurred before his eyes as the mocking roar of the ocean swept him into unconsciousness, a merciful prelude to his drift into the afterlife.

*

"There!" bawled Kranidas against the shrieking winds. "An island! We'll have to make for it before we break up."

The ship's crew had lashed themselves to the oars in desperation, fighting with the tenacity of fear for their lives, slowly forcing the war galley up and over another massive wave. It seemed the craft must plummet down into the deeps, but its nose rode up once more, like a live beast intent on defying the freakish elements.

As it crested the wave's peak, something broke from the sea ahead of them, an immense tentacle, thrice as thick around as a man, and lashed at the waters, its wriggling tip almost gripping the prow of the ship. Two others rose up and thrashed the waters, turning them into an even more turbulent, boiling cauldron of surf and spume. Miraculously none of the crew were flung overboard, but it was clear now that they would never make it to the island, not with this undersea creature set against them.

"It's Ceraphis, the guardian!" Kranidas shouted above the staggering din of sea and wind. "The coils will fling us back, or else rip us apart."

Three times the craft attempted to bypass the colossal sea beast that protected the island, but even the spells and curses of the Druid were of no avail. If his gods heard him, they were unable to weaken the powers of the frightful Ceraphis, whose flailing limbs swung this way and that, more than once coming no more than inches from the ship and splintering its prow and snapping its spine. The efforts of the crew to keep the ship afloat were heroic, and as men began to tire, they were forced to turn again, riding yet more waves that would have swamped lesser craft or oarsmen not as determined.

Once clear of the immediate danger of the guardian, they got into waters that were less threatening, gradually restoring control.

Volnus was back on deck, though hardly able to stand. He gripped Emmaneus' arm. "Is he lost? Artugol! Is there no sign?"

The Druid shook his head. "We cannot pass the guardian. No ship has ever done so. The Dreaming Isles cannot be reached. No man has ever set foot upon them. I fear your friend has joined the gods. Pray for him."

Volnus gave a great cry of outrage. "No! While there is a chance –"

"We must go back to Epharra, where the King awaits us. There is nothing in these waters but a chilling death. Our gods cannot help us here."

*

Artugol felt himself floating gently, moved to and fro on an invisible current, less violently than before. Time had lost all meaning for him. He opened his eyes. Around him there was only the deep, dark green murk, and occasionally something slid by on its near horizon, unidentifiable and silent. The roar of the waves and the shrieks of the wind had abated as his memory began to kick in.

Have I drowned? he asked himself. *Is this undersea world my grave?*

He was able to move very slowly, hanging in suspension. The light, such as it was, came from all around him, more of a glow, an unnatural green radiance, perhaps diffused by submarine life. At the perimeters of his vision, shapes were coalescing, wisps of greenish mist, curling and unfurling, breaking up into numerous individual forms. They drifted around him, over and under, as curious, it seemed, as dolphins might be. The more he tried to focus on them, the more their details eluded him. *How am I breathing? I cannot be alive.*

The shapes drew closer, apparently morphing like mist, never fixing their forms, ghost-like, beings perhaps, from an afterlife, spirits of the former living, slipping like dreams through his consciousness. There was a sudden urgency to their movements as a group of them gathered around him. If he sensed anything about them it was fear, though not of him. They conveyed a unified terror of something else in those deep vaults of the ocean, something from which they must flee, and with him. Somehow he understood that he must go with them.

As the shapes wrapped him, becoming a pale shroud, he felt himself borne along, as if in a dream, unable to resist, but in a bizarre way comforted by the efforts of the swarm. Out in the invisible deeps, something else was moving, heading his way, another shape, hidden by distance, but exuding a solid miasma of malign intent. Artugol felt himself wracked with an instinctive horror. He allowed himself to be transported by the spirit-like cloud. His blood pumping. *I am alive!* his mind cried. *This is sorcery at work, but I yet live.*

Other things were pulsing through the waters around him, never quite coming into view, though they were no less a threat, both to his sanity and his physical being. Abruptly he was plunged into utter darkness, and coupled with the silence, his mind was again tested to the limits of endurance. On the brink of mental collapse, he felt himself flung forwards, free of the sea's grip and he tumbled on to a bed of cool, yielding sand. Coughing the last of the sea water from his lungs, he knelt on all fours and raised his head, to gasp in amazement at what was before him.

He was on a beach, the sand unlike any other he had ever seen. It sparkled like a million jewels, as if each tiny grain was a miniature diamond, or precious stone. Beyond the narrow strip of beach, the tangled mystery of an island's undergrowth spread to left and right of him. Like the sand, its composition was unique, for these were not trees or shrubs or any other kind of vegetation he was familiar with. It all looked alien, more like the flora of the seabed, dark green and brown-hued, slick and shiny like weed, as if only recently uncovered by a receding tide, though such a tide would have been extraordinarily high.

Shaking himself, he stood, taking a few moments to accustom his body to its return to a physical state. Apart from the muscular aches resulting from his buffeting in the seas, he was relieved to find himself unharmed. Movement beyond the beach drew his eyes and he felt a renewed stab of apprehension. More shapes were materializing. At least a score of them, wraith-like and ethereal, like warm air rising from the sands, gathered. Their features were more substantial and recognizable than those under the sea, for these had the look of men, or at least of creatures akin to men.

Ghosts? he wondered, though they were substantial, flesh and bone. He could not make out their faces, their heads being amorphous, like extensions of their upper bodies, without neck or throat, and if they had eyes, they were so deeply sunken as to be invisible in the folds of their pale flesh. Their arms were short, hairless and gleaming like the appendages of a squid, or similar marine creature. Artugol felt no repulsion, however. There seemed no sinister intent among these things. Had they, like the sea spirits, been part of his fetching up here?

Before he could attempt to communicate with them, he heard the sea behind him, its waves abruptly breaking, and he swung round to gaze on a new horror. From out of the water, twisting serpents were advancing through the shallows, countless scores of them, each the thickness of a man, and in place of a serpent's head there was an opening, a yawning mouth, ringed with suckers, the like of which Artugol had seen in lampreys and other similar marine predators. Silently these nightmares were about to invade the beach, as Artugol felt a sudden rush of air. The wraith-beings rushed past him on both sides and others formed a ring around him. They were protecting him from attack, he realized.

There followed an incredible conflict at the shoreline as dozens of the beings who had risen from the jewelled beach clashed with the serpent-things. It was an exceptionally violent battle, for battle it was, as both parties flung themselves into the affray, the land beings ripping and tearing with claws and what appeared to be beak-mouths, and the serpent-things wrapping themselves around their assailants and clamping their ghastly mouths on to the flesh.

Blood and ichor mingled in the waters, and limbs were severed, serpent heads smashed and pulped. Artugol watched in stupefaction, mesmerized by the frantic encounter and the impossibly fierce nature of the combat, where a kind of madness had taken over.

Beside him his protective guardians urged him away and he followed them without a word being spoken or conveyed to his mind. He knew only that, just as the things in the water were hell-bent on killing him, these land ghosts were not intent on harming him. They led him to the weird jungle and a path opened for him, its plants curling back on themselves to form it. Uneasily he went forward, trying to probe the silence ahead, but failing to detect a sound there, as if this whole region were nothing more than a vast mausoleum, a monument to life beyond what he had known.

*

The Druid's war galley was not the only ship that had been mauled by the storm. The *Arrow*, a sleek pirate vessel captained by the she-wolf, Eskarra, had parted company with the ship from Epharra, the King's capital, several days prior to the storm hitting, and had been ploughing a course for a remote northeastern isle, whose only settlement offered a harbour for the likes of the independent *Arrow*. Unable to sail into the teeth of the storm and confused by it, Eskarra's vessel was turned around and forced to run before the worst of the waves. Inevitably it ran across the Druid's ship once more.

Now that the winds had died down and the seas had ceased heaving, Emmaneus was able to hail the *Arrow* as it came close. "Is all well with you?" he called.

Eskarra stood in the prow, her lithe figure a picture of defiance and determination. "We shipped enough water to sink a dozen lesser ships," she yelled. "But we came through. What of Volnus? Has he found his feet yet?"

"Yes," called Emmaneus. "But there is sad news. Artugol was taken by the storm."

"Taken? How? What happened?" The anguish in Eskarra's voice was very clear.

Emmaneus explained and the girl cursed as crudely as any of her male crew. "Are you looking for him?" There was a challenge in her words.

"I'm sorry, but in those seas, he had no chance. We have to return to Epharra and King Elak."

"He would never abandon a single man!" cried Eskarra. "Not until he saw with his own eyes proof that he was dead. You must continue the search!"

Emmaneus shook his head. "I have my duty."

The bulky figure of Volnus appeared at his side. "I'll not go back until there is proof Artugol is dead," he shouted. "I'll join you again, Eskarra."

Emmaneus tried to pull him back, but Volnus shook him off.

"Don't make me confine you," said the Druid.

"You'll not do that!" Volnus growled, and before Emmaneus could prevent him, he leapt over the side of the ship and plunged into the sea. Moments later his head reappeared and he swam with swift, powerful strokes towards the *Arrow*.

Eskarra was grinning as she had a line thrown to him and in moments Volnus was clambering aboard, dripping like a seal. He looked across the waters at Emmaneus.

"It's a fool's errand," called the Druid. "You'll never set foot on the Dreaming Isles. All of you will be lost."

"We'll take that chance," said Eskarra. With a final, dismissive wave, she turned to her crew and bawled out instructions to Zendullo. His face splitting in a huge grin, the helmsman turned to obey. When the crew realized their captain's intentions, they roared with delight.

"What are the chances?" she said softly to Volnus. "Can Artugol yet be alive?"

The big man's face clouded. "Unless those mad gods have plucked him from the storm's fury, I fear for him."

*

Artugol had travelled for some distance along the path, which had opened out now as he came deeper into the heart of the island. On either side the banks of weird vegetation had thinned out, leaving walls of what might have been dead coral rising, sharp and angled, towards high ridges where nothing stirred – no leaves, or birds or any other sign of life. The place appeared to be a dead rock, abandoned and sterile. Clouds scudded by overhead, casting the landscape into a gloom that barely lit the place, and Artugol again felt as though he had passed from the world he knew into some other, desolate region, a land between worlds. His guardians were like wraiths, milky and insubstantial, drifting around him like mist, as silent as the riven terrain.

Ahead of him rose numerous columns, also comprised of the coral-like growths, and although they had a vaguely constructed nature, they were set randomly like an unfinished work, some leaning over, others snapped or deeply fissured. They might have been the ruins of a forgotten city, or a failed experiment of nature. Either way they cast bleak shadows, and the air around them was cold. Artugol entered the passage between the central columns, where wide steps led down to an open area. As he descended and walked into this place, light suddenly speared down from overhead, and although he shielded his eyes and looked up, he could not penetrate it, turning away. The wraiths had pulled apart, secreting themselves among the jumbled columns.

Artugol felt himself growing drowsy, sleep threatening to slide over him like a susurrating wave, and he stumbled. Although he tried to rise, he could not, and sank down, as if into a soft bed, rather than a hard floor. Darkness closed in swiftly and then there was nothing.

*

When he opened his eyes, it was to gaze on an impossible sight. He was floating once again, but this time not in a sea, but in clouds, like a great bird, which his mind immediately associated with the dreaming world. As the clouds parted to reveal what was spread beneath him, he gasped in amazement. It was like a living map, a view from far above a seascape, a brilliant blue ocean, speckled with scintillating jewels that were islands. The central island, he knew intuitively, was the one on which he had fetched up after the storm. As he studied it, it took on a recognisable shape – it was like the torso of a gigantic being, a half-submerged man of impossible size. *A fallen god*, he thought.

"Yes, Artugol. That is exactly what you see." The voice spoke beside him, deep and with no trace of malice. He tried to turn his head, but could not. His gaze remained fixed on the island. The smaller islands around it varied in size, from outcrops that could have been the partially sunken fists of the figure, to tiny islets, like spilled precious stones, gleaming in sunlight.

"I am Dagnann. Once I was a powerful sea god, master of the oceans, and I shared my powers with others like me, a race of beings that the first people of your world worshiped and honoured. For eons I was content, and knew my place, until I grew restless and greedy for more power. Foolishness! My fellow gods grew angry until, convinced I would never cease my rebellion, they put a curse on me. There, below, you see me now, as I have been for long centuries in human terms. Time for the gods is meaningless, for we are deathless. I am that island, surrounded by the other isles and islets that make up my whole. I am held there, surrounded by another of my pantheon, Ceraphis. She sought what I sought and we fought, bitterly and furiously, until neither of us could master the other. Had we compromised and joined our energies, what power we would have had, and how we would have thrived among the other gods!

"As a punishment, I was cast into the sea, and Ceraphis was set around me, my jailer, although she, too, is chained to her fate. Not only does she hold me in thrall, but she also wards off any who come near to the Dreaming Isles. She sends storms and wrecks any ships, drowning their crews. Neither of us can break the sorcery that holds us here."

Artugol felt the deep sense of frustration and sorrow that augmented the words. "Why have you brought me here?" he asked.

"Many times I have sought to guide a ship through the protective storms of Ceraphis. Those that have succeeded were met by the terror that is the goddess, and all were destroyed, taken down to the ocean's abyss, drowned and dreamless. In despair, I tried a final time, thinking to bring just one human ashore, one that could somehow avoid the traps set, unnoticed, like so much flotsam. Ceraphis did eventually become aware of you, but she was too late to prevent your landfall. My servants, created from dreams, my ailing powers, pulled you through."

"But what can one man do?" said Artugol. "I have no power, other than my sword arm, and I have no sword, no weapon save my fists."

*

Stars littered the heavens in a cloudless night sky as the *Arrow* rode the soft swells of the ocean, where jewelled light reflected in the dark waters. Volnus was alone at the ship's prow, studying the horizon, though nothing broke its regular line. Occasionally he thought he caught a glimpse of something, an islet perhaps, or a short stretch of coast, but they were illusions, smudges of wish fulfilment. A soft movement beside him made him turn. Eskarra had joined him, framed by the slight billowing of the sail. The oarsmen were asleep, rested after the fierce blow of the previous day's storm, and Zendullo's deputy helmsman held the ship's course steady, aimed into northeastern waters.

"No signs?" said Eskarra. Suppressed anger shaped her expression, mingled with frustration and anxiety. Volnus read them all in her eyes and in her manner.

He shook his head. "The seas are empty. After such a storm you'd expect something, but not even a knot of weed or a broken branch. It's unnatural."

"Yes. There was something behind that storm, I felt it. Artugol is alive," she added, glaring stubbornly at the swell.

"I feel that, too," said Volnus. "It's as if there's a distant light, but I can't bring it into focus."

"Zendullo was deeply uneasy about venturing here, though he would not give Artugol up for lost. Of all the islands we've seen, Zendullo claims the Dreaming Isles are the ones we should avoid above all others. The sea goddess, Ceraphis protects them, and Zendullo said it must have been her who sent the storm."

"Then if we approach them, she'll send another."

"I'll not give him up, Volnus. Not while that light shines."

He watched her face for a moment, and caught the gleam of starlight reflected in her tears. Again he studied the horizon but it continued to hide its secrets.

*

Artugol came out of the darkness of sleep, the dreams or visions that had threaded it slipping back into its shadows. He rose from the solid floor, his muscles surprisingly refreshed, as though he had indeed slept in a warm bed. Around him the massive pillars of this bizarre construct – or growth, he could not tell which – loomed over him in arches that formed a vaulted ceiling, a place that was totally alien and forbidding.

You are safe here, said the voice of Dagnann inside his head. *Go beyond this hall and you will find another, smaller chamber.*

Artugol did as bidden, entering a place that appeared to have been carved from bone, though from what monstrous creatures he could only guess. In the centre of the chamber was a sarcophagus, hewn from a single lump of cartilaginous material into its rectangular shape, and resting on it was a coffin that was either cut from glass, or some other material from the ocean's treasury. Inside the coffin, stretched out lifelessly, was a corpse, wrapped in cerements, mummified.

Come closer, said the god's voice. *You see my mortal remains.*

Artugol felt compelled to obey and stood as close to the glass as he could, Mesmerized, he watched as the shape defied the weight of centuries and slowly lifted an arm, pulling aside the wrappings to its face.

*

"There!" said Zendullo, pointing directly ahead.

"Gods," said Volnus, leaning as far out over the *Arrow's* prow as he dared, "you have the eyes of a sea eagle! I see nothing—no, wait! Yes. An island."

"One of the Dreaming Isles," said Zendullo, scowling menacingly. "And it would be madness to attempt to land."

"Nevertheless," came Eskarra's sharp retort behind him, "that's what we'll do."

"Then I'll rouse the crew and get the oars manned. It's calm now, but as soon as we show our intentions, the sea goddess will give us the full benefit of her anger."

"And *she* can have the benefit of mine," said Eskarra, turning away to call out her own orders.

Zendullo gaped at Volnus. "She's hell-bent on drowning the lot of us."

Volnus clapped him around the shoulders. "It's love, my friend. All other powers shrink to nothing beside it."

Zendullo snorted. "You should be a poet," he growled, heading back to his shipmates. But he was grinning.

Shortly thereafter, the *Arrow's* speed picked up as the oarsmen pulled hard. The breeze had stiffened, as if in response to the ship's sudden lurch forward, and the sail had to be furled once more to prevent resistance to progress. As the *Arrow* ploughed through seas that were becoming quickly more choppy, the wind swirled and the waves rose up, the tops blown away in white clouds of spray.

"She knows we're coming," said Zendullo, now at the helm.

Volnus braced himself against another swell. Eskarra and the crew who were not at the oars were also lining the deck, prepared for the worst of the elements.

"It's not just the storm," said Zendullo. "These islands are said to be protected by sea creatures along every inch of their shores. That, or it is Ceraphis herself, wrapped around the archipelago, jealousy hugging it. How am I supposed to guide the *Arrow* through such a barrier?"

As the first of the islands rose up from the dip and rise of the sea, something broke from its edge, a huge, writhing length of living cable, either a sea serpent or a tentacle that defied belief. It struck the sea as it fell back and an immense wave surged away from the impact, racing across the treacherous waters and rocking the *Arrow*, which rose up and almost corkscrewed down into a deep trough.

Zendullo howled in anger and fear, his words blown away like spray.

*

Artugol staggered back at sight of the face. It was *aged*, but by centuries, mummified, yet alive, the bright eyes glittering with the last vestiges of the god's energy. Painfully slowly, Dagnann slid the transparent top from the coffin and rolled from the sarcophagus, to stand shakily, gripping its edge. Artugol sensed that one blow would turn the being into a cloud of dust, disintegrating it in moments.

Follow me, came its voice. Amazingly the stooped figure, little larger than a young boy, bent over by the weight of its impossible years, shuffled to the edge of the chamber, to where a corridor had been bored into the coral-like walls. Artugol stepped after the old god, ducking down in the shadowy confines. Beyond was a small room, little more than a bubble, and here there were jewels and other strange chunks of rock and perhaps bone. A single elongated casket rested on top of one heap and Dagnann pointed at it, though the effort clearly exhausted him.

Open it.

Artugol went to the casket, which appeared to be made from polished wood. He went to undo its single metal clasp, but as he touched it, the wood fell apart like rotted cloth, revealing a dull blade that had originally been wrapped in rich cloth, probably velvet. This cloth also turned to dust. Artugol hesitated, but gripped the haft of the blade with both hands, as it was long and wide, not meant for protracted bouts of fencing, but instead for single, brutal blows, possibly to bring a horseman down, or to cleave the head and limbs from more powerful opponents. As he lifted it, he felt something travel along his arms, as if the blade transferred power to them, so that its weight lessened. Instinctively he held it aloft, and as he did so, light ignited it, a soft suffusion that heated its haft, making the weapon almost a live thing.

You feel it! came Dagnann's excited voice, the mummified figure trembling.

Artugol nodded, now able to sweep the blade to and fro in low arcs, its weight nothing to him.

Come, said Dagnann, and again Artugol followed him. They went through a number of convoluted passages, the way lit now by the sword's glow. For untold centuries these lost tunnels would have been in total darkness, Artugol realized, as he swept aside curtains of dust-hung web.

Invisible things, larger than he would have liked, scuttled back into numerous crevices. Far down another chamber opened out, a low-ceilinged tomb, for at its its centre was an oblong, stone memorial to another age.

Here lies Ceraphis, said Dagnann. *The gods placed us both in this remote place, in a time beyond all memories of man. A time when this world boiled and seethed with the conflicts of many star-spawned demigods and demons, when humanity as you know had barely stumbled up onto its feet. Ceraphis and I desired the same powers, and fought each other for them, causing much disruption in a world that was beginning to rise from the mires of its god wars. Our punishment was to be chained here. Over time, my powers have almost died, and me with them. All that is left of them now is in the sword.*

Artugol would have dropped the miraculous weapon, but he found he could not release his grip on it.

Ceraphis prevents anyone from approaching. She cannot be killed, but if you use the sword against her – now! - her defence of the islands will be weakened for a time at least. If there are ships out there, seeking a landing, they can pass through her barriers.

Artugol used the sword to pry the stone lid from the casket, easing it aside. Darkness rose like a cloud from within as the lid fell noisily to the floor. As this dissipated like a black miasma, light shone. Artugol stood back, knowing he was merely a puppet, the tool of the ancient god. A long, pale arm rose from the stone coffin, in contrast to the mummified Dagnann, for it was young flesh, unblemished, perfect. The figure that sat up and studied Artugol was no crumbling relic of antiquity. It was a young woman of inimitable beauty, her long, golden hair sweeping down over her shoulders. Her eyes, brilliant green gems, fixed on him, and when she smiled, it was a like a blow, rocking him to his core, as irresistible as the ocean's tides.

Strike! said Dagnann's voice in his head, almost smothered by the sudden, seductive whispering of the risen goddess.

There is a ship! said Dagnann. *Out on the ocean, coming towards the islands. She is not yet aware of it, being so enraptured at being woken. Strike her and the ship will land!*

Artugol's mind was racing. A ship? Had the king's ship of Emmaneus returned? Volnus would be aboard it. Maybe they had decided to search for Artugol. That must be it, for what other ship could possibly dare these waters? Unless...by the ocean's gods, could it be the *Arrow*? Could Eskarra be looking for him?

Close your mind, you fool! Dagnann's voice was a hiss, reptilian and threatening. *Strike! Do it now!*

Ceraphis had climbed from the coffin and stood before them both. She was tall, extraordinarily regal, and her skin diffused light like perfume. She offered a hand to Artugol, and her smile promised him treasures beyond imagining, love, worlds, empires, possibly even godhood. He felt the great sword wavering. It was possessed of stunning puissance, but it would need his hands to steer it and bring it down upon the form of the goddess. *Would you toss all that away?* Her eyes seemed to speak the words, her lips moving, implying that a kiss was all it would take to free him for mortality.

Strike! said Dagnann's mind-voice once more, but this time there was sheer desperation in the faltering command.

*

The *Arrow* continued its direct approach to the island, though its crew shuddered at the possibility of an assault from whatever horrors lurked beneath the waves close to the shoreline. Numerous sea serpents burst up from the waters and circled the ship like discoloured dolphins, their flattened heads darting forward to beat at the keel. Mercifully it withstood their initial attacks. However, when the huge tendril of a larger marine horror rose up, preparing to come down across the hull, all seemed lost.

Zendullo could see breakers at the nearest cove, and yet that massive tendril only had to fall and the *Arrow* would be reduced to matchwood, everyone hurled into waters that churned with the massing serpents, eager for the kill. He and his companions, Eskarra and Volnus among them, shrieked their defiance, but curses and their bright blades would be no match for the coming destruction.

*

Artugol focused his mind on the thought of Eskarra and the crew of the *Arrow*, praying to all the sea gods that it was indeed them approaching the island. Dagnann had said a blow from the sword would enable them to get through the things guarding the shores. Sweat stood out on his brow as he fought a mental battle. Dagnann hobbled forward, his skeletal fingers groping for the goddess. It was enough to deflect her attention for a brief moment. Artugol stepped in and drove the blade, point first, at the vision. Ceraphis staggered, face wreathed in pain. Encouraged, Artugol raised the sword and brought it down mercilessly. There was a blinding flash of light as it struck. Both Dagnann and Artugol were flung back into the doorway of the chamber, light flooding it.

For a while Artugol lay crumpled, every bone singing with pain. He had dropped the blade, but he got to his knees and fumbled in the brilliant glare for it, finding it and holding it out against any attack. None came. After the detonation of power when the light had flared so dazzlingly, all was now silence. Gradually the light began to fade, and Artugol's eyes again grew accustomed to his surroundings. He made out the still form of Dagnann, curled up like a foetus at the base of the stone sarcophagus, his arms and legs tucked up tightly.

There was no sign of Ceraphis. Gingerly Artugol rose and went to the stone, from which the last of the glow was emanating. He peered inside the coffin, preparing to strike with the blade once more, but there was nothing within, just a few wisps of smoke, curling upward like mist. He bent down to the tiny body of the god. Had Dagnann expended the last remnants of his energy to help him?

I live, came the mental voice and agonizingly slowly, the shrivelled figure began to uncurl, its limbs stretching. The cerements fell from the body as Dagnann got his feet. Like a butterfly emerging from its chrysalis, the god had changed, becoming a man, very lightly clothed. He was old by human standards, but no longer wizened or gnarled with age, his face lined but not excessively wrinkled. "Yes," he said, using his voice. "I live. Such powers as I have retained are little more than a mortal man's, but that will change with time. You did well, Artugol. The distraction you caused allowed the ship through Ceraphis' defences."

"What ship is it?" Artugol could not keep the excitement from his voice.

"I think you know that," said Dagnann, laughing softly. "What else but the *Arrow*?"

Artugol cried out in joy. The sound was cut short, however, as a distant scream from beyond the passageway rent the air.

"They are here," said Dagnann. "Your work is not finished yet. Make haste!"

Artugol did not hesitate, knowing how much power

resided in the blade. Having tasted it, he felt a deep urge to exercise it again. Another scream prompted him and he followed Dagnann eagerly, racing up the passageway. They quickly reached the main chamber, where Artugol was brought up short, his heart lurching at the numbing vision of horror that greeted him.

*

"Drive them back!" snarled Eskarra, ferocious as a huge cat, her blade ripping into the serpent-things as they swung in over the ship's rail. All along its length her crew fought with these marine terrors, hacking and slashing at them, severing heads, which dropped back into the foaming sea. Overhead the colossal tentacle of the island's guardian swung down, but missed the *Arrow*, subsiding, preparing, as Eskarra thought, to rise up and strike again. Yet it did not. The seas had become wildly disturbed, so it seemed that the ship must surely founder, but somehow it stayed afloat and miraculously held its course.

Scores of the serpents were repelled, their gore dripping from the rail, until slowly their assault failed and one by one they slid into the creaming waves. Eskarra looked at Volnus beside her. Sweat poured from him but he was smiling, a maddened wolf at the kill.

"We're through!" yelled Zendullo. It was true. They had breached the defences of the goddess and come to the calmer water of a lagoon, with a shore ahead of them. It was a curious sight, no ordinary sand or stones, but a glittering expanse of apparent jewels, like a spilled treasure. Zendullo brought the *Arrow* as close as he dared and dropped anchor. The frenzy of the battle, the roaring of the winds and fury of the sea had all abruptly subsided. Out in the bay, the sea had become calm, as though what had gone before was no more than a dream. On the deck, however, the smashed remains of serpents and the slick mess of their gore attested to the reality of the encounter.

"We've lost two men," said Ormullah, the oarsman. "Others are wounded, but they'll be fine."

Eskarra nodded, her face clouded with anger. "Whoever did this will pay. We'll hold sea burials later." She glared at the strange forest beyond the beach. "Let's see how these mad gods like the taste of our steel."

*

Artugol was rooted, unable to move. In the centre of the chamber was a large group of men and women, the bulk of the crew of the *Arrow*. They'd broken through Ceraphis' defence as he'd struck that blow with the blade, and they had come up here to this citadel. Ceraphis, however, had not been destroyed or blasted into some other dimension. She was here!

Eskarra was on her knees, the right hand of the goddess gripping her hair, twisting it cruelly as she stared at Artugol. Beyond them the crew stood back, afraid to interfere lest the goddess dealt their mistress a killing blow. Ceraphis was standing tall, glowing with unmistakable renewed power. Whatever the blow with the sword had done to her, had only been a temporary setback.

"Well, Dagnann," she called. "Your treachery will be your last act against me. That sword will do you no good now. You've expended its energies."

Dagnann remained calm. "The power of swords, however divine, is not all that shapes our lives, Ceraphis."

She laughed, and the sound was cold, filled with

bitterness as she twisted her fingers in Eskarra's hair. The girl swore, but her efforts to free herself were not enough.

Artugol snapped out of his trance and took a step forward, brandishing the blade in spite of what had been said. "Let her go. Face me. Come on, face me!"

Ceraphis laughed again, releasing Eskarra, who stumbled to her feet. At once Volnus and Ormullah stood beside her, their own blades held in readiness to defend her.

"I am sure your love for her has burned brightly, Artugol," said the goddess. "But I will show you so much more. Why waste your time on a mere mortal? You can step into another realm and become a demi-god. It is simply a matter of choice. The power that was in that sword was nothing to what you can experience – with me!"

Eskarra gasped, watching Artugol's face. His features had clouded with uncertainty, confusion. Slowly he stepped forward, crossing the floor, towards Ceraphis in all her glory.

"Yes, Artugol," she said. "*My* love transcends all human love. I give it to you freely. And with it we can break the shackles of time that have held me here, and go out into a new life, new worlds beyond your wildest imaginings."

Artugol stood before her, motionless as a small animal trapped by the stare of a predator.

"I am lost," whispered Eskarra. Yet she lifted her face, straightening, and called to Artugol. "She is poison, Artugol. What she offers you is not love. Only I can offer you that."

Artugol turned, as though he had only just noticed her. "You -"

Ceraphis laughed again, a mocking sound, vicious as a serpent's strike.

Eskarra nodded.

Artugol moved with a speed that defied the eye, swinging round and using the sword once more, raising it and bringing it down in a gleaming arc that flared as it chopped deep into the body of the goddess. Ceraphis, taken completely unawares, screamed, the sound reverberating around the twisted columns of the chamber. Light flared brilliantly as it had in the lower chamber. When it subsided, Artugol went to Eskarra and held her. The sword was smouldering where he had dropped it, and soon it had become nothing more than a sooty stain.

Ceraphis had fallen, her body stretched out, doll-like and motionless. Dagnann had also fallen. Both were either unconscious or dead.

"Let's get back to the *Arrow* as quickly as we can," said Eskarra, aware that she and Artugol were pressed together, her face betraying her embarrassment.

"That was well done," whispered Volnus as Artugol passed. "The right choice, I'd say."

The company was leaving, but Artugol looked back. "Are they dead?"

Before Volnus could answer, the two bodies moved, crawling towards one another. The youths watched in amazement as they seemed to embrace, but something more was happening. They were merging, becoming one figure. Presently it stood, like a man coming out of a deep sleep, a long dream.

Dagnann smiled. "Ceraphis and I are one, as we were before the gods punished me. For my greed they split me and set us both here, neutralizing each other. All human failings are also to be found in the gods. Lust, greed, envy, desire for power, jealousy, and as many other weaknesses as you can name. And you, Artugol, have shown that man's better nature can overcome the darker things."

"You are freed?" said Artugol.

"Well, that's a matter of choice. You made yours, and if

I may say so, it was a good one." Dagnann laughed, and this time it was a warm sound. "I must make mine. I am no longer required to remain here, imprisoned as I was. My future lies with the gods who imprisoned me. There will be fresh choices, new temptations. Perhaps I'll be wiser this time. Go. Your ship will carry you away safely."

The two young men took the opportunity and left, quickly catching up with the others.

*

Volnus watched the stars from the ship's rail as the *Arrow* gently ploughed her way through the glass-like waters. Artugol stood beside him. For a while both men were lost in private thoughts.

"Maybe Dagnann will watch over us from now on," said Volnus. "He owes you, Artugol. If you'd chosen Ceraphis, he'd have gone the same way as that sword."

Before Artugol could answer, he felt a firm grip on his arm. Eskarra was there, a fierce gleam in her eyes. "He used you, Artugol. The gods mock we humans. And I want no further part of those two, who are one. We don't need them."

Artugol put his arm around her waist, and for once she did not pull away or berate him. "You are right. There are far greater powers here among the mortals. Isn't that so, Volnus?"

But his burly companion had already slipped diplomatically away into the darkness, leaving the lovers to enjoy their moment beneath the indifferent stars.

WHEN THE SEA GODS RISE

History teaches us that the time of the various Atlantean periods were defined by tumultuous events in the greater scheme of things, both in the burgeoning affairs of Man, and that of the warring gods. The world was a focal point for a unique conflict, one that could never be resolved, and which will rage for millennia. Within this there were balances of power to be struck, and at times these could be defined by the smallest of the world's denizens, for all the star-forged powers of the gods.

Elak, who had become the prime ruler in the Atlantean world of men, had learned much of this from his many voyagings, and by listening to the sacred histories of the Druids, to whom he always looked for guidance. From his magnificent palaces at Epharra he exercised his duties as Emperor, bringing all but a few of the people of his world under his sway. When the time came to meet the ultimate challenge of the gods from beyond time and space, he needed that support.

- Helvas Ravanniol, **Annals of the Third Atlantean Empire**

Prologue

In the oceanic deeps, far beyond the range of human eyes or thought, shrouded in darkness and guarded by monstrous, shifting creatures for whom the light of day was as alien as the planets beyond the stars, a jagged plateau spread along the endless sea floor, its curious, hybrid corals and banks of thick weed rising upwards as if in search of freedom from this cold, crushing domain. Enmeshed in these rampant growths, the pinnacles of the plateau also groped upward, gnarled fingers of impossibly gigantic beings, birthed on far worlds, hurled across the incalculable vastness of space when the world was barely cooling after its ejection by the sun. It was a city, the first ever to grace the world, long before indigenous life crawled from the foaming seas, beginning its struggle towards primitive Humanity. Over immeasurable distances of time, the city had expanded, strata by strata, drawing to it other entities foreign to this world, beings cast out from their own hideous realms by masters far more frightful. Weird, distorted sorcery prevailed here, and unthinkable gates were opened into realms beyond human imagining. The universe turned like a great wheel, time driving it on inexorably to its multitude of conjunctions. Some of these were minor, portending circumstances that impacted only in local star systems. Others were more significant, the coming together of eons, the melding of galactic forces and dimensions that made even the gods dizzy. In such times it was possible for a single world to become the focal point of one of these omniscient conjunctions.

In the endless corridors and tunnels of the submarine city, there was light, emanating mostly from peculiar corals and phosphorescent growths, cultivated over the city's history by those who controlled it and who siphoned its powers and the dreams and desires of its gods. These were the sorcerers, the Vannadril, quasi-humans leeching off grotesque powers, the gift of even more monstrous beings who dwelt at the fringes of reality, waiting patiently for the synchronization that would potentially introduce a great change, a coming of elder gods whose reign would sweep all before it and establish their kingdom for all eternity.

There were many chambers at the citadel's heart, at all levels. In the lowest, where the sea pulsed with the tidal ebb and flow, creatures both alien and quasi-human swam or crawled, communicating with others on higher levels, or those that swam beyond the plateau's walls, a mixture of beings hybridized by centuries of existence, where evolution had exercised its own twisted development, like the mad workings of scientists experimenting with life forms intent on infecting the world's oceans, a toxic virus at the command of the star-born. In the higher reaches of the citadel, chambers more suitable for human life afforded the Vannadril sorcerers their base, although even they spent time in the colder, more watery regions, their own forms mutating over time, becoming as their masters were.

Within a small chamber, spread around its circumference above a dark pool, a dozen of these creatures gathered. Above them the walls opened, revealing the skies, where storm clouds raced and raged, and strange light filtered down as if through deep water. In the pool a single shape raised itself, an aquatic thing, its skin mottled and slick, its features highlighted by the strained light, a face from primal deeps, cold and devoid of humanity. Its great eyes observed the gathered sorcerers, unblinking and moist, its lipless mouth opening and closing as it gulped air. The water's darkness made it impossible to judge the thing's size, but it gave the impression of singular girth, its gathered tendrils barely below the surface, hinting at disturbing powers.

It communicated with the sorcerers by invading their minds, probing and exposing them, but it found only obeisance, a slavish devotion to its powers and those of its oceanic lords. The Vannadril had long surrendered themselves to the plans and ambitions of these aquatic monsters, all too eager to accept their place in the new age, the corruption of the world, which they would straddle like kings.

Soon it will be time for this plateau, Shunn-Ul-Darza, to break free of its moorings and rise to the surface. From its ramparts and the waters surrounding it, the invasion of the world will begin. What has gone before, the testing of humanity and the failings of our initial incursions will mean nothing. We have studied and learned enough about the creatures who infest this world to know they cannot repel our greater powers, once unleashed. Each of you will be given access to the energy of star lore, enough to counter any puny sorcery the people of this world invoke against us. It will be an unequal battle. The seas will rise and flood the world. Thereafter, as they recede, they will leave a new landscape, a changed world, where humanity has become a shadow of what it was, all chained to us.

Each of the deep gods is preparing. Ctuthfathak of the Ice Wastes, Xeraph-Hizer, the Leviathan Lord, and all the other former denizens of the distant star reaches. Their armies, among their number the Orugllyr, the Gnorl and the serpent men of the remote past, will go forth in far greater number than anything humanity has previously experienced. Cities will fall, continents will founder. Soon Shunn-Ul-Darza will rise and it will begin.

The Vannadril uniformly understood and absorbed this in silence, sitting like huge birds with folded wings above the being in the pool. A tremor of disquiet rippled through them as it spoke of past failings, which it had mercifully dismissed. More than once the forces of humanity had rallied and beaten off incursions into their empires, and the defeat at Skaafelda, where Pict and Atlantean forces had used Druidic sorcery to repel the Orugllyr, still rankled. There were to be no recriminations, however. Whatever cosmic wheels were turning were not stalled.

When the aquatic being sank into the depths once more, the sorcerers felt its mind presence recede, and with it relief. A calmness settled over them and Aarrzoruuk, their primary leader, spoke. "In human time, the unleashing will be no more than months away. That much has been made clear. Several of the great denizens of the deep are preparing to rise. Among them is Xeraph-Hizer, the Leviathan Lord. His fury at the failure of his servants to destroy the island of Grimfallas and those around it, has fuelled his desire to begin the great work." The sorcerer turned, raising his white hands and skeletal claws, and in a sweeping gesture took in the various openings and holes that peppered the circular walls of the chamber. Within these, creatures of the sea, things that swam or slithered both on and off the rocks, swayed as one as if conducted by the sorcerer, slaves to his powers, eager as hounds to obey instruction, to begin the workings that would stir the greater creatures of the deeps and unleash the alien sorceries required to rip Shunn-Ul-Darza from its ocean bed and bring it to the surface.

In the skies overhead, clouds forged themselves into a single blurred shape, like the face of a god, and through its distorted eyes light filtered like discoloured fire, shot through with energies birthed in realms far beyond the knowledge of man, realms of madness and despair. Such a wealth of power for the sorcerers to tap into, to wield like weapons against those they would subdue.

Chapter One: The God-Heart Stone

The huge aerial sky lizard used its powerful wings to slow its flight through Atlantean skies above the city of Epharra, braking and dropping like a stone to the buildings far below. On its back a rider felt the rush of air, the exhilaration of flight, a joyful experience that never failed to thrill, whatever the purpose of the flight. Together man and beast plummeted down through the night skies, and if there were other creatures in those skies, they kept well away. There were guards on the highest parapets, but as they saw the downward onrush of the creature, they spoke softly to one another, and not from fear, for this was one of the elite royal messengers from far across the sea. There was not a man among the night guards who did not envy the magnificent beast's rider.

It dropped lightly to the central area of one of the tallest towers, its rider alighting and saluting the approaching three guards. "I am Carraverin," he said. "From the island of Illyrin. I bring urgent news for King Elak. Can you see my sky lizard is fed and watered?"

Two of the guards nodded and quickly tended to the creature's needs. It raised its head, snorting, used to the procedures after such a long flight. Since the King and his companions had won the trust and service of the fabulous lizards of the former island of Umaarsquu, their potential savagery was never a danger to the Atlanteans and they lived in harmony with men. Carraverin was escorted below by the officer, Thelbrin.

"It is late," said the sky warrior. "Is the King asleep?"

"My orders are always to wake him if messengers arrive. As with the High Druid, Dalan. Word has been sent to rouse them. Speak freely when you see them. They are the eyes and ears of Atlantis."

Carraverin's expression softened. "Their protection of the Empire is legendary. Those of my companions who have flown with them speak of them as they would of gods."

Thelbrin, a rugged, stern man, laughed softly. "They are men and would not welcome such extreme reverence, but they are deeply committed to their people, no matter how far they live from the heart of empire."

A chamber had been prepared lower in the tower, and as the two men entered it, they found both the King and his High Druid awaiting them. Both wore looks of uneasy anticipation.

Carraverin bowed. "Sire, I bring word from Illyrin's commander, Vargan."

Elak waved another man forward and he carried a small salver, on which there was food and water. "You must be in need of refreshments. Go ahead and eat."

It was true. Carraverin had travelled a great distance over the ocean, and at speed, so was deeply gratified for the food. He tried not to rush it, and as he drank, the King and Dalan waited patiently.

"Our Royal Wing outriders have been returning from deepwater searches, all with the same reports," Carraverin began. "I, too, have seen what they have seen. There is an area far out in the ocean, furthest from any inhabited islands and south of Vaarfrost and the rest of the ice continent, where the ocean has begun to seethe with new life. It heaves and boils like a living thing, an immense whirlpool, within which many of us have glimpsed sea beasts unfamiliar to us. The largest of these are never fully seen, but they are truly vast."

"Leviathans?" said Dalan.

Carraverin nodded. "Others are smaller, but thrive in great shoals, packed tightly, covering areas as big as any sizable island. It is as if the seabed has dredged up all living things. For now all are contained in the whirlpool. From the skies above them, strange lights flicker and stab down, pouring twisted energies into the ocean. We dare not investigate. Our mounts would be tossed aside like leaves in a storm."

Elak turned to Dalan. "What does it mean?"

"It is beginning, as we feared," said the Druid. "They will raise their island from the deeps, redolent with all their evil powers. It is from there the final assault on our world will be launched. All the powers of the deep gods, and their masters from across the vaults to the stars, will feed their sorcery."

"Can we withstand them this time?"

Dalan gently waved Carraverin away to a night's rest, taking Elak to one side. Together they gazed from a window at the open expanse of ocean beyond the city. Tonight it was dark and motionless as glass, daubed in cold, white moonlight.

"We need powers of our own, Elak. Ancient powers that have not been unlocked in living memory. I have read of such things in the secret books of my order. Things left untold and unbidden. Their release brings dangers, as with all power. To control it is never easy. It can twist and turn itself into something that could threaten destruction, not avert it. However, against what comes upon us, it may be all we have."

"Then we have no choice."

"Tomorrow at dawn, you and I must go up into the mountains. There is something I must show you."

*

The cleft in the higher reaches of the mountains behind Epharra was so well hidden that anyone passing even as close as a few yards to it would easily have missed it. Vegetation overhung it like a static green waterfall and large, splintered boulders were tumbled around the vague pathway nearby. Dalan, however, knew the way in, having secretly visited this remote place previously, though only when particular circumstances demanded it. Among his Druidic order, this was the most hallowed of sanctuaries, and only the most senior of the religious sect were admitted. Beyond the initial entry, in darkness, a way into the mountain wove a zigzag path, reaching a solid stone wall, apparently its impassable end. Dalan, however, spoke softly in an ancient tongue, and a small section of the wall opened, admitting him and Elak, his sole companion. They had left their horses with an armed escort of men further down the mountainside.

Once inside, natural light from overhead indicated the narrow way forward as the door closed. There were no guards here, no sign anyone had ever been within. Dalan led Elak down the pathway until they reached its sudden widening and an open chamber, bathed in sunlight that made them squint after the darkness of the way in. Several statues lined the place, and Elak started as he realized they were not cut from stone, but were actual beings, members of Dalan's order, guardians of this place's secrets.

They came forward, recognizing Dalan and bowed. He introduced Elak. "The time has arrived," he said, "for the King to be shown the ancient mysteries. Beyond these walls, the world of Atlantis faces its greatest perils. We must turn to the God-Heart Stone's power."

One of the Druids, their spokesman, Morgannis, studied the King briefly, as though his piercing blue eyes could see deep within Elak, judging him and his fitness to be admitted into such hallowed places. Elak was impatient, but Dalan had forewarned him he'd be scrutinized and judged. This was a place of dangerous knowledge, its potential formidable.

The small party descended more passageways, coming at last to a vast opening at the heart of the mountains, a huge crater that might have been scooped from the naked rock by the hand of a god, or certainly immense powers. After a moment contemplating the place, Elak could see what had caused it, for in the centre was a stone, as large as an island, its upper half above the heaped scree, the rest buried. It was shaped like a huge, bulging menhir, though Elak felt certain no human hands had fashioned this thing, and its stone – or was it metal? – was smooth, polished, as if impervious to weathering.

"The God-Heart Stone," said Dalan beside him. "It came to earth before life began on our world, so it is believed. In our books of lore, much has been written about it. Opinions vary as to its source, though all agree it is from the stars, its material derived from them, resistant to change, everlasting."

"It will help us?" said Elak.

"It has the potential to create and to destroy. We believe such stones were set strategically throughout the stars to protect all life from evil powers. In this world, it is a shield from the Elder Gods who would overrun us." Dalan pointed to the scree around the base of the great stone. "Shards have fallen from it over the vastness of time. From the smallest of these, our smiths have forged weapons, great swords and spears. None of them has yet been used, for to wield their power is dangerous. A warrior using such a weapon becomes one with it, entering a life partnership, unique and demanding. Whosoever wields these weapons becomes the servant of the God-Heart Stone."

Elak frowned. "You have it in mind for me and my commanders to bear such weapons in the coming war?"

"It is not my choice, Elak. You must decide. For the

moment, the God-Heart Stone is silent, dormant. To awaken its powers I must bring the three great staffs here. The Valusian Staff, the Scourge of the Night, and Ishtar's Fury. Their own powers, combined, will harmonize with the God-Heart Stone's and bring it fully to life. The weapons we have made will be imbued with it. Whatever vile sorcery the enemy brings to bear upon Atlantis will be matched by the power in the weapons."

"Enough to triumph?"

Dalan's face clouded. "Possibly. We are entering unknown waters. The scale of the conflict will be far beyond anything known before. Nothing will be the same afterwards. The very shape of our world will change. No power can be utterly destroyed, only subdued. But we must strive for that, or Man will face an eternity of darkness."

*

Shiveeri left the small chamber where the two children had at last fallen asleep. She found Elak brooding on the balcony, overlooking the splendid Bay of Gold and the countless ships moored there, bobbing up and down in the twilight. Shiveeri came to Elak and put her arms around him, hugging him to her.

"Since you came back from your last meeting with Dalan, you have not been yourself. Will you not tell me what it is that troubles you?"

He nodded. "I told you of the sacred place of the Druids, and of the great God-Heart Stone kept there. There is more to tell. Powers that must be unleashed in this coming war, but of such a nature that I am loath to use them. All that I hold most dear would be at risk, and no kingdom is worth that to me."

Chapter Two: Lair of the Serpent Men

Deep down in an ocean trench, far from the shores of Atlantis and the coast where the towers of Epharra rose proudly and majestically to the skies, far below the seabed, the tunnels and caverns housing another city sprawled in a dim light, the product of countless creatures, packed together in masses. They coated ceilings and walls like a malignant fungus, leaching whatever nutrients they could from otherwise naked rock. Along one of the narrow tunnels, hacked from the stone in a time beyond memory, a lone figure moved sluggishly, its weight hampering progress, its mighty limbs low to the ground, its thick tail a counterbalance to the figure's stoop. It wore a harness and armour like a carapace, embossed with designs unlike anything seen above the waves or in the cities of men. For this was a serpent man, a warrior in a race that had long since hidden itself in the deep places of the world, harried and hunted almost to extinction, though its kind had existed for untold centuries. In their time of glory they had fought the mighty Atlantean empires, and the Valusians, as well as Picts from the first glimmers of time. Eventually they had been driven into a few extremely remote strongholds.

This warrior, Azzarak, had travelled from the mainland, where he had spoken to the spies slinking through its underworld, culled from the quasi-human servants of the serpent men, spurned by the men of Epharra, cast out from it. Such beings were one with the night and had learned well how to survive in it, as worms do. Crude mutations, they squeezed their secret way between rock and soil, into the lower chambers of the city, unseen and unknown to the occasionally patrolling men. Men who assumed, wrongly, that all subterranean exits to the city had been sealed.

Azzarak reached the end of the tunnel and climbed the slippery stairs, at the head of which an iron-bound door was sealed against him. He took a key from his thick belt and thrust it into the lock, twisting it until it clicked. The door resisted him, but Azzarak was thickly muscled and tugged it open. Warm air gusted outwards. There was light beyond, given off by several cressets in a passageway. Azzarak entered, closing and re-locking the massive door. He heard a heavy tread and moments later a trio of serpent men guards met him. They recognized him and stepped aside with a brief show of deference.

Azzarak went higher into the lower workings of the city, for such it was. By human standards it was an alien place, more suited to the serpent beings who dwelt here. The passageways had been bored, as if by great worms, and such dwellings as branched off from them were little more than caves, rank and dripping with moisture, as if the seas above leaked into these stony deeps. Higher up there were more sophisticated structures, hewn from the living rock, like the workings of insects, a hive or a nest. Azzarak was met here by others of his kind, who knew him to be a royal courier and stepped aside for him.

He wasted no time in pausing to refresh himself or to speak to anyone other than very briefly, but went directly to the heart of the city, where the palace of its ruler had been erected from rough-hewn blocks, a final bastion against intrusion. Azzarak considered it a poor reflection on the mightiest days of his kind, the days of empire when they had ruled most of the world. Days when they had spread across the surface, legions of them, whereas now they were forced to burrow ever deeper into the last caverns. It would change, though. Soon that work would begin, and the serpent men would return to the light, and there would be a reckoning.

In the palace, Azzarak was escorted to the chamber of the rulers, the Trine, three of the most powerful of all the serpent men. They were the spawn of the great ruler, Quarrass-Theen, who had been killed by the hated human monarch, Elak, now incumbent upon the Dragon Throne of Atlantis. Seated on their own thrones, single blocks of obsidian, they were Issathass-Vekk, Quaran-Zaan and Vathaan-Raal, and each of them stared unblinkingly at Azzarak as he bowed. He was about to deliver his report, when he noticed a fourth figure in the shadows by the side of the three rulers.

Azzarak peered into the gloom, but the shape moved, its exact nature disguised by the strange floor-length robes it wore. It was globular, its arms wrapped within the robe, though its head was visible. It belonged not to a serpent man, nor a human, but to another race with which Azzarak was familiar, that of the Orugllyr. This specimen, however, was unlike any of that race Azzarak had seen before, for the head was less bulbous, the bright, wide eyes gleaming with unusual intelligence, and it had better developed facial features. A hybrid, perhaps.

Issathass-Vekk indicated the Orugllyr. "This is Urzook, king among the Orugllyr, appointed by the Vannadril. Your return to us is timely, Azzarak."

Azzarak bowed to the Orugllyr.

When Urzook spoke, it was with a soft, sibilant voice not unlike that of the serpent men, caressing the mind with its syllables, emitting an almost hypnotic power. Again, Azzarak was surprised, for the only Orugllyr he had known were almost without speech, apparently devoid of self-expression, beings who existed purely to obey commands. Urzook was not such a creature.

"I gather you are mighty among your people,

Azzarak," he said. "One destined to command legions in the coming war against the creatures of the surface."

Azzarak kept his ambitions to himself, but was pleased by the comment. "I hunger for the flesh of my enemies."

Quaran-Zaan, largest of the Trine lifted his head, the eyes widening as they settled on the warrior. "There are preparations to be made first. Tell us what you found beneath Epharra."

"There are ways in, although too large for our kind. The city has been sealed both physically and by the use of Druidic sorcery. There are no doors, no pathways, but there are narrow crevices, drains and other broken sections of wall, inadequately sealed, that will allow certain creatures within. I have spoken to such." Azzarak looked unflinchingly at Urzook. "Creatures who can transform themselves and slip through many a gap like water through a sieve."

"Rest assured," said Urzook, "I can provide such servants. The Orugllyr are changing, evolving. The sea is their home, but we adapt, and can penetrate the darkest realms below the ocean and beyond. Epharra's walls will open to us."

"What have your spies seen?" hissed Issathass-Vekk, again fixing Azzarak with his gleaming gaze.

"Although King Elak is at peace with the world, settled in his palace with his family –"

"His family, yes, tell us of his family," said Vathaan-Raal. "That is of special interest to us."

Azzarak nodded. "His wife, Shiveeri, is never far from the King's side. They have two children, a son and a daughter. The girl, Elara, has reached her fourth year, and the boy, Shivak, his second."

"They are well guarded?" said Quaran-Zaan, pressing

forward, forked tongue flicking from his mouth as though tasting the air and Azzarak's very words.

"Always. Many guards surround them. In the palace, Elak has stationed his warriors on constant alert, expecting invasion at any time. He has aerial spies, his accursed Royal Wing, riders of the sky beasts. And in the Bay of Gold, his fleet is kept readied."

"And the High Druid?"

"He and his cult have a strong grip on power. They have many sources, numerous ancient weapons as well as access to the lore of the ages. Force alone will not be enough to overthrow them. In such a war, the balance would not necessarily fall in our favour."

Issathass-Vekk nodded. "We will not rely on force alone, Azzarak. Not the weight of bodies, an army, more. No. Our physical armies are merely a weapon, part of the means to our end. We have our own ancient powers to draw upon. And such powers! From Xalkara, mother world of the Orugllyr and others, and further far-flung star rovers. The Vannadril prepare. The world will shake."

"We have it in mind," added Quaran-Zaan, "to weaken King Elak's confidence, his assurance he can match us. How would his armies be if their ruler were to be broken in spirit even before the war begins?"

"He is a beacon to them," said Azzarak. "There are legends surrounding him making him a god in the eyes of many, across the entire continent."

"They think him immortal?"

"Some might. But I doubt if he is vulnerable to assassination. Every precaution has been taken to protect him, including whatever secret sorcery the High Druid has used. Shiveeri is also protected."

"And the children?"

Azzarak could see the hunger in the cruel eyes of all three of the Trine. Each of them leaned forward, studying him as if he were on a sacrificial slab before them.

"Protected, yes."

"Could they be taken? Could a small unit penetrate the palace, shielded by sorcery, and abduct them?"

Azzarak hesitated, but nodded. "Possibly. The odds against success would not favour us."

"Yet the reward for success would be sublime," said Issathass-Vekk. He waved a long talon towards Urzook. "Our ally is prepared to attempt this abduction. He and his servants can breach Epharra's defences. Take them there and show them the means of ingress."

Azzarak bowed. "I will take a unit of my own fiercest warriors to shield the Orugllyr from pursuit. Elak will never recover. It will be the beginning of his fall. And that of all Atlantis."

*

Eskarra, captain of the *Arrow*, swung down from the mast as lithely as any cat, and faced the startled expression of Artugol, who ducked barely in time to avoid the blade that almost parted his hair. The girl was laughing as she slid her weapon back into its sheath.

"Stay alert," she said.

Artugol grinned wryly. She was right, and also right to treat him like any other of her crew, in spite of the relationship they now enjoyed discreetly. In these and any waters lives were cheap, constantly under threat from numerous dangers. They were currently berthed in the cramped harbour on the island of Mallomas, a former pirate stronghold that had not entirely given up its independence in favour of allying itself to Atlantis' King. As such it proved a useful place to indulge in gossip, rumour and news from afar that might otherwise have been repressed.

"Something's wrong," said Eskarra. "I've been to the masthead. The open ocean is restless. I can sense it. Don't ask me how, Artugol."

He knew her instincts well enough, her uncanny power to read the seas, a gift from her ancestral line, of witches maybe. "And?"

"There's something out there, in the most open reaches."

"Your expression tells me this is not good."

"No. I think we should take a look."

"I'm not sure Dalan would approve. Aren't we supposed to be awaiting orders?"

"We're not doing a lot of good stuck here on this rock. We'd hardly be missed for a week or so."

Artugol sighed, knowing her moods. If she'd set her mind on going out to sea, the *Arrow* would inevitably sail. He looked out at the open expanse of water. It was calm, perhaps too calm.

Chapter Three: Abduction

Shiveeri and Darruvia were engaged in an amused conversation in the private chamber where they spent most evenings, usually with their respective husbands, although today Elak and Lycon were busy attending to the prolonged process of organizing the defences of the city and in particular the harbour. Outside the open window, Epharra was quiet, with little sound rising from the streets, and few lights. The atmosphere of unease was spreading along with rumours that something dark infected the far north. Atlantis was not at war, but it would not be caught unawares if one did suddenly burst upon it.

If the streets were quiet, the palace was not. Beyond one set of tall doors, those leading to the royal bedchamber of the children, where Elara and Shivak slept, an alarm sounded, a high-pitched shriek, bringing Shiveeri to her feet in an instant. She rushed to a table where her scabbarded sword was always at hand and pulled out the rapier blade. Darruvia, who was less lithe than her companion, was nevertheless not far behind her, pulling a spear from a rack beside the bedchamber door.

Shiveeri flung the door open and a scene of horror met her gaze. Her two children sat upright in the centre of the large bed, hugging each other. Several guards were here, usually secreted in quiet corners where they would not be noticed, though always alert for anything amiss. These were all engaged in a ferocious conflict with creatures that Shiveeri only recognised from her husband's descriptions. He had fought an army of them in a bloody sea battle at the island of Skaafelda, some years in the past. They were Orugllyr.

These quasi-human beings were pale of skin, scaled like sleek fish, arms and legs extended like bloated tendrils, as though more suited to being in water than on land, and their rounded heads glistened, faces morphing into grimaces, with ichthyoid eyes and a great gash of a mouth, like that of a sucking lamprey or similar denizen of the deeps. Yet they fought with swords, short, stabbing affairs, moving with deceptive speed. The guards drove into them and as they thrust their blades at the creatures, the flesh of the Orugllyr appeared to absorb the steel and reject it, with no sign of damage or bleeding.

Both Shiveeri and Darruvia tore into the conflict, the former swinging her rapier in a glittering arc that ended with its point rammed hard into one wide eye of her nearest opponent. This did draw fluid, and the creature sank back, mouth gasping as Shiveeri followed up her first thrust with another that drove into the open mouth and up into whatever brain the thing possessed. Darruvia used her spear to probe at the Orugllyr, jabbing viciously and with considerable strength, the equal of many a male guard.

"Secure the children!" Shiveeri shouted and at once three of the guards gripped Elara and Shivak, hoisting them off the bed. Both were more than happy to be whirled away, although Shivak looked anxiously at his mother as she carried the fight to the intruders.

"Lock the doors behind you!" Shiveeri called as the guards exited, her voice filled with the power of command. Within moments it was done, the huge bolts drawn.

In a brief pause Shiveeri turned to one of the three remaining soldiers. "How did these fiends get in?"

"It should be impossible," gasped one of them. "The walls are thick, and there's no way through them."

"Sorcery!" exclaimed Darruvia, lunging at another of the Orugllyr, plunging the point of her spear into its thick neck and twisting it aside so the creature was swung to the ground. Three more came at her, and in the darkness at the back of the chamber, more of them were gathering.

Two of the guards were brought down and dispatched by the Orugllyr blades, leaving Shiveeri, Darruvia and the remaining guard to defend themselves against a new onslaught. They realized the numbers were against them, and were soon fighting with their backs to the door, but Shiveeri would not have it opened. She kicked and drove her rapier into more Orugllyr faces, and Darruvia swung her spear in a ripping arc that tore through the resistant enemy flesh. Beside them the guard fought like a demon, his own sword a blur, but it was impossible to stem the tide and he was hewn down and torn to pieces.

In a brief respite, Shiveeri and Darruvia faced a wall of Orugllyr, the women's chests heaving, blood and the leaked fluids of the slain smearing them from head to foot.

"Do your worst, you filth," Shiveeri snarled.

The leader of the Orugllyr, a larger being than his companions, regarded her with his saucer-like eyes. "We don't mean to kill you, queen of Atlantis. We came for your children, but since you have foiled us, we will take you and your companion instead."

"I don't think so," said Darruvia, preparing to launch her spear at him. He waved a group of his Orugllyr forward and they flung a steel net over both women before they knew what was happening, tightening it: within moments both were snared, tangled and dragged to the ground.

"Bring them," said the leader.

"They'll never get us out through the walls," hissed Darruvia.

Shiveeri grunted agreement, but was deeply uneasy about this apparent abduction. She would have snarled a curse at the Orugllyr, but before she could twist her head to voice it, a length of cloth was pulled tightly around her mouth as she and Darruvia were both gagged.

At the back of the chamber, a small door, usually locked and triple bolted, had been smashed inwards and lay on its side. In the corridor beyond, a dozen Atlantean guards had been cut down, none surviving, and yet more Orugllyr waited. The entire company, with the two netted prisoners, was borne along the corridor until it reached a metal covering, pulled from a vertical shaft that Shiveeri guessed must lead down into the palace's water system. Both women were thrust downwards and the entire party slid down the chute and into a wide pipe below, splashing through its waters. For some time the Orugllyr worked their way through a maze of conduits, barely wide enough to let the netted women through, until a grille was reached. Beyond was the Bay of Gold.

Two of the Orugllyr removed the grille, the remainder going through and onto a sloping expanse of mud. In the darkness a single shape waited in the gently lapping waters—a low craft without sails and a narrow ramp leading up to its deck. Shiveeri cursed inwardly as she realized she and Darruvia would indeed be taken away. This had been carefully planned. As the two women were hauled aboard and hidden in the low hold of the craft, the night closed in. *At least the children are safe*, Shiveeri thought.

*

The *Arrow* knifed through the calm seas by night, moonlight barely breaking through constantly scudding clouds that heralded cold air coming from the north, deeply and unexpectedly chilling, like the icy breath of hostile gods. The island of Mallomas was well behind the sailors: they'd left it in silence and no one had raised a cry. In its independent port, ships often came and went. If any of Dalan's spies were watching, they did nothing to prevent Eskarra from sailing.

She leaned on the rail near the prow, watching the darkness ahead, though its shifting shapes revealed nothing.

Artugol came to her. "What do your instincts tell you?" he asked.

"Can you not feel the atmosphere? A sense of threat. Perhaps I'm over-sensitive."

"No. You've a unique bond with the sea. I knew that

from the first. Volnus has noticed it, too. If you say there's something out there, I believe it."

"If we find nothing after five days, we'll go back to Mallomas and wait for Dalan's instructions."

They did not have to wait for five days, however. On the third day a cry from the masthead drew them back to the prow. Eskarra, Artugol and Ormullah studied the skyline and all saw the first smudge of land appear where none had been known to exist before.

"What island is that?" growled the huge oars master.

"Unknown," said Eskarra. "There should be nothing between us and the northern ice shores."

The seas around them were often troubled, swirling in cross-currents and the whimsical shifts of prevailing winds, but the sea passage was not hampered. Reaching the island would be straightforward, but Eskarra was cautious. Previously uncharted islands often proved dangerous, many relics of a bygone age and cursed with buried sorcery, a threat to any curious sea hawks. As the *Arrow* approached, more of the crew studied it.

Scores of the numerous known islands were volcanic in nature, with overgrown central cones and calderas, in most cases almost inaccessible. Although the vast majority were extinct, beyond active, smoking life, some yet emitted their clouds of sulphurous gas, swirling high into the heavens. This island had no such plume, and its rounded shape lacked the characteristic central cone of a volcano. It was far out in the ocean, a single fist of land in some of the deepest waters around. How, then, did it come to be here? If not volcanic, how had it thrust up from such deeps? Eskarra and many of her companions were pondering this as the ship came within sight of the island's shoreline.

"What kind of vegetation is that?" said Artugol,

pointing to the thick banks of living growths hanging over the low cliffs into the sea. He had his own view, that it was weed, something more likely to be found underwater. It was brown, not green, and its fronds were surely marine.

"See how it glistens," said Ormullah.

"This island is new," said Eskarra. "Lately risen from the ocean bed, if indeed it came from there. I don't think it did."

"Is it *floating*?" said Artugol.

"Such places exist," she said, nodding. "We'll circumnavigate it and see what its shores reveal. And we'll look for a place to land."

Ormullah roared out instructions to the crew and the men scattered, quickly resuming their places at the oars. There was a breeze, but not enough to sail the *Arrow* at any great speed, so the crew's muscles were required. They laughed as they set their backs to the work, but even so, there was a current of disquiet among them, the influence of this incongruous island.

Eskarra leaned into Artugol and said for his ears alone, "This island is not the prime cause of my sense of foreboding. That lies further north. But if we get ashore and scale the island's heights, we may learn more."

The *Arrow* circled the island, a matter of a few hours' steady rowing, its circumference proving relatively small. If there was life of any kind upon it, man or beast, there was no sign of it, and silence hung over it like a pall. Its strong smell of weed wafted to the sailors by shifting winds, and the concept of the place having lately been submerged strengthened. At length, at the southwestern end, a narrow indent into the shore between two high banks of weed was opening enough for the ship to manoeuvre inwards and moor.

Eskarra prepared to disembark with a picked handful of the crew. Before she clambered ashore, she turned to Ormullah, who yet growled at being left on the ship. "Be ready at all times to take us away again. When I return, I may be in a hurry."

Chapter Four: Island from the Deep

Shanatarl Vaarst watched the moored fleet of the Atlanteans as his craft slid through the pitch-dark waters of the Bay of Gold. The Orugllyr sorcerer's thin, ascetic face was serene, belying the emotions coursing through his veins. He had failed to abduct the King's children, but surely the Vannadril would reward him for the delivery of the two women who were at this moment trussed up in steel nets in the craft's hold. This was a real coup for him, and must lead to his elevation to the highest position of his order, beside his masters. Vaarst studied the ships, all of which were lit by a few lanterns, their seamen watching the waters of the bay. This craft, low and sleek as an alligator, would not be seen, cloaked as it was in darkness Shanatarl Vaarst himself had conjured. It did not need sail and once it had pushed off from the shore, it required no oarsmen to propel it either. Instead there were creatures below the water, relatives of the Orugllyr, who got beneath the craft and sped it on its way, heading for the open sea.

Neither Shiveeri nor Darruvia were able to shout their protests, gagged as they were, and they had ceased struggling for fear of tearing their flesh. Once the craft had passed beyond the wide mouth of the Bay, on either side of which the tall observation towers rose like frozen statues, it sped northward. The sorcerers' underling called softly to the leader of the Orugllyr, Urzook, and had him release the two women, although several of the Orugllyr were close on hand to secure their wrists and ankles, chaining them to the deck. The craft was far enough out at sea for their gags to be removed so they could drink fresh water. Their captors obviously wanted them in good condition.

Shiveeri immediately spat at Urzook, but the bloated figure merely opened his gaping mouth further in a mocking grin. "Save your energy for the voyage, human vermin," he said in a voice barely above a hoarse whisper.

"Where are you taking us?" snapped Darruvia. "There's nowhere in these seas you can hide us from our people."

"Tell that to Shanatarl Vaarst," said Urzook, his shoulders heaving, indicative of his laughter. "Spit and scream as much as you like. No one will hear you, nor will they ever find you. Not until your carcasses are tossed back on to the waters for your King to find." He turned away towards his master, who ignored the women and watched the northern seas.

Shiveeri said softly to her companion, "They have not brought us this far to kill us. We must feign weariness, despair. There will come a moment when their guard will be down. We must be heading for an island and a docking. At that point, if we can get them to free us of these chains, we'll take our chances over the side."

"But, Shiveeri, have you forgotten? I cannot swim."

*

Eskarra held up a hand and her small party stopped, waiting while she assessed the way ahead. The island was still a mystery, its entire surface a mass of knotted weed, some of the branches as thick as tree trunks, suggesting they had formerly been bedded deep down on the ocean floor. Rough paths could be made through the grotesque weed forest, upwards towards the rising crown of the island. It was far larger than the sailors had first thought, sloping away on either side through more banks of weed and what looked like glistening coral outcrops, torn from their beds.

The company, a dozen of them, which included Artugol and Volnus, listened to the island, but were rewarded with a dull silence. If there was life here, it kept to itself, far down among the weed banks, slithering and sliding through them, well out of the light, although there was precious little of that this night. Fat clouds obscured the moon, and the only light from it created a vague blur to the northwest. Satisfied that their progress was not being studied by anything obvious, Eskarra led them on and up. They reached the uppermost ridge and looked out at the ocean beyond the skirt of the island, which dropped in continued profusion to the shoreline. However, it was not this island that now snared their attention. It was what reared up on the northern horizon like an unexpected range of mountains.

"By Ishtar," gasped Volnus, "what is that? There should be no land there, and that is no island."

Eskarra and Artugol stared at the distant shape that rose, darker than the ocean. "It's what brought me here," said Eskarra. "I told you I sensed something strange, an atmosphere, call it what you will. That's it, that place."

"Gods," said Artugol, "has it risen from the deep, as this place has?"

"It must be huge," said Volnus. "Judging by how far away it is. And those are mountains."

"The King must be told of this," said Eskarra. "We'd better get back to Mallomas. Dalan may have come."

Artugol was craning his neck, his eyes fixed on the island's shores far below. "Is that *smoke*?"

Eskarra and Volnus also studied the distant weed banks. One of the crewmen called to Eskarra. "There's someone else on the island," he said. "Could be a camp."

"Can you see a vessel?" said Eskarra. No one had.

"Do you think we should investigate?" said Artugol. "If there is anyone down there, they won't be friendly to Atlantis. They might know something about that larger island."

Eskarra nodded. "Let's find out," she said, drawing her rapier, her face brightening.

*

"It's disgusting," snorted Darruvia, scowling at the bowl of thick fish gruel.

Shiveeri managed a grin: Darruvia looked horrified. She, like her husband Lycon, was fond of food and at times for her, life was a constant battle against over-indulging, as it was for Lycon, whose love of wine was legendary.

"Eat," said Shiveeri, spooning some of her own mixture into her mouth and trying not to grimace. "I told you these scum want us alive. There's no fine food aboard this vessel, but what they're giving us comes regularly enough."

Darruvia shuddered but got some of the mess down her. "When we get back to Epharra, I shall order a banquet and eat for a week."

Shiveeri laughed softly. "The food will keep us warm if nothing else, although these fleeces they gave us are welcome. We're in frigid waters now, and Ishtar alone knows how far from civilization." She pulled her fleece tighter.

"Why do they want us alive?"

"It'll enable them to taunt our husbands. And make demands they'll find hard to refuse. Either that or they want to sacrifice us on some remote altar to whatever repulsive gods they worship."

Darruvia almost coughed up her food. "Do you think that's possible?"

"Most likely they'll use us as hostages." Shiveeri lifted her head. The two prisoners were in the hold, but the craft was shallow, open to the winds.

"What is it?" said Darruvia, seeing her companion's sudden interest in the sea around them.

"We're slowing, and turning. I think we may have reached our destination. It's hard to tell without sailor oarsmen."

Darruvia shuddered. More than once she had wondered what did propel this weird craft. Something below it, she had concluded. Hidden creatures of the sea. That or sorcery. She knew Shiveeri had an instinctive understanding of the sea, having spent most of her life sailing with pirate crews before becoming Elak's mate.

"There's an island," whispered Shiveeri. "I can't make out the details, but it's a strange place. And in these northern waters, there should be none. Occasional drifting icebergs, but not islands."

The craft slowed and shortly afterwards was directed into the small bay of an island and up on to a narrow strip of beach. Shiveeri and Darruvia were forced to their feet, still hobbled, and a plank was lowered so they could struggle down it on to the harsh chips of coral that comprised the shingle. Beyond them was a packed mass of growths that could not have been trees. They dripped like weed, their sagging fronds as dark as anything below water, and a powerful saline smell arose from them.

"What is this place?" said Darruvia.

"Nowhere known to man, I suspect. If there's life here, it's not human."

*

Elak stared in horror at the carnage beyond the bedchamber, where the murdered guards were being carefully collected and carried away. The men had evidently fought hard to defend this position, but whatever had come among them had completely overpowered them. Beside him, Lycon gasped, his fists knotted in anger and frustration. He had fought beside most of them in the past.

"How has this happened?" Elak said, turning to Dalan.

The High Druid was scowling, clearly puzzled. "This section of the palace should be impregnable. And yet our enemies breached the walls." He bent down and studied the pools of blood and other liquids. He stood up with a grunt of recognition. "The sea creatures, Orugllyr."

"How could they have got in?"

"Their bodies are not as ours. They partly liquefy, like those of an octopus. They must have found crevices within the stonework and thrust themselves through."

Lycon cursed. "That's as may be, Dalan, but how did they take Darruvia and Shiveeri back? If they had meant to kill them, the bodies would be here somewhere."

Dalan nodded. "Yes, this was an abduction."

A shout from further down the passageway turned their heads and shortly they were gazing into a chute to the drains below. Dalan examined the open mouth and again nodded. "Here was their exit."

It was not long before the truth of the escape became evident.

"A ship of some kind?" said Elak. "How is that possible? The Bay of Gold is full of our own ships. No one could pass among them and out to the open sea without being discovered."

"There is more to this," said Dalan. "Sorcery. The Orugllyr, or creatures like them, could easily have swum away and, I suspect, propel a small, dark craft with them."

They were standing on the small strip of beach at the harbour's side. Elak gazed out at the dawn light, breaking over the Bay of Gold. He, like Lycon, swore in fury, barely containing his temper, and his horror at the loss of their wives.

"They become more daring," said Lycon. "They took me once and used me as a lure." He recalled vividly the battle at Skaafelda, the culmination of his own abduction. "This time they have something far more valuable to bargain with, if that is their purpose."

"We must hope it is," said Dalan.

"What do you mean?" said Elak.

Dalan did not speak his grim thoughts. *In this coming war, the enemy will stop at nothing to overpower us. There are no gods so black they will not summon them. I dare not contemplate what rituals they will conduct, or what frightful uses they will put their prisoners to.*

"We cannot know their plans yet," he said.

"You must use your powers to find our wives," said Elak. "We'll hunt them, though we'll set out with caution. Every king, every ruler in our Empire, must be told of this."

"Our enemy will expect this. They will want us to sail into their jaws, and they will have prepared for that, as a commander sets out his troops and prepares the ground for a land war. Somehow we must find a subtle way of taking the war to them."

"I'll not risk the lives of Shiveeri and Darruvia," said

Elak, and Lycon recognized the tone. Neither the High Druid, nor any other power in Atlantis would deter Elak from whatever course he chose.

Chapter Five: Prisoners

Eskarra and her companions peered over the top of a low ridge beyond which the tightly compressed weeds ran down to a small bay. There were taller weeds on this north side of the island, crude variations on trees, their branches smooth, their leaves like clots of underwater weed, damp and sodden as if they had recently emerged from heavy rain. But it was not the bizarre vegetative scenery that drew gasps of surprise from the company. What caught their attention were the jutting blocks of, what? Coral? These formed a rough village of some dozen buildings, if such they were, and from at least two of these, smoke arose into the morning light. There was the narrowest of beaches along the shoreline, and a few smudges of shadow that suggested small, sleek boats, but otherwise no signs of life.

"Pirates?" whispered Artugol. Around him the world might have been cast in stone, for nothing moved or made a sound.

Eskarra shook her head. "Not in those craft, whatever they are. No sails, no oars. I'd like to find out who is in those buildings. Enemies of Atlantis, for certain. Come, let's go down."

They all made their way to the edge of the ground around the blocks, where Eskarra had them take cover. "Watch for me," she instructed them. "Artugol, you come with me. Up there." She pointed to the roughly flattened roof nearest to them. Then, shinning up the wall like a spider, she clung to the darkness before disappearing over the lip. Artugol, no mean climber himself, followed and quickly joined her. Apparently they were unobserved.

Eskarra indicated the first of the buildings from which smoke was rising from a low, crude chimney. Cautiously the two figures approached it. They leaned as close as they could to the opening without breathing in the smoke. Voices came from below and Eskarra listened, Artugol pressed close beside her.

"Something about waiting for three days," Eskarra whispered.

"Who is speaking?"

"The other refers to him as Shanatarl Vaarst. They speak our tongue, but none of them are men." She listened again, her eyes widening. "There! He refers to the prisoners. Women, but who?"

"Human prisoners? From our lands?"

Eskarra gave a sudden intake of breath. "Shiveeri! They have her prisoner! The King's wife! How is that possible?"

Artugol drew back, appalled. "But that's disastrous!"

"The leader refers to two women, so Shiveeri must have a companion. In three days' time something is planned."

Artugol looked across the ocean to the distant mass of the island on its horizon. "Could they be taken there? Could that be the base of the enemy?"

Eskarra gripped his arm. "Gods, you're right! We can't let it happen. One way or another we have to prevent this."

"Of course. Yet if we're to intercede, it should be by cover of darkness. Are the prisoners in the building below?"

"I can't tell. We should find out before we attempt anything. At least we'll have surprise on our side. They won't be expecting anyone else to be here."

They withdrew from the chimney, careful to keep hunched well down, and clambered across the roof, studying the adjoining buildings. In all there were seven of them, closely packed, so that Eskarra and Artugol were able to cross over to each of them. They noticed that one of the buildings had a number of figures around its rectangular perimeter.

"I recognize them from Emmaneus's description of them, when he was discussing the kind of enemies we'd be likely to come across. They must be Orugllyr," whispered Artugol. "They sent an army to the battle at Skaafelda. Sea dwellers, not human."

Eskarra indicated the roof of the hut these strange beings were stationed beside, and she and Artugol crossed over to its roof to where its chimney jutted obliquely. No smoke came from it, making it easier for Eskarra to hang over its lip and listen. For some time there was no sound from inside the building. Then, faintly, she heard a cough and was convinced it was a human sound. She waited patiently, then heard voices. Yes! It was the women.

"Are they alone?" said Artugol.

"I can't tell. I daren't risk calling to them."

Artugol studied the inside of the chimney. Its sides were comprised of bricks, old and worn, and although they were sooty, the chimney did not appear to have been used for some time – there were several trailing weeds here, their roots poking through the brickwork.

"I can clamber down inside," he said.

Eskarra scowled. "I've seen you climb a mast as nimbly as any rock monkey," she said. "But this is too dangerous. There's a big drop if you lose your footing."

"I just need to look. If the women are alone, we can speak to them." He handed her his blade. "Toss it down to me if I get into difficulty."

She shook her head, but watched as he climbed over the

chimney rim and let himself down until his feet found the first of the cracked brick courses. As a youth, he'd spent days on the treacherous rock faces of his native islands, where he and Volnus had been like twin spiders, masters of the dizziest heights. Slowly he went down, Eskarra watching uncomfortably. Then, to her utter amazement, he swung round, feet and arms holding him in place in the cramped space and turned himself almost upside down. He continued the descent until his head was at the level of the opening into the room. From below he must have been in shadow.

Eskarra waited for the bricks to collapse, or some other slip to take him down in a tangle of limbs, probably breaking a few, to the floor, but Artugol remained fixed impossibly in place. Then he was whispering, but not back to her. More long moments passed, until eventually he began the ascent, again turning before coming upwards. Eskarra would have helped to haul him out, but there was no need. He again clambered over the chimney lip, covered in soot and dust, but lowered himself to the roof with ease.

"So you really do have rock monkey blood," she said, handing him back his sword.

He grinned, wiping muck from his face. "It's them. Shiveeri and her companion, Darruvia."

"Wife of Lycon, the King's right-hand man?"

"Yes. And it was a party of Orugllyr who abducted them, under the command of one of the underlings of the sorcerers, Shanatarl Vaarst."

"Can we get them out?"

"They are both chained. But Shiveeri says the floor is made of compacted roots. It can be cut."

"Tonight, then."

He grinned again. "That's what I told them. They'll be

fed before sunset, then left alone. There'll just be the guards outside to deal with."

Eskarra returned his grin. "I'll fetch the others. They can deal with the Orugllyr while we drop down and cut the women loose. We'll be gone back over the island before the sorcerer notices."

*

Dalan, Elak and Lycon stood before the immense God-Heart Stone, in the sanctity of its mountain retreat. Lycon, seeing it for the first time, gaped in wonder. He could feel its latent power, a living force within it. He held one of the three staffs of power, the Scourge of the Night, while beside him Dalan held the staff of Valusia, and Elak the Gift of Ishtar. Lycon knew that the High Druid had thought long and hard about the bringing of the staffs to this place. Dalan's fear of the use of the great powers stored in the staffs, especially combined, was palpable, but Lycon had only one desire in mind. To recover his wife, Darruvia. He knew Elak felt the same way about bringing Shiveeri home.

"I'm always uneasy about using sorcery," Elak had said before they left the capital. "Too often it turns and becomes a force for darkness, the tool of evil. Few men can resist the tug of its energies. Perhaps, Lycon, you and I and Dalan will be strong enough together to resist such things."

"I'm willing," Lycon had said.

Dalan turned to them both. "Morgaal, prime guardian of the God-Heart Stone approaches. See, he brings shards of the great stone with him."

The others watched as the Druid and two others came to them and set down three groups of various flattened pieces of stone. "These have been stricken from the Stone," said Morgaal. His face was no more readable than the Stone itself, though he had an air of unease about him. "There is still time to put aside this working," said Morgaal. "You know the dangers, Dalan. None of us truly understands the powers of the Stone."

"Atlantis is under a dire threat," said Dalan. "We have weighed it and without the use of the Stone's power, the balance may well dip dangerously in favour of the darkness. We will begin."

"Then each of you stand before one of the stone selections," said Morgaal solemnly. He watched as Elak, Dalan and Lycon did so, then indicated the huge stone towering over them all. "Raise your staffs and direct them at the God- Heart Stone." Again the three men complied and Morgaal began an incantation. His words grew in strength, his voice becoming a deeper, sonorous sound that swelled in the air and swirled around the huge stone like a strong sea current. Light from the three staffs of power crackled and struck the stone, and it began to hum, the ground around it pulsing like a mighty heart. Elak and his companions braced themselves against the vibrations of the earth.

Reflected light from the God-Heart Stone dazzled the eye before striking down at the three individual collections of shards and they glowed, white hot, too fierce to look upon. The air fizzed and a smell of burning pervaded it. Elak became dizzy, knowing he would stumble if this blaze of light continued for long. Then, abruptly, it shut off. Before him he saw the shards glowing softly, no longer slivers of stone. They had become three segmented suits of armour.

"Wear these when you face your enemies from beyond the deeps of night," said Morgaal. "For now you must put them aside in your palace at Epharra, where they cannot be found." He turned to where a number of his priests were gathered, awaiting his commands, waving them to him. They brought three large casks, bound in iron, and presently opened them before lifting each suit of armour and placing it within. They locked the casks and presented Elak and his companions with a key each.

Morgaal bowed to them. "It is done. We pray you have chosen wisely."

Soon afterwards the three casks were being loaded on to the cart that Dalan had arranged to be brought to the mountain retreat. As the three men prepared to return to Epharra, there was a slight commotion on the rocky path leading out of the mountains. Moments later a single figure rode up to the King and bowed.

"Sire. A great sea beast has entered the Bay of Gold."

Elak gasped. Had it begun already?

"And with it," said the messenger, his face flushed, "are many sea dwellers. They call themselves Aquarri."

Elak turned to Dalan, his fears modified. "They are our allies," he said.

Dalan nodded. "They are. But something must have disturbed them greatly to have brought them to Epharra. They rarely leave their sea havens."

Chapter Six: Swords in the Moonlight

Volnus and the others around him, ten of them in all, watched the roof of the building closely, now the moon was up, although mostly obscured by clouds. At last a shadowy figure up there appeared and broke the tension among the pirates, hidden by the fringes of the weed forest. It waved at them before disappearing from sight. Below, around the perimeter of the building, a handful of Orugllyr had posted themselves, blending with the walls, daubed in shadows. Volnus grinned and whispered to his nearest companions.

Swiftly they spread out and on an agreed command from the big man they broke from cover, hugging the roughly flattened ground, and bore down on the Orugllyr. The Atlanteans had the advantage of surprise and went for the kill, but the Orugllyr were abnormally difficult to dispatch, their rubbery skin resistant to sword strokes, their fat necks not so easy to slice open. Volnus told his men to go for the eyes and mouth, and when the first two Orugllyr fell, it was by killing blows into their brains. The pirates spread around the building, attacking with speed and venom, but as it was one of the Orugllyr almost broke free and was in danger of reaching others and raising the alarm.

Volnus rammed into the creature with the strength of a bull, bringing it crashing down, its head smashing up against another of the buildings. Before it could recover, Volnus got astride it and rammed his blade deep down into its throat. Its life fluids gushed up and the fish-like eyes turned to glass. Behind him, the pirates were fighting the last two guards, and although hard pressed their combined efforts were too much for the Orugllyr, who were driven up against the nearest wall. Swords ran into them, but they writhed like huge maggots, resisting death.

Again Volnus drove at one of them as it made ready to give vent to whatever sound these creatures made, but it choked off as Volnus's blade tore through the roof of its mouth and upwards. It died in a welter of gore and Volnus swung round to see the last of the Orugllyr suffer a similar fate. The company paused, all heaving with effort. Silence had fallen again. Swiftly Volnus led them round the building to its door. It was double bolted. He listened, but there were no sounds within.

While the fight had ensued below, Eskarra and Artugol had swung over the lip of the chimney and carefully made their way downwards. The Orugllyr had not lit a fire in here in spite of the coldness of the air. Instead they had left their two prisoners to settle down and sleep for the night. Neither Shiveeri nor Darruvia had done so, so that as Artugol dropped lightly to the floor, they were watching him. He grinned and bowed.

"I am Artugol," he said. "And yours to command, queen Shiveeri."

She raised her arms. "You'll have my undying thanks if you'd rid me of these."

Artugol studied the chains as Eskarra dropped behind him. "Our swords would likely break on them, but can we free you from the leg irons?"

"We've loosened them," said Darruvia, straining at hers to demonstrate how much.

Artugol set to work on Shiveeri's irons and Eskarra did the same with Darruvia's. Both had been fixed in place by bolts driven into the thicker parts of the weed floor, and after a while they came free.

"We can at least walk," said Shiveeri.

"On the ship, we have the means to rid you of the chains," said Eskarra.

"You have a ship?" said Shiveeri. "Praise Ishtar for that."

Artugol touched his lips for silence and went to the door, listening. He heard the sounds of steel clashing with steel. Volnus and the others were battling with the Orugllyr guards. The fight seemed to go on for some time, and Artugol was praying that no reinforcements came. They had no idea how many of the creatures were here on this island.

Silence fell at last, and then a long pause. The outside bolts of the door slid open and very slowly the door was pushed inward. Artugol watched moonlight leak in, and with it the silhouette of a warrior he recognized. It was Volnus.

"You took your time," Artugol growled, though his face was split in a grin.

"They're not easy to kill," Volnus replied. "You had the easy task. Did you manage it?"

For answer Artugol waved Shiveeri and Darruvia through the door and into the chill night, their leg chains clinking. Volnus bowed to them both. Artugol and Eskarra followed, and he pulled the door shut, sliding the bolts back into place.

"Let's get going," he told Volnus, who nodded and led the company back into the weed forest and along the narrow path they had used to get here. Behind them in the buildings, all remained motionless and silent, as if they had quit a graveyard. No one spoke as they made their way upward. The going was slow, the weed floor treacherous, an easy surface on which to twist an ankle. Behind and below them, they suddenly heard a howl, a strange, ululating sound. The Orugllyr had discovered their dead and inevitably would now begin the hunt for their killers.

As the runaways worked their way up through the clinging weeds, slipping perilously but aiding one another, they heard more sounds behind them. It seemed as though the Orugllyr had suddenly burst from wherever they had been based and were coming up the slope in great numbers. They made no attempt to disguise their chase and emitted a cacophony of demented howls, like wolves hunting down their prey. It was evident from the noises that they were closing in on the escapees. Volnus came to a more level area not far below the crest of the ridge.

"We'll have to make a stand," he said. "Artugol! Take Shiveeri and Darruvia up to the ridge. The rest of us –"

"Give me a sword!" said Shiveeri. "I'll not run while you're fighting on my behalf. And one for Darruvia!" The latter nodded, her expression as determined as that of the queen.

"But you are the queen," protested Volnus. "We must get you to safety –"

"*Give me a sword!*" Shiveeri almost snarled. There was no time for further discussion and spare swords were tossed to both Shiveeri and Darruvia, who stood shoulder to shoulder with Eskarra, Artugol and Volnus. Minutes later the first of the Orugllyr horde burst through the weed banks, attacking. Swords flashed in the dim moonlight, sparks zipping through the air as steel bit into steel. The small plateau was narrow and the defenders were able to close ranks and prevent the Orugllyr from surrounding them, having to press their attack from one concentrated area.

Again the pirates used the tactic of jabbing at the eyes and mouths of the enemy, knowing the sleek bodies of the Orugllyr were resistant to steel, which either slid off or penetrated to no avail, finding no organs within to slice. It was difficult, exhausting work. Volnus urged his companions to work their way backwards, moving up the last of the winding trail to the ridge. Slowly they managed this, although two of their number were lost, cut down and trampled by the Orugllyr, who fought mechanically and with low growls. The deaths served only to infuriate Shiveeri and Eskarra, who fought with redoubled efforts and fury, smashing aside one after another of the Orugllyr. Both Volnus and Artugol marvelled at the fighting skills of the queen, and no less those of the ferocious Darruvia, who cursed and swore with an imagination that made the men grin.

The group did reach the ridge, where they were able to pause briefly. Whoever was calling out the orders to the Orugllyr was invisible, but Shiveeri said it must be either their leader, Urzook, or possibly the servant of the Vannadril, Shanatarl Vaarst. Neither were in sight.

Volnus voiced his own crude curses as he surveyed the dark path that would lead them down the southern slope of the island to the *Arrow*. He could see more Orugllyr there. They had surrounded the ridge and it would now be a simple matter of closing their ring and they would re-take their prisoners, doubtless killing everyone else.

"We fight to the death," said Shiveeri, her blade dripping with the thick ichor of those she had killed.

As they waited for the Orugllyr to synchronize their attack, something moved in the higher weed bank to one side of the ridge, a huge shape that came out of the night and gave vent to a snarl. The beast raised its head, revealing a mouth filled with rows of gleaming teeth, and it snorted, pawing at the weed in readiness to launch an attack of its own.

"Mider's blood!" cried Artugol. "They've brought death upon us!" Nevertheless he stood before the terrifying creature, sword raised, ready to defend the queen to the last. Eskarra leapt to his side, her own blade readied for what would surely be a hopeless defence against this thing's power.

*

Elak, Dalan and Lycon rode down to the quayside, where a group of guards awaited them. Out in the Bay of Gold many of the ships were lit up, as if in preparation for action. The waters seemed calm, and there was no sign of the sea beast that Elak's messenger had spoken of up in the mountains. The King and his companions dismounted and were taken into one of the larger warehouses, where a further group of guards awaited them. With them, huddled together in obvious fear, was a small number of beings that Elak immediately recognized.

They were Aquarri, little sea men half the size of the humans, toad-like in build, with skin that gleamed as with the scales of fish, slightly green in colour. Their huge eyes gazed on the King and as one they bowed.

"You are welcome here, my friends," said Elak, standing before them.

One came forward and Elak recognized him at once. He was Marequarl, who had helped the King once before, in a desperate battle against the serpent men of Quarrass-Theen, whose plans to overthrow Atlantis had been thwarted, with no little thanks to the Aquarri. "I would not have presumed to come to your city," said Marequarl. "But I am here in desperation. Terrible things are occurring in the deep oceans of the world."

"It is good to see you, Marequarl. Atlantis will always be in your debt."

"There is little time for explanations."

"You know my companions, Dalan the High Druid and Lycon."

"Of course," said Marequarl.

"You may speak freely. Is there anything you need before you do? Food? Other refreshments?"

"No, sire. Time is against us. We have accompanied one of the Deepwhales to your waters. It rests on the seabed beneath your ships. Your sailors have not harmed it, but they fear it."

"A Deepwhale?" said Dalan. "Such a creature does not surface in the realms of men, let alone in a harbour. This must be rare news you bring us."

"It is, master. They watch the deepest of the oceans from the north to the south ice sheets, and from the east to the west and around the world. There are things stirring in those deeps, things that have been dormant since time began, since they came here from the outer vaults of space, between the darkest of its stars. You must come with us, when you will learn of these things."

"Come?" said Elak. "To where?"

"The deep oceans, beyond their night."

Chapter Seven: Claws from the Sky

"Wait!" shouted Shiveeri. She stepped between Eskarra and Artugol as their swords were poised to strike at the beast, and to their horror she went closer to it. She spoke words no one else could hear, and at once it bowed its head and to everyone's amazement the queen stroked its nose as if it were no more than a favourite horse.

"What in the Nine Hells?" began Volnus.

Shiveeri turned to the pirates. "It's a sky lizard. From its home island of Illyrin. I have flown on the back of one of these. They serve Atlantis."

"Indeed they do, madam," came a voice from beyond the weeds, and a tall warrior emerged. "I am Carraverin, in service to your King, Elak." He bowed to the queen. "But, majesty, what are you doing here? You are in the gravest danger."

"There's no time for details," said Shiveeri. "Are you alone?"

"Yes. There are others scouting the oceans and islands for you both, but we have spread far and wide."

"Darruvia and I have been rescued from the Orugllyr, who have surrounded this ridge. We need to get back to our ship. Can you help us fight off the enemy?"

"Of course, majesty. But surely I should carry you away. The sky lizard is strong enough to take you, the lady Darruvia and me."

"I'll not abandon anyone. They've risked their lives to break us free of our captors."

Eskarra stepped forward. "Shiveeri, if we can get to the *Arrow*, we'll be safe enough. We'll be out to sea before they catch us, and we've a strong enough crew to prevent the Orugllyr from boarding us."

Shiveeri nodded. "Very well. Carraverin, you must distract them while we get to the ship. We'll fight our way down to it together."

"But, majesty -"

"That's an order!"

Carraverin paled, but nodded. He could see the queen was in no mood to be denied. Swiftly he mounted the sky lizard and took it into the air. It circled the ridge and at once dived down and began harrying the Orugllyr, who shrank back in consternation as the beast's claws raked for them.

"Hurry!" said Shiveeri, waving the company to the far side of the ridge and down the slope beyond. No one had time to argue further. Shiveeri and Darruvia were unable to race downwards, their chained legs an impediment, but with the sky lizard driving the enemy back and the pirates cutting into any that were adventurous enough to press the attack, they made progress. The weed path was narrow and the massed banks of the growths made it difficult for the Orugllyr to harass them.

The sky lizard's claws ripped into the sea creatures with deadly effect, and the pursuit became more ragged, falling behind as the company went ever lower down towards the shore. At last they came to the inlet where the

Arrow had been moored and immediately were seen by a lookout.

Carraverin brought the sky lizard down in a small space, and at first the crew on the *Arrow* were poised to unleash a hail of arrows at it, until Eskarra shouted to them to desist. She turned to the Queen. "You must go with the sky rider. We'll be safe now. Go! You must. We did not release you to risk being recaptured. You must get back to the King."

Shiveeri looked up at the rising weed banks and the path they had descended. The Orugllyr were not yet in sight, but they were coming, and by the sound they were in even greater numbers now, a swarm of them, like angered hornets protecting an overturned nest. Carraverin urged her and Darruvia forward and the sky lizard bent its neck to allow both women to climb on to its back behind Carraverin.

"I don't like to leave you," Shiveeri called to Eskarra.

The pirate laughed. "Leave the Orugllyr to us. Go!"

As the sky lizard took to the air once more, Eskarra and the others swiftly ran up the plank into the *Arrow* and at once the crew released the ropes mooring her. The oars were lowered and the craft slipped into mid-stream, just as the first of the Orugllyr appeared on the shore. Without hesitation they dived into the water, and the pirates gathered at the decks, led by the massive Ormullah, swords drawn, prepared for a fresh onslaught. More of the creatures poured from the weed, and as they dived beneath the ship Eskarra turned to Artugol.

"They're in their element now. Let's hope the gods are still with us." As she spoke, the hull rocked to the first of many blows. Getting to the open sea was going to be the most difficult challenge yet.

High above them, again circling, the sky lizard's riders watched, barely able to discern the events below in the gloom, but they could hear the shouts of the pirates as they defended themselves from the massed Orugllyr.

"If they can reach open water, they'll stand a chance," said Darruvia.

Shiveeri nodded. "Carraverin, dive. Do what you can to aid them. Help them break free of the inlet."

The man scowled, wracked with indecision and reluctant to risk his precious passengers, but he would not defy the Queen, so swooped downwards. By now the Orugllyr had become used to the sky creature's attacks and were afraid of it, so as it swooped, no more than a few feet above the surface, they dove underwater, many dropping from the sides of the *Arrow*, bludgeoned by Ormullah and speared by his companions. Repeated passes by the sky lizard reduced the assault on the ship and it made faster progress, out of the inlet and beyond the shoreline. Although the Orugllyr pursued it, it got free of the island.

On its deck, the company watched as the sky lizard rose up, quickly becoming one with the clouds. This time it would not dive again.

*

Although the Aquarri had come to Epharra under the sea, having no need to sail in a ship to reach the city, they had brought with them a craft the like of which Elak had never seen before. It had a low hull and no masts, almost as if it had been lying on the seabed, damaged in some storm or unfortunate act that should have crippled it. Dalan, however, told Elak that this was a craft with unique qualities, something which the Aquarri had imbued with special powers, their own brand of sorcery. It would, avowed the Druid, be their means of reaching the places the

Aquarri wanted them to see. Elak and Lycon had exchanged uneasy glances at this, as they had known strange undersea voyages before. Such voyages seemed to them at times no more than dreams, as if those aquatic exploits had occurred in the mind, events no human traveller could really have endured physically. And yet they had brought up from the ocean deeps the potent weapons of lost Valusia, and used them subsequently.

"Is there word yet from the Royal Wing?" Elak asked several of his guard, men who had been stationed at all times to watch the skies for any sign of the sky lizards, who had been sent to scour the oceans for Shiveeri and Darruvia.

No word had yet come, he was told.

"I should wait here in Epharra," Elak told Dalan. "I cannot function until I know the fate of my wife."

"It is the same for me," said Lycon. His cheerful nature had subsided under the combined grief and fury at having Darruvia abducted. Both men looked weary, deprived of sleep, unable to focus their thoughts on anything other than recovering the two women.

"You can do nothing while you wait in Epharra," said Dalan. "Better that you accompany me and the Aquarri. They may know something. Their people travel to places below the ocean that others cannot visit. It is possible they may have news."

Elak snorted in frustration. For long moments it seemed as if he would give vent to his anger and go against Dalan's suggestion. In the end he simply nodded. "Very well." Beside him, Lycon also nodded.

Marequarl and his fellows led the company to where the strange craft had been moored. Beneath it, in choppy waters, there were other Aquarri, silently waiting, heads bobbi ng on the surface like those of seals. Dalan followed Marequarl on to the craft, Elak and Lycon behind him. Elak gave strict instructions to his commanders on the quay and they acknowledged them with looks of grave concern. Elak knew when the Councillors heard of this latest voyage, they would voice their objections, but the King was used to verbal conflict with them.

Once the trio had boarded, the craft moved swiftly out into the Bay of Gold, propelled by the creatures below the surface. Only their leader, Marequarl remained on deck. He sat at the narrow prow of the craft, wide eyes fixed on the sea ahead as the craft prepared to go out into the open ocean.

"What of the Deepwhale?" said Lycon, trying to peer down into the dark waters. His instincts told him something vast moved down there.

"It is our protector," said Dalan. "There are numerous enemies around us, especially in the oceans. Without the protection of the great sea beasts, we would quickly be snared. The darkness we face has redoubled its efforts, and the war it will unleash is much closer."

Beyond the harbour, where the waves strengthened, driven by cold winds from the north, winds that brought sleet and the constant threat of storms, the strange craft turned westward, increasing its speed, racing across the water, faster than any sail could haul it, or men row it. Far from the shore, with no land visible on any horizon, it began a slow slide downwards.

"We will go *below*?" gasped Lycon.

Dalan put a hand on his shoulder. "Have no fear. The Aquarri have prepared the way for us."

Nevertheless both Lycon and Elak stiffened as the sides of the craft dropped level with the water line, and then, miraculously, they were below it, and they watched in bewilderment as the sea curved up and over them, forming what looked like a glass roof, enclosing the craft in a bubble.

Their descent increased and soon they were at the limits of light, the window around them intact. Before they slipped down into the black vaults, a cloud of miniature sea creatures appeared around them, each a tiny light, and as the craft dropped, Elak and his companions saw by it other denizens swimming by in the distance. There were sharks and smaller fish, some single, some in shoals.

"Is this real?" said Lycon.

Dalan laughed softly. "It is. These are ancient powers at work, thought lost by many of my fellow Druids. There was a time when ancient Atlanteans knew of these things. Put your trust in them."

Elak pointed to a huge shadow in the near distance that would not quite reveal itself.

"Yes," said Dalan. "It is the Deepwhale. If we are attacked, it will drive away such creatures as would seek to kill us."

"Such as those?" said Lycon, pointing beyond the stern of the craft, to where a shoal of some dozen sea creatures, as big as the largest sharks known to them, were preparing to surround the craft, their several rows of teeth gleaming in the glow from the tiny light-creatures.

Chapter Eight: Lost City of Legend

It was evident that the *Arrow* was not going to escape easily from the island. As the craft cut through the incoming tide, the sea boiled with countless forms as the Orugllyr determined to halt its progress and swarm aboard. There was a stiffening breeze, presaging a storm, so the sail was billowing, few men needed to supplement its power at the oars, which enabled as many as possible to get to the rails and repel the sea creatures. The fighting was furious, swords flashing in the fading light, and for a time it seemed that the deck would be overrun with the Orugllyr, so many of them were there in the waves.

However, the determined defence of the ship, whipped up by the fury of Eskarra and Artugol beside her, held strong and as the craft made its way out into deeper waters, the Orugllyr fell back. Instead they attempted to slow the ship's progress by clinging on to its keel like limpets, but its smoothness and the increasing speed of the vessel defied them, until at length the *Arrow* was out in open sea, the Orugllyr falling behind.

"They know they've lost their prime targets," said Volnus. "It was Shiveeri and Darruvia they wanted. They attacked us from spite."

Eskarra frowned, wiping blood and the slick muck of sea creatures from her arms and sword. "Maybe. But we'll keep a constant watch for them. Set a course for Mallomas, Zendullo. We'll get a message to the High Druid, although with luck the sky lizard will have delivered its riders by then." She looked back at the northern skyline, but the island had already slipped below it, possibly back beneath the waves.

*

Elak and his companions braced themselves as the huge sharks bore down on their undersea vessel, the bloated bodies of the killer fish seeming to double in size as they tore forward through the water, pink mouths agape. Even Dalan seemed at a loss to know how to soften what would be terrible blows as those monsters hammered home their assault. The Aquarri were clearly not able to propel the craft away any faster, and a shuddering contact seemed inevitable. Something rose up from the dark waters below, like a huge fist punching upwards from the unseen deeps.

Its massive weight struck right into the oncoming sharks, driving them upward and outward like so many scattered toys, and as the thing rose, dazzlingly fast, Elak saw a single eye, huge as a man's head, and only then realized what it was that had diverted the sharks.

"The Deepwhale," said Lycon. "Look at the size of the beast!"

Elak laughed, though his nerves were on edge. The immensity of the creature, however friendly it might be, was terrifying. Its full-size tore upward and the tail, thrice the size of the craft, swung sideways and smashed into more of the sharks. Some of them had recovered and instantly tore at the bigger creature, but it moved through the waters with the grace of a seal. Numerous sharks were sinking downwards, their white bellies upward, life pulped out of them.

"Worse things will come for us," said Marequarl. "But for now the sharks will scatter. Their masters will know what has happened."

"Who controls them?" said Elak. "Sorcerers?!"

Marequarl nodded. "Yes, master. You will see once we reach our destination."

After that the downward plunge continued without incident, and the vast shadow of the Deepwhale kept its distance, while on all sides there were other such huge shapes, as a large pod of the creatures stationed themselves as an escort to the craft. The light in these depths was minimal, coming solely from the accompanying creatures, many of which were smaller than a human hand, and Elak wondered if the craft would eventually sink into depths that even their light could not brighten.

"We are nearing the citadel of Yllythur of the Meruvians," said Marequarl. "Its gates will open to us."

"The city of legends," said Dalan. "It is said to watch

over the impenetrable abyssal deeps. No living man has visited it. We are privileged."

Elak and Lycon joined him as they watched more shapes rising from the ocean floor, not living things, but the dramatic towers of this mythical city. Their dark green stone shimmered with its own iridescence like precious stone and between their tall columns other blocks of chiselled rock spread throughout a plateau that sat astride a ridge overlooking the utter darkness of the abyss. The craft wove between several of the reaching towers like a living entity, knowing its course, and it came before a large rectangular rock that Elak took to be a building, although its architects must have been possessed of extraordinary powers to have created such an amazing structure.

A single portal near the base of the building opened like a pitch-black eye and the craft entered. Its movement stopped and Elak felt suddenly as though he was standing in his own grave, so silent and dark was this place. He felt the craft rising and after a while there was more light. A chamber spread out around them, with a dock, and the Aquarri moored the craft to it. They were no longer under water and the bubble-like sides of the craft slid back to allow unexpectedly clean air to envelop the travellers. A set of stone steps reached up from the water to the dock and Marequarl climbed them, waving Dalan, Elak and Lycon to his side as he stepped on to a narrow ledge.

Armoured figures came out of the shadows, each the height of a man and bearing a tall trident. Their heads were encased in steel helms, cast in a unique style, the faces hidden behind a thin mesh. Marequarl spoke to them and they formed two ranks, allowing the company to pass between them and beyond into this strange place. Sounds echoed from distances in the corridors, and soft light danced as if reflected from water as the surface dwellers made their way through this deepest of labyrinths. The corridor opened out once more and they gasped in wonder at what was revealed.

It was another chamber, but its walls were not cut from stone or coral, but seemingly from crystal, forming a huge convex dome, beyond which the ocean pressed in, as pitch black at the outer reaches of space, a starless, impenetrable void. There was light in the chamber, diffused by sections of the floor around its semi-circular boundary, and at its heart a small group of beings waited. Dressed in long, flowing robes that looked as though they had been woven from the silk of spiders, they were not unlike the Aquarri, though these were as tall as the men, with narrower heads and features more human than Aquarri, though they had gills and the fingers of their tapered hands were webbed.

"Welcome to Yllythur," said one of them, stepping forward with a slight bow. "I am Eldarvel, the Protector of the City."

Dalan approached him and also bowed. "It is an honour to be brought to the domain of the Meruvians," he said. "Our lost legends did not lie."

Eldarvel smiled. "It has been many millennia since my people shared the company of Men," he said. "You are Dalan, High Druid of Atlantis. You and your work is known to us, who see far into the oceans and above it. And you are Elak, Emperor of the Atlanteans, who you have united."

Elak bowed in silence.

"And you, Lycon," Eldarvel continued, "are Elak's most loyal of friends and defenders. We honour all of you, for among Men, none is more worthy of trust and respect than you."

"We thank you for your kind words," said Elak. "It is a great pleasure to know your city of marvels is more than just a legend."

"It would have remained no more than a myth," said Eldarvel. "Yet these are days of a new darkness. Nothing is safe from the greed and avaricious desire of the Star Gods and their terrible spawn. All of our world, from its skies and mountains to the greatest depths of the ocean is threatened by them. If they are to be defied, all races must combine powers in the coming war."

"How much of these things do you know?" asked Dalan.

"It is given to us to watch the world and to see great distances, not only below the waves but above it. The elements themselves are our messengers: the breath of the wind, the course of the tides, the shifting of lava beneath the ground. There are things we must show you, which is why we have brought you here. We have little time, so come."

Eldarvel waked across to the centre of the crystal dome and pointed to the darkness without. The three men joined him and studied the black void. Gradually the darkness trembled and grew lighter, until a vision opened up into the distance, the seabed, disappearing into a remote haze. A city spread out there, its magnificent buildings, towers and bridges a marvel of engineering, a place of exceptional wonders, where the numerous streets, perfectly rectilinear, thronged with life, beings akin to Eldarvel as well as the Aquarri and other related species.

"Yllythur at the peak of its glory," said Eldarvel. "Living in harmony with all the oceans and seas of the world. A time that is no more than a far memory. On the world's surface, there was ever strife, as empires rose and fell, some to great wars, others to cataclysms. Your own Atlantis was almost destroyed, but enough of your people survived to rise again."

Elak was nodding in agreement. "We have seen visions

like this in other places. Histories of devastation, great waves that inundated whole land masses. It is said that such things will come again."

"The war to come would unleash them, yes. Unless we prevent it. The past, the city you see out there would have given help to the surface dwellers, but they were all jealous of each other's power. Man against man. It was not a war that we could contribute to. We chose to turn from them and to live as we have done. This time, however, it is the entire world in danger. Divided, our races will succumb to the Great Darkness."

Eldarvel took the three men across to one side of the curved crystal, where another view of darkness awaited them. "Let me show you what it is that seeks to rise up from the deeps." Once again the obscuring pitch darkness lightened to reveal another ocean vista. Its floor swept away from the window, dropping down into an abyss whose depths were completely shrouded. Along the sides of the gaping canyon there were buildings, these in direct contrast to the majesty of Yllythur, being roughly hewn, mere blocks, cracked and hung with black weed, windows empty, like holes bored into the stone by sightless worms, some of which slithered around the squat towers.

Other creatures shifted down in the abyss, some rising, their bulbous heads crowned with fat clumps of cilia, their barrel-like bodies trailing tendrils. These deep dwellers varied in size, some no bigger than a man, others almost as vast as the great Deepwhales above Yllythur. Some met and clashed, entwining their tendrils in a wild, chaotic dance, driving the beasts down into the darkness where the conclusion of their terrible conflicts was hidden from sight.

As Elak and the others watched, they sensed something truly vast moving toward them from the far end of the trench, a colossal, living entity, and from its dense mass, a palpable evil flowed, a vile, poisoned light. Elak felt his heart pounding as he fought the waves of nausea. This was the bringer of the final darkness, the end of all light.

Chapter Nine: Storm-Tossed

High above the ocean, wings beating powerfully against the increasing buffeting of the winds, the sky lizard flew far to the east of its home island of Illyrin carrying its three passengers to Epharra. The worsening storm and the weight of the three humans made it difficult to maintain height and speed, and the creature dropped lower in spite of Carraverin's attempts to coax it higher. He knew this storm was no natural thing, its elements commanded by the enemy's sorcery, and if he did not take evasive action, the valiant sea lizard would be dragged into the ocean, where inevitably its riders would be drowned.

"What's wrong?" called Shiveeri over his shoulder, her grip on his belt tightening as the sky lizard swayed dangerously in another great gust.

"We are being hunted. We must search the ocean for an island."

"How far to Epharra?"

"We'll not reach it without rest. This storm intensifies, seeking to drive us back to the north."

"Then find an island," she said. "What about your companions, other sky lizards?"

"If there were any of them in these skies, our mount would know it, but there are none. They may well have found their own sanctuaries." So saying, he guided the sky lizard downwards in a fast glide, and the winds around it eased slightly. They swooped through the clouds that rose in thickening fog banks from the surface of the sea, like its breath, emerging into clearer air, the choppy surface boiling with white-capped waves. Carraverin attempted to guide the sky lizard southward, but again the winds arose and beat at it, driving it in a curving glide that veered it eastward. For a time they held the course, until Carraverin saw a smudge on the horizon.

He leaned back to Shiveeri. "There is an island, not much more than an atoll. I think we should land there, at least until the sea lizard has its strength back. It will be hungry by now."

They had little alternative as the winds now were laced with sleet, driving at them in fierce, irresistible blasts. Quickly they turned and made for the distant island, and in doing so benefited from the storm's fury. In no time they were gliding towards the island, a hummock of greenery, a tangled mass of vegetation, incongruous in these northern waters. Shiveeri saw it was not formed of knotted weed, but of something akin to the jungle isles of further south, as if it had broken away from a chain and drifted here.

Behind her Darruvia spoke, her words almost snatched away by the wind. "This is no natural place. We'd do better to avoid it."

"I don't think we can. The storm has penned us in."

Carraverin took them lower, dropping the sky lizard on to the beach, where it churned the sand as it landed. The riders dismounted, Carraverin bringing with him a backpack that contained food and water. Somehow, and again the three humans suspected sorcery, the winds rose up over the island and bypassed it, as though the place had power of its own to deflect the storm. Sunlight broke through the raging clouds, and although its light was vivid, it seemed tainted, as was the silence that hung over the place like a thick shroud.

With a piercing cry, the sky lizard took to the air and skimmed over the calmer waters of the bay, abruptly diving down into them, lured by the teeming fish.

Shiveeri turned to Carraverin, holding out her arms, in one hand the sword she had brought from the island of her imprisonment. "Can you get rid of these?"

He studied the manacles. "The lock is primitive." He took a long knife from his belt and worked it into the lock, grimacing with effort as he turned it and presently snapped its mechanism. Shiveeri gave a little cry of delight and moments later Carraverin had freed both her wrists from the manacles and those of Darruvia. "I may have more difficulty with those round your ankles."

"Let's find shelter," said Shiveeri. "We can all eat and you can try and free us there."

He nodded, leading them across the beach to the tree line. The trees and plants looked to be no different to those on many Atlantean islands, although none would have been expected this far north. There was a rough path through them and carefully Carraverin parted ferns and bushes, easing the way along it, sword poised to defend himself. There was no birdsong, and no drone of insects. In the sky, there was nothing to suggest the storm churned there. A bubble of serenity enclosed the place. Soon they had reached the heart of the island, the path debouching into a lake, little more than a large pool. Its water was like glass, its depths a deep green.

"I would not drink from it," said Carraverin, instead pulling a leather pouch from his backpack, holding it out to Shiveeri. "Take a little."

She handed it on to Darruvia, who drank sparingly before returning it. Shiveeri drank and handed the pouch back to Carraverin, who had a single sip before putting the pouch away. They ate a frugal meal, sitting on the bank of the pool, all careful not to dangle a foot into it. The place remained uniquely still, and while they waited, Carraverin worked on the foot manacles of the two women, though without the success of those he had removed.

Evening had fallen by the time he gave up. "We need a smith," he said, exasperated.

"I can move sufficiently," said Shiveeri. "With my hands freed I can use the sword if I need to." Beside her Darruvia nodded. "What about the sky lizard?"

"It will sleep in the sands, half buried for its own comfort and protection," said Carraverin. "We can spend the night in the shade here. In the morning, with luck, the storm will have blown itself out."

Shiveeri nodded, but her mind was in turmoil. *We have been brought here. And whatever brought us will show itself. Probably when we least expect it and are unprepared.* She stared at the pool, but could not do so for long. Something about it repulsed her. It was connected, she thought, to their situation.

*

Elak drew back from the horrific vision as the deep-sea dweller rose from a bed that was now illuminated in sickly green light, revealing a city spread throughout the chasm. Yet what a nightmare city this was! Its buildings seemed to defy the eye with their bizarre lines and angles, its streets like jagged rents in the seabed, spewing forth growths that looked malign and diseased, while around the distorted towers creatures drifted like tangled weed, hideous mouths gaping, sucking in smaller life forms. In his dreams Elak had pictured such grim architecture, imagining it to be something clawed together on distant worlds among hostile stars, remote from the reality of his own world, and yet he knew intuitively that what he was seeing here was not such a vision. This place of terrors and malefic life was on the seabed, the spawning ground of real entities, servants of the incomprehensible evil gods that were coming to subjugate his world.

As he watched, nauseated, the huge ocean dweller rose higher above its submarine base and as it did so, three shapes appeared from the black waters around it and attacked it. Deepwhales! He saw, with mounting disbelief, they were no more than a third of the creature's size, dwarfed by its terrible dimensions. And yet they tore into it like maddened hounds savaging their prey, drawing back and coming again. The sea dweller swung its trailing tendrils around in a sweeping circular motion that ripped into the three Deepwhales, completely enveloping one of them. Its death was horrible, the creature torn apart, its leaking components blurring the vision. The others continued their ferocious attack, damaging their opponent, gouging chunks from its bloated trunk, which bled clouds of thick, oily life-fluid.

"It is but one of that hellish city's monstrous servants," said Eldarvel. "There are not enough Deepwhales in the entire oceans of the world to subdue them all. When these horrors are released, it will take the hand of a god to stop them."

"What place is that?" said Elak, hypnotized by the challenging features of the buildings that grew out of the seabed like an infestation, a rampant plague.

"Whatever it calls itself is unknown to us. It is the dwelling place of Xeraph-Hizer, the Leviathan Lord. He is there, underneath the city in caverns beyond our contemplation. I could show you other such places, some buried deep under mountain ranges, others in the ice wastes of the world, yet more in deserts. In all places usually shunned by Man, they slide and crawl and hop and fly. Waiting for the war to begin."

Beyond them, over the city, the last of the Deepwhales had been smashed aside, forced to flee, although the attack on the vast creature had injured it enough to force it to subside, and it sank back down, engulfed by the abhorrent buildings, its graveyard as darkness shrouded the entire scene.

"Is there enough power in the world to defeat these Star Gods?" said Dalan. "If they coordinate their resources, how can Man stand against them? We'll be driven into the ground, far from light."

"Light," repeated Eldarvel. "It is the one thing capable of destroying these gods. Both the light of the sun and that which you have already tested in the staffs of power. Imbue all your weapons with it."

"Is this war to be fought in the oceans?" said Elak. "Both below it, as we have seen, and on the surface?"

"The enemy hordes are controlled by the sea gods. Those that dwell in the world's remote places answer to them and are controlled by them. Defeat the sea gods and the others will slide away into the uttermost wells of the world."

"We are disadvantaged," said Elak. "We can command a vast navy from our people and all our allies. However, war at sea is far more hazardous than it would be on land."

Eldarvel nodded. "Yes. Perhaps you should take the war to the enemy, and deprive them of any advantage."

Dalan frowned. "You know how we could do this?"

Eldarvel nodded again, leading the men to a third curved window. The vision now was one of the surface, where the restless ocean broke its waves on the shores of a land mass that rose up out of it in a shoreline of towering cliffs. Numerous waterfalls fell from the great heights, suggesting that this land mass had lately risen from the sea. Strange aerial creatures swooped and dived around the rocks, and clusters of dark weed choked the walls, within whose cracks pulsing bladder-like clumps spread like a fungoid infection.

Elak drew back in revulsion. "It mirrors the city of Xeraph-Hizer."

"It is exactly that. It has lately risen from the seabed in the north. Shunn-Ul-Darza, the island of the Vannadril, the sorcerers of the Sky Gods. We believe the war will be conducted from there."

"Then we strike at its heart," said Elak. "With all our power."

Eldarvel turned away from the towering image of the island. "The Aquarri will aid you. As will the creatures of the oceans. Light against darkness."

Chapter Ten: The Pool of Horror

Although Carraverin took the first watch, he was unable to keep his eyes open. While the moon rode high, casting a lurid light across the island, mirrored in the flat surface of the pool, Shiveeri and Darruvia slipped into the sleep of exhaustion. Carraverin, lulled by the still, silent night air, and by the subtle scents of the unique plants surrounding the island's heart, drooped and sank into oblivion. As he sagged to one side on the turf, the pool's surface stirred, but he was too deep into sleep to be woken. Gradually a shape rose from the water. Larger than a man, with darkly mottled skin and a head that glistened with scales and orb-like eyes widening in the moonlight, it glided through the water, its lower body invisible. As it came ashore, its many limbs, tentacular and trailing behind it like those of a large squid, writhed as they slid it forward, like a nest of serpents. It reached the two women, as motionless in sleep as two carved statues, and reached for each of them with its long, spatulate fingers. Each hand rested on the head of a sleeper as the creature began its work.

Shiveeri was dreaming, her mind soaring over strange landscapes, which opened out beneath her to reveal a city of startling magnificence, a place of wonders, with glittering towers, covered in jewels, and sun-lit boulevards, lined with trees. There were palaces and gardens, all splendidly wrought, and in the skies beautiful birds and other exotic winged creatures swooped and dived in a spectacular aerial ballet.

Thus will your Epharra become, said a mellifluous voice beside her. *Ruler not only of Atlantis, but of the entire world, with all its people living under her banners in harmony. Your King, your many nations, will enjoy its splendours and all the benefits of its new gods, your glorious lords from across the universe.*

In her dream she turned to see the being who had spoken. Dressed in magnificent robes, woven with gold, it was a man of striking beauty, his features perfectly carved, the physical embodiment of a man, with hair like woven sunlight. He bowed to her.

"Who are you?" she asked him.

I am simply a messenger, whispered his voice inside her head. *Sent to you from the gods to bring you word of the coming new age. This will not be a time of war, but of celebration, of joy among all your people and those of the travellers from afar.* He came towards her and she did not step back, even though his presence filled her with uncertainty.

Do not be afraid, Queen Shiveeri. You are blessed. Before she could resist, he took her hand and pressed his lips to it. The kiss was warm, and the power within it coursed through her veins, making her shudder. *Go back to Epharra and speak to your husband of the dawn of the new era. Prepare him to receive the joyous arrival of those who would elevate him and all his subjects to triumph.*

Before she could collect her confused thoughts and answer, the golden figure receded into the light and was gone. Somehow, Shiveeri knew, he had left something with her, a feeling that she could not shake off, and although it subsided, she knew it was within her, hidden away, like a serpent that would rise at some future time, when she would be powerless to overcome it, or whatever dark plans it would reveal. She came awake, the dream already dissolving, like water slipping through her fingers.

Beside her, Darruvia stirred, then also came awake. The two women stared at one another. "There was a man, a golden warrior," Darruvia said, also trying to hold on to what she, too had dreamed, but like mist before bright sunlight, it had dispersed. A sound behind her made her and Shiveeri turn.

Carraverin was awake, his face a mask of terror as he came towards them. "Step aside!" he called, his sword raised as he got beyond them and faced the pool, which once more was a mirror of the night.

"What is it?" said Shiveeri.

"Do you not see it?" he gasped.

Both women shook their heads, moving lethargically. Carraverin, however, saw through eyes whose vision had not been distorted by the mind-sendings of the thing from the pool, the monster sinking back into its depths. Carraverin leapt forward and swung his blade at its head, but it raised an arm and a flash of green light exploded in a glowing host of stars, vivid embers that fell to the earth, winking out. Carraverin was tossed backwards, tumbling on to the knotted grass. He was entirely at the mercy of the pool dweller, but it simply slipped under the water, a few ripples remaining to mark its passing.

Shiveeri came to Carraverin's aid, helping him to his feet. "I think you have had a bad dream," she told him as he shook is head to clear it.

"Did you not see?" he said again, staring at the pool, which was as flat as glass once more.

"No, there was nothing to see."

He looked into her eyes. Something was not quite the same about her. A lethargy, tiredness? Not something he was used to in her. Before she slept she had been vibrant, her powerful emotions evident, her manner decisive, forceful, but now she seemed tired, almost listless. He turned to Darruvia, and she appeared no less so. He would have commented, but he felt a sudden nausea, a wave of unease that came over him slowly, calling him back to sleep.

*

On the Aquarri ship back to Epharra, Elak paced the narrow deck, face clouded, fists knotted in frustration. Beyond him, at the rail, Lycon watched, understanding well enough what it was that so tested the king's sanity. What had been revealed in Yllythur of the Meruvians was bad enough, and would have brought anguish and a sense of dread to any man who had witnessed those appalling revelations, but Elak's spirit was being tormented by more than that: Shiveeri's abduction. Lycon, too, felt the fears that went with the crime, his own wife part of the enemy's machinations. He prayed to the gods there would be word of the two women when they got back to Epharra.

"You fear for him," Dalan said softly beside Lycon.

"And for us all, Dalan. Elak has been cut deep by this abduction. I have watched his love for Shiveeri grow since he first met her. It burns in him as brightly as any star. He'll not know peace until he has regained her."

"You, too, Lycon. Your own loss is as great."

"Aye. Years ago I lost a love and spent too many years half killing myself because of it. Then Darruvia came into my life. I was initially insensible to the depth of my feelings for her, but no longer. Now I burn to have her back. And when I do, I will exact such a revenge on those who took her that the world will talk of it for ages to come."

Dalan smiled. "You and Elak have been riled by the abductions, goaded to a kind of madness. It is what our enemy wants. You must both exercise control in the reckoning. Without it, our cause will fail."

Lycon growled deep in his chest. "We'll not fail."

The Aquarri ship took them swiftly across the ocean and as they came within a day of Epharra, they saw a great sky lizard in the heavens above them. It swept down, wings beating the air, its lone rider waving as the beast dropped to sea level, alighting alongside the ship. As it contented itself with diving for food, the rider, Hannaster, came aboard and bowed before the King.

"You have news of our wives?" said Elak, trying to keep a note of desperation from his voice.

"Aye, lord. They are both safely returned to the capital. They await you there."

"Are they harmed?" said Lycon, his face like thunder.

"No, sire," said Hannaster. "They are tired from their exertions, but not harmed."

Elak gripped Lycon and lifted him from the ground, which was no small feat, for his friend was not a small man. "Gods be thanked!" Elak swung round to the watching Marequarl. "Redouble the speed of this craft! Get us to Epharra as fast as you are able."

When his relief had eased, he turned again to Hannaster. The young man looked agitated, gripping the ship's rail as the craft skidded over the surface and broke the waves across its bow, bucking at times like a beast.

"Is there other news – of the north?" said Elak.

"Yes, lord. An island, a huge, soaring mass of rock, has risen as by sorcery from the deeps, for there is no central volcano to explain its sudden birth. It -"

"Shunn-Ul-Darza," said Dalan. "We know of this place."

"Several of the Royal Wing attempted to fly around or over the island," said Hannaster. "But it was impossible. It has so many defences. Fogs and foul winds are a perpetual threat in its upper air, and there are creatures within that do not belong to this world. They spit fire and rend with claws that could pull a sky lizard apart if they could catch one."

"And its shores?" said Elak.

"Black cliffs, sheer and sharp, rocks and coral that would deter any climber. From what little our patrols could see, the upper island is a city, but one of immeasurable size, rising, layer upon layer, tower on tower, an impregnable fortress. We saw creatures there, swarming like rodents, or bats. Strange fires lit the walls, and in the seas around the foaming rocks there were other creatures, large and small, an aquatic host that choked the ocean with their numbers."

Elak gazed out at the northern waters. "The Vannadril sorcerers will be strutting about its battlements with confidence, expecting to sweep all before them. They'll not expect a hammer blow from our own force."

Hannaster's shocked expression made Elak smile grimly. "Lord, you cannot mean to attack that place?"

"We fight fire with fire, power with power. And our gods will rise with us, and defend their world, as we do."

Later, as the afternoon faded into evening and the sun began its final submergence into the western ocean, the ship berthed once more in the Bay of Gold. There was a royal company on the quayside to meet the King and his companions, although Shiveeri and Darruvia were not among them, which surprised Elak.

"They will have had an exhausting experience," said Dalan reasonably. "You heard the sky rider. They are unharmed."

Nevertheless Elak and Dalan were impatient to get to the palace and confirm the truth of those words. They quickly mounted horses provided for them and galloped up the streets of the city as if all the devils of hell pursued them.

Dalan turned to Marequarl. "Thank you for your service."

"It is only the beginning, master. When war begins, our people will stand in the first ranks beside you. We are already preparing."

Chapter Eleven: Forgotten Dreams

Elak and his companions returned to the royal palace after nightfall, and within its quiet chambers, the King and Lycon were reunited with their wives. Elak swept Shiveeri off her feet and although she laughed, he sensed she was abnormally tired, her usual high energy level compromised by her grim ordeal. Lycon and Darruvia embraced no less enthusiastically, but she, too, was clearly suffering from the effects of the abduction. Both men insisted on at least going to see their children, all of whom were sleeping comfortably in their chambers, outside of which the guards had been trebled.

Although Elak was anxious to hear the full account of what had happened, Shiveeri insisted they all get some sleep, saving discussions until the morning. Elak would have insisted on at least a basic hearing of events, but it took Dalan's persuasive, patient tones to calm him.

"There will be much to discuss," said the High Druid. "And much to plan. Get all the rest you can."

Elak retired and soon after, Lycon and Darruvia also. In the King's bedchamber, Elak and Shiveeri lay on the bed and held each other among the shadows, and he realized whatever had transpired across the ocean, it had left its mark on her. She was not withdrawn from him, but she was tense, uneasy and unsettled. When he fell asleep, she remained awake for a long time, her eyes fixed on the darkness outside, though her thoughts were a vacuum.

It was some time after dawn when Elak woke. He cursed himself for sleeping so late, turning to Shiveeri, only to find she was not beside him. He rose and sluiced his face with cold water to revive himself and washed, donning fresh clothes. Shiveeri was in another room, seated near the terrace that looked out over the spectacular Bay of Gold. He put an arm around her, kissing her lightly. She smiled but did not respond with her usual ardour.

"We must join the others," she said in a slightly mechanical way that puzzled him.

She is not herself, he told himself. *For all her natural strength and fierce determination, she, too, is human.*

When the two of them joined Dalan and Lycon, with a few other dignitaries in attendance including Zerrahydris and various Councillors, they sat around a large table and enjoyed a modest breakfast, with chilled water. Lycon drank this without complaint, and Elak noted the fact. Once, his companion of many years would never have settled for less than wine.

"You slept well?" said Elak softly to Lycon, who sat, as always beside him, as the others talked among themselves while eating.

"I did. And without dreams, though my memory of the things we were shown returned quickly enough when I woke."

"And Darruvia? Did she say anything at all about her abduction?"

"No. She seemed listless and fell asleep almost as soon as she got into bed. I didn't disturb her, much as I desired her. I think our wives had a far worse experience than we realized."

Lycon's sensitivity surprised Elak. The King knew him well enough for a kind, considerate man, but he was nothing if not lively, the first to brush aside emotions and drive on with the business of living. Darruvia had changed him, and listening to him now, Elak could feel his deep concern.

"Shiveeri also," Elak said. "Who brought them home, do you know?"

"It was Carraverin."

Has he returned to Illyrin?"

"No, I believe he awaits us, and will make his report."

"We'll hear it privately." Elak was conscious that Shiveeri was looking at him, her face bland, although he wondered if she had heard his soft exchange with Lycon. The moment passed, however, and Elak rose.

"Events in the wider world are conspiring to bring about the war we have been fearing," he said, his voice carrying around the high walls of the chamber. No one spoke, all eyes on the King, the faces of the Councillors lined with their grave anxiety. No one underestimated the threat to Atlantis, or to civilization itself. "I have seen what is gathering." Elak went on to describe in great detail what he and his companions had been shown in the undersea citadel of Yllythur of the Meruvians, and when he had finished, his revelations punctuated by the gasps of astonishment of the assembly, both Dalan and Lycon added to the King's summary.

"We know the plans and conspiracies of our enemy are devious and completely callous. Shortly before I was taken by the Aquarri to their city, there were events in this very palace to make one's blood curdle. As you know, an attempt was made to abduct the children of myself and Lycon. Mercifully it failed. The gods alone know what horrific purposes lie behind this, and we'll not linger on this. What does concern us, however, is the abduction of the Queen and Darruvia.

"They are with us now, and have consented to share with us the details of their abduction and of how they escaped the clutches of the sorcerers behind it, the accursed Vannadril, creatures who work for the monstrous forces behind all this perfidy." He turned to Shiveeri and Darruvia, and slowly both rose, ready to contribute to the discussion. Both were remarkably composed, and when the Queen spoke, her voice was firm, with no hint of distress. She delivered her words bluntly and with little emotion.

Elak was surprised she did so without showing signs of her customary anger at such things, her temper that could so easily flair when she was roused by fury. He glanced once or twice at Lycon, and it was clear to the King that Lycon at least was as puzzled by this as he was.

*

In the darkened chamber, far below the upper palace, Elak, Dalan and Lycon waited while the guards brought Carraverin to them. The sky lizard rider appeared relaxed. Elak would have forgiven him for being a little nervous in front of him and his companions, but the young warrior simply bowed patiently before the three seated men, preferring to stand.

"You are to be thanked for your part in the rescue of our wives," said Elak. "They have both given us a detailed account of it, but I should like to hear more."

"Of course, lord. It was a frantic experience." Carraverin went over the events in which he had been involved, talking quickly but smoothly, leaving out no details, his eyes fixed on a point ahead of him as though he were seeing and re-living everything. As he spoke, Elak looked sideways at Dalan, who listened to every word with deep concentration. He and Elak exchanged a discreet look, a reference to unspoken questions.

"This pool on the island," said Dalan when Carraverin had concluded his report. "You all slept beside it?"

"We did, sire."

"Was it a troubled sleep?"

Carraverin frowned for a moment, but then shook his head. "No. We were all exhausted. If we had dreams, we do not recall them."

"The Queen said that?" said Dalan.

For a moment Carraverin's brow creased in a frown. "Yes. We do not recall the dreams."

"The Queen and Darruvia both had dreams?" Dalan persisted.

Carraverin hesitated, again frowning, apparently puzzled. "Yes. But none of us can recall them."

He's using the present tense, thought Elak, and could see

Dalan had also noted this. The High Druid had brought with him a flattish, rounded pebble, its dull surface marked with various sigils. He handed this to Carraverin, who reached out and took it automatically. "Hold it tightly," said Dalan.

Carraverin did so and almost at once the sweat broke out on his forehead and he shuddered. He could not release the stone.

"Tell us about your dreams," said Dalan softly, his voice coaxing.

Carraverin's eyes opened wide, and he looked out at something beyond the chamber. "I saw... I saw the pool move. Something rose from it. The two ladies were asleep, not moving. I had tried to stay awake, to guard them, but could not. In my sleep I saw the pool move." He became agitated, his body trembling. "There! See it rising! They are awake! It steps towards the Queen!"

"Describe it," said Dalan, quietly, though his voice held power.

"Taller than a man, a thing of the sea, with long arms, claws, its lower body is...is...not a man! A sea-thing. It reaches out, touches their heads. I cannot move. Gods, help me, I am transfixed. Sorcery! My blade is useless." Tears were coursing down the young warrior's face and he struggled as though his body was caught in a steel grip. Eventually he twisted aside. "It's leaving. Going back into the pool. I can break free. Get between the women and the creature. I try to attack it, but it brushes me aside with its evil.

"Shiveeri helps me to my feet. Neither she nor Darruvia are harmed. The thing has gone back under the water. Did they not see it?"

"What did they say?" said Dalan.

"That I was dreaming. That there was nothing to see."

Dalan took back the stone and put it away. "But you saw this thing from the pool?"

Carraverin shook his head. "No! It was just a dream. I cannot recall it. Neither can Shiveeri or Darruvia."

"Very well," said Dalan. "Get more rest. You have served your mistress well."

Elak and Lycon watched as the guards lead the bemused warrior away. Elak's anger was scarcely under control, as if he would strike out at anything that moved. "This explains my wife's lethargy. She is under some spell, the work of this creature from the pool."

"As is Darruvia," said Lycon. "I knew something was amiss. What does it mean, Dalan? Are they in danger"

"It is they who are dangerous. They may be used –" His face clouded as a new, terrifying thought struck him. "We must go to them at once."

*

When the three men reached the upper palace, they found a number of the guards milling around outside the royal chambers, panicking.

"Open the doors!" shouted Elak. "Quickly! The Queen may again need our help."

"We cannot open them, sire," said the captain on duty. "They have been barred from within."

"Who is in there?"

"The Queen and Darruvia. No one else, other than the royal children."

A look of absolute horror twisted Elak's face. "The children! By the Nine Hells, this is another attempt at their lives!" He swung round to Dalan. "The doors! Dalan, use whatever force is needed, but blast them aside! Let us pray we are not too late!"

*

Far from Epharra, high up in Shunn-Ul-Darza's vast citadel, the Vannadril sat on their stone thrones and watched as the creature rose from the pool below them. Its aquatic features studied them, its wide eyes gleaming with reflected light from the moon beyond the open ceiling. A twisted joy was in those unblinking orbs. Its telepathic voice spoke clearly in their minds.

Soon, masters, it will be done. This time the King's offspring will be dealt with. The abduction may have failed, but this way will be better. Elak and his consort and all the others closest to him will be racked with grief and ultimately madness. Epharra and all her minions will be dealt such a blow as they will never recover from. What better time to launch the invasion, while all in Atlantis is in chaos?

Chapter Twelve: Return of the Serpent

Moonlight silvered the wharves and quays of the tiny port, nestled on the western coast of Mallomas, once a stronghold of the renegade pirate confederation. In the taverns, a mixed company of sailors from many parts of the Atlantean world, men and women who had voyaged to its far reaches and who had defied fate's attempts to send them and their ships to the ocean's bottom, drank together and exchanged wild tales, vying for the limelight, showing their samples of treasure pilfered from one lost temple or another. Among the crowd in one of the smaller taverns that backed on to a tall cliff, Eskarra and the bulk of her crew revelled with the best, or worst of them, filling the pungent air with song and noise. Artugol and Volnus were among the company, though they, like their captain, were not abandoned, even if they gave that impression. All three of them were on alert.

Since returning from the strange island where they had helped the Atlantean Queen and her companion to escape the clutches of the Vannadril, they had been holed up here on Mallomas, awaiting word from Dalan, High Druid of the King. After a week, no word had yet come, and the ship of Dalan's right hand Druid, Emmaneus had not appeared. Eskarra had become impatient and swore whatever the weather brought on the morning tide the *Arrow* would sail. Artugol had given up attempting to dissuade her, but he knew there were times when Eskarra was immovable in her resolve, and this was one of them.

"We should be out there, searching as many islands as we can for more signs of the peril in the north," she said, mouth set.

Artugol turned to Volnus, but his big companion shrugged, about to voice his capitulation to Eskarra's plans, when another of the *Arrow* crew abruptly joined them, his bright eyes hinting at news.

"What is it, Rastak?" said Eskarra. "Is it the King's ship?"

"No, captain," said the youth. "But there is a ship. You know its captain, Andarban, who once sailed with you."

Eskarra grunted. "A renegade if ever there was one. I always knew he'd command his own ship one day. His crew will be as rough and ready as any other on the ocean. Why should I be interested in him?"

"He's berthed at the far end of the harbour."

"Hardly surprising," Eskarra said, her look one of disdain. "There aren't many here on Mallomars who'd make him welcome. If the Druid comes, he won't mince words with Andarban either. It might even mean a fight."

"He wants to talk to you," said the youth, clearly nervous.

"The last time I saw him, before he jumped ship and made for the open seas in search of his own private glory, he tried to persuade me to share a tussle in the pelts with him." Artugol scowled. "You never mentioned him before."

"Why should I? He was a rat. He thought his sword would persuade me to accept his gross attention, but I used my own to teach him otherwise. I would have opened his gut with it if the others hadn't prevented it. So, Rastak, what is it the sea scum wants?"

"His men caught me unawares and forced me before him. He was guarded in what he said, but hinted at news about the enemy. No more than that. He said you'd know what he meant."

Eskarra looked at both Artugol and Volnus. "The enemy? There was a time when Andarban would have called Elak enemy, whom he swore he would never serve. But now, I think he means something else."

"Our mutual enemy," suggested Volnus. "Perhaps he has word of those in the north."

"It wouldn't do any harm to find out," said Artugol.

Eskarra fell silent for a few moments. "How many are with him?" she said to Rastak.

"His ship, the *Red Wolf*, is not a large vessel. Fifty hands, no more."

"Do you think he has abduction in mind?" said Artugol.

This time Eskarra laughed. "Here on Mallomas that would be a foolish ploy. There are rules in this place that even vermin like Andarban would adhere to, if he values his hide."

"So you'll see him?" said Volnus.

"Call the men together. We'll pay Andarban a visit, but if he wants to conduct business, we'll do it on the quayside, with plenty of swords behind us and under the eyes of the harbour watch. Even so, be ready to use your blades."

*

The night was almost cloudless, the moon full, a brilliant eye overhead, the quay side well lit. Torches on the harbour wall fluttered in a light breeze, adding to the glare as the two parties moved towards each other on the neutral dockside. Eskarra could see the bloated figure of Andarban leading his cut-throats towards her. He was overweight, but she knew in a fight he would use his strength to great advantage, and he was no mean swordsman, a dangerous opponent for anyone. No doubt the half dozen pirates he had chosen to accompany him were equally as skilled. For now, all their swords were sheathed.

Andarban raised his massive be-ringed right hand in greeting. "I've not come for a contest," he said in his deep, phlegmy voice. "No need for bloodshed here."

Eskarra stood several feet away from him, more than ready to use her rapier on him if he as much as blinked with evil intent. Never a man to be trusted, he stood before her a little uncomfortably, as if unaccustomed to being on land, and his words were slurred, though not, she thought, with drink. Maybe he was afflicted by something. She studied the men around him. They, too, had a strange bearing, their eyes narrowed, observing Eskarra and her companions coldly.

"What is your business with me?" she said.

"There has been enmity between us," he said. "You went your way and I mine. But a time is coming when all pirates need to stand together. I have seen a storm coming that may wither the world."

"The lone wolves won't survive."

"I understand that. I have seen strange islands in the uncharted ocean. Heard things. Something powerful stirs in the deeps. I fear it, as all men should."

"And?"

"You serve the King. It is known you have dealings with the Druid, Emmaneus."

"Why should that concern the likes of you?"

"It is said that pirates who cast off their independence and swear loyalty to the King are pardoned and permitted to serve him." Andarban turned his gaze into the shadows behind Eskarra, where the large form of Ormullah was part of her company.

"And you would do that?" She looked at him sceptically. He looked even more shifty and untrustworthy than she remembered.

"I would. I have nothing to gain by lying. I have seen many sea colleagues turn to the King's banner. Some fought for him at Skaafelda."

"And earned his trust."

"When the next conflict begins, I will fight for Elak."

She nodded, though her face remained fixed in a scowl. "You've come to your senses. So how does this affect me?"

"Take me to the Druid when he next comes. Speak on my behalf. My crew and I will lay our arms down before him and swear loyalty. I ask no more than that."

She studied him for long moments, then nodded.

"My ship is the *Red Wolf*. It will remain moored here until you send for me."

Andarban turned and with a few words to his men, headed back along the quay to where his vessel awaited him in the shadows. Eskarra watched them go, her face a mask of suspicion.

"Is this a trap?" said Artugol.

"Perhaps, and yet, what has he to gain? He knows it would be a fool's game to remain his own master. There are few such now, with war coming. The enemy has no need to recruit vermin like him. His only hope for survival is under the King's flag."

Volnus was nodding. "It's true that others like him have already capitulated. As he said, men died at Skaafelda who were once privateers."

"It's a matter for Emmaneus," said Eskarra.

"So we wait here a little longer for him?" said Artugol.

Eskarra swore softly. "Yes. At least I can warn him about Andarban's nature. Not that his manner wouldn't give it away."

"There was a stench of deceit about him and those seamen," said Ormullah behind her. "When I quit privateering, it was through Shiveeri, whom I'd always respected. Andarban's greed is poisonous."

Eskarra nodded. "When we next meet them, we'll keep up a pretence of acceptance."

*

In his cabin on board the *Red Wolf,* Andarban bolted the door and opened a drawer of an old cabinet, lifting aside a number of charts and papers. There was a small bundle of cloth beneath them, and he took it out, unwrapping it to reveal a brightly gleaming jewel the size of a plate. He set it on the table and pressed the largest of the rings on his right hand to the centre of the jewel. At once it flared, glowing like a mirror, its surface opaque but becoming clearer until it revealed a chamber where torches kept the night at bay. Several figures sat in the chamber, the Vannadril on Shunn-Ul-Darza.

Aarrzoruuk, their leader, spoke, his voice coming clearly through the jewel as if he were in the cabin. "Have you made contact, Azzarak? Did your disguise fool the pirate bitch?"

Should anyone else have seen into the cabin, they would not have observed the sea captain, but instead the bulky form of the serpent man, who had taken on his true guise for this conversation. "Yes. She and her crew saw only the human wretch they knew as Andarban. They have no love for him, but it is no matter. His plea for sanctuary would have sounded genuine to them, given the danger he'd have been in if he'd not offered service to the King."

"Where is Andarban and his crew?"

The jaws of the serpent man opened, revealing the rows of pointed teeth in a vague semblance of a human smile. "Feeding the fishes in the deep waters off the nearest reef. When Emmaneus arrives, it will be me and my crew waiting to embrace him and his master. It will be an easy matter to dispatch them all."

"No. Maintain your disguise. We need spies among the King's fleet. To bring us word of his every move. While our forces prepare for the invasion, you will work from within, like rats gnawing at Elak's innards."

Azzarak's serpent smile widened. "As you wish, master. It will all end the same way, with the extinction of the humans."

*

Elak and Lycon had almost lost their patience, both waiting outside the royal bedchambers, wanting to beat at the doors, but knowing they would hold fast against any attempt to shatter them. After what seemed an eternity, Dalan returned, carrying with him one of the long staffs of power. He ushered Elak and Lycon aside and set the tip of the staff against the centre of the door, beginning an incantation. At once the rod began to glow and in moments it emitted a high, whining note, culminating in a brilliant flash of light that sent everyone staggering backwards in the blast. The great door shattered like glass, smoke billowing.

Elak was the first to leap through the opening. There was dim light beyond, and in its thin rays, the King saw into his children's bedchamber. The Queen stood over the bed where they were laying among the bed sheets. She turned to Elak and smiled, but it was a strange, unemotional smile, and it sent a cold shiver through him. *Am I in time?* his mind screamed.

Chapter Thirteen: The Kiss of Evil

Emmaneus leaned back in the chair, considering Eskarra's report. They sat across a narrow table in the Druid's cabin in his ship that had docked in Mallomas shortly before. Artugol and Volnus were also in the cabin, their faces as creased with unease as Eskarra's.

"Is it possible," said Artugol, "that Andarban has been won over by the enemy, and sent to spy on the King's forces?"

Emmaneus frowned. "All the evidence so far demonstrates the enemy's contempt for us and our allies. And there have been a number of other pirate captains, just as unscrupulous and self-seeking as Andarban, if not more so, who have come over to us. Did he say what he has seen?"

Eskarra shook her head. "No, but he has voyaged to remote regions, so may have useful information about islands taken by the enemy."

"That could be invaluable. If I accept his request to serve the King, it will be a risk, but if it wins us such knowledge, it could affect our war strategy. Possibly vitally." Emmaneus studied his hands, as though the answer resided in them. He did not seem to the others to be an indecisive man, but they understood how crucial his next words would be. "Rejecting him might do more harm than good," he said at last. "It could rebound on us. What does he want most? Riches, treasure, the usual spoils of piracy?"

"Greed was always his failing," said Eskarra. "And he would never accept anyone else as his master."

"Then I'll meet him. Confirm his command of his ship, in the name of the King. And promise him a hull fold of gold if he truly fights alongside our line of battle. But you, Eskarra, must keep close to him. Work with him."

"He won't accept my authority," she said contemptuously.

"No, but he'll accept mine, as a condition of his service to the King."

"It will be a dangerous game," said Artugol.

"It's war, Artugol. There will be few compromises."

*

Elak went to Shiveeri cautiously, not wanting to trigger anything that would endanger the children. They appeared to be unharmed, fast asleep.

"I was about to kiss them goodnight," she said, bending over them in preparation. Her lips were slightly parted as she lowered her face over the boy, Helmas.

Elak barely had time to take her arm and tug her aside. She resisted at once, a sudden hiss escaping the lips that would have, what? planted a deathly seed? As Elak pulled her back, her eyes were filmed over, slitting in a way that made his blood curdle, and her hands swept towards him, fingernails tearing at him like the claws of a jungle beast. Something dreadful possessed her, infused with her and that remote island. He lurched back to avoid her vicious lunge. There was a low stool behind him, and his calves hit it as he ducked another swipe of those claws, knocking him off balance, toppling him to the thick pelts on the floor.

Shiveeri stood over him triumphantly, a look of wild fury transforming her into something demonic as she prepared to administer what could have been a bloody death. As she was about to launch herself, a bolt of white light struck her and deflected her. She fell and rolled, sitting up slowly, dazed. She looked confused, her expression less feral. Dalan had entered the chamber and he went to her and put a hand on her head, speaking the words of an incantation or prayer, as Elak watched in horror, getting to his feet. Beyond him Lycon had rushed towards the bedchamber of his son.

He almost collided with Darruvia, whose hands reached out for her son, but Lycon was faster, dragging her back. Behind him Dalan flicked his wrist and a ball of white light struck her chest and sucked the fury from her, dropping her to her knees. Lycon bent over her, holding her gently. "Is she mad? What has happened?" he gasped.

"The boy!" cried Elak. "Is he safe?"

"He's asleep. But what has happened?"

Dalan went to Darruvia, touching her forehead. "Something on that island," he said. He coaxed Darruvia to her feet and guided her into the main chamber and set her beside Shiveeri, getting both to kneel. Once they were side by side, he placed a hand on each of their heads. Both were supine now, eyes partially closed. Again Dalan spoke and as he did so the two women began to shiver, then shudder, growling like animals. Dalan fell back and both Elak and Lycon watched in stupefaction as something began to emerge from the mouths of both women, a greenish mist that started to solidify.

Elak snatched his rapier and prepared to rip into the thing, but Dalan checked him. At first the entity was a misshapen, humped being, the size of a man, but with no clear features, and elongated arms and legs like the fat tendrils of a sea creature. Dalan reached for the rod he had set down and, lifting it, jabbed at the thing. Light fizzed like an ignited fire, and as it dimmed, the creature changed, becoming more human, a warrior in golden armour, dazzling, its facial features possessing rare handsomeness.

"I am not your enemy," it said, its voice musical and seductive. "I have come to welcome you to the new glory, to the kingdom of the Gods from the Stars." It opened its arms and as it did so, Elak rushed forward, ignoring Dalan's attempt to forestall him, and plunged his blade deep into the creature's throat and beyond. There was another blinding flash of light and then darkness, an impenetrable cloud that plunged the chamber into total oblivion.

*

They met again on the quay side, Emmaneus and his immediate guards standing alongside Eskarra, Artugol and Volnus as the pirate captain, Andarban, came from the shadows, his ship behind him outlined by the rising sun's rays. He bowed low before the Druid, his teeth showing in a wolf-like smile. A dozen of his own crew stood beside him, as silent as the rocks overhead.

"Thank you for this meeting," said Andarban. "I know the Empire sees me as a thorn in its side, as with many of my sea-faring brethren. But these are troubled times, my lord."

Emmaneus, a large man, puffed himself up, enjoying his position, and spoke solemnly. "I gather you are prepared to swear fealty to the King. If you do, it must be without compromise. You will be under instruction from me. There will be no more private enterprises, and when the time comes to use your sword, it will be in the King's name."

Andarban carefully slid his curved weapon from his belt and lowered it to the quay. His men did the same. "That is agreed, lord. We are yours to command, our swords at your disposal."

"I have a small fleet here," Emmaneus went on, his arm sweeping back in a gesture that revealed the panorama of the bay and its moored craft, most of them pirate vessels, all now an element of the King's fleet. "Your ship, the *Red Fox*, will join it?"

"It will. Give us our orders and we will carry them out happily, from this hour, if it is your wish."

Eskarra and her two immediate companions were watching the burly pirate like hawks, in particular his face, searching for clues as to what it was that yet made them uneasy in his presence, the shadow behind him, which all of them had sensed.

"There is one thing," Andarban said. "You have good reason to question my honesty, as it has not been a feature of my nature until now." He laughed softly at his own jest. "Why should you trust me, eh? Well, let me give you something, a token of my desire to serve your master."

Emmaneus's expression remained formal. "Very well."

"Information, lord. Something which helped to decide my coming to you. Information about the enemy, and his movements."

Emmaneus's attention was now fixed clearly on the pirate. "What have you found?"

"As you know, these waters have many islands, some too small to warrant much attention. They are in the main disregarded, a haven for the gulls and other sea birds. They are, however, useful to the likes of me and other freebooters, a good place to shelter in a storm, or from the attention of your spies. I can give you details of several of these."

"Small beer," Volnus said to Eskarra and Artugol softly. "Hardly of value."

"Not in itself a prize," said Andarban, as if he had heard Volnus. "But there is one island in particular you should know about. It has no name and is generally ignored. But not by the enemy."

"You have seen something?" said Emmaneus.

"Yes. By chance, when we were taking on water. There's an old ruin there, a crumbling remnant from a remote past. We saw men there who were not men, more like creatures of the sea. They had made the temple a base and were gathering in numbers. As if in preparation."

"For what?" said Emmaneus.

Andarban shrugged his broad shoulders. "I could only guess, lord. But they had weapons, and there were small ships moored off the shore. I could show you this island."

Volnus moved closer to Eskarra and Artugol and again spoke in a low voice. "It's a trap. He's a fool if he thinks Emmaneus will fall for it."

Emmaneus was silent for long moments. He considered Andarban's words and the silence closed in around him as he deliberated. Eventually he spoke. "This is of great interest to me. Very well. We will visit the island. But under certain conditions."

"Name them, lord. I merely wish to establish my genuine desire to stand with you and the King."

"We will take several ships. You, Andarban, will join

me on mine, and some of your crew will join others. If there is to be any treachery – no, I am not accusing you of anything – but if there is to be duplicity, which, as you say, you have been a party to in the past, you and your men will be executed and fed to the sharks." Emmaneus said this with a convincing firmness.

Andarban laughed, a hollow sound. "Well, lord, that's no more than I would have expected. Very well. I agree. We will spread ourselves. And what of the *Red Wolf*? Will you have your men board her and sail with the rest of my crew?"

"Yes. This will be a good test for our new alliance."

Eskarra turned to her companions. "He puts himself at a strong disadvantage," she said. "One false step and we'll cut them all down."

Artugol kept a straight face. "Maybe. But I'm wondering what's on that island."

*

Elak was the first to raise himself. Light was returning to the chamber. He felt renewed panic as he rose, reaching for the rapier he had dropped. Lycon stirred beside him and the two of them went to the bed, where the two children were still asleep, mercifully unharmed. Lamps glowed anew and Dalan stood with Shiveeri. Darruvia, who appeared to be as alert as any of them, emitted a gasp and rushed out of the chamber, returning in a few moments with her son gathered to her. He appeared to be half asleep, but unaware of the previous chaos. Lycon joined them and hugged them to him, hugely relieved.

Dalan pointed to the fading pool where the golden warrior had stood. "Your strike sent it back to whatever hell it emerged from," he told Elak.

The King went to Shiveeri and studied her bewildered

face. She looked as if she had just woken from a particularly potent nightmare.

"What has happened?" she said, confused.

The pool reduced and became no more than a dark stain on the tiles. Elak put an arm around his wife. "You don't remember?"

"There was an island," she said hesitantly. "In my dream. A golden warrior, who promised a new dawn of glory for Atlantis. Darruvia shared the dream."

"It's over," said Dalan. "One more failed attempt by the enemy. It won't be the last. We must treble our vigilance."

"Everyone get some sleep," said Elak. "In the morning we will conclude our preparations for war. We are agreed, Dalan? We strike first, at this newly risen island, Shunn-Ul-Darza?"

"Yes. Word has come from the Picts, united under Kaa Mag Borga, and from as far south as Zangarza, where Hamniri already has a fleet ready to sail north to swell our numbers. And there are many others. We must move with all speed."

*

"Azzarak has done well," said the Vannadril leader as the latest vision from the jewel faded. "The humans think they are dealing with the pirate, Andarban. He is taking them to the Isle of the Serpent. This pompous Druid, Emmaneus, will take a strong party ashore, no doubt to protect himself, but Azzarak will be with him. There will be a full moon, a fine omen for the serpent men, who worship it as Saaraaza, their Moon God. Urzook of the Orugllyr is ready in the waters beyond the island. Its ruined temple is so much more than heaped, crumbling stones."

Chapter Fourteen: The Isle of the Serpent

Ormullah crossed the beach with the second wave of Eskarra's crew, lifting his head like a great hound scenting the air. He growled deep in his chest, a sound his fellows new well: it presaged a burst of temper, usually vented in a curse. However the huge man held himself in check, not wishing to disturb the tranquillity of this island. Instead he pressed forward through the first ranks until he reached Eskarra and her immediate companions, who were preparing to follow Andarban and his men from the *Red Wolf* up into the trees.

"You look puzzled," Volnus said to the *Arrow's* oars master.

"I captained a crew of my own once," Ormullah muttered. "Before I threw in my lot with Shiveeri, and was ultimately assigned to Eskarra and this crew. In those days, I visited many places, islands off the chart. A lot were alike, small islets, no more than sources of water and supplies. But I recall one of them that was unique."

"How?"

"The smell. Stale, rotten, a nest gone bad, choked, maybe with carcasses of creatures that died to feed whatever lived there. We never found out, but I knew that smell. The stench of a snake pit."

Volnus scowled. "There is something in the air here."

"It's the same smell, the same island. I've been here before."

"Does this island have a name?"

"None that I know."

Eskarra had seen the two men talking quietly and joined them. "You are ill at ease," she said to Ormullah.

The oars master repeated what he had told Volnus.

"The smell, yes," said Eskarra. "Like a stronger scent of Andarban and his men. Have they been infected by this place?"

"What is it?" said Artugol. "Something animal?"

"This is not a place for men," said Ormullah, hand tightening on his sword hilt.

"We knew that before we came," said Eskarra. "Andarban saw men who were not men. Orugllyr. If they've been here in number, their stench would permeate the place."

"It's not a smell of the sea," said Ormullah.

Emmaneus, some distance ahead of them with a party of his own crew, waved them forward. As the company moved, they did so more warily, weapons drawn. Overhead the skies were cloudless, the sun strong, but among the trees and low vegetation, there were shadows.

Eskarra joined the Druid. "This is a well-beaten path," she said. "Many have been here before us."

"Andarban was right," Emmaneus replied. The pirate captain had gone on ahead, though he and his crew were still visible among the undergrowth. "Not human. This is clearly an outpost of the enemy."

"Do you smell something in its air? Something rank."

"Yes. It has tainted Andarban and his men, as it may us if we linger here too long. We will remain here only as long as we must to learn its secret and then go back to Epharra."

"What is it?"

"I did not want to set fear among the sailors. These anonymous islands are steeped in legends. One of which concerns an ancient cult, worshipers of snake gods that existed at the time of the Valusian Empire. Long extinct, though they have left their mark, it seems."

"Serpents!" said Eskarra. "Yes, that smell – I recognize it now."

"You must not panic the men. If we are attacked by the Orugllyr or whatever else haunts this island, we must be prepared. Fear will weaken their resolve."

Ahead of them, Andarban waved back, ushering them to him, and Emmaneus moved forward again, his own blade unsheathed. Soon the entire company had assembled in a small clearing and Andarban pointed ahead to a steeply rising but low bank.

"Beyond that," he said. "It's where the enemy gather, by night. Send scouts if you like, Emmaneus. If it is clear, we should find out what the sea vermin are about."

The Druid selected men from his own crew and others from Eskarra's and they followed Andarban up the slope, fanning out before cresting it. Artugol was among them and at the top of the bank he looked down into a wide space with the distinct appearance of an amphitheatre, something certainly artificially made. At its heart was a jumble of rocks that could once have been blocks of stone, hewn by whoever had set them there originally, in the form of a building, possibly a temple. The huge stones were cracked and overgrown, long disused.

"A perfect base for the Orugllyr," Artugol said softly to Eskarra beside him. She nodded, watching as Andarban and his crew moved down the inner side of the bank, which was devoid of undergrowth, cleared down to the thick, knotted grass. The amphitheatre was also open, the only weeds and twisted vines clinging to the ruins, a dark green blanket. A shift in the breeze brought a sudden gust of the nauseating smell to the intruders, as if it had emerged from the ruins and any number of their gaping holes.

Andarban came to Emmaneus and Eskarra. "The enemy isn't likely to come until nightfall. I suggest we camp on this bank. Set guards around us."

"What is that place?" said the Druid, indicating the ruins.

"The enemy uses it to hide," said Andarban. "My men and I have seen them emerge. It must lead to tunnels beneath the sea, connecting this island to others. A network that would be part of the enemy's bridgehead."

Emmaneus nodded. "If so, this will be vital knowledge for the King. Very well, we will camp here and wait for the moon. It will be full tonight."

*

Emmaneus had spread his crew and those of both Eskarra and Andarban around the circular bank, under cover of its stunted trees and shrubs. The tension among the watchers heightened as the day wore into evening, Andarban's men keeping their distance from those of the Atlanteans, who yet viewed them with suspicion. Eskarra was like a caged tigress, barely able to sustain her patience, and Ormullah was in favour of checking the ruins at the heart of the clearing, in spite of the brooding atmosphere that clung to them. Some of the company dozed, while others indulged in quiet small talk or banter, but all were relieved when the sun fell into the west and the moon held sway. It was particularly effulgent, the silent landscape vividly lit by its radiance. Soon after it reached its zenith, dull sounds were heard, emanating from under the earth.

Artugol pointed to the ruins. "Something stirs within."

Volnus had been studying the vegetation outside the mound. "We are not alone," he said. "Movements out there." Those around him craned their necks, everyone alerted.

"It's a trap," said Eskarra. "We're surrounded." She

was about to call out to Emmaneus, when shouts and the clash of steel rang from along the top of the bank. Figures broke from it and in the garish moon-glow Andarban could be seen, leading his crew down the inner side of the bank, sword raised as if in salute to the huge orb.

"Blood for Saaraaza, Moon Goddess!" he shouted, and as one, his crew raised their own weapons in salute. In the wash of light, he changed, his shape shifting, his face blurring and then becoming a new visage, its elongated features highlighted by the moonlight.

"Serpent man!" cried Volnus. "I have heard of these creatures. That's not Andarban. That monster replicated him."

Azzarak's followers sloughed off their human guises and now formed a line of snarling beasts, waiting for the command to attack.

Eskarra watched the trees beyond the bank, down on the slope of the island, where massed ranks of more enemies were climbing upward, closing the net. "We must hold this high ground!" she shouted and Emmaneus called back an affirmative as he readied his own defence. They all watched as the vegetation came alive and disgorged whole ranks of Orugllyr. Although the sea beings were not armed, their extended claws were as deadly as any weapons, and as they came up to the bank, their eyes gleaming in the moonlight, they presented a formidable mass, a powerful tide.

Artugol looked back into the inner clearing, expecting to see the serpent men come back up the slope to hack into them with their blades, but they were holding their line, apparently waiting for a signal. Azzarak was facing the ruins, from which the deep sounds were increasing in volume, like oncoming thunder. As Artugol watched, several of the biggest chunks of stone tumbled to one side, revealing a wide black opening, from which emanated a sickening stench, a far stronger version of the smell permeating the island. The concentrated reek of serpents.

As he watched, mesmerized, Artugol saw a huge, flattish head emerge from the darkness, its mouth opening to reveal a fat, darting tongue, its slitted eyes ablaze with reflected moonlight. The serpent was vast, uncoiling itself and pushing yet more stones aside with ease. Azzarak shouted out to it, bowing down, and his serpent warriors did the same. Before Artugol could react, the Orugllyr were coming up the bank towards its defenders and within moments the battle had begun, with the violence of a storm tide crashing on a rocky shore.

All around the circumference of the bank the fighting seethed, wave upon wave of Orugllyr pouring forward, their numbers hugely outweighing the defenders, who were forced inexorably backwards, down the bank and into the amphitheatre. Many of the attackers were cut down, swords driven into their eyes and throats, and they fell, to be trampled by a succeeding wave. Eskarra paused from the relentless killing only for a moment to lock stares with Artugol.

"At least we'll die together!" she said, laughing.

"Maybe not," he shouted. "See! Not one of our number has fallen."

"You're right," she said, amazed. "I don't understand—they're not trying to kill us."

Artugol's attention switched to the towering shape of the serpent, its shadow falling across the amphitheatre, a premonition of doom. "They're trying to herd us!"

"To feed that thing!" Eskarra gasped. She called out to her crew, reorganizing their defence, coming down off the bank.

Azzarak's teeth were gleaming in a rictus of triumph. "Come to us!" he snarled. "Come and bow to the Serpent God!"

Artugol gasped as he realized what Azzarak really intended. "Once they've sacrificed us to that monster, they mean to replace us with replicas, just as they did with Andarban and his crew. When the King's forces reach these islands, they'll be infiltrated by serpent spies."

Chapter Fifteen: Under the Eye of the Moon God

Elak stood in the high prow of his warship, the *Epharran Queen*, gazing around him at the immense fleet he had gathered to his banner. Not only were the finest of Atlantean vessels here in line, but also numerous smaller fleets from around the coastal waters of most of the continent, all of whose kings and rulers had answered the call to action, to take the war to the Vannadril and the dark gods from the stars. Elak's Royal Wing, the powerful sky lizards of Illyrin, were here in force, used to fly messengers with all speed to as many far-flung ships of the massed navy as possible, and already had established regular contact with the great Pictish force from the western isles and the assembled fleets of the Atlantean eastern seaboard, as far south as Zangarza. All were sailing northward now in a sweeping arc that would form a wide net around the southern coast of the alien island, Shunn-Ul-Darza, in a rapid entrapment that was expected to take the invaders by surprise and pre-empt their own assault plans.

In the hold of Elak's flagship were the casks that held the armour wrought from the God-Heart Stone, locked away until the moment came for the prime warriors of Atlantis to don it, and with them were many of the ancient Valusian weapons taken from the golden city of Amon Thuul as well as the three great staves of power in readiness for the oncoming battles. In the seas below and around the ships, a secondary fleet moved forward as sleekly as sea beasts, the combined strength of the Aquarri from their scattered undersea realms. With them, in the deepest parts of the ocean, the Deepwhales had gathered in an unprecedented show of power, and with them were countless shoals of smaller sea-killers, including sharks in their countless packs.

Beside Elak stood Shiveeri, no less intent on leading the attack than the King, and for once he had not tried to dissuade her from coming into what would be a dreadful cauldron of conflict. Whatever fate had in store for them, they would face it side by side, to the last stroke of their blades. Darruvia stood likewise with Lycon, equally as committed to him, and he to her. Across the entire fleet its men and women warriors were ready for their mettle to be tested, and for victory if the gods willed it.

Dalan joined the King, his face set grimly, studying the open ocean ahead of them and the racing, troubled clouds above it. "I have heard no more from Emmaneus," he said. "He went to Mallomas, where Eskarra awaited him on her ship, the *Arrow*."

"She has proved a valuable ally," said Shiveeri. "Darruvia and I owe her and her crew our lives."

Dalan nodded. "She and Emmaneus sailed north, in search of something, among the unknown islands. She left word of that, but no more. I wonder if she's learned of our enemy's movements in those islands. They'll have their own spies at work."

"Is the Royal Wing pursuing her?" said Elak.

"Yes, though there are numerous aerial horrors in the skies around Shunn-Ul-Darza."

*

The moon was swollen, a huge ball in the skies above the ruins, which formed a rumpled silhouette against the sky. Towering over them, the weaving serpent's head dipped, its long, forked tongue flicking from its mouth, its breath hissing. Azzarak's sword wove patterns in the air, as though conducting the movements of the great beast, and his serpent men warriors lined up beside him, swaying rhythmically. Others had come forward from the darkness, beings who the company guessed, were to be the vehicles for the replication.

"The serpent's eyes!" shouted Emmaneus from somewhere among the assembled crews of the Atlantean ships. "Do not look at them!"

Eskarra tore her gaze from the twin saucers of the serpent's baleful gaze, and together with Artugol, Volnus and others, rushed forward to attack the serpent men. Having realized they wanted the humans as living sacrifices, they knew the serpent men would be at a disadvantage, defending themselves and not wanting to press home their greater strength and speed for the kill. It meant the rush of the attack pressed them back, under the shadow of their oncoming serpent lord.

The fighting became furious, the tide tipping in favour of the humans, but Azzarak and his immediate warriors were powerful and fought off their assailants, whose stamina would be tested as the night went on. Eskarra knew she and her comrades could not keep this battle going indefinitely. The serpent men seemed to take strength from the huge serpent, as if it poured energy into them, drawing on dark magic from whatever dread regions fuelled its own black heart. Eskarra turned again to stare briefly at Artugol, who was bathed in glistening sweat, his chest heaving with effort. All they could do was nod to each other.

Further along the line, two of the seamen sagged, their sword arms falling to their sides, and by the garish moonlight, their assailants stepped in for the kill, dispatching them with sweeping cuts of their blades, and as the two bodies collapsed, their serpent men killers began the immediate process of transformation. The process had begun and within moments they had replicated the fallen seamen, lifting their bloodied swords in triumph. Eskarra knew this fate was to befall them all as the night wore on: the opposing powers were too much.

She cursed, looking up at the serpent as it yet shifted its head from side to side, preparatory to striking at any moment. Beside it, high among the ruins, a single figure emerged, its long robe torn and muddied. It was the unmistakable bulk of Emmaneus. He was not a fighting man, his physique and age not allowing for that, but he had braved the awkward climb, and carried with him a long spear. As Eskarra watched, he leapt from the block on which he stood to the back of the serpent's head. Then, picked out by the brilliant moonlight, he struck down with as much strength as he could muster, driving the spear into the space between the serpent's eyes, sinking the weapon into its scaled flesh almost to its entire length.

The serpent's head snapped back, tossing Emmaneus from it, and the Druid was flung through the air, tumbling among the blocks, bouncing awkwardly into darkness. As he disappeared, the serpent shuddered, blood leaking from the wound, and the serpent men swung round as one to gaze at it in horror. The humans were quick to take advantage of the abrupt confusion, and many of them hacked off the heads of the serpent men. Whatever power the serpent had been exercising had withered, and within moments the beast had dragged itself back into the stone mound, withdrawing into whatever dark chambers twisted below it.

Artugol faced Azzarak, who also had lost his advantage, as if the insuperable strength fuelling him had been withdrawn. Artugol drove his blade deep into the gut of the muscular figure, and beside him Volnus swept down his own blade, splitting that huge skull in two. As the serpent men's leader crashed lifelessly to the ground, the others became confused, their movements lacking coordination, as though the sudden fall of the serpent had drained not only its projected power, but their own strength. Their demise after that was swift and merciless. Every one of them fell and was quickly decapitated. Ormullah and his blood-drenched companions roared in triumph.

Eskarra raised her sword. "Make sure none gets away alive. Their masters on Shunn-Ul-Darza must not hear of this. They must be made to believe their deceit worked."

Artugol knew her well enough by now to understand she read more into this business. "You think we can turn this trickery to our advantage?"

She gave him a wry smile. "Certainly. They would have had plans for these serpent men, in the guise of humans. So if they still think that scheme is working, then we'll play along. They'll think we are their servants."

Artugol was grinning as he digested this. A shout from Volnus turned his head. Volnus was pointing to the crest of the ruins. "Emmaneus! He fell." He threaded through a dozen serpent men corpses and clambered up the stones, watched by Ormullah and the others. It took the two men a while to find the Druid. They knew at once Emmaneus was dead, his body broken, his neck snapped in the fall. The broad shadow of Ormullah fell across the corpse and the oars master gazed at it with a growl of anger.

"Help me get him up from here," said Artugol, but

Ormullah was already bending down and gathering the body, ignoring its weight: he gently heaved it over his shoulder. Together they climbed back down to the others.

"He had more courage then all of us," said Artugol.

"A brave sacrifice," said Eskarra. "Without it we would all have succumbed to these foul creatures. We will give Emmaneus a sea burial and honour him before his gods."

"Shall we return to Mallomas?" said Ormullah. "By now the King's fleet will be coming north. We could join it somewhere near the island."

"We need to see if we can track the serpent. If it has not died, it cannot be allowed to return to the enemy."

"Track it?" said Artugol. "Gods, you mean, *follow* it? Underground?"

"If it means confirming its death, or finishing it, it will be worth it."

"If it's still alive, it'll be almost impossible to kill in its lair."

A stony determination straightened her. "Are we less brave than Emmaneus? Did he strike that creature for nothing?"

Artugol felt a flush of embarrassment. "No, of course not. I'll come."

"And I," said Ormullah and Volnus together.

They wasted no further time clambering back up the jumble of blocks. Most of the crew would have joined them, but Eskarra gave strict orders for them to wait. Then, without further hesitation, she dropped down into the dark hole into which the serpent had retreated. Both Ormullah and Volnus brought lighted torches with them, their flames throwing the tunnel below into gaudy relief. The stench of serpent down here was almost overpowering, but the four humans padded on down the sloping tunnel, treading in thick muck they thought to be mud, until the light revealed it as blood, a trail leading into the darkness. No one spoke, but clearly the serpent was sorely wounded.

When they came to the small cavern, they saw the creature, curled up as if in sleep, under an overhang. Emanneus's spear haft shone in the glare, most of its length buried deep in the serpent's brain. It opened its eyes, but they were opaque, misted over like frosted glass. The mouth opened, but only for more blood to pour out. Ormullah approached cautiously, his blade before him, but before he could use it, the huge head sagged to once side, the forked tongue sliding out, stiffening as he watched. The eyes turned to stone.

"Our work is already done. This thing won't be returning to the masters that summoned it," Ormullah said.

Eskarra sheathed her own blade, relieved. "We need to cast every serpent man corpse into this pit and bury them from prying eyes. We must not leave any clue as to what happened on this isle."

Later, when the work was done and the burrow of the serpent sealed with blocks from the surrounding ruins, Eskarra led the company back on to the bank surrounding the clearing. By the dawn light they could see shapes moving down among the trees beyond, a gathering that blocked their way back to the *Arrow*.

"Orugllyr!" said Volnus, tugging out his blade. "It seems we have more work yet."

"Wait," said Eskarra. "We may not have to fight our way out."

A small group was coming up the slope to meet them, led by one of the Orugllyr. This being was not like the others, its body less alien, bearing some resemblance to the human form, and its facial features were the same, though distorted. Its huge eyes fixed on Eskarra and her immediate companions, then singled out the larger bulk of Ormullah.

"Is it done?" the creature hissed, addressing the oars master. "You are Azzarak?"

Ormullah grunted. Eskarra had told the company of the serpent men's plan while they toiled at hiding the corpses from the battle. "Who are you?" snapped the oars master.

"I am Glizzak, right hand of Urzook, king of the Orugllyr." The bulbous eyes swivelled, taking in the entire company. "You have disguised yourselves as humans perfectly, almost too much so."

Ormullah leaned forward and bared his teeth in a wolfish snarl. "Does anyone doubt it? Or wish to see me as I am? Feel my lizard breath on their face?"

Glizzak shrank back in horror. "No, no. Not necessary."

"Good. We have work to do. Where is the pirate ship?"

"Out in the bay, untouched by the Orugllyr. Its small crew remains aboard. I suggest you kill them before sailing south to mingle with the unsuspecting humans."

"Go back to your king," said Ormullah. "Tell him and those he serves that their spies are being planted."

Glizzak bowed and swiftly led his companions away.

"By the Nine Hells," said Volnus. "You make a convincing serpent man, Ormullah. I think the threat of your breathing on him really did the trick."

The huge oars master laughed. "You mind your manners, underling. Azzarak doesn't take lightly to insults. You mind it isn't your face I breathe on."

For one short moment they all laughed, but as the sun rose and they went back down to the shore, they felt the stirrings of a deeper unease, knowing that all future paths led to the war in which the fate of all humanity rested.

Chapter Sixteen: The Dawn of War

West of Elak's fleet, the Pictish ships were met by scores of craft manned by the servants of the Vannadril. There were

Orugllyr and other creatures from the sea, mingled with warriors from the island of Shunn-Ul-Darza, and in the waters around their ships, others churned the seas into bank after bank of waves. It was the first test of the war front, and as the two great forces fell upon each other like the blows of a storm, the fighting was furious and wild, two immense armies locked together in a devastating conflict, with no quarter asked or given. The seas heaved with the fallen, dead and dying, the white waves turned to the colour of blood.

Kaa Mag Borga, leading the entire Pict force, pressed home the attack with absolute determination and with all the fury that characterized his nation in war, and as the day progressed, the casualties among the enemy were huge, for the Pictish war axes drank thirstily of their blood, and countless enemy ships were scuttled and sent to the ocean depths. Above the attacking fleet, numerous sky lizards swooped and dived, adding to the utter mayhem, using their claws to devastating effect on the sea beings, destroying many.

While this tumultuous sea battle raged, a similar conflict boiled in the seas to the far east of Elak's lone line of attack, where another huge navy, led by kings and rulers of the eastern side of the Atlantean continent and its southern realms unleashed its assault. As with the Picts, these naval warriors drove their ships into the heart of another massed array of Orugllyr craft, coupled with the spawn of Shunn-Ul-Darza, and the fighting was no less intense than it was to the west, with the seas curdling into blood. Men fought heroically and tirelessly against quasi-men, driven on by a ferocious determination and the intensity of their hatred for anything smacking of sorcery. Above them, more of the Royal Wing of Elak's sky lizards added to the mayhem, ripping into the aerial demons from the Vannadril island.

By early evening, some of the sky lizards flew around the *Epharran Queen*, taking turns to drop down and deliver their messages to Elak. One of the fliers, Carraverin, alighted on the high deck of the royal flagship and bowed before the monarch.

"I come from the seas directly north of you, sire," he said.

"Have the Vannadril released their central forces? Should we engage as our eastern and western fleets have done?" Elak was impatient to get involved in the action having received news all day of the violent engagements on the wings of his invasion force.

"No, sire. The island is silent, its waters clear. But one ship comes—the *Arrow*, the pirate vessel commanded by Eskarra."

"What of Emmaneus and his ship?" said Dalan, beside the King.

"There is no sign of him, or his craft. Some of its crew, though, are with Eskarra on the *Arrow*. It will be with you before the dawn."

*

Far beneath the ocean, in a deep trench that reached to the lowest levels of Shunn-Ul-Darza and the bizarre growths that attached the roots of the island to the seabed, a vast bulk was stirring, a deep ocean leviathan, a unique life form, dredged up from centuries of existence in the muddy chasms in which it lay dreaming. It unflexed endless lengths of tendril, thick cables of tough, spiky arms that wove patterns in the silt and the utter depths of the sea, its blind eyes opening, its mind absorbing the disturbances around it in the water as though messages had been transmitted to it by other than physical means. As it lifted itself from the nacreous deeps, its mind was turned by the workings of the Vannadril on their island so far above it, and the sorcerers shaped the creature's purpose, to destroy whatever it found in these waters.

Somewhere nearby, on the surface, the massed central fleet of Elak was forging its passage to Shunn-Ul-Darza. The sea monster became aware of the ships and life forms swarming in them, and directed its attention to them, its immense mouth opening to reveal a vast maw, eager to swallow countless numbers of these intruders. As the beast rose, the darkness of the seas around it was lit by thousands of bulbous creatures, akin to great jellyfish, whose domes gleamed with internal light. In their wake came the first of the Deepwhales, a dozen of the creatures propelling themselves forward at remarkable speed. They drove to the attack like missiles hurled by a subterranean god, and tore into the flailing tendrils of the great sea beast.

As the contest ensued, with several of the Deepwhales enmeshed in the tendrils they sought to rip to shreds, others attacked its long tail, a thick knot of more tendrils, woven together in a long, drifting appendage. The monster pulsed with cosmic power, a gift from its predecessors that had come here at the dawn of the world's history, power from the stars and the world of Xalkara, mother world of the Star Gods. It was indestructible, but the massed attacks of the Deepwhales rendered murderous damage to it, ripping apart its tendrils and severing its long tail, so that it rolled over and floundered, its sense of direction muddied and confused. Many of the assailants died in that onslaught, but the immediate destruction of Elak's central navy was spared, at least for the time. Out in the endless landscape of the deep ocean floor, other vast shapes were waking from their eon-old sleep.

*

Elak stood in the prow of his flagship, an arm around Shiveeri. They had watched the sunlight daubing the eastern horizon as dawn spread its glow. In the distance a lone ship approached.

"Should I have stayed with the children?" she asked him.

"They are in good hands," he reassured her. "I can think of no safer place for them than with the Druids of Morgaal in his mountain retreat. This war will not reach there. I am glad you are beside me."

"Can we win this war? Do we have enough to combat these alien gods?"

"We must hold to that belief." He kissed her, pointing to the ship ahead. Soon it had come alongside, showing itself to be the promised *Arrow*. Eskarra and several of her companions clambered up the lowered ropes to the central deck of the flagship, where Elak and Shiveeri met them with Dalan.

Eskarra quickly gave an account of all that had transpired on the Isle of Serpents. Dalan stiffened at the telling of the death of Emmaneus, but remained stoically silent. When she had finished, Eskarra turned to Ormullah, who stood at her side. He bowed to Shiveeri. and undid the neck of a sack he had been carrying.

"Show them," said Eskarra.

Ormullah upturned the sack and a grisly, bloodied trophy fell onto the boards. It was the severed head of a serpent man.

"Azzarak," said Eskarra. "I wanted you to have proof that my story was not a myth."

"With Ormullah at your side, I would never have doubted it," said Shiveeri.

The huge oars master bowed to her again.

Elak gazed at the foul object in disgust. "Dalan and I have seen the like of these creatures before. We know well enough their powers. What you've told me about their transformations is not new to us. You've prevented what could have been catastrophic circumstances, for which I am deeply grateful."

"We buried the corpses on the Isle of the Serpent, but kept certain segments of their armour which we can wear if need be, to fool any of them we meet in future, though the smell of these creatures is enough to unsettle the strongest of stomachs."

"Better the disguise," said Lycon, though he screwed up his visage, an even more grim sight than usual.

Dalan spoke at last. "And it's given us an unexpected advantage. Since the Vannadril do not know about their failed plot, they may well assume that you and your companions, Eskarra, are *their* spies, serpents in human guise."

Eskarra and her immediate pirates were grinning, and in spite of the gravity of the situation, Elak laughed. He turned to Shiveeri. "That may go some way to answering the question you asked me about winning the war."

She, too, laughed.

"Then let us plan anew," said Elak.

*

In the upper temple of Shunn-Ul-Darza, the Vannadril gathered, considering the reports of the war constantly being brought to them by the commanders of their own armies.

"Elak may have thought to surprise us with this abrupt

invasion," said Aarrzoruuk. "Yet he is simply playing into our hands."

"Can we be sure he will not drive our eastern and western forces back and press his advantage? Elak has amassed a far greater navy than we might have expected. And his aerial creatures, his sky lizards, are greater in numbers than we knew. He has been preparing for this war longer than we understood."

"We can hold them," said the huge Vannadril. "This war will not be won by the massed warriors in the field, or on the seas. They will tangle and enmesh themselves, and while they are thus engrossed, from the deeps our lords will rise and sweep the ocean over all of the land masses to the south! Whatever sorcery the High Druid and his acolytes summon up will be wasted in their sea battles. There will be nothing to stop the unleashing of the sea."

"There are reports of other waking creatures of the deep abyss, summoned by the Aquarri, the sea people. Xeraph-Hizer and his fellow gods are not alone, nor will they go unchallenged."

Aarrzoruuk waved away the concerns of his companions. "These are not gods! No more so than the Deepwhales they send against us. Mere creatures of the ocean. Fodder for our masters!"

"What of the other plan? The creation of the serpent men spies?" The Vannadril turned to the hunched figure of Issathass-Vekk, principal of the Trine.

"Our warlord, Azzarak will have performed the ritual under the eye of our moon god, Saaraaza. By now he will have killed all the interfering pirates and supplanted them. When they go to Elak, he will imagine he has a company of his own spies, whereas he will have a team of assassins at the very heart of his followers."

"Primed and prepared to eliminate him and his closest allies, including the accursed High Druid, Dalan?" said Aarrzoruuk, the words almost lost in another snarl of anger.

"Of course. Their minds have been cultivated. They will not fail to comply with their orders."

"The death of the King and all his Council will bring about the collapse of the human forces. It is as inevitable as the rising of the next full moon, the Killing Moon, and the coming of the exalted ones from Xalkara itself!"

*

Elak sat back, a deep frown on his face, his mind clearly racing. With him were Dalan and Lycon, Eskarra and Artugol, whom the King noted, was never far from the girl's side. Not only is he her personal bodyguard, but he is also much more than that, the King was thinking. *Just as I was to Shiveeri, my own pirate lover.*

It was late, the inner cabin secured from the wild weather outside, where the deck of the *Epharran Queen* was washed by continual waves, the crew fighting to keep the ship steady as it ploughed northward. The gathered company had been running over the details of a plan, instigated at the suggestion of the spirited young pirate captain, Eskarra. Slowly, with Dalan's significant input, the plan evolved from the wildest of gambits into a passable strategy.

"It's certainly daring," Elak said eventually. "Some might say foolish."

Lycon grunted. "Reminds me of many a lunatic venture you and I used to undertake."

Elak chuckled. "I never thought I'd hear myself echoing the words of my Councillors." He looked warmly at Eskarra and Artugol. "They berated me time and time again for setting out on what they called my adventures, when they wanted me safe on the throne, looking after the affairs of state."

Dalan's face did not crack in a smile. "You took risks, and were more than a little fortunate."

"The gods must have favoured me!" Elak said with another smile.

"If we are to undertake this plan," replied Dalan, "we'll need their favours again."

Chapter Seventeen: Awakenings

Carved deep beyond the floor of the ocean bed, the night-black canyon ran for a thousand miles from the northern fastness of the Vaarfrost continent to the widest sweeps of ocean and the tides that fetched up on the western shores of the Atlantean lands. For millennia this vast abyss had held its darkest secrets, lost to antiquity, almost forgotten by the denizens of the deep, unknown to the races that spread across the world's land masses. Now, in this time of ultimate war, the ink-black fissure that probed the very bowels of the earth stirred, its icy currents moved by the waking of a monstrous entity, a being that had entrenched itself here at the end of its journey from the distant stars, from the world of Xalkara, a centre of Star God rule, vassal of the Old Ones. This being resembled none of the creatures of this world, known to mankind only by its name and the obscure references to it found in texts, tablets and long-rotted temples in overgrown jungle citadels. For this was Xeraph-Hizer, the Leviathan Lord, and he was rising, breaking free of the murk and mire, lifting from his bed of primal ooze and unfurling his limbs, great, sweeping fin-like appendages, and bunched tendrils at his lower end. His enormous, bulbous head, capped with streamlined spikes, lifted to the upper waters, the twin eyes, immense saucers, focused on the remote surface.

Around him his underlings swam in shoals, submarine beasts the size of earthly whales, their own distorted shapes blurring together in a chain, like alien ships steering towards the light. The colossal jaws of the Leviathan Lord opened to reveal row upon row of teeth, each the size of the whale-like company, and the creatures kept well away from that cavernous mouth. Far beyond this stretch of ocean, other shapes were stirring in their beds, summoned by the voices that had penetrated Xeraph-Hizer's mind and woken him. Somewhere on the churning ocean surface, the great war of wars had already begun. The navies of Mankind already clashed with the Orugllyr and other servants of the Vannadril, the conduit for the Star Gods, waiting in the void, ready to descend to their new realm.

*

A few days after the company had agreed on their strategy for taking the war to the enemy, Elak waited impatiently for the return of Dalan, who had taken to the skies on Carraverin's sky lizard and gone to the mountain retreat of the Druids to collect what he needed to strengthen the company's plans. These plans, and those who would undertake them, were known only to a few of Elak's immediate warriors. Not for the first time the Atlantean Council was kept in ignorance of what their king intended.

Shiveeri and Darruvia were part of the company, as no amount of persuasion by their husbands would have them remain with the royal fleet. Present also were Eskarra, Artugol, Volnus and Ormullah. The huge oarsman had endeared himself to the others, and although there were more of Eskarra's crew who would have readily stepped forward to join the company, Dalan had said the success of their plan depended on stealth and secrecy. When the sky lizard returned, the Druid was dropped lightly to the deck, together with two bags, one light and one heavier.

"At last," whispered Eskarra to Artugol. "Now we can begin."

Dalan opened the smaller bag and pulled out a number of golden arm-bands, embossed with ancient writings and tiny, glittering jewels. "Elak, Lycon and I have worn these before."

Lycon's face twisted into another of his gruesome scowls. "That is so. Some years ago we fought the serpent men when Scuvular attempted to have them set him on the throne of Epharra."

"What do they do?" said Darruvia, her own face creased with a frown.

"Wear these," said Dalan, "and your disguise as serpent men will be sustained. Only if you take them off will your true human form be revealed." He handed them out, and the others put the arm-bands away.

Dalan then went to the larger bag and revealed its contents. "More light suits of armour. Enough for all of us now to be protected by the power of the God-Heart Stone. Each suit will be like a second skin, and although they won't make us immortal, they will protect us from the worst of the enemy's assaults."

"Let's waste no more time," said Elak. "We'll dress ourselves and begin."

"We have other weapons to help us," said Dalan. "The three great staffs of power. Rather than have each of them deployed among the three prongs of our naval attack on

Shunn-Ul-Darza, I have placed other powerful rods with the main flagships, our own, that of the Picts and that of the Zangarzan confederacy. We have the Valusian staff, which I will bear, the Scourge of the Night, to be carried again by Lycon and Ishtar's Fury, in the keeping of Elak. They are disguised, of course, but if we reach our objective, they will be instrumental in bringing the Vannadril to their destruction. Be warned, though, I do not know what other consequences may be unleashed."

The last of the daylight faded and a full moon bathed the ocean around them and the accompanying fleet. Among the countless vessels, thousands of sky lizards were bobbing up and down on the waters, resting, their riders sleeping on their backs, the beasts calm, bellies filled with the rich fishing of day's-end. Every captain had been given his orders for the forthcoming day, and each of them believed Elak and his immediate followers would be on the *Epharran Queen* to lead them into the dawn attack.

Elak and his company donned their inner armour and on top of it fitted a second layer of the armour taken from the serpent men killed on the Isle of the Serpent. They wore, too, their arm-bands, and when Dalan spoke the words of his incantation, the head of each of the group transformed, becoming that of a lizard man. For a while they all gaped at each other, Shiveeri, Darruvia and Eskarra in particular, all of them murmuring their disgust, but the disguise was remarkable. They pulled their hoods up and minimised the effect on the startled crew of the flagship, who watched as Elak led the company over the side, into the smaller ship awaiting them.

Ormullah took the helm, and in moments they had cast off from the *Epharran Queen* and sailed swiftly away from the fleet, heading northward. The moon remained bright, but as the ship dipped and rose among the choppy waves, it was well disguised by the night, its single sail dyed black, its sleek hull like the body of a sea beast. Ahead of them a small patrol of Aquarri swam like dolphins, testing the waters, watching for any signs of Orugllyr or other enemy patrols, but the sea ahead was empty.

In the depths far below, however, the conflict began to rage as it had done on the surface where the huge fleets had fought by daylight. Xeraph-Hizer and his accompanying servants sensed the coming of countless undersea creatures, a vast subterranean army, spurred by the Aquarri. These had used their own ancient sorcery to summon sea dwellers from remote places, none as huge and powerful as the Leviathan Lord, but marine beings who possessed power, which, combined, made of them a formidable foe. In the aquatic darkness, numerous contests began, far from the moonlight, and blurred shapes rammed each other like icebergs in a storm. Among them the Deepwhales drove hard at the enemy, ripping many of the servants of Xeraph-Hizer apart.

The Leviathan Lord exuded waves of evil power, the direst sorcery that could be conjured, waves of it permeating the seas around him like oil, but the Aquarri deflected it through their quasi-gods, and for long periods during the contest, one force nullified the other. High above these dreadful clashes, the small ship of Elak and his company sped on across the surface, unnoticed and unhindered in its passage.

A few hours before dawn it had sighted the island on which Shiveeri and Darruvia had been held by the Orugllyr. Ormullah steered the ship around the island to its northern shoreline and found the narrow bay where the Orugllyr had made their base. The huts that constituted the rudiments of a village were still there, silent as heaped stones, but there were lights betraying the presence of the sea beings.

Dalan waved a lantern that those onshore could not miss, and presently there were shapes in the water around the ship as it tacked into the bay's shallows, dropping. Surrounded by Orugllyr, the entire company climbed down into the surf and up the beach.

"I am Azzarak," said Ormullah to the nearest of the sea beasts. "Who is your leader here?"

The Orugllyr stood back from what they saw as a huge serpent man, uncomfortable in its presence. One of them spoke up. "Shanatarl Vaarst, second in command to our king, Urzook. We will take you to him."

Elak and the others, still hooded, looked around them, relieved to see that their disguise was fully effective. The three staffs of power had also been disguised, and now appeared to be no more than spears, sturdy and fit for war, but with no visible elements of power. Led by Ormullah, the small group went up the beach, watched by the Orugllyr. Inside the largest of the huts, lit by twin crystals that glowed green, a large Orugllyr waited.

"We meet again, Azzarak," he said, studying what he assumed to be the muscular serpent man. "I remember you from your visits to my master, Urzook, in the halls of the citadel at Shunn-Ul-Darza. You led the expedition to Epharra and brought out the King's woman, and her companion."

"They were housed here," said Ormullah, quickly caching on. "Yet you could not hold them."

The round face of Shanatarl Vaarst exuded anger, his wide mouth twisted in barely concealed resentment at the reference to his failure. "Those responsible will be made to pay, rest assured." He looked at the group around the serpent man and for a moment Elak and his companions wondered if their disguise had been breached, so direct was the Orugllyr's stare.

"Never mind that," said Ormullah, his voice almost a snarl. "There is other business to attend to. I am on my way back to the citadel."

"Yes, I gather you sail in an Atlantean ship, now beached below us."

"My warriors and I took it from them and cut the crew to pieces, making it easy for us to slip through their incompetent watches. Their navy will be no match for that of our masters."

"Quite so. And soon, as Xeraph-Hizer obliterates the rabble beneath the waves, he will rise, along with other gods from the deeps, and smite them all. He is near." He closed his eyes and shuddered, though not in fear.

"I will sail to Shunn-Ul-Darza immediately. Is there another ship I can use? It would be more welcome than an Atlantean craft."

"Of course. I can provide you something more suitable."

"Good. Burn the one we came here in. Leave no trace of it. And continue your own preparations."

*

In the dawn light, Elak and the company sailed in another craft, a much cruder vessel of the Orugllyr, who preferred to travel in the water than by ship, but one which would not be challenged by whatever watches had been set on Shunn-Ul-Darza. When they at last arrived under the shadows of the southern cliffs of the towering island, there was considerable movement as units of Orugllyr left the place, heading for the battle front, as well as other beings, Gnorl, spindly creatures more arachnid than human, crammed into yet more ships.

As Ormullah took his craft into a sheltered cove away from the activities of the main shore, the company got ashore, apparently unnoticed and thankfully unchallenged.

"Now," said Dalan. "We need to find a way in."

Chapter Eighteen: Dawn of Fury

As Elak and his resolute company had been sailing in the dawn light to Shunn-Ul-Darza, the war had burst once more in all its furious intensity along the entire line of the battle front. The fleets of the Picts, the Atlantean spearhead from Epharra and the Zangarzan confederation drove into the massed Orugllyr and ship-bound servants of the Vannadril, and the fighting intensified as the day broke, the seas churning, thick with the fallen on both sides. Under the waves, other forces smashed into one another like the waves of a colossal storm, the Aquarri amassed in unprecedented numbers, together with other creatures from the deep places who had been dormant for centuries. Added to this were the ferocious denizens of the ocean gulfs, gathered into battalions that tore into the enemy, down in the darkness, invisible but no less potent.

Xeraph-Hizer swam close to the surface, confident of victory over these lowly beasts of the ocean, but he was attacked on all sides, as Deepwhales in their thousands supported the other god-like leviathans that the sorcery of the Druid Morgaal had raised from his secluded sanctuary in the sacred mountains beyond Epharra. Ineffable power from the God-Heat Stone pulsed like a living thing, sent in waves across the ocean to shatter the creeping mists of the

Vannadrils' own sorcery, brewed into a storm that roared southward, skies packed with demonic forces. Morgaal, as Keeper of the Sacred Archives, had long held the wind elementals of his world in chains, but now he released them, their freedom won in exchange for their aid in this tumultuous conflict. Now, together with the swarming sky lizards from Illyrin, they tore into the demonic forces of the enemy in a dreadful aerial maelstrom.

While the war raged and the world shook, Elak and his companions made their way inside the tortured crevices and tunnels of Shunn-Ul-Darza. The sea had unknowingly made a passage for them, the bludgeoning currents and violent rip tides of centuries opening up dark wounds in the mass of the island, underwater for eons, penetrating the very foundations of the island. When it had risen, the sea sluiced out of it, revealing its brutal work. While the storm blasted the heavens far above the island, its light boiled down into its deepest parts, affording light to the small company as it made its laborious but determined way upwards towards the foundations of the Vannadril citadel.

There were enemy warriors here, more of the chitinous Gnorl, but when they saw the serpent men rising up from the stairway to the sea, they stood aside, knowing them for agents of their masters. Ormullah, as Azzarak, led the way. They came to a tall door, barred and guarded by other creatures, dressed in armour that disguised their nature, and for a while it seemed they would oppose the company's progress and must be fought.

"I am Urzook's messenger," said Ormullah. "I bring important news for him and the Vannadril."

After another pause, the creatures stepped aside and the door swung inward. Ormullah and the others went through and on to the first steps of a long stairway that rose upwards into the light that streamed from overhead. It was not this world's sunlight, but shimmered with alien spells and sorcery, blazing through a vent into the outer void. Elak felt the sudden heat of the arm-band he wore as it deflected the probing fingers of the air around him. The serpent men disguises held good, and the party climbed ever upward.

When they at last reached a plateau, high in the upper halls of the citadel, a line of serpent men awaited them. One of them stepped forward, its eyes fixed on Ormullah as though seeking to peer into his, searching for the truth of his identity. "They tell me you have brought word to your king," said Urzook, for this huge serpent man was none other than their ruler. "Do you know the exact whereabouts of the Atlantean King and his accursed High Druid?"

Dalan whispered something to Ormullah, key words in the strategy the company had agreed upon. The oars master reacted at once, drawing his wide blade. "Let this blade speak for me," he said, and with a great shout that startled even the fierce serpent men, leapt forward.

Urzook was taken by surprise, but he was exceptionally fast, having won his kingship through physical skill and strength, and his own blade flashed as he took the full impact of Ormullah's attack. Around him the other serpent men, a score of them, also erupted into life, and in moments the air sang to the clash of steel as the intruders fought tenaciously. Dalan had warned his fellows not to use the hidden power of the staffs until absolutely necessary, knowing that if the Vannadril learned of them, they would lock themselves in some part of the citadel where they could not be reached.

The fighting was intense, and the two parties well matched. Ormullah broke through the defence of the huge Urzook more than once, wounding but not seriously harming him. The serpent man king would have downed Ormullah and killed him, but for the inner armour the oars master wore, and although bruised from the blows he received, Ormullah stood his ground, pressed forward, and eventually found the blow that brought Urzook to his knees. The king snarled like a demon from the pits, but Ormullah's blade sliced into his neck, his blood gushed, and he toppled forward, gasping out the last of his life.

Elak and Shiveeri fought side by side, and as Urzook fell, they redoubled their efforts and brought down more of their opponents, whose staunch defence waned at the loss of their leader. Lycon and Darruvia likewise tore into the foe, wreaking havoc, and the trio of Eskarra, Artugol and Volnus had similar gory success. When it was over, with all the serpent men slaughtered, the level area fell silent, as though the air breathed in the knowledge of what had transpired. There were more stairs beyond and Dalan urged the company upwards. As they went they heard the scurrying of feet down shadowy corridors that led off the wide stair, but no further attacks from serpent men or other defendants of this inner sanctum were yet forthcoming.

There were more great doors ahead of them, but these were not closed, opening instead into a tall oval chamber, where even stranger lights danced like malefic spirits, transforming the palatial surroundings into a shimmering arena. Three huge thrones dominated the place, and on each of them sat one of the serpent men Trine, waiting patiently and without a trace of fear for the arrival of the intruders. Their great jaws opened, teeth glittering like rows of daggers as their leader, Issathass-Vekk, leaned forward, a sound that might have been contemptuous laughter rising from his throat.

"A creditable disguise," he snarled. "Enough to fool

our common warriors. But we are the Trine, and we see through you, worms of Atlantis. Take off your amulets!"

Dalan whispered something to Elak and Lycon, who lifted their spears as the Druid slid the leather covering from the top of his own weapon to reveal the crimson jewel of the Valusians set there. It pulsed with energy as though the light from above had ignited it. "And do you see through these?" said Dalan.

The three huge serpent men rose as one, their terrible claws reaching for the swords at their belts. Dalan was faster, and directed his staff at Issathass-Vekk, a stream of crimson light arcing across the chamber and striking the creature full on the chest, shattering his sword in a cloud of metal shards. Elak and Lycon similarly used their staffs to send bolts of energy at the two remaining serpent men, and they, too, were hurled backwards. All of the three tried to rise, crippled like insects smashed to the ground by a huge fist. As they did so, a score of serpent men guards rushed in upon the Atlanteans, but they were swept away in a combined blinding flash as the three staffs unleashed another stream. Dalan was quick to leap up on to the dais and drive his staff down into the body of Issathass-Vekk, which burned with a vivid fire. Elak and Lycon dispatched the others and it was quickly over as the last of the screams of the Trine died away.

Once more silence fell in the chamber. It was broken by the thundering storm high overhead, and by its flickering light the company, now strained through the alien starlight, saw a spiral stairway, woven around the walls of the chamber, climbing upwards. Dalan led the way upwards, past gigantic columns twisted into statues, representations of the things that sought ingress into this world from the opened stellar tunnel to their world of Xalkara. These statues shimmered, their towering shapes seeming to shiver, reacting to the garish light, and overhead a swarm of aerial horrors plummeted downwards, screaming and ripping with their talons, only to be met with another surge of power from the three staffs. The creatures exploded and tumbled far down on to the solid stone floor, bursting as they landed.

Bolts of light ripped down through the air, but Dalan and his companions deflected them, so their power tore chunks from the statues, damaging one so badly it fell, crushing another company of pursuing serpent men. Dalan led them to the final steps and up into another chamber, the heart of the Vannadril citadel. Around its far wall, arranged in an arc of defiance, the Vannadril waited. Each of them held a deep blue globe, and when Dalan directed power at the one held by the centre-most of the Vannadril, Aarrzoruuk, the beam simply sank into the globe, absorbed by it. Elak and Lycon had no more success as they attempted to bring the Vannadril down. As the air stilled, their caustic laughter broke out in a wave.

While this was happening on Shunn-Ul-Darza, the sea gods were preparing their onslaught on Epharra and the northern coast of Atlantis. Xeraph-Hizer rose from the waters, as did Ctuthfathak of the Ice Wastes, and Quazzir-Rahan in the eastern ocean. In the mountains behind Epharra, Morgannis had been waiting, and now he spoke the ancient words that released a torrent of long-forbidden spells, waking the final powers of the God-Heart Stone. These flashed in the blinking of an eye outward to all the great singing stones from the Pictish Isles set along the coast to protect it. From them, the power of the earth, deep and inexorable, vast as the volcanic energy of its deepest parts, spread out across the ocean, a storm beyond any ever previously experienced by this world.

Power from the Star Gods, invested in Xeraph-Hizer and his fellow sea gods, clashed with this earth-power and the alien beings were brought to a halt, rocked back by wave upon wave of terrestrial sorcery. While they faltered, the Vannadril in their citadel felt the massive blows against their masters, and as they uniformly gaped in horror, each of their globes exploded, their powers fizzling out. Instantly the roof above them blurred and the light of sorcery was scorched by incoming natural sunlight, its power enhanced by the earth's.

Elak rushed forward and drove his staff into the heart of Aarrzoruuk, and within moments the sorcerer had turned into a melting, dripping mass of flesh that slithered to the stone.

From the central pool in the chamber a great head emerged, its baleful eyes taking in the company, but before it could lift an arm to destroy them, Lycon and Dalan plunged their staffs into the water. It effervesced, becoming lava red and the being writhed and twisted in agony, boiled by energies it could not resist, sinking down out of sight. Deprived of their globes, the remaining Vannadril were no more powerful than any human warrior, seared by the sunlight, and found themselves fighting hand to hand with Shiveeri, Darruvia and Eskarra, who wrought havoc among them, exacting a bloody revenge for the tribulations they had suffered.

In the open skies above the chamber, the storm had ended and whatever dark channel had opened to the Star Gods' home was closed, its power sealed off. Out at sea, the massed fleets of Elak's allies watched as their enemies sank back into the deeps, leaving behind numerous rafts of their dead. Whatever dreadful powers had been unleashed by the Druid and the God-Heart Stone had done their work with staggering effect. Confounded, Xeraph-Hizer and his allies went back to whatever subterranean haven they could find, their powers severely crippled, perhaps for all time.

Epilogue

Lycon turned to Dalan amid the carnage they had wrought in the Vannadril chamber. "Can we take these accursed armbands off now? I don't think I can stomach being a serpent man much longer."

Dalan managed a smile. "Yes, but there may be more of the creatures in the citadel, although I suspect any survivors will have gone to ground, back into their subterranean tunnels."

As the company removed their amulets and became their true physical selves once more, Lycon and Elak embraced their wives, and Artugol similarly hugged Eskarra, who for once was more than happy to exhibit her love for him publicly by wrapping her arms around him and kissing him with a fervour that surprised him. Volnus clapped Ormullah on the shoulder and the two men laughed in sheer relief.

"Once this war is over," said Elak, "it will be a time for love."

Shiveeri took his left hand and placed it on her stomach. "And new life."

Elak's smile of realization widened, and beside Shiveeri, Darruvia also laughed, gripping Lycon. "New life indeed," she said, patting her own abdomen and Lycon's embarrassment was plain for all to see. He hid it by suggesting that they all go in search of any wine cellars to celebrate, for which he received a cuff from Darruvia which would have felled many a strong man.

Later, sailing through the wreckage of the defeated forces of the Vannadril, its wrecked ships, its scattered knots of Orugllyr dead and dying, Elak's company saw the oncoming Atlantean fleet and gave it a rousing, unified cheer. The King stood beside Dalan, whose own delight at their success seemed mildly coloured by a thoughtful frown.

"The tide has turned," said Elak.

Dalan nodded. "For now Atlantis will enjoy a new era, and I expect great days will follow. Morgannis released dark powers into the world to counter the threat from the Star Gods, and they will need to be managed with great care from now on. Things will always be set at such a fine balance."

"Then we will enjoy whatever time we have, and make our empire a place of celebration."

*

After the brief but cataclysmic war with the agents of the darkness from the stars and their undersea envoys, the Atlanteans began swiftly rebuilding what had been lost, for the tides and abnormal waves had wrought much havoc, in spite of the protection afforded by the singing stones and the power of the God-Heart Stone. Epharra, already a magnificent city, grew in size and beauty, its spires and temples, its great galleries and its supreme harbour becoming the envy of the world, welcoming ships and nations from even further away, and for once the numerous tribal feuds that had been an inevitable part of existence in the past, eased so that new trade and prosperity burgeoned.

Elak's second son, Dalannis, named in honour of the High Druid, was a healthy child, as was the daughter of Darruvia and Lycon, Brannach, and it was not long after their births that Artugol and Shiveeri had their first child, the bright-eyed girl, Shivasta.

Shunn-Ul-Darza sank once more beneath the waves, where it gradually disintegrated, leaving no trace of what had been there. Of Xeraph-Hizer there were no signs as he, too, subsided and dived deep down into some unfathomable abyss, stripped of his powers, in time to become no more than a memory, a reference in the secret histories written by the Druids and stored in the hidden vaults in the mountain temple of the God-Heart Stone. Of the Orugllyr, serpent men, Gnorl and others that had served the cause of the Star Gods, little was seen or heard, as they, too, sought the oblivion of the ocean abysses.

The seas rolled forward, embodiment of time itself, waiting, perhaps, for another era, a time when they would stretch their unique powers and inexorably re-establish their sovereignty over all the places and peoples of the world down to their final dawn in a time beyond knowing.

- Helvas Ravanniol, **Annals of the Third Atlantean Empire**

Tough Guys contains three previously unpublished novellas and a short. Based on the title theme, these four works are completely different in subject matter and tone. There is, of course, A Nick Nightmare story herein, *Wait for the Ricochet*, in which the gumshoe is entrusted to convey a message about "The Malleus Tenebrarum", a book that names the properties and powers of dark and light, to the Mechanic, one Oil-Gun Eddy... His adversary is the sinister Lucien de Sangreville, plus assorted non-human denizens of the murky lower levels, and his sidekick the sword-wielding business-woman Ariadne Carnadine. In contrast, in *If You Don't Eat Your Meat* the reader enters a post-apocalyptic world where the very unsavoury Ryan relates his story of rival families and cannibalism. It is gruesome and unflinching horror. In *A Smell of Burning* a hospital patient finds he is having out-of-the-body experiences. On his astral journeys he visits a man recalling his abused childhood and this leads to a shocking revelation... Finally, *Not If You Want to Live* explores the fate of Razorjack, who is a Redeemer, a dead man used by a shady organisation to bring back others from death. An intriguing and engrossing story of love between Razorjack (aka Jack Krane) and mobster's moll Rebecca Fellini, with science fictional and satanic elements.

Published as a paperback and kindle eBook

by

PARALLEL UNIVERSE PUBLICATIONS

READ FREE

JANUARY '21

SAVAGE
REALMS
M O N T H L Y

TALES OF
SWORDS AND SORCERY

FEATURING THE TALENTS OF:

WILLARD BLACK   STEVE DILKS

DAVID SIMS   AND   KELL MYERS

https://bit.ly/SavageRealmsFreeMag

TuleFogPress.com

Crimson Quill Quarterly is proud to present the authors to be featured in Volume 5, set to release in January

Teel James Glenn - Choices

Thomas Grayfson - Cold Blood

Daniel Quiogue - Feast of the Fallen Gods

David A. Riley - Essayan's Terrible Machineries of War

Ismail Soldun - Between the Devil's Maw and the Serpent's Fang

Gregg Stewart - Good Luck, Utz Grelk

Jason M. Waltz - Trades